Sea Buzzards

Sea Buzzards

JAD DAVIS

Copyright © 2021 by Jad Davis.

Library of Congress Control Number: 2021910165

HARDBACK: 978-1-955347-74-7
PAPERBACK: 978-1-955347-73-0
EBOOK: 978-1-955347-75-4

All rights reserved. No part of this publication may be reproduced, distributed, or transmitted in any form or by any electronic or mechanical means, without the prior written permission of the publisher, except in the case of brief quotations embodied in critical reviews and certain other noncommercial uses permitted by copyright law.

Ordering Information:

For orders and inquiries, please contact:
1-888-404-1388
www.goldtouchpress.com
book.orders@goldtouchpress.com

Printed in the United States of America

Dedicated to:
"The fishermen of Tangier Island"

CONTENTS

Chapter 1	Liverpool	1
Chapter 2	The First Leg	47
Chapter 3	Middle Passage	78
Chapter 4	Slave Revolts	127
Chapter 5	Charlestown	167
Chapter 6	New York	218
Chapter 7	Black Sam and the Indians	272
Chapter 8	National Betrayals	315
Chapter 9	King George's War	356

CHAPTER 1

LIVERPOOL

Captain Jonn Kimber stormed out of Charles Hayes's office after slamming the front door so hard it jarred loose the elephant and castle logo of The Royal African Company that was bolted onto the wall. He crossed Wapping Street and walked directly toward the Huskisson Dock where the 'Thomas' was being readied for another triangular run.

Kimber had once again been humiliated in front of the same bunch of marginally respectable merchants that Hayes liked to refer to as his 'board of directors'. The same thing happened before but this time Hayes had hit too far below the belt!

It was true he had lost the 'Cheshire' twelve years earlier but that ship didn't go down because of neglectful leadership. It was sunk due to the R.A.C.'s failure to belly-up to the modern-day realities!

Had the slaver been given enough space to build some adequate living quarters for a reasonable staff of officers and had it been equipped with some descent cannons to protect itself from pirates then the bloody slaver would still be afloat! Instead, the company's owner who by the way had never been any further out to sea than the sight of the shoreline chose to use that necessary square footage to house more cargo.

Strangely, the company's owner was no longer enamoured with the sale of human cargo to the new world. His latest interests were now leaning toward the exporting of gold dust, cocoa and ivory.

This was why the dickless Mister Hayes had begun to surround himself with the second and third generation white-breads of Liverpool. He was starting up a side business of his own!

With the subtle withdrawal of the giant Guineamen from the midlife of the lucrative people-selling game, Charles Hayes began to feel that he was a very special entrepreneur. In reality however, Hayes knew nothing about the business of moving large numbers of Africans to the Americas.

Captain Kimber kept mulling these thoughts over and over in his brain as he watched the initial caravan of mule driven wagons offload the textiles and such into the aft section of the lower deck. He was confident the 'Thomas' would set out on her first leg in six days. This would give him just enough time to sell off his properties and get his affairs in good order!

Tomorrow morning at 0600 he is to meet his officers for breakfast. Supposedly There were supposed to be ten seaworthy men in attendance of this long practiced and traditional first meeting. It was said that such occasions were used as a precautionary measure to ensure that the ship's captain felt confident of his officers' compatibility!

Kimber turned toward the skyline of Liverpool with distain written all over his stubby face. He despised that city more than men hated hell!

Things didn't make sense anymore. The R.A.C. had a goldmine going on in the human cargo business so why would they abandon a downright solid money-in-the-bank enterprise? "The truth may never be known," reasoned Jonn.

But in actuality, it didn't make a damned bit of difference to the Captain because when he got to America, he was going to steal the 'Thomas' anyway!

Five dongs from the distant Saint Luke Holy Catholic Church alerted Jonn to the exact time. He was to meet with someone in an hour.

The Three-Legged Dog Tavern was the litmus test for traces of irregular scheming which seemed to blow in as frequently as the mist off of the Mersey. House rules were different there.

The most telling 'rule' was written above the doorway leading into the establishment. It reads, "We welcome only those who are blind, dumb, and deaf!". Jonn chuckled to himself as he braced himself for what was about to come. After entering through the door to the tavern, two enormous men came up behind him. One of the brutes sporting a blood red mustache, slipped a stick between Jonn's thighs! He turned his fist to the side like a striking prizefighter and then lifted the hundred-and-twenty-pound seafarer off the floor as if he were a loaf of bread. Man number two, the inquisitor, jumped in front of Captain Kimber like a jackal in heat! Through rotted teeth he started questioning Jonn.

"Now, what would a bloody Guineaman be doing in a lowly joint like this one at five o'clock in the afternoon? Maybe you might be bringing us a little present since I didn't see your name on today's guest list! You do have an invite, don't you?" asked the quizzing ruffian.

Jonn Kimber instantaneously replied, "Well, yes, sir, I certainly do!"

The mustached man lifted his leg-sized forearm another quarter of an inch upward, hoping to remedy the Captain of his smart-alecky mouth.

No one saw what really happened at the Three-Legged Dog Tavern that afternoon but two carcasses had been shoved into a booth. Both were propped up as though they were passed out!

Captain Kimber moved to the rear of the tavern. He positioned himself so he could watch the front door. It was six o'clock on the dot.

At eleven minutes after six, a knock interrupted the white noise in the otherwise buzzing tavern. Except for an occasional burst of laughter, the only sounds within the walls of the Three-Legged Dog Tavern were the beelike vibrations of valuable whispers.

The barmaid opened the humongous tavern door. A pretty blond girl curtsied as her sky-blue eyes met the hardened stare coming from the bedraggled tavern maiden.

"May I speak with my Father, please?" asked the girl.

"And whom might your father be?" snarled the barkeep.

"His name is Jonnathan Kimber." sweetly retorted the polished young lady.

Confused, the greying worker abruptly slammed the door leaving Captain Kimber's caller demurely standing on the tavern's front porch. With a practiced hog calling type of bellow, the wrinkled barwoman hollered.

"Jonnathan Kimber, your daughter is at the front door! She ain't allowed in here!"

Captain Kimber haughtily marched toward the tavern's entrance. He had ordered nothing so he just left the place without saying a word.

"Daddy, I was getting so worried about you! Mamma has taken a turn for the worse! Doctor Biddle asked me to fetch you! You're not mad at me are you, Papa?" theatrically queried the precocious girl.

Captain Kimber picked his pretend princess up in his arms and gave her one of those ubiquitous father-daughter hugs! It must have slaked the curiosities of the tavern onlookers because their faces disappeared behind the shaded windows.

Still in character, the angelic faced actress looked up and smiled while kissing her fake daddy's hand. She then parlaying to him his assignment!

"Now, listen very carefully to me, you are to walk in a northeast direction for about ten minutes. When you come to Booker Avenue you will take it west until it intersects with Woolton Road. There will be a roadside stand selling various kinds of produce at the intersection of the two roads.

A gypsy woman wearing a blue scarf will ask if you still like her spiked apple punch! You are to answer, 'No', and then spit on the ground!

You must say nothing more and then continue to the west on Woolton. Two men will come along and ask you if you need a lift to the abbey. Jump onboard with them; they will escort you to your contact. Do you have that, Slick?" The blue-eyed girl said through a more than mature sneer on her face.

"Yes!" curtly answered Jonnathan.

Liverpool had greatly improved its infrastructure over the last five years. The streets were better lit these days. Tile lined gutters had been constructed along both sides of the major roads to prevent washouts and other nasty things that go along with longstanding pools of water!

Jonn surmised that the children looked healthier than he had remembered them as being. Maybe, it was because of the better rubbish disposal boxes recently set up by the city government, Jonn thought.

At the top of Booker Avenue Captain Kimber saw the sparkle and then the flash of reflected sunlight shooting toward him. He was sure someone was watching him through a telescope!

The sound of thunder rumbled behind the apex of what Kimber had once named, "Gypsy Hill". He continued to walk up its sharply angled sidewalk.

Three sets of mule ears were the first things the Captain saw coming over the top of 'Gypsy Hill'. Two drivers of a nine-mule transport wagon were beckoning the mules to slow their pace before the tons of merchandise pushed them down the steep road. Both drivers were pulling their brake levers like skilled pump men!

Jonn watched the monstrous load go by and all the while selfishly prayed it made its way safely to the 'Thomas'. Jonn had worked through almost every night since his last three-legged trip ended in February. 'That was forty some days ago', he said to himself as he topped the hill.

What the Captain had done during those forty laborious days was to build a façade within the slave quarters and thus increased the ship's dry goods capabilities by a few pounds. What was even more incredible, no one else in Liverpool knew about it!

A twig-thatched box with a sign out front advertising the sale of fruits and vegetables got Jonn's mind back on his task at hand. He was to walk by the fruit and vegetable huckster and respond to nothing except the correct que.

In an attempt at emulating the typical road traveler in those parts, Jonn picked up a handful of grey sand and commenced to throw it about six feet above his head and willfully endured the shower he received when gravity did its thing! He then removed his seaman's cap and nonchalantly dusted himself off.

Kimber then pulled together enough of his pedestrian experience to make his gait look pretty much look like the real thing. The woman who was described by the rude blond girl looked more like a fair skinned negro than a gypsy Jonn thought. As the Captain walked past the twiggy hut the voice of an elderly woman broke the early evening air! She was wearing a scarlet hat!

"Hey there, Captain Kimber, fancy seeing you this far from the water! We were all real sad to hear about your wife running off like she did! You reckon, Jonn, you'll be able to get your girl back?"

The Captain fought back his anger. He had to glance away to avoid showing his failure to do so.

Jonn's messenger told him two men would meet him on Woolton Road once he had headed west a bit! They were the conduits to his operative, the only ones.

Without looking too obvious, Jonn quickened his steps to the nearest dip in the road that would block his whereabouts from the lenses of a telescope! He reversed his western directive and crept behind the ridgeline of a good stand of black walnut trees.

His plan was to cut off his legitimate pair of contacts before they ignorantly rode into what Jonn believed was a trap.

Captain Kimber had camouflaged himself within the roadside undergrowth. He laid parallel with the road so that even a wary traveler would not pick the silhouette of his body. He waited.

The sun's position on the city's outline allowed Jonn to gage the approximate time he had left until dark. He had thirty minutes of light left.

There are few smells in this world that are as unmistakably recognizable as Caribbean cigars! The type of man who emits such a scent is also not without a cloud of mystery about him. They, most often, are dangerous people.

This confused Jonn because he had not heard anyone pass from either direction on Woolton Road. But he did smell the very strong whiffs of the cigar smoke. At the peak of his internalized terror, a couple of voices split the evening air! Jonn gave a sigh of relief.

"What the hell are you doing laying in the goddamn woods like a copperhead for, Captain? We've been less than sixty yards away from you since you got into this bunch of trees. We had to make sure you weren't followed! We are glad to say, you were not!" said the two men in unison from the seat of an opulent six-seat carriage.

"You boys really know how to make a man shit his pants don't you? What brings you fellows to this side of the pond?" quizzed Jonn.

Once again as though speaking with the same vocal cords, they answered.

"Jump in, Jonn. We're taking you to the abbey."

David and John Deas were monozygotic twins. Right down to their teeth, the twins were identical! They even used the same Charlestown tailor who obviously fitted both men from the same bolt of cloth.

Each brother wore the same ring with identical markings on their right middle fingers and both carried a thirty-two-caliber walking cane with their company's name on its' solid gold head. "D. and J. Deas Exporters" is what was embossed on it.

"You might as well make yourself useful, Captain. Grab that blunderbuss from between our seats and keep a lookout for uninvited visitors! We've got about an hour's worth of woodsy road ahead so keep your eyes peeled!" the twins said in precise unison.

No one spoke a word after that. There was a quarter moon gradually trying to take over a darkening sky. It was eight o'clock.

The shiny leather bodied carriage powered by two solid black quarter horses slipped through the wood lined turns like a hungry mamba. The twins turned around in their seats and offered comforting smiles along with a duet of consoling words.

"Since Reverend Green bought this tract of land, about seven-hundred acres of it, a field mouse would shutter at the thought of stealing one grain of corn from him! The wharf's scuttlebutt has it that in December a couple of blokes were caught by ole Isaac attempting to chisel off one of the copper gutter spouts from the new chapel he is building onto his castle or whatever you would call it!"

Jonn blankly stared at the strip of remaining sunlight and then asked the obvious question.

"What did he do to them?"

The Deas brothers looked at one another and then smiled as if they had boiled eggs in their mouths. With matching shrugs paired with their foreboding expressions, David and John turned around and silently plopped back into their fine leather seats.

"What did you mean when you guys referenced Isaac Green's castle? I know of no castle in Liverpool, I'm just curious, that's all," asked Kimber.

John leaned over to his brother and asked him a question.

"Should we tell him now or might we cause him to soil his britches again?"

"Naw, go ahead and tell the good captain!" answered David.

"Jonn, Isaac Green's 'whatever-you-want-to-call-it' looks exactly like a giant witch's hat! It really does!" said John.

"Why?" asked the captain.

David who was getting more red-faced by the second, blurted out what sounded like a cross between the punchline of a dirty joke and a soothsaying.

"Because, Captain Kimber, the man has gone bloody bonkers if you ask me!"

"David, why do you believe our financier has lost his marbles'?" seriously asked Jonnathan Kimber.

"You'll see, Jonn! We also asked ourselves the very same questions and we ain't sure they'll ever be answered!" said the Deas twins.

The three men rounded the last bend on Woolton Road, the top of what appeared to be a mammoth spear tip rose into the sky. The brothers curiously glanced back at Jonn and then harmonized the same grunt.

John and David said Reverend Isaac Green's "castle" was like nothing Kimber had ever seen before! The sanctuary's steeple did resemble a witch's hat much like the one illustrated in his daughter's storybook! Jonn painfully remembered.

The high intensity of the estate's security lamps remarkably heightened the amazement of seeing firsthand Isaac's year-long project. He had constructed in red sandstone a sizeable chapel with a peaked tower which ended up resembling a spike intended to puncture the sanctity of heaven!

As soon as the pair of black horses were drawn to a halt, thirty bush-covered men surrounded the Deas's carriage. Each camouflaged soldier was armed with a four-barreled 'mares-leg' shotgun.

That too, was something the veteran captain had not seen until then. Jonn wondered how the gun would fire. Would each barrel shoot individually or in doubles? He mused.

"Gentlemen, I'll ask you to get out of the carriage, please! Do not reach for any of your belongings! Kindly, stand away from the rig and lift your hands, palms front, in the air. Do not speak!" barked the detachment's leader.

Four of the commandos after swinging their slinged weapons behind their shoulder blades, frisked the visitors thoroughly and then placed black hoods over their heads. The commander of the security unit then placed nooses around the three men's necks so they could be led like blind goats into the tower's entrance.

Seven men, three being Isaac Green's invited guests and his four bushmen guards, huddled together as they quickly shuttled into a water-weighted lift. Once the above cauldron was filled, the counter-weight of the water allowed their bulletlike compartment to elevate all the way to the top of the spiked turret. The elevator doors opened.

"You men, step forward four paces and stop!" said a rough voice from behind the hooded invitees.

By the sounds of things, thought Jonn, the guards had left. All that could be heard were the wheezing lungs of air taken in by their host sitting in front of them.

Two gloved hands sliding across rolling wheels caused an assortment of consternations within the minds of the awkwardly treated guests. None of the men thought their situation would end well.

Neither of the Deas brothers nor Captain Kimber had previously met their financier. The only communications received by any of the three came through a child aged courier.

Kimber as well as the Deas boys had done business that way for more than a decade but something very out of the ordinary recently happened! Captain Kimber received a visitor at his countryside flat a week ago.

Not that visitors were an abnormal occurrence because Jonn often had one of Madam Lucky's girls ride out to his home for a conjugal get-together every once in a while. But on one of those particular occasions something quite odd took place.

What was so different about that particular incident as Jonn recalled, the prostitute was the spitting image of his wife! What felt like a narcotically infused session turned out to be an event in which he had almost no recollection of what happened during the woman's visit!

Upon awakening, Jonn discovered a pound of sacked-up gold coins laying on a signed employment agreement. The Royal African Company had contracted him to pick up "some special cargo" in Senegal.

In that Jonnathan planned to never return to Britain anyway, he didn't particularly care what 'special cargo' meant. All he knew was that a woman looking like his wife, left him a bag of elephant headed coins worth more than the cost of a brand-new ship! Suddenly a voice interrupted Kimber's thought.

"Gentlemen, I am pleased by your punctuality! I apologize if a mild bit of paranoia swept over you boys during your travels here. Given the cloak and dagger mindsets we are seeing acted out these days, ya'll did well by making it here!

Those hoods are annoying I know, but they are necessary. Should any of you ever get caught up in a quagmire, my identity could never be compromised no matter how skilled our enemies' torture experts are! Although, if we do our jobs correctly those kinds of irritations won't come into play and we'll retire as wealthy men!" said Isaac Green.

One of the guards in the Reverend's study slid three chairs into the backs of the hooded guests' knees. Reverend Green then went on with the preamble he had already begun.

"I have been your paymaster over the last eleven years! The Royal African Company has pretty much been defuncted for quite some time now!

Although several of the local merchants along with a few deep pocketed politicians believe they are investing in their own export concerns, they are actually buying stock into my company!" gloated Reverend Green as he rolled closer to the seated men. He then began to whisper.

"You see, Gentlemen, I am this century's czar overseeing the distribution of human cargo coming off the continent of Africa! I am the man who manipulates although I prefer to call it 'regulates', the prices paid for every negro shipped across the Atlantic Ocean!" tyrannically yelled Green.

Several shots were heard from below the tower! The voice of the guard ensconced behind Kimber and the Deas twins gave a breathless report to his boss.

"Sir, two men were spotted crossing in on the northeastern perimeter about fifteen minutes ago! It was assessed by one of the 'zebras', the intruders were attempting to do some poaching in the forest! Both men had shotguns and consequently were dispatched! Sir, do you wish to examine their bodies?"

"No, Tonka, that won't be necessary. What kind of weapons did they say the poor blokes were toting?" inquisitively asked the Reverend.

"Just shotguns, sir," stated the bodyguard.

"In that case, say a nice little prayer over their bodies and dispose of them in the usual manner!" sullenly said Reverend Green.

"Absolutely, sir!" replied Tonka.

The room became silent again. In an evangelistic manner, Reverend Isaac Green rolled his wheelchair within inches of his hooded guests and began his oenomel.

"As I was saying and I will be brief, I called you here because I wish to inform you men that I have drafted you into my cabinet! In seven days, Captain Kimber will command the 'Thomas' and take her on its normal leg to Sierra-Leon. You Deas boys are to become part of the ship's crew until you make it to the coast of Western Africa! This is a brand-new game, Gentlemen, and one with very high stakes! Good evening!"

Isaac Green turned his wheelchair around and pushed the leather treads on his chair's wheels toward an empty room on the other side of the steeple's slanted wall. He was retiring for the night.

The three hooded men sat quietly in their seats. They could hear the cadence of three competing hearts which sounded as if all three men were pounding a dead cow's ribcage.

When the elevator doors opened, Kimber, David and John Deas were returned to their carriage. Only the guard removing their hoods was present.

Thunder rumbled about thirty miles to the east. Jonn clutched the extra blunderbuss. It was a long and wordless trip back to the wharf.

At four-thirty a loud thud jarred Jonn from his otherwise ragged sleep. The bad dreams had returned so being awakened was not such a bad thing at all.

The Captain made sure he held the lantern three feet away from his body! Shooting at lone lanterns from a passing boat had recently become an international sport. He cautiously opened his cabin's door.

A grinning black boy was standing very close to the door. Jonn invited the lad into his room.

"Young man, if you will step back about two paces, I'll certainly grant you your deserved entrance given the monsoon that's upon us! Please, come in, I'll fix you a mug of cocoa!" kindly stated Captain Kimber.

"Sir, I mustn't tarrsy. I have a message for you! 'When you pass into the Caribbean Islands, you are to send up your mast the Spanish flag! Britain will declare war on Spain within the next forty-eight hours!'" said the boy.

The young negro then pulled from his pocket a sack of gold coins and handed it to the Captain. He said not one word before his return into the rainy dark. He then peddled away on his rusty bicycle.

Captain Kimber crossed four pieces of dried kindling in his oven's fireplace and sprinkled about a teaspoon of coal oil on the pine sticks before setting them ablaze. Miniscule bubbles clung to the duck eggs as the temperature of the pan began to boil. He prepared a pot of tea while he sponge-bathed. There was a scarlet red line across the dawn's horizon.

Jonn looked at himself in his full-length mirror. It had a rude crack at the bottom of it. He remembered the scuffle that took place over the thing.

The four-foot glass covering had a barrel of nails roll onto it during a night of rough sea. He had to pay for the thing so he kept it!

Sheets of cold rain swept across the planked roads near the dock area. The wooden planks were slippery because of the buildup of coal dust. His new boot soles were no match for the slick inclines so Jonn made his way down Copperas Lane via the sandy path paralleling Carriage Avenue. He could hear the beginnings of a busy morning before he reached the overlook at James Street.

The mercantile wagons had already fashioned their ques. It was the "early-bird rule," Jonn mused.

From seventy-five yards away and despite the rain, Kimber spotted a major breach in the security of the 'Thomas'! His cabin's lights were on!

Kimber was positive he had blown them out. No one was permitted into the Captain's quarters at any time!

Jonn needed to move to a higher elevation in order to get to a better vantage point. When he did, Captain Kimber could see someone sitting behind his desk!

Having sustained only one stain on his britches from his slippery reconnaissance climb, Captain Kimber didn't have much difficulty neatening himself up. He felt for his bone-dry pistols and then assured himself that his cane's rifle barrel wasn't stopped up! He then stepped onto the 'Thomas's' gangplank with a dagger clinched in his left fist and a cocked pistol in his right!

Jonn made every effort possible to quiet the turning of the brass key through its two-part lock system. The lock took one three-hundred-and-sixty-degree twist to the left and then a one hundred and eighty degree clockwise turn to get it to unlock.

It was a French devise as the captain recalled and one he would never buy again. He never trusted the French anyway! He opened the door.

"Top of the morning to you, Captain Kimber! Now, sir, in that I am assuming you are as jumpy as I am, I shall ask you to place your weapons gently on your very nice conference table!

Please understand, my intentions are not hostile. I am simply here at the request of a mutual friend of ours, Reverend Isaac Green!" said the man hiding behind the bookshelf.

"Then show me your face!" shouted the perturbed Captain.

An impeccably dressed gentleman stepped out from behind Kimber's collection of log books. His eyes bore into Jonn's much like a lion's gaze into the pupils of an elephant. He wasn't that confident of himself, the captain noted.

"Captain Kimber, my name is James F. Stanfield. Sir, in less than an hour your crew of ten will be sitting around this very table! I do not have the luxury of time to explain the details but let me say, your staff has been carefully selected. They are specialists in every sense of the word. And, Jonn, they will follow your orders! Perhaps it would be to both of our interests to have dinner together this evening! I'll pick you up here at eight!" said the intruding Mister Stanfield before he exited the 'Thomas'.

From outside, Jonn heard what sounded like a command sounding-off. Captain Kimber walked toward the closest porthole and peeked out.

He rushed back over to the conference table to gather his side arm and sat down in the chair which provided the most optimal view of the door. He checked his watch.

At six o'clock, a moderate three-strike knock was instantly responded to by the anxious Captain.

"Please enter," said Jonnathan.

A well-groomed naval officer entered Captain Kimber's cabin. He was wearing a meticulously tailored uniform. He immediately came to attention, saluted, and then introduced himself.

"Sir, Commander Devgru reporting for duty! Captain, may I have your permission to ask these men to enter, sir?"

"Granted," said Kimber.

Nine scraggly sailors meandered into Kimber's conference room as if they had chosen to lounge in it for the day's entirety! Captain Kimber became enraged and reached for his pistol beneath his jacket!

With the speed of striking vipers, Commander Devgru's gang of ruffians drew their weapons and aimed them at Jonn's chest! The confused Captain quietly remained in his seat and angrily stared at the violating commander.

"Captain Kimber, there is no doubt an irregularity is occurring here! Soon, I shall explain in full detail the reasons for these precautionary measures. There is absolutely nothing for you to worry about. No harm will come to you nor to your ship!" consoled Devgru.

"So, why is this cloak and dagger bullshit necessary?" asked the out gunned Captain.

"Captain Kimber, I shall repeat, the necessary precautions are of a security concern! Sir, I strongly urge you to be patient! Colonel Stanfield will fill you in tonight but in the meantime my unit and I have a great deal to do! Kindly gather your gear, sir, and leave the 'Thomas' immediately! We will be standing tall by the morning and ready for your inspection! Good day to you, Captain Kimber!" said Commander Devgru.

The rain had stopped. Jonn had no idea where he was going to go for the next twenty-four hours. He took his brass telescope out of its case and scanned the docks.

Seagulls were working the fishing boats harder toward the north than they were to the south. Jonn considered this as an omen.

More fish meant more money for the fishermen! Fishermen with bulging pockets would be drinking as soon as their captains paid them out. Drinking men also talk a lot, he reasoned.

The tavern called "Slim Jim's" was an old dock house that had been transformed into a working man's drink house. There were no frills to be had at Slim Jim's. The only thing their customers got was a place at the bar, a mug and a pint of whatever kind of booze they had in stock that day.

Jonn found an empty stool between two older gentlemen. A huge man inquisitively raised his eyebrows as the Captain sat down. Jonn assumed he was the bartender.

"What will it be, Bub?"

"Scotch"

"Ain't got it!"

"Well then, whiskey," conceded Kimber.

Seeing as how the captain saw that the pig-headed server was moving, he pulled out a small silver coin and put it beside the empty cup setting before him.

A minute later, Jonn's pint of liquor was slammed down in front of him. The ham-handed barman then tried to pick up his silver piece with a magnetized rock. When it didn't stick to the magnet the boorish brute simply put the coin into his money pouch, grunted, and walked away without even a hint of appreciation.

Once the first mouthful of rotgut had its required twelve seconds to take effect, Captain Jonn Kimber began going over in his mind the jagged edges surrounding the past twenty-four hours. He couldn't stop thinking about that girl back at the Three-legged Dog Tavern.

"Who in the hell was Reverend Isaac Green and what had caused the radical change in the Royal African Company's way of doing business?" Jonnathan queried to himself.

Jonn dug into his pocket for another shilling. Just as he was about ready to flag the bartender down, the guy sitting to the right of him gently touched his arm.

"The next one's on me," said the stranger.

"No thanks." Captain Kimber curtly said.

"Well, sir, if you don't mind me saying so, I'd bet you are a man…"

"I do mind!" interrupted the semi-inebriated Jonn Kimber.

"Then I am to understand, you do not wish to unshackle yourself from the albatross of ignorance? It's plastered all over your face, you know! Captain Kimber, I was sent here by our mutual boss to help clear up some of the oddities that have suddenly fallen upon you! I believe you will feel better after we talk a bit! So, what do you say? May I buy you another pint?" softly asked the intrepid fellow.

"If you insist then I'll accept your offer; but I'd like to know who's buying the drinks!" kiddingly prodded Jonn.

"Captain Kimber, my name is Bill Bosman. I've been running the triangle even longer than you have, Jonn!"

"How come you're still alive?" Jonn wryly whispered.

"Just lucky, I guess. But maybe unlucky, who knows, right?"

"I've puzzled over that myself," said Kimber.

As if scripted in a Shakespearean play, a silly looking seaman stumbled into Slim Jim's Tavern. Although the colorfully clad sailor was apparently drunk, he was somehow able to engage in a brief conversation with the bartender.

"Jim, you might not have noticed but I am wearing my happy clothes today!"

"Why is that?" sneered Jim.

"Because I'm for certain going to die soon, that's why!"

Jonn and Bosman looked at one another. Both grimaced.

The bartender, swung his body across his teakwood bar top and commenced to jack-slap the drunken young man about eight or nine times!

"I've told you before, Son, drinking is not for you! Your goddamned mother, bless her soul, was a full-blooded Cherokee so for that reason alone, among a thousand others, you ain't allowed to drink!" yelled Jim.

"But, Daddy, it's for real this time! The 'guarda costas' cut off Captain Jenkin's ear last week! He was somewhere in the Caribbean they say. The Spanish done it! We're going to war, Papa!" slobbered the wobbling teen.

"Boy, get out of those ridiculous clothes right this minute! If you ain't back there scrubbing them damn pots in the next five seconds, I will most certainly beat you like a circus monkey!" hollered Slim Jim.

"You see, Jonn, this is an example of why we need to talk!" joked Bill Bosman.

"Correct. Where do you suggest we go?" asked the Captain.

"How would you feel about a nice little boat ride?" quizzed Bosman.

"Let's go; I'm ready if you are?" quipped Jonn.

William Bosman had invested most of the money he had earned and even more of it he had not gained honestly into his estate! Its rolling grounds spread out over three hundred acres, he said.

Above ground, Bill Bosman's home was a modest rock dwelling surrounded by a ten-foot wall made of the same limestone used to build his house. Below his ground level floor was a labyrinth of hallways that shot beneath the hill overlooking Bootle Point.

If one were to calculate the worth of Bosman's living space by square footage Kimber figured, it would make his newfound drinking buddy one of the wealthiest men in Liverpool! Briskly, both men shuttled to the end of a hallway which gently rose in altitude by way of almost unnoticeable ramps.

Jonn checked the tiny compass at the butt of his cane. They were walking toward the northeast.

Unexpectantly, Bill threw up his hand with a halting signal! He turned toward Jonn with his right forefinger pursed against his lips. This needed no explanation because one could hear the distant voices of working men.

As if moved by involuntary tendon contractions, the captains untied the complex knots before winching down Captain Bosman's bullet-shaped craft into the channel below it. To Jonn, the thing appeared to be a sealed metal tube that's contour resembled a dead dolphin.

"Captain, what in the hell have you made here?"

"Why, it's a phallic-symbol, Captain Kimber!" Bill smartly responded.

"No shit, what the fuck is this thing?" said Jonn.

"Jump in and I'll show you!" comically warned Bosman.

With little effort, Captain Bosman turned an inset lever. A hatch opened.

Bill smiled at Jonn much like a kid would do after launching a stone through a church's window!

"Watch your step," firmly spoke Captain Bosman.

"Bill, do I smell fuel oil?" asked Kimber.

"Hush, you'll ruin the surprise!" teased Bill.

Restlessly, the awestruck guest sat in what 'Captain Billy' called, the copilot's seat. Jonn tried to take it all in without up-turning his reputation for having a smooth demeanor; but he failed.

"Jesus Christ, Man, what have you done?" cried Jonnathan.

"An old friend of mine and I have been fiddling around with this boat for about six years, I recon!" said Captain Bosman pensively.

"You, call this a boat, do you, Captain?" Said Jonn as spittle spewed from his lips.

"I'd call it a 'submarine'; but Tom doesn't like that name!" Whined Bill.

"Tom?" Pressed Kimber.

"Yea, the guy helping me with his 'sub boat'! He goes by the name of "Newcomen", he's an old salt, like us!" Bosman teased.

"What does it do?" Kimber asked with a quickish grin. "You'll see!"

Captain Jonn Kimber's jaw flew open when he felt the vibrations from the spinning propeller. Bosman released the unneeded steam from the fuel-fired boiler into a pipe that followed along the top of the vessel's ceiling all the way to the back of the floating tube.

"Where does it go, Bill?" "Where does what go, Jonn?" "The goddamned steam!"

"I'm impressed by your zealous question, Captain Kimber! Exactly the kind of inquiry expected from a seaman with some experience in the evasive arts, no doubt!

And you are so correct; white smoke would certainly be a dead giveaway as to your whereabouts, now wouldn't it?" chortled the submarine pilot.

"So, how do you hide it?" further pressed Jonn.

"That particular genius deserves to be crowned upon Mister Newcomen's head! That rascal figured out a way to compress boiling saltwater so compactly that the acceleration of the craft is enhanced threefold just by the release of that pint-up steam!

What's even more amazing, that underwater release also spins the armatures of a generator which lights up the gages of our control panel! It gets dark in here!" boasted Bill.

"So, when can I get a test ride?" Jonn anxiously asked.

"Maybe tomorrow night. We should have a full moon. If the weather holds out, we'll give it a whirl then. We'll see!" slyly said Bosman.

"Please tell me then, Captain Bosman, what is it that you needed to speak with me about that required all of this secrecy?" Jonn playfully questioned.

"I'll tell you what, let's get out of this metal coffin and go someplace where we don't have to smell each other's breath!" countered Bill.

"I'm right behind you, sir, you, lead the way!" remarked Jonn.

The two men climbed out of the Bosman and Newcomen experimental craft as if they were escaping from their tombs. Claustrophobia, admittedly, was the authentic reason for Bill's exiting suggestion; however, he playfully told Jonn it was because of his farting that expedited their departure!

They sat down in a shady spot. Both captains shared a swig or two from Jonn's terrapin flask. A couple of church bells competed in announcing the noon hour.

"Captain Kimber, the 'Thomas' is about to become the spearhead if not the flagship, in the most clandestine naval operation ever recorded in the dark annals of history! Although our efforts will never be recorded, they will retool the construct of what we currently call a normal world!"

Captain Bosman paused as he fingered Jonn's turtle shell. He took another deep swallow, grimaced, and then continued.

"You and I, Jonn, in less than a month, will release into the Americas hundreds of highly trained and lethal agents onto their soil! We are to be the first of thousands of more insertions to follow! The Colonies are to become the headquarters for what is to be named…"

With the speed of a rattler, William Bosman withdrew from his shoulder holster a pistol and fired it at an aspen tree. Seeing as how the apparent spy was dead before he hit the ground, Bill took his time measuring the distance of his shot.

"As I was saying, America, primarily speaking of New York, will become the home to what Isaac Green calls, the 'world capitol'," Captain Bosman said.

"Bill, what in the hell is going on?" questioned Jonn Kimber.

"Jonn, I swear upon my Mother's grave, I know very little about it!"

"So where does Isaac Green come into play here?" nervously muttered Jonn.

"I've asked that same question to myself a thousand times! If my hunch is right, Jonn, our good reverend, financier, and confidence man is up to something naughty! He's sure as hell spending a lot of money on something!

Green claims to know exactly when the "Rapture" is coming! His congregational followers who by the way serve as his grounds' staff, have been taught that 'all whom are faithful to him will be the forerunners into the pearly gates'!" preached Bosman.

"And what do you think?" snickered Jonn.

"Captain Kimber, I have lived to be almost fifty years old! My eyes have seen a lot and my ears have heard even more!

When I run across one of those kinds of 'human-puzzles' like the one you just presented to the floor, I do as my Grandpappy said to do; that is, 'Follow the Money!'."

Jonn stared across the Mercy. Eight seagulls by his count were diving into the wake of 'The Comet' as it arrived from its morning catch. Fear began overtaking him like a freezing fog. He thought about what had happened that day and he wondered if the seagulls ever thought about that kind of thing.

"Captain, you mentioned you were expecting a James Stanfield at your place tonight around eight, you said?" asked Bosman.

"That's right. What're your thoughts on that?" asked Jonn.

"My boy, from what I have already observed over the past few hours and taking into consideration my fifty-yard bullseye, I'd say it's a good day for a crapshoot! I believe one should not struggle when caught in a riptide; therefore, not that we have another option, I would think it best to just go with the flow, Jonn!" said Bill.

"Unfortunately, I see it the same way! But I can say this, I will feel a lot better when I get back out to sea. At least there, I will have more control over my fate!"

"Maybe." solemnly said Bosman.

"Listen, Mate, why don't you help me upload that nosey bloke into the back of my wagon. We'll dump him in a spot where a single splash will rid us of our load!"

"Look at this, Captain Bosman, your ball went through this lad's telescope as well as his brain! That was a remarkable shot, sir!" marveled Kimber.

"It was a 'spitzer', not a ball."

"Pardon me, Bill, did you say the word, 'spitzer'?"

"Yea, it's a new bullet the Austrians are playing with. It's not a ball; it is a conically shaped piece of lead. Interestingly, it can only be fired from a rifled barrel. The difference between a spiraling cone and our regular speeding ball is obvious isn't it?" Bill said with a cocky air about him.

"Boy, that's an understatement! Where did you learn to shoot like that?"

"Probably from the same place you learned to use a wrist garrote!"

Captain Kimber said nothing but did jump up into the shotgun seat of Captain Bosman's wagon. Jonn then reached into his breast pocket and retrieved his terrapin flask. He took the next to the last swallow and handed the shell over to Bill. Both men knew the bull sharks would be waiting for them but they took their time just the same!

"Who do you think that guy was?" pocked Jonn.

"His name's Richard Turpin." flatly answered Bosman.

In a more serious tone this time and postured far differently, Captain Kimber walked over to his buddy, Bill Bosman and looked directly into his eyes.

"Bill, I'm going to ask you again, who the fuck was the man whom you shot out of the tree?"

"Dick Turpin was nothing more than a common thief! Mostly, his shtick was robbery, the highway style! The only thing that made him any different from the rest of the hoodlums was ole 'Dick' had turned pirating into an artform!

I was under the impression he was in prison. Frankly, it baffles me as to why he was here!" said Bill.

"You say he was locked up?" asked Kimber.

"Yeah, I did." answered Bill.

"Did you take a close look at the telescope he was looking at us through?" remarked Jonnathan.

"No, I didn't but I did consider keeping it as sort of a trophy in that you bragged about my shooting and all! joked Bosman.

"Well, I did! It was the standard brass type. It's the kind given to seamen in basic training!" spouted Captain Kimber.

"Maybe ole 'Dick' down there was here on a reprieve from the hangman's rope! Is it possible that our infamous highwayman was sent by none other than King George to extrapolate whatever he could from someone or some group who may be under his suspicious eyes?" poisonously questioned Bill.

"That's a possibility. Go on!" prompted Kimber.

"Could it be that this invisible King of ours is not as flawlessly noble as we would have hoped he was? Could it be, our pure and noble Reverend Isaac Green is up to something that his Majesty deems as a threat to his kingdom? Further, what would prevent George II from marching up here or over to Isaac's place and killing out the whole lot of us?" loudly wailed Captain Bosman.

"Bill, it is true, we don't know the people we are working for nor what their ultimate objectives are!" said Jonn.

"That is very true but can you show me at least one example of what we have been hired to do that would be considered breaking the law?" said the red-faced Captain Bosman.

The two captains seemed to run out of arguing ammunition simultaneously. Ragged bits of the burlap bag that Dick Turpin's body was wrapped in was floating in the froth below. Hungry seagulls dove for the scraps the bulls had left behind.

A snap of Captain Bosman's whip ignited his quarter horse into a jolting start. Just as the Deas twins had done, Bill handed Jonn a double-barreled mares-leg. Fire was in the hole, Captain Kimber feared.

As the two Guineamen were trotting across the northern perimeter of Liverpool, something quite out of the ordinary was observed by both men at the same time! A hundred and fifty yards below the hilly road an enormous cloud of smoke rose into the air.

The sounds of men humming in very low tones vibrated the ground beneath the canopy of trees the group of hooded men were huddled under. From what could be seen through Captain Kimber's telescope there appeared to be a ceremony taking place!

For a closer look, Bill tied 'Gin Nose' his horse's name, to a nearby fencepost and then motioned for Jonn to follow him. He whispered that he knew of a path which would put them into a better hearing range of the humming ritualists!

Jonn's new boots proved once again to be dangerously slippery. He grumbled as he fought the sharp angles toward Bosman's suggested spot.

"I'd say there's two hundred of them, wouldn't you?" Jonn excitedly whispered.

"At least!" responded Bill.

"What in the hell are they wearing, Captain?" asked Kimber. "Jonn, what I am seeing is hard for me to describe! You take a look!" Bosman said as he handed Jonn his telescope.

"I'll be a sonofabitch!" Jonn not so silently exclaimed.

"Jonn, we need to get the hell out of here! We can talk about this when we get back to the wagon!" breathlessly said Captain Bosman.

Without warning, the sound of a screaming cannon ball whizzed over the men's position. Two seconds later, they heard the field weapon's report and witnessed Bosman's carriage along with 'Gin Nose' being obliterated.

Stunned, the two captains stared at one another in disbelief. There was nothing that either of them could do without giving away their hiding place.

But as luck might have it and to certainly compound the confusion even further, Bill and Jonn saw the hundred or so men, all of whom were wearing papier-Mache animal heads, cluster together as a herd of cattle might do and shuffle away into a deeper part of the surrounding forest.

All during their passive retreat the monk clad men with their hoods covering the specie they represented, continued to buzz until the moss and the ground foliage muffled their sounds. This left the perplexed Guineamen in quite a lurch!

With almost the same spirit in which a man would take his first step toward the gallows, both vintage warriors slowly snaked their way through the thick hedgerows and into the heavier tree line. At least there, they would have a chance against the cannoneer set-up over to the southeast of them.

"Bill, I believe it would be prudent of us to head toward my place. I wouldn't think returning to yours would be wise at all!" exclaimed Kimber in a whisper.

"Whoever the bastard was that killed Gin Nose will soon die by my hand! I loved that damn horse." pined Bill.

"We'll mourn together, Brother! For now, we have to move as far away from your horse's killer and as fast as possible! I think it best if we move below that ridge over there…"

No sooner had those words left Jonn's mouth when another flying ball exploded seventy feet above the fleeing men's heads. Although knocked to the ground and still ambulatory, neither man could hear. The explosion's concussion had split their eardrums!

Now left with only hand signals to communicate with, Bill pointed to the west and hand formed the mouth of a cave.

"Are you saying you know where a cave is?" lip-synced Jonn. Bill nodded.

"I'm right behind you!" grunted Kimber.

After a reasonably unobstructed trek, the mouth of a cave gaped open behind a veil of ivy. Bill led the way in.

Jonn reached into his pea-coat pocket for the candle he always had in there. While he was fishing around for it his fingers ran across something he had forgotten to mention to Bill. It was about the elephant coin he was holding in his hand.

He nudged Bill and then handed him the gold piece while he held the burning candle above the golden thing.

"Where did you find this?" asked Bosman.

"It was in Turpin's pocket. That's all that was there in it and I did search the man pretty damn well! What do you think it is?" tauntingly quested Jonn.

"My guess is, it's a symbolic token of some sort. We'll figure that out later but right now, we need to get through this passageway. It gets rather tight up ahead so we had better utilize our candlepower for as long as we can," commanded Captain Bosman.

Kimber learned very quickly that Bill had been correct about the tight spaces they would have to get through! Finally, light broke through the darkness like an angel opening her wings!

As soon as their eyes adjusted, the men left the cave as quickly as jackrabbits on fire! They sprinted toward a wood lined cart road Bill prophesized would take them a mile north of Jonn's cottage. It was six o'clock.

Given there was only about a half hour of daylight and a three-quarter moon above, any directional choices made would have to be well thought out. Predators wait until dark to do their work and so do highwaymen!

From their prone positions, Jonn and Bill could see through their naked eyes, Jonn's house appeared to be undisturbed. As a precaution, Jonn motioned to Bosman to carefully glass his place over before committing to cross that much real-estate. There was still enough sniping light left in the day to consider!

Jonn had set up several contraptions which would tip him off to any intrusions made during his absence. His ingenious devices were subtle in appearance and yet effective. They were natural looking things.

After examining his 'signal-traps', Kimber returned his attention toward the decorative front gate used by folks like the postman and tax collectors. It had a little bell on the top of it so when anyone opened it, the ringing noise would politely announce their arrival at his address. But the bell wasn't part of the trick!

The tell-tale deal was, the thing that told the seamen his place had been breached was nothing more than a thin strand of wire attached to the gate's hinge! You see, once the four-foot slatted gate was opened, the wire would invisibly tighten and cause the wooden-rooster, a yard ornament, to turn toward the house! It was that eloquent!

If Stanfield were coming, he would most likely be along within the hour. Entering the house was very risky. They already knew their pursuers were adapt with pyrotechnics. Whomever their cannoneer was, it made crossing the separating field like rolling dice with Satan. Bill was the first to detect the vibrations of horses coming their way! Kimber and Bosman slid deeper into the undergrowth. Pistols drawn and cocked, they waited.

With bullets zipping through the trees behind him, James F. Stanfield came over the hill like a bat out of hell! The Clydesdales pulling the cyclonic coal wagon were about ready to drop in their tracks!

Stanfield's jaws were clinched so tightly it made his taught face look as though it belonged to a mythical demon! When he saw Kimber and Bosman stand up with their cocked pistols in hand, Jim turned the team toward his perceived nemesis!

With the reins in his teeth, Stanfield drew back both hammers of his sawed-off shotgun and prepared to shoot his assailants as he rode by!

Through a stroke of pure genius, Jonn Kimber at the speed of lightening tore his jacket off, balled it up, and then threw the woolen mound into the faces of the oncoming Clydesdales! Both giant animals then sat down on their haunches in an effort to brake their body's momentum!

Within seconds, the massive beasts had managed to come to a complete stop in the middle of the road! James Stanfield on the other hand, did not. Fortunately, he was not injured even though he may have been airborne for forty feet or more!

With Kimber's help, James Stanfield was able to climb over the bullet ridden tailgate of the stolen coal truck. Kimber continued to revive Stanfield by pressing on his ribcage. The breath had been knocked out of him, Jonn said to himself.

From more than a mile away, a fiery ball streaked into the evening sky! Preempted by a loud bang, the entire area lit up as if the sun had replaced the moon.

A bullet zipped through the walls of the coal wagon splintering bits of wood and coal dust on top of Kimber and Stanfield. When Captain Bosman snapped the backs of the Clydesdales, chunks of black coal began falling just before the rest of it toppled onto the recuperating Stanfield and his medic, Captain Kimber.

The eighteen hands tall animals were being terrorized by their new maniacal rein holder. Bosman cursed the beasts every time he stung one of them with the tip of his buggy whip!

By their frothy mouths, it was apparent to Bill the highjacked workhorses had never been pushed harder than a couple of miles per hour! He smacked the quadrupeds into an eyewatering speed but not fast enough to escape a speeding bullet!

Instantly, a hissing round passed through the haunches of the Clydesdale on the driver's side! The beige and white giant crumbled beneath the coal truck's powerful inertia.

The other unscathed horse tried to compensate for the coal wagon's lack of balance but could not do it. Consequently, both Clydesdales ended up skidding off the road and down a grassy embankment and into a waterfilled ditch!

In an attempt to save the horses from drowning, Bill withdrew his boot knife and began cutting the tackle loose from the gasping brutes. Seeing that he was doing nothing more than slicing strips of loose rawhide, he ran to the back of the upside-down coal truck. Both rear wheels were still spinning.

Two bullets slammed into the 'O' belonging in the inverted word, 'COAL'. A third round joined the other two outlining a triangle. An egg would have covered the grouping.

Captain Bosman dove into the ditchwater and hid behind the now listless Clydesdales. All around him, he could hear the buzzing sounds of the animal headed people but he could see any of them!

Trying to not panic, Bill ran back around to the rear of the painted coal box and began kicking the roof as if it were a rabid dog. Desperately, he called for the men to answer.

"Bill, can you get the door open? We've got a half ton of bloody coal between us and you!" Jonn angrily hollered back to Bosman.

The animal heads were closing in! Bosman had only enough time to save his own skin or get the men out of the coal truck. A miniscule number of choices making seconds remained. But then as though coming from out of the heavens, a familiar voice cut through the night air!

"That's right, Men! Always triangulate your quarry! One mustn't leave a single avenue open for its escape; the minute you do, he will strike out at you!" bellowed the vaguely remembered voice.

Captain Bosman couldn't see a thing and yet he could distinguish the buzzlike hums coming from a large number of men. Feeling as though he had no other option, Bill Bosman clinched his pistol in his right hand and his sheath knife in his left and rushed toward the invisible voice with the fury of a warlock!

The wildly attacking captain raced about ten yards before he was swooped up in a net which then cast him up into the treetops. Had a passing nun overheard Bosman's curse words, she would have most certainly turned into a pillar of salt!

From high above, William Bosman looked down upon a platoon-sized circle of full-grown men each of whom were sporting some type of exotic animal head! Bill glared down at his captors as he discovered why he had been unable to see his pursuers.

The monk-like outfits the animal heads wore had tiny ferrotype threads woven into their fabrics. When seen in lowlight, the garment would actually reflect the surroundings making the wearers virtually impossible to see!

Having been in precarious situations before, Captain Bosman knew he had to remain levelheaded. He then tried to take control of the situation by using intimidation.

"Just for your information, you gaming lads down there are in violation of His Majesty's Code number, eight-one-six-three! It's a hanging offense to obstruct the operation of any overseas export activity whether it be on land or sea…"

Clapping noises filled the ground below the suspended captain. For at least a one-hundred-yard radius beneath him, hundreds of reflectively camouflaged animal heads began slapping their hands against the butts of their rifles while humming their obnoxious buzzing noise.

Below, the men according to their mocked specie, herded together while communicating across the congregation with distinctly different buzzing inflections. The Zebras used a high-pitched wheeze while the Jackals hummed more of a nasally buzz.

Six 'Elephants' each pulling a wagon, paraded around the inner circle of men while passing out torches to the rifle shouldered animal heads.

By now, Bill could feel the heat coming from the dozens of blazing lanterns below him. With an abrupt change in the cacophony of buzzes, the netted captain knew his sentence was soon to be announced.

A ceremonial platform was being put together by the Hyaenas. From behind the ranks of the seen animal heads, Captain Bosman saw the forming of an entourage! They were about to escort their leader to the stage below him.

An immediate silence fell over the torchlit army as an approaching gold shield followed by six lion heads made their way up the steps of the makeshift stage. Bill looked very closely at the shield's markings.

From the Captain's perspective, he saw a four by four-foot repoussage which was backdropped with an iron cross. Attached to the front of the hammered-out shield was the antlered skull of an elk.

Captain Bosman pulled from his pocket his brass monocular and glassed the petrifying spectacle below him. Jonn and Stanfield were still in the coal box as best he could tell.

Four Latin words were inscribed between each arm of the iron cross on the gold shield,

'Deum, Diligite, Animalia, and Diligentes'. "Honoring God by Honoring his Creatures" was a preposterous thing to put on a goddamned golden shield, Thought Bosman.

Finally, after thinking about the ridiculous animal headed people parading around underneath him Bill decided that the only possibility he had left was to infuriate them!

"Let us examine your quite stupid set-up! Here we have god's animals who are actually a bunch of eunuchs wearing silly masks, prancing around the forest like a gang of rowdy school boys!" yelled

Captain William Bosman who then proceeded to urinate upon the upwardly looking elephants.

The buzzing hums grew louder! The true candor of the people revealed itself when a troop of monkey heads formed into a triangular formation. One man moved into the center of the three-sided configuration. His job was to shoot a dart into the body of their netted catch!

After the initial sting of the dart had subsided, Bosman grew quite melancholy. Not knowing whether the poisonous dart was going to prove out to be a deadly one, Bill made a fading perusal of his life. He even prayed some.

Just as the buzzing below began harmonizing with the legs of katydids, Bill was able to put a face with the familiar voice that both he and Jonn had recognized! Bosman then slipped into a comatose state.

An unkind breeze shifted the smoke from the burning Clydesdales and trapped the oily fumes within the reunited prisoners' hoods. Laughter filled the air as if a carnival were in full swing.

From left to right, Captain Jonn Kimber, James Stanfield, and Captain William Bosman had been tied to three separate posts situated as though each were to face a firing squad. A bonfire roared so close to the staked seamen the candle in Jonn's pea coat pocket began running down his britches leg. The animal heads were singing from a distance not so far away.

A drumroll began, marking in the minds of the captives that what was to happen next would probably involve them! The animal heads began marching.

From beneath their sweltering hoods the men could pick out through only bits and pieces some clues as to who their captors were. Certain accents, Austrian in particular, seemed to permeate sporadic chats going on between the buzzes. Some of the animal heads apparently didn't know where to stand or what to do.

This led Jonn to assume that whomever the animal heads were, they were not regulars at meeting together. For that one isolated reason, Kimber surmised that what was taking place was some sort of ritualized convention.

The bonfire had settled for the rich fuel of melting horse flesh rather than opting for the hardwood. It seemed to hiss with satisfaction over its decision.

After an hour of hearing nothing more than the normal night sounds, James Stanfield once again took a chance. This time however he wasn't so blatantly impudent.

"Jonn, I have a question," whispered Jim.

"Yea? What about, Jim?" queried Kimber.

"You just answered it! I have another question to ask you," stated Stanfield.

"Well?" Jonn asked.

"If you are next to me on my left side then who is on my right?" James Stanfield asked.

"I'm hoping it's the fellow they had in the boar net! The one I mentioned to you, remember?" Jonn questionably responded.

"Bill… right?" asked James Stanfield.

"I'm here, Jonn. Sir, whomever you are, I'm pleased to meet you! I would shake your hand although I am a bit indisposed at the moment." mirthfully stated Bosman.

A loud boom shattered the hooded men's nerves down to their bones! A voice whispered from the other side of the blaze!

"Gentlemen, let me be the first to make an apology for the miserable welcoming you received from us. As you will soon learn, we are gentlemen of the highest order and certainly not the type of chaps who would normally stoop to such barbaric measures; but the boys got itchy for a chase and elected to use you fellows as their evening's play-prey!

I decided to hold back from the others to afford us the opportunity to pull the cat out of the bag so to speak, but I am quite positive that you men are already thinking you know who I am! You would be correct in assuming that Reverend Isaac Green is the man speaking with you; however, you would be only half right if your bets were placed on that assumption alone! As I have mentioned to you before, I have been your employer for more than ten years.

"During those years, it was my responsibility to make sure your ships were in top working order, your supply of trade merchandise was on time, and your cargo was always disease free! But now the world cries out for new commodities! The affluent are clamoring for opulent tangibles and desiring more exciting intangibles as well! Pretty young white girls are bringing a premium these days!

Parsimoniously speaking, the wealthy inhabitants of North America namely those in the port towns, wish to purchase items that will greatly enhance their peer recognition standings as well as flaunting their 'new stuff' in front of their buddies! Interestingly though, they also want some major thrills and chills! This is where we come into play. So, Jim, Bill, and Jonn, listen up!

"There has been a huge spurt of interest in hunting throughout the colonies! I don't mean your typical rabbit or quail shoot with grandpa kind of hunting; I'm talking about going after the big stuff! Put in your minds for a moment, a second or third generation plantation owner, bored out of his mind, sipping on a mint julep and trying to figure out what he could do for some excitement. Oh, he's already seeded most of the hot darkies on his place; but, that's not what he really wants anyway, he thinks! What he desires more than anything else is to let go of his responsibilities and to give way to his primal inner self! In essence, the man wishes to return to the primitive way of obtaining elation!

"What do you suppose a wealthy ole Georgia boy would pay to belong to a century old hunting club? One known throughout the world as being the most elite fraternity existing on it! And what if that 'organization' provided for that blue-blooded young man an opportunity to earn his way into that coveted group and at the same time slake his animalistic yearnings…" spoke the lion head.

Captain Bosman's loud voice interrupted Reverend Green!

"What in the hell does this have to do with us? Are these animal headed jokers really necessary? For god's sake man, come to your senses!"

"Silence, Captain Bosman! One more of your impudent pipes and I'll invite those 'animal heads' to come and eat you!" Isaac Green said with a half-smile on his face.

"As I was saying, 'prestige', is the optimal objective of these gentries. What I have recreated, will give them exactly that!" yelled the masked Reverend Green.

The lion head then walked around the burning coal truck so he could stand more closely to his captives. He then spoke again.

"In a couple of minutes, a flare will ignite from some three hundred yards away. It will signify the beginning of the 'Burning of Care

Ceremony'. It is the culmination, the graduation, from an unbelievably difficult training institution known as 'SPORCK'. But for right now and I'll fill you in on the details later, we have a ceremony to attend! I trust you will allow me to remove your hoods and introduce the 'other' Isaac Green to you!" somberly spoke the reverend.

With that said, Isaac put back on his lion's head and proceeded to the rear of the posts where he removed the leather hoods from the heads of the three mariners. From the shock of light coming from the blazing horses, the sailors' pupils almost closed shut!

"Jesus!" exclaimed the infuriated Captain Kimber. Jonn began lambasting the away walking lion head as well!

"How dare you treat men under your employ, honorable gentlemen, as though they were common slaves! What gives you the right to interdict, to tamper with, the centuries old Rules of the Seafarers? Sir, I hereby place you under arrest!" screamed Kimber.

The great lion head clad with his reflective camouflage stopped in his tracks. He turned back toward the three bound men and saluted them. Jim Stanfield chimed in after the lion head's venomous reaction.

"Boys, I believe I'm beginning to understand the gist of what is going on around this place!"

"Then kind, sir, please guide us toward the light!" sarcastically stated Captain Kimber.

It was then at that ironic second, the flare Isaac had promised ignited in the sky. The night lit up like a cloudy afternoon. At the sound of a distant bugle, the mock carnivores split off toward the right side of the field while the omnivores marched to the left side of it. What remained was the perfect military formation designed for visiting dignitaries!

What sounded like a command for 'Call to Arms' caused the animal heads to snap their rifles into a 'present-arms' mode. It was then for the very first time, Jonn and Stanfield got to see the spectacular plate baring the iron cross and the elk's skull!

Following the four-man detachment of symbol-carriers came a lion head adorned in a purple and gold cape. As he passed through the gauntlet of saluting soldiers each man when the timing was right, snapped his heels together and then bowed his head out of respect to their 'Fuhrer'!

With the precision of a crack drill team, the animal heads began spinning their weapons like dervishes. They wove around into a broad circle until they had completely surrounded the fire and the makeshift stage!

The three Guineamen tied to the firing squad posts were in the dead center of the circle! The lion head wearing his flowing purple and gold cape, stepped up to the podium.

"Brother Sporckians, the sun is once again in the clutches of the lion, and the encircling season bids us to the forest— there to celebrate… the awful mysteries! Sporckians, come! Find home again in the woods! Burn CARE and hurl his ashes, whirling, from the bushes! Come out, Sporckians! Come out to play and bring all of your buoyant impetuous rush of youth with you!" bravely spoke the Fuhrer (a.k.a., Reverend Green).

Following the initial address to his followers, a single glowing candle was passed to every man standing within the Sporckian circle. Once the candle had made its round and after a minute of silence, every animal head yelled to the top of their lungs!

"Weaving Spiders, come not here!"

What came next would remain emblazoned in the minds of Stanfield, Bosman and Kimber forever! At exactly ten o'clock, a procession of priests carrying an urn filled with the ashes of 'Mister Care' came slowly walking out of the forest. They wore bright red, blue, and orange hooded robes.

Five black men approached the ceremonial circle dragging a stone owl which had been mounted on the bed of a tobacco sled. The weight of the eleven-foot carving caused the sled's runners to sink more than an inch into the soil!

The harder the negroes pulled the more often they received the sting of a bullwhip thrown from the hands priests! The buzzing noise returned.

With the assistance of a field-winch and a couple of dozen back-snaps, the slaves finally got the owl set up on the stage behind the podium. When their job was done, a red cladded holy man shuffled the black men off the sacred stage. Their chains rattled as they disappeared into the night.

Two hamadryads, men dressed up like tree spirits, joined a couple of other priests on the stage. The four of them bowed to the stone owl.

A leopard head walked toward the speaker's podium. He cleared his throat and began chanting in Latin a message to the Sporckians.

Since Stanfield was the self-appointed interpreter for Jonn and Bill, he gave an extra effort as if he were performing at the "Globe"!

"A man's heart is divided between reality and fantasy. It is necessary for a Sporckian, a real man, to escape to another world of fellowship among his brothers! The 'fairy unguents' will free you to pursue warm fellowship in these woods!" yelled Jim.

A procession of condor heads carrying a large box upon their shoulders slowly toted the heavy load toward the center of the Ceremonial Circle of Brotherhood. With their two free hands available to them since their weapons were now slung over their backs, each animal head proceeded to do his part with the assembly of a hot air balloon!

Within ten minutes after the orchestrated uncasing of the basket and the silk balloon skin and yet another two minutes to inflate it, the Sporckians had themselves a genuine hot air balloon! It stood ready at fifty feet high. An antelope head gave a mournful cry for the delivery of the urn filled with the ashes of 'Mister Care'!

"Oh, please thou great symbol of all mortal wisdom, Owl of Sporck…grant us thy counsel!" An antelope head said as he collapsed into a prostrate spread at the base of the sculpted stone idol. He pleaded some more.

"Our wise Sage, guide us through the dark passage of ignorance. Help us to see, as you can, when the density of responsibility denies us our sight. Take caring from our souls, we beg of you, sir!"

A black robed priest appeared from behind the stone owl. With the urn clutched in his gloved hands, the faceless man sat down in the balloon's basket. Without any pomp or warning, the hot air balloon silently lifted into the night's sky and rapidly ascended into the heavens.

Once the priest holding 'Mister Care's' ashes had reached an altitude of a thousand feet, the holy man opened the vessel inviting the ten-knot winds to steal the contents and to scatter the ashes into the sea. The land beneath remained dark and silent.

With that being done, the ghost of 'care' was gone. The animal heads buzzed. But then through a ventriloquist's voice, these soothsayer's words blared out from the beak of the stone owl:

"Fools! When will ye learn that me, ye cannot slay? Year after year ye toss me into the Atlantic… But, when you return to your craft, am I not waiting for you, as of old?" Another flare streaked into the midnight sky!

"I certainly do hope you boys enjoyed the ceremony! I was hoping ya'll might come up to the house for a bite! You fellows have got to be starving to death by now! Let me get Bill loose first and then he'll set the rest of you blokes free! Jonn, if you will, 'give me a push'." innocently said Reverend Green.

Isaac Green wheeled himself up a thirty-five-degree slope toward the 'witch's hat'. By the time the four men reached the entrance of the Reverend's seventeen storied home, Isaac was the only one not panting.

"Gentlemen, kindly watch your heads as you step into the elevator." Isaac said as he pulled a brass lever.

Bill and Jim looked up as they heard the ballasts filling with water. With a comforting smile, the former lion head explained how the transport system worked.

When the metal doors opened, a lavish spread of exotic foods welcomed them. Jim gasped when he gazed upon the collection of uncorked wine bottles backdropping the epicurean delights.

An exquisitely manicured man wearing a butler's jacket came out from a backroom holding a sword with all sorts of steaming meats impaled onto it. With a gold toothed grin and a gentle bow, the four men were shown to their places. Reverend Green's wheelchair fitted perfectly under the table head's spot.

After the gargantuan feast, Isaac picked up a tiny silver bell hidden beneath an overturned tea cup. He rang it for five seconds. The elevator opened.

Four jackal heads entered the dining room! They pointed their shotguns at the three captains' chests! The elevator disappeared down the empty shaft while the metal doors remained open.

"Gentlemen, I shall now insist that you kindly leave your seats and walk over to elevator's passage. Please place the back of your heels over the edge of the shaft! At this time, I shall ask the jackals to ready their weapons in case you guys are noncompliant! In any case, it is a lifetime decision that must be unanimously made!" Reverend Green sternly said before rolling backwards. He spoke again.

"As I promised, we're going to let the cat out of the bag! So here it is in a nutshell and I urge you to listen closely to what I have to say! After that, you'll have to make your own choices! The King wishes to invade the colonies! He believes that war with them is better fought before they grow strong enough to defend themselves! From a financial perspective, America is by far our best customer! They buy every slave we can catch by the toe! The Brits want to see human cargo banned forever while the good ole southern boys want us to bring them even more than they're already getting! So, should our loyalties remain with our homeland? Or should we honor our commitments with our business partners?" Isaac said. Sporck had more to say.

"The Spanish have offered their loyalties to the Americas! Additionally, they have forwarded to me enough gold to equal the profit generally yielded from ten triangular voyages! Accordingly, I will pay my men at a tenfold level as well!

These "Sporckians" that you call 'animal heads', happened to be amongst the most highly skilled hunters on the planet. But that is not all they do!

Most of them are aristocrats; that is, they own boo coos of rich farm land from which they sell their crops to further enhance their coffers. Additionally, these wealthy individuals band together not only to fix the prices of their monopolized produce, they also bond into a formidable political faction!

With the world teetering on the edge of war, these gentry clusters are reaching out for some sort of guaranteed safety net just in case their country is overrun by one of the big three! In other words, Gentlemen, they want assurances from the Spanish, French and the British that no matter who gets a port or capital city, their holdings under no circumstance will be jeopardized!" preached Ike.

Isaac Green then made a one hundred and eighty degree turn and began pointing at a world map hanging above his fireplace mantel. He then beckoned the captains with an arm wave to step a little closer to the wall atlas. Anton von Sporck then spoke again.

"Just a few years ago when I was full of piss and vinegar, I founded an organization of which I named, 'The International Order of Saint Hubertus'. It started out as nothing more than a rich man's hunting club.

As time moved onward, I found that there were hundreds of wealthy men in need of a place where they could go and be with others of their same ilk. An innocuous club catering to the protection of endangered species seemed like the hot ticket!

It has turned out that our little sportsman's group has grown into a membership of over a thousand men each of whom can buy or sell the country they hail from! That being said, one might see how the fate of this world could be determined around a roaring campfire!

Just imagine if you will, Captains, one dead elk being field- dressed by the kings of those afore mentioned 'big three' countries! Can you fathom what their semi inebriated conversations might entail?

Is it logical to ask then, if practically every world leader falling under the realm of Christianity were to belong to the same elitist hunting club, wouldn't that fraternity of hunters also become the most powerful force on that same planet? Well, it has!

Clearly, over the past ten years every decision, every act of war, every enactment of an embargo, as well as the seating or unseating of someone's king have been made right here on these grounds! Also, as can be measured, these 'decisions' are being decided upon by the unanimous applauding of Sporckians and none others!

Their general motive is for the wellbeing of mankind; however, to be very transparent, a great deal of pocket lining does take place during the milieu of these biannual events. This is where you men come into the picture!

The Sporckians have made the decision to side with the Americans during the up and coming war. Economically, it would be foolish to abandon such a resourceful virgin as the Colonies!

It was then that Isaac Green rose from his wheelchair, ripped off his priest's tunic and replaced his lion's head arrogantly back upon his shoulders. He then turned angrily toward his three captains and vociferously spoke.

"As, Count Franz Anton von Sporck of Austria, I hereby sentence you men to life or death! If 'life' is your choice then you lads will launch the 'Thomas' into the unforgiving pages of history!

If a noble death is preferred, then step backwards and allow gravity to splatter your carcasses on this church's basement floor! The jackal heads will dispose of your bodies and even say a little prayer on your behaves before dumping you into the river!"

Captain Jonn Kimber, red faced, stepped forward to speak. After looking curiously at one another, both captains Bosman and Stanfield, also stepped up beside of Jonn.

"Count Sporck, I am asking this question only on behalf of myself! These brave men beside of me have nothing to do with the authorship of my query! I am acting on my own! Therefore, I ask you this question, 'are you suggesting that I betray the Crown, Sir?'" questioned Kimber.

"Yes! But, not to harm it! Our intentions are only to help America and other nations like England to dig themselves out of the delusional mindset of self-aggrandizement!

The Sporckian goal is to teach the monarchs a new way of controlling the worlds' population!" said Green.

"When you said that about controlling the worlds' population, what did you mean, Sir?" asked Jonn in a hangdog manner.

"Son, I'll tell you why and pretty soon I'm going to show the world why! You see Jonn, if we do not manage the population as one would a robust herd of antelope, that unfortunate group of mammals will grow weak and perish!

All living things need to be checked! They must have an overseer, someone who can make the decision to rid the populace of those among them whom are no longer useful to the whole!

Therefore, I made the decision to utilize the talents of my well trained Sporckians to reweave themselves into the fabric of their indigenous territories and to stand ready for whenever their cleansing services are required!

As captains of the 'Thomas', your assignments will be a slight bit different than your normal runs would generally call for. Your new routes will require extreme navigational savvy along with a goodly amount of stealth!

These changes will require a more formal briefing which we will do before tomorrow's departure. But for now, I must have your commitments!

All I want to know is, 'will you swear an oath of allegiance to The International Order of Saint Hubertus and will you serve its cause until your dying day? If so, then say, 'I will'! Or, if not, then say, 'goodbye!'" warned the screaming lion head.

As the captains waited for the transport cauldrons to fill with water, each man found it rather difficult to look at themselves in the elevator door's reflection. All three had unanimously chosen life instead of death! They had done it at the expense of their integrities.

Jim Stanfield was the first to speak. "Pride cometh before the fall", was all that he said but he said it with a big smile on his face. It eased the tenseness.

Jonn looked over his shoulder at the 'witch hat' spire, he thought of his daughter and then proceeded down the walkway where Jim and Bill were already prepping for what was to come. The guards opened the gigantic front gate.

Before the three captains stood the same Sporckians who had played havoc with them earlier. But now, they were no longer wearing their animal heads. Instead, each man held their animal heads in their left hands while they saluted with their right ones.

A brass band dressed in straw hats and peppermint-striped jackets burst into a medley of Wagnerian styled rallying tunes! One of the combo's trombonists who was actually Isaac Green, marched to a spot no further than six feet away from the departing captains and began to blow an exciting melody from his instrument.

Four former giraffe heads, brought out an empty horse trough and placed the metal tub at the captains' feet. From that point forward each animal head passed by in single file and urinated into the trough.

Once that part of the so-called ceremony was completed, two more men approached the slosh tub and began spiking it with five gallons of spiced rum. A deck mop was then used to stir the concoction.

The scene was permeated by a kind of kitsch Black Forest imagery backgrounded by the rhythmic taps of a snare drum. One by one, each Sporckian kneeled beside the horse trough, clamped his hands behind his back and as if he were dunking for apples, stuck his head into the bubbling liquid and took a deep swallow!

An earsplitting boom shook the ground below their feet as the last flare of the night illuminated the sky. As if being commanded by a single ghost, the Sporckians mechanically stood straight up, replaced their animal heads, began buzzing, and shuffled into their appropriate positions within their company. It was midnight.

From the top of a not before seen tower came the earthshattering voice of Count Franz Anton von Sporck. The Sporckians now holding flaming torches in their free hands, looked up at their leader as he prepared to bid them his farewell address.

"My brothers of the hunt, I wish to express my deepest admiration for the amazing strides you have made during your three-month visit with us at the Sporckian School. You have learned many things here, haven't you?"

"To the Furor!" yelled the excited animal heads.

"Tomorrow morning or I should say, this morning, at 0600 the 'Thomas' will set out for the west coast of Africa! Captain Jonnathan Kimber will command the first leg of the voyage!

Captain Kimber's port of call is to remain an unknown until he reaches the Gulf of Guinea at which time his point of destination will be disclosed to him. I take these added precautions for security reasons. Why, you might ask, well, I'll tell you why!

Even at this moment, the King's spies lay among us! They are here and their purpose is to derail, to snuff out, our ultimate objectives!

Those dastardly under miners are determined to stunt the growth of mankind! They want us to bow under the wave of the puppet master's hand! Those wannabe controllers wish for all of you to break your backs in order to fill their own money chests!

These flea inflicted vermin intend on weakening you with the sickness they spread! Their royal doctrines and toothless snarls are aimed at those pedestrians who lack the fortitude to get for themselves their own sustenance!

Instead, the 'whipped by intimidation' subjects fall to their knees, eat their meager rationings and cast the pearls of their labors at the cloven hooves of their kings! Preposterous!

Our duty as Sporckians is clear! We are to supervise if not to cause the downfall of the worlds' enablers!

"You, the crème de la crème, will plant in the soil of your plantations the seeds of not only revolution but you Sporckians are laying the cornerstones of democracy. America will become the land of the free!

The 'Thomas' will soon deliver to the Americas five hundred more slaves! Those enchained men however will not be your normal run of the mill cargo! They, just as you, have been schooled in the 'tricks of the trade'! They too are Sporckians!

Under your command, these pretend-like slaves will act as the strike force you will utilize when the time comes! That time by the way, is just around the corner!

Already, the British are beefing up their port patrols. Riots are breaking out all over the eastern seaboard in defiance of the tariffs being hammered on them.

The fanatical humanists are crying out against the immorality infused issues of slavery itself; while, the Christians are hoisting the other end of that 'Jesus approved' banner with equal zeal. In other words, Sporckians, the time is nigh!" screamed Sporck.

Below, the torch raising animal heads began buzzing louder than anytime heard before. The pitch of the collective buzzes grew higher and higher until finally a cheetah head marched up to the base of Isaac's tower and saluted. He withdrew his spotted cat head, came to attention, and then spoke.

"Permission to ask a question, Sir."

"Granted!" said Isaac.

"Count Sporck, how will we know when we are to rally our forces for battle?"

"Son, I always use children to deliver my messages! When the day comes for you, Mister McRae to clean-up a problem down there in Beaufort, I shall send out to your farm a nice little girl selling apples. Then you will know, Sir!" Forcefully stated Sporck.

Isaac Green's attention abruptly switched over to the three captains standing at the rear of the lauding crowd. He called the Guineamen by their names as he wanted to speak specifically with them.

"As you can see, Fellas, we have a 'rough and ready' bunch on our hands! Your first job will be to pass these men off as your crew members. If done with finesse, they should satisfy the curiosities of George's dock detectives!

Captain Stanfield, you will see to it that these spoon-choked gentries are in good standing by the time we set sail tomorrow afternoon! Drill the shit out of these men if you must; but, have them looking like veteran sailors by sunrise!" said the lion head.

Jim Stanfield stepped forward and saluted the Sporckian king.

He snapped to a rigid 'attention' and sharply spoke.

"As commanded, Sir! The men will be ready!"

"Take charge of your men, Captain Kimber!"

"Aye-aye, Commander." answered Jonnathan Kimber.

With that, Captain James Stanfield began removing his clothes as if he were preparing to go skinny-dipping. Seconds later, he yelled out a vicious command demanding that the animal heads follow his lead. He then remarked further.

"Remove your masks! I want to see who you men really are! Once we can see your smiling faces, we can then move forward with our morning jog to the sea!

I have some songs in which I would enjoy teaching you along the way! Then, if you are ready, 'Ladies', kindly follow me!" barked Stanfield.

Captains Bosman and Kimber quietly stood below the lion head. Isaac looked down upon the two men who had made him a fortune over the past decade. All three had been remarkable seamen.

Sporck secretly admired their courage. He felt a tiny bit ashamed of himself for pressing their loyalties into a bargaining chip. But as it turned out, they had won!

"Captain Kimber, it will be expected of you to do your usual pre-sailing side deals with the wharfmen. It is most important that you make this appear as if it were just another adventure into the wild blue yonder.

Oh yes, and another thing, Jonn, that very fine secret storage space you so ingeniously crafted may be used for what you intended it to be used for! You can keep your profits from the sales from its storage but, Jonn, this new phase of your career will require that you not have contact with those 'tariff-dodgers' again! So, make this your last wholesale event, alright?" Said Sporck in a fatherly fashion.

"Yes, Sir!" answered the embarrassed Captain Kimber.

"Captain Bosman, you will take command of the 'Thomas' as soon as she docks in Senegambia. You will receive a courier delivered map giving you the specifics as to your next destination."

Jonn looked up at Isaac Green with a face of pure befuddlement. In response to Jonn's disheveled expression, the lion head stepped down from the lectern and walked over to the two captains.

"Gentlemen, there is a whole lot of everything in this world balancing on the success of this voyage! Unlike any you men have captained before, this voyage will be the crown on your seafaring heads!" Isaac said as he removed his lion's head.

"Boys, this world is getting ready to turn upside down! We must protect our assets from the changing political tides.

Britain believes she has evolved onto a higher platitude of being! Their entire kingdom has soothed itself into thinking the country is safe from predators!

It'll be the poor, the sick, and the hungry who will toot the notes which will crumple the single last brick of their goddamned empire! The Catholics and all sorts of fanatical Christian groups are already wielding signs and singing songs about the wrongs of slavery!

Goodness, loving our enemies, helping the afflicted, are the intended messages by those well intending folks, no doubt! In the meantime, they are strangling their top producing colonies' manner of harvesting their British-taxable products!

Meaning, King George is shooting himself in his own foot! Oh yes, ole George is surely welcomed by the fat and sassy populace who have forgotten the stings of enemy spears. But just wait until they feel the heat from foreign cannonballs rolling down their streets!

The way I see it, the King and his subjects have overlooked the evidentiary fact that all people must have their physiological and safety needs met long before they can ever be expected to respect his leadership! Yet he continues to bully around the Americans and her contiguous allies!

Now after a decade of fucking with the Colonists and the French and the Spanish, King George believes he can avoid their backlash? Not a chance!

The reason the Sporckians are in existence today is to prevent this type of complacency from spreading to the new world! Only the strong will thrive there!

Even today within the Colonies, no quarter is giving to those unwilling to tote their part of the line. Production, imports, exports, manpower and aggression will become the needed implements for use at the American dinner table. Sleepy royalists will grow quite thin on that side of the ocean once the Sporckian ideology takes hold!

It will be a cold day in hell before the new America will tolerate any sort of freeloading within or on the outside of its elected administration! No man under the sun will be exempted from their dues and no working man will be denied the benefits of his labor!

Therefore, a healthy and vibrant nation just as any mammalian herd, needs to be managed! To head off the diseases of sloth and entitlement a checking mechanism must be set into play! A game referee if you will, has to be put into place!

And that, my Boys, is exactly why the both of you are alive at this moment! You men, all three of you for that matter, are by far the most recognizable Guineamen in Liverpool.

No one will suspect there is anything out of the ordinary going on! But of course, there will be!" Chuckled Isaac.

"In less than a dozen hours the mighty 'Thomas' will sail out of Huskisson Dock and into the Atlantic Ocean. Commanding that great Parr-class slaver will be three highly skilled captains along with a crew of fifty Sporckians!

The 'Thomas' will during various stops, pick up a total of five hundred and fifty-six additional Sporckians. Together, you will make your way up through your usual Caribbean haunts to drop off your promised goods. After that, you can expect it to get rather dicey!

You may be required to raise several flags as well as fire on your own countrymen! But, in the end, I know you will be triumphant and complete your mission!

In order to do that, you, maritime marauders, must figure out a way to smuggle the negro Sporckians onto the assigned plantations without being sold through the authorized brokerage houses!

Each of the men whom you are transporting to the colonies have been designated their own squad of twelve pseudo-slaves. The plantation owners will absorb these men into their current populations until the time comes for them to be called into action!

It will be up to you three captains to see to it that these units every damn one of them, are inserted into their proper environs without being detected! The good news is, we will have operatives offloading your animate contraband into low profile boats under the cover of darkness!

I would suspect your greatest challenges will come from the British who will certainly wish to assure themselves that you have the proper authorization stamps to proceed into the American ports! Don't despair, the Spanish know you're coming and they have assured us they will deflect as much of their attention as possible!

My greatest concerns deal with the other slave traders. Americans as I mentioned to you are a hungry bunch. They don't appreciate competitors horning into their trading-grounds without paying their fair share to get into the game! And they make a good point; but, that's not what this is all about!

The 'Thomas' will be the first of hundreds of ships to embed thousands of Sporckians throughout the Americas! Their responsibilities will weigh upon the actions of the Colonials themselves.

Providing the Colonial government adheres to our philosophies, we will be an asset to them! All we want is for the Americas to be the catalyst of an economic energy the world has never seen before!

The American continents will soon be divided into two equal parts! Spain will manage the southern ports while the Colonists take control of the northern ones. Britain will not like this arrangement in the least; consequently, they will declare war against the Colonies as they recently did with Spain!

To sum up, Gentlemen, I want a piece of everything that goes in and out of North America from now until kingdom comes! And if I get my men situated in the right spots, I'll own the whole goddamned seaboard!

Once you have completed this mission, I shall pay each of you a total of ten years of your normal salary! On top of that, I will establish in your names, a plantation of your own!

Your belongings here in England will be sold or sent to you!

Liverpool will no longer be your home!

You men must now report in to the 'Thomas'. Do not and I repeat, do not return to your houses! Go now!" said Anton von Sporck.

CHAPTER 2

THE FIRST LEG

Charles Hayes stared at the coocoo clock setting on his office's mantel piece. A pair of Spanish pistols laid parallel on his desk with their triggers positioned for an instantaneous doublehanded grab.

The hand carved bird sprung out of the pirated antique announcing the five o'clock hour! Charles cocked both silver hammers back until he heard the set triggers click into place. If a fly were to land on either one of those triggers Charles thought, anyone standing in front of the door would be shot deader than a doornail.

Sub-Governor Charlie Hayes was a defeated man. His physician had placed him under orders to restrict his diet to nothing more than goats' milk and crème of wheat.

No booze, no tea, no salt, no tobacco was Doctor Tibble's professional advice! Otherwise, Tibble would no longer send in to the Royal African Company Charlie's 'doctored' medical reports!

All of the Royal African's employees had to be 'fit for naval duty' and the sub-governor most certainly was not! Hayes had one of those bleeding ulcers which normally befalls upon men whom have been promoted to their highest levels of incompetency.

"All I ever wanted to do was be a goddamned chronologist!" yelled Charlie.

The coocoo clock pinged a mid-hour note but had no further reaction to Charles Haye's whining. It was five thirty and still no word.

Charlie picked up one of his pistols and placed its silver barrel into his mouth! He pointed the muzzle toward the center of his crown and began to weep.

Realizing he was making a fool of himself even though he was alone, Charles Hayes opened his desk's top righthand drawer and pulled out a bottle of scotch.

Charlie Hayes then took three deep swallows and fired his Spanish dueler at his ill-gotten coocoo clock! A slight tap on the front door interrupted Charlie's second shot plans.

"Hi, my name is Blanche. Reverend Green sent me over to bring you a basket of all kinds of goodies! May I step in for a moment? I do hope I haven't dropped in at an inopportune time?" pleasantly greeted Blanche.

"Yes, yes, my child, do step in! You've come at a fine time!" said the R.A.C.'s disturbed supervisor.

"I promise, I won't be here but for a jiffy!"

"May I get you something? I believe there are some spiced biscuits in the cupboard and if I am not mistaken…" gently asked the sub-governor.

"Look, Chuck, I don't want any of your bloody cookies or your raunchy ass goat milk! All I want from you are a couple of minutes of your allusive sobriety!" seethed Blanch.

"Who are you?" Spewed the red-faced sub-governor.

"Oh, I'll assure you, I'm your worst nightmare, Curly! So, don't piss me off!"

Blanche then marched over to Hayes's desk, shooed him out from behind it, sat down on his fur padded chair, reached into his top right-hand drawer and commenced to gurgle down the last bit of his scotch! She then heisted one of his cigars from an ivory box, lit it, and then asked the defrocked governor to have a seat.

"Here's the scoop, gramps! Isaac has asked that you remain vigilant about your business! Has he ever seen this pigsty? Anyway, he, being Reverend Green, strongly recommends you focus on your responsibilities instead of skimming off the 'cherry' runs for yourself and your cronies! Furthermore, if you're still paying attention, Ike wanted you to know he will honor the agreement he made with your father! What'd your old man do, did he buy his little runt a job?

"Despite your personal views, the Royal African Company is in the business of transporting people to many corners of this world!

Your approval of what or who is exported to the Americas is of no concern to the powers that be! In short, either you get your act together or go find yourself a ship to sign onto! Either way, Bucko, it's 'shape up or ship out' time! Here, I almost forgot, Ike sent you a couple of bottles of scotch. Strangely, he suggested that you throw them away! Well, maybe I misunderstood that part; but just the same, I bid you a fair adieu!" Blanche said with a smirk on her face.

Charles Hayes thought about putting a bullet square in the little cunt's back as she left on her rusty bicycle! He even went so far as to aim his pistol at Blanche but then the coocoo returned. This time he nailed it!

Stoked with excitement over his excellent shooting, Sub-Governor Hayes powdered his wig, grabbed his seventeen-caliber cane and left his office without even closing the door behind him!

Charlie was ready to make his big political move! That little bitch was the final straw! He might become the city's constable after his strategic ploy's execution! He thought. It was seven-thirty.

Chaloner Ogle swirled around a bit of tobacco that had backwashed into his almost empty glass of scotch. He poked at the particles as if attempting to spear a barracuda.

The Royal Investigator checked his pocket watch. Whomever this crackpot was Cal thought, had better be able to back up the wild tale written about in the note slid under his door!

Sir Robert Walpole had sent a courier to his home ordering him to immediately investigate a matter which was 'window-dressed' as a 'huge' breach of the Kingdom's security! Prime minister Walpole had personally written the word 'urgent' on his directive and had done so under his formal signature.

After a grueling two-day horseback ride from London, the naval commander was ready for a hot bath and a descent night's rest. A hundred and seventy miles escorted or not, is one hell of a long way for anyone to go in forty-eight hours! Cal grumbled.

"Sir, how about another cocktail? I'm sure your guest will be along shortly! After all, it's always a lady's prerogative to be fashionably late!" jokingly quipped the well-dressed bartender.

"Yea, what the heck, I'll have another. Thanks!

It's still early, whomever I'm supposed to meet and I have no clue as to what the other looks like these days! Anyway, he's not due for another hour yet.

So, how long have you been working at the Royal Clarence?" politely asked Cal.

"Oh, let's see, I guess about three years now, and you? Are you passing through or are you one of Liverpool's finest gentleman with whom I have not yet had the pleasure of meeting?" nobly asked the likeable bartender.

"Neither, sir! I am but a simple traveler looking for a little work and one hell of a big payday!" Chaloner said as both men laughed.

"No, seriously, I am here in Liverpool doing some shipping work and I thought I'd touch base with an old friend of mine from way back in our Edinburg days! We were roommates for two years, we were. Hey, come to think about it, you might know him! His name is, Edward Teach. Does that ring a bell?" Cal said with a pan face.

"Vinibal" or so his name tag read, stood like a gargoyle suspended in midair! A thin smile cracked across his stone shaded face.

"You bloody joker! laughingly said Vinibal.

The two men broke all kinds of the house rules with their bawdy carrying-on's! They went way beyond the bounds of the Clarence's protocol and thus were given the 'evil eye' by the hotel's penguin-looking general manager, Robert Barbara!

Nevertheless, somewhat of a friendship between Cal and Vinibal was kindled that night.

"Actually, the gentleman I am expecting, goes by the titled name of Governor Charles Hayes of the Royal African Company. I would guess he has aged beyond recognition by now!

Can you give me a description of what the booger is looking like these days? Is there something, Vinibal, I should have forewarning about?" asked Ogle.

Vinibal Baggott gazed out of the window probably searching for the safest answer to give to the hotel's important guest. He then looked over at the dining room on account of Mister Barbara's persnickety ways. Chaloner thought.

When he saw that the weaselly hotel manager was occupied with a complaining employee, Vin leaned over Cal's table as if he were smelling his drink. He motioned for Ogle to lean closer. A secret was coming.

"Just between you and me, I never thought much of the R.A.C. anyway! The whole place started to fall to pieces as soon as they screwed the Crown out of it's agreed upon gold! Instead, your old school buddy sold George's coin allotment off to the Spanish for a measly half-point increased bid! Can you believe that? In the end though, our ole crafty King got his pound of flesh back, yes, he did! He declared the Royal African Company a monopolistic swine and started allowing private investors to jump into the slave auction for only a ten percent levy! And did the locals ever jump in after that? You bet they did, big time! Ever since, the whole damn operation seems like it's nothing more than a brokerage house for somebody else's slave ships! As a matter of fact, I walk by their office on my way to and from work and about half the time, the place is shut up tighter than a whisky drum!" hastily whispered Vinibal.

Some new guests arrived and were being introduced around to the Clarence's availabilities as well as its staff members. This allowed Commander Ogle some time to scribble a few notes down.

Cal then concluded that his theory about the unauthored note leading to a wild goose chase was beginning to fray. Although plausible, Vinibal's description of a multimillion-dollar company being run by an idiot didn't make any sense!

It then became nakedly obvious this case was going to be one of those stalactite-stalagmite ordeals where one can never quite guess whether the villain is hiding in the top or the bottom of the dark opening. It was already beginning to stink.

So far, Chaloner knew a very big rat was rotting somewhere amidst the billowing sails of slavers headed toward the western coast of Africa. Admittedly, Cal had his doubts about Hayes's viability; hell, he wasn't even sure if the man was a player in the game!

He was sure however that whatever kind of criminal activity was seeded had roots spreading into some mighty deep pockets belonging to someone! 'Two-hundred-year-old companies don't just close their doors during business hours' was the oblong marble rolling around in Cal's mind.

"How about another one, sir?" asked Vinibal Baggott.

"I believe I will, Vin." responded Ogle.

"The last time I laid eyes on him was around Christmas. As I remember, it seems like there was some trouble over the tab being paid but I'm not really sure about the exact timing of it. That's been some time ago!" somberly whispered the bartender.

"Vinibal, is there a more private place where Mister Hayes and I can meet?" asked Cal.

Sure, it's a nice evening, why don't you both go out to the gazebo? It'll be just out through those doors. Speaking of the devil, here he comes now!" shockingly exclaimed Vinibal.

The steps leading up to the Royal Clarence Hotel offers a challenge for even a sober person to walk up. The steps however were not the forbearing issue but the part about sobriety was.

You see, ole Charlie had polished off both bottles of Isaac Green's gift. But to hear Sub-Governor Hayes's point of view, 'he was as fine as a frog's hair!'. Nonetheless, it took both Robert Barbara and Vinibal Baggott ten minutes to finally get the wobbling mass up to the gazebo where Chaloner Ogle was waiting.

"It is great to see you again, Charlie!" cheerfully yelled Chaloner.

Cal guided his schoolmate imposture to a seat after he embraced the souse as if he were his long-lost brother. A large turtle tear even trickled down the side of the King's investigator's cheek as he dismissed the hotel's bartender with a grateful smile. Charlie and Cal were alone.

"Who are you?" slurred Charlie.

"I am Commander Chaloner Ogle. I was sent here by my boss, Sir Robert Walpole of the Royal Admiralty Board!

It is my understanding that you, and I quote, 'wish to blow the lid off the greatest breach of security since the Trojan horse'. Does that sound remotely familiar to you, Governor Hayes?"

"Why, of course, it does, Commander! I wrote it all by my little lonesome self! And how is ole Bobby doing these days? I was wondering if he hadn't tired of wiping Compton's ass by now! I expect he has been doing that all along or you wouldn't be here now would you, Sport?" aggressively slurred Hayes.

No one saw it or even heard it but as swift as a pit viper's strike, Cal Ogle surreptitiously leaned over Charlie's shoulder and thumped the poor bastard in the nuts! This of course caused the R.A.C. man to stumble over to the edge of the Clarence's gazebo and begin hurling into the grass below!

"Sonofabitch! Why did you do that?" cried the sub-governor. "Because you, I fear, are wasting my time! Plus, I don't appreciate your condition one single bit!" screeched the Commander.

"Hey, look, I'm the guy with the information you guys need! There is no reason for you to rough me up when I'm the one who is trying to be the loyal subject here!" spoke the sobering man.

"Then get on with it!" spat Ogle.

"Okay, but let's order a drink first!" gayly proclaimed Hayes. "We speak first and then we drink, got it?" said Ogle.

As soon as Charles Hayes sensed he had a sympathetic ear, he broke down into tears. With an overly dramatic waving of his arms, Charlie began his well-rehearsed repertoire.

"I have been under the threat of being sent to our fort on Cape Corse if I ever came forward with the truth about the Royal African Company! Yet, despite the duress I have endured for the past ten years, I alone, have managed to skillfully keep the company's ledger sheets in the black!" said Charles.

"Excuse my abruptness, Governor! But I don't have the time nor the patience to listen to your sad story! You have five minutes to spin your yarn so therefore I would advise you to get on with it!" Commander Ogle shouted.

"I don't think I am really working for the R.A.C. anymore at all! I believe that Reverend Isaac Green has taken over their properties! I mean, this man whom I've never met, seems to dictate what goes into what ship and who is taking the stuff out to sea and where it is going! I therefore, have nothing to do but watch the sailing ships go by! Oh sure, I get paid with the same elephant and castle coins every week but for what? I really don't do anything to deserve it!" whined Hayes.

"Stop there! You say you are being paid weekly with 'elephant and castle guineas'?" questioned Cal.

"Yea, that's right! Every Friday afternoon around three o'clock a courier comes by the office with a jar of pickled peaches. In that container are always ten of those coins." softly spoke Charles.

"That's a lot of money!" exclaimed Ogle.

"You betcha it is! But where in the hell is it coming from? All I see leaving our docks is just a smidgen of desultory trade every now and again! We're not doing very much slave trading these days and plus, I'm not even allowed to know what profits we earn from the few places we do sail to!" pouted Charlie.

"Charles, why don't you just sit back and enjoy the easy ride? You seem to be very angry at this phantom employer of yours! Why is that, Charlie?" pried Chaloner.

"Because my pride has been crushed for one thing! Secondly, I suspect that Reverend Green's exports have a far different purpose than for mere profit! I have reason to believe that what Isaac Green is up to is in direct contrast with the objectives set out by King George!" gasped Charles Hayes.

"Tell me more about these 'suspicions' of…," Ogle was saying.

There was a rustling noise coming from underneath the gazebo! A blond girl ran out from beneath the lonesome gazebo and hopped onto a bicycle and rode away as fast as her little legs could pedal.

In a maniacal frenzy, Charles Hayes leaped from the fancy platform and began chasing after the pedal-pumping child! He then stopped in the midst of his pursuit long enough to fire a round off at her from his walking cane!

Curious guests began oozing out of the Clarence like hungry ants. Chaloner Ogle left a gold coin on the gazebo's table and made a beeline straight toward the hotel's livery stable. He summonsed his escorts and together the six men rode out of Liverpool. It was ten o'clock.

Charlie's head felt like it was about ready to explode. He found himself in a fetal curl just so he could catch his breath. A western breeze made it very clear to him that his clothes were soaking wet.

Hayes had been exposed! Soon, Isaac Green would retaliate.

Charlie had to make some fast decisions.

Blanche was exhausted. She had underestimated Charles Hayes's stamina. As a result of her miscalculation the miniature woman found herself having to walk her bicycle up the gravelly road to the All Saints' Church.

Reverend Green was waving at her just as she crested the hill. No sooner had the four-foot woman locked in her kickstand when Isaac reached out for her with his arms spread wide open. They embraced and then they kissed.

"Sweetheart, I was beginning to worry about you! Were you able to find out what our friend Mister Hayes was up to?" calmly asked Reverend Green.

"Baby, I did more than that! I caught the varmint being a dirty rat!" chortled Blanche.

"Well, come on in the house! You look like you just crawled through a jungle!" joked Isaac.

Charles Hayes's chest ached like he had been kicked by a horse. Blue streaks interrupted his normal vision as he fumbled with his key ring.

After four tries with six different keys, the distraught man elbowed out a window pane and then climbed into his office. He lit only one lamp but turned the wick down so low the only light coming from the crystal globe was a tea colored amber.

Hayes was at his wits end. He had to figure out what to do.

Everything had gone very wrong!

"That little bitch is probably up there right now spilling her guts out to the Reverend! It won't be very long before he'll have some thug come down here and that'll be the end of that! Jesus, I gotta get out of this place!" Charlie wailed into the darkness.

'First things first', he said to himself as he dragged out a leather trunk from beneath his dusty conference table. Hayes figured he had maybe two hours to evacuate his belongings before some bad company would show up!

Charles carefully lifted the lamp onto the table so he could identify what he had months ago packed into it. Just as the dull light struck the chest's contents the sub-governor shrieked with glee!

"What a beautiful thing!" Charles said to the night as he lifted a well-aged bottle of cognac toward the heavens. He nodded at his invisible god and muttered a small prayer of thanks!

With the anesthetic kiss of relief now swishing around in his brain, Charlie did another very stupid thing; he polished it off! After that, his sense of urgency passed. He became interested in the various knickknacks he had previously packed into the chest.

Reminiscence set in along with its time-consuming consequence.

The 'sandman' sat patiently nearby.

Commander Chaloner Ogle waited at his Downing Street address for the King's carriage to arrive. He was wearing the same uniform he had worn when he was knighted.

Finally, a small carriage arrived at the end of his driveway. The driver hopped out of his seat and then tied the single Cleveland Bay to the hitching post.

The driver casually walked up to Cal Ogle's home as if he were a delivery boy. He had a colorful suitcase in his hand.

"Greetings from King George, sir," the man casually spoke. "And, how might I help you?" asked Fredrick, the Commander's ancient butler.

"I'm here to pick up a Mrs. Callie Ogle!"

"Pardon me, kind sir, but you must have the wrong address!" corrected the agitated servant.

"Oh yea? Well, I'm supposed to give you this and then return in thirty minutes to fetch her! I expect there is a note in the clutch which will more than likely get everything squared away for you!" The driver said with a wink as he handed 'Fredrick' the traveler's bag.

"Very well, my good man, she'll be ready in two shakes of a lamb's tail!" said Fredrick.

"See ya in thirty, boss!" the driver said.

Fredrick was startled when he turned around to find Chaloner was standing behind him! With a confused look on his face, the old aide slowly handed over the bag to his long-time captain.

"It's started up again, hasn't it?" vociferously asked the butler. "I'm afraid so, Fredrick. Maybe, just maybe, it won't be so bad this time!" Gasped Ogle.

"Captain, I wouldn't be so sure of that! Ole George is a war-dog too, sir!" Chatted Fredrick.

"Are you insinuating that I am a crusty old salt?" humorously asked Cal.

"Indeed, sir!" the old seaman answered.

"Well then, since you think so little of me how about helping me put this damn dress on! And what pray tell is this contraption?" painfully asked Chaloner.

"A corset, Commander." Fredrick said.

Port Royal, Jamaica is not the place a normal man would want to be in the early weeks of July. The average temperature of a ship's deck during a windless spell will get you two eggs over-easy about anytime between ten and four on most days!

The British and the Spanish were constantly taking pot shots at each other during the blurry strings of calm sea. It was not uncommon to have three or four bodies or at least parts of them, wash up on the island's shores. But a lot of them survived!

Career mariners who had served in a navy or who had worked aboard privateers under government commission, were suddenly finding themselves unemployed but alive! So, it would then be logical for such men to declare themselves miserably idol.

Because Port Royal is surrounded by water and the disaffected men from 'nowhere' roamed the streets, a fomenting culture of low boiling anger incubated the unpleasantries normally associated with an anomic bunch of horny men.

Organized fistfights, wrestling matches, knife and hatchet throwing contests were the social highlights of every week. That is, until Benjamin Hornigold washed up on shore.

Within the first six-months of his miraculous arrival, Ben had revamped the entire insides of a Spanish trading vessel. He had used rolling logs to move it to higher ground.

Along with eating monkeys and bananas for sustenance, August was spent leveling the ship so the customers' drinks wouldn't slide down the bar by gravity's thoughtless pull. Benjamin was able to scour out from a couple of jungle villages a fairly large group of teenaged girls.

He made two promises to the girls' tribes. He promised to send the mothers half of whatever he sold them for and he had to cross- his-heart he would never bring them back again!

Six months after Benjamin Hornigold's arrival he had himself a genuine gentleman's club! His establishment offered anything and everything a man could desire. The place even had membership requirements which included a black-ball system of acceptance.

In order to acquire membership into Ben's by-the-seashore clique, one had to sign a 'Document of Promise'. This piece of legalese was then read to the charter member mainly because none of the candidates were literate. What it said in a nutshell was, 'All Charter Members Must Work A Year For Mister Hornigold'.

With free labor and an army of island scroungers things started to look up again for Benjamin Hornigold. What was offered as pay was plenty of booze, marijuana, fruits, monkey meat, fish and willing women at the end of each day of work! So being as that's what the marooned sailors would have spent their money on anyway, all seemed quite pleased with theirs' and Hornigold's arrangement.

Pretty soon Hornigold was able to get his hands on a fast little schooner. How he got it will never be known.

But, the important thing to remember is, 'The Club' then had the ability to make some really big money! By pirating mostly Spanish ships which they certainly did, Hornigold was able to pretty much buy the island his gentleman's club was setting on.

The Bahama Islands presented an ideal base of operations. The archipelago abutted the main shipping channel for vessels heading for Europe and was made up of some seven hundred tiny islands which provided harbors and waterways for hiding.

The Bahamas' main island of New Providence was sparsely populated and had no government to speak of. The isle even had the skeleton of a town, Nassau, which had been burned to the ground by Spanish pillagers, nicely served as the pirates' new home!

By Hornigold's second Christmas, he and his accomplices along with their expectant 'wives', installed themselves amid Nassau's ruins. They built small but swift boats and organized themselves into bands. They began attacking Spanish trading vessels and a few sugar plantations for which they were rewarded by bringing back silk, copper, rum, sugar, silver coins and slaves back home to Nassau.

Soon the club members began calling themselves the 'Flying Gang' and surprisingly had grown to the point of outnumbering Nassau's law-abiding citizens. Greed and power however as expected, raised its viperish head!

To expand his reach, Hornigold sought out a larger and more sophisticated boat. What he wanted was an intimidator with plenty of guns!

The prize would be a battleship from any navy but Britain's. After all, he was King George's bastard brother and a loyal subject of England. Stealing a ship from his own blood was unthinkable!

King George was standing by the fireplace in his study when Windy, the head housemaid announced the arrival of Commander Ogle. He had missed his old war buddy. They hadn't seen each other in almost two years!

Caroline stuck her head in the half opened sliding doors and studied her husband for a few seconds before he realized she was looking at him. He was getting those headaches again and was sporting a greenish pallor which substantiated her thinking.

She knew Gus despised being cooped up every day! He hated even more going about a king's duties!

The Queen was quite aware that the man she married was a warrior! He detested the helium spines of politicians almost as much as he deplored the pomp and circumstance involved with making regal show-ups!

She knew it would lift his spirits to speak with Cal again. Therefore, she had taken the liberty of cancelling the day's usual quest attendees. That way, 'the boys' would have some time to catch up!

"Caroline, I cannot begin to express the horror I experienced when I looked at myself in the mirror! What I saw reminded me of an old troll attempting to dress up like a princess." said Chaloner in his first sentence spoken to the King's wife. He schmoozed some more…

"I am embarrassed, no, down-right ashamed, to be in the presence of the runner-up to Athena in the 'Grand Goddess Contest'! It seems totally impossible to make a wart-hog such as I, something of beauty when you do it so naturally!" Concluded Commander Ogle as he bowed to the Queen.

"Oh, cut the horseshit, Cal! We're alone now, by all means be your normal wonderful self! It's been a long time; how have you been?" happily, asked Caroline.

"Well, I was beginning to start liking the idea of retirement until your husband's Secretary of War joggled me back into a more realistic state of mind! Sir, Robert Walpole sent me north to track down a wharf-rat and I am here to report my findings."

"Ah, I see you're consorting with the enemy again! You better watch out for that one, Cal, especially when she gets tipsy! The Queen can order your head chopped off you know!" greeted the King.

The two men embraced one another like school boys. They even played an electrically swift game of 'rocks-paper-scissors' as it had been done between the two since Chaloner had served as George's father's letter boy some years before.

Although the men had grown older and further apart while pursuing their ambitions, they had never forgotten the bond that emerged during the din of battle in Belgium. Together, the two lieutenants fought off an entire detachment of marines after being cornered in a collapsed building.

That particular skirmish lasted just under ten hours. In the aftermath, it was discovered that the pair of them had wiped out the entire bunch of Frenchmen. Amazingly, neither of them got a scratch from it!

"Gentlemen, if you will excuse me, I shall retire to my quarters in hopes of my husband's return to my bed before the cock crows in the morning! All I ask of you charming young men is that you keep the noise down to a low roar and that you smoke only outside!" blurted Queen Caroline.

As soon as King George heard Caroline's door shut, he turned to his old friend with a worried look on his face. He then checked the windows to assure himself there were no eavesdroppers.

"Tell me, Cal, what's going on in Liverpool?" asked "Gus".

"I don't know for sure but I believe there is some sort of underground movement going on up there. The poor fellow who Sir Walpole demanded that I interview, apparently had written a letter to the Prime Minister disclaiming himself from any wrongdoings going on by the Royal African Company!

This Charles Hayes the man I was sent to investigate, dropped several indicators there was indeed something of a nefarious nature happening within the R.A.C.! Although quite drunk, Mister Hayes did manage to throw out a few usable tidbits which caught my attention right away.

Hayes mentioned he was always paid by a lone courier which interestingly was a child bearing a jar of pickled peaches for him! A little girl in his case, would pay him his weekly salary of ten elephant and castle guineas packed within the delivered jar of peaches.

Another piece of intelligence I extrapolated from the 'sub- governor' was the Royal African Company's leadership is actually under the control of only one man, a Reverend Isaac Green."

"Bingo!", shouted the King. "Sir?" asked Ogle.

"Oh, Cal, you have caught yourself a big one this time! Yes, sir, and it is a monster at that! Our guys have been trying to smoke that rodent out for nearly a decade now! We didn't know who the bastard was for sure, but, we had a pretty good idea! Out of six possibilities, Reverend Green was in the top three 'likeliest' candidates! Your elephant and castle coins discovery cinched our theories about this character! Here, let me get his file. Hey, Cal, may I fix you a drink?" asked George Augustus.

"A bottle of scotch if you please! I won't need a glass." answered Cal.

Chaloner's mind drifted back to the girl speeding away on her rusty bicycle. 'Usually a child bearing a jar of pickled peaches' kept cutting into his mind.

"Were you able to find anything helpful in my report?" asked Ogle.

"Oh yea, plenty! Come look at this, Cal!" shrieked the British king.

King George II spread out the time line that his detectives were unable to completely fill in.

"What's been such a conundrum for us was finding out where Green got the money to do what he's doing." said the King.

"What is he doing?" asked Cal.

"Patience, my child, I'll get to that!" teased Gus.

George Augustus motioned for his childhood friend to walk over to the table where there were neatly arranged files on a person named, Count Franz Anton von Sporck.

"Who is this?" curiously questioned Cal.

"'That' is what you hooked, my friend!" solemnly said Gus. "Are you suggesting that this von Sporck is also Isaac Green?" Asked Ogle.

"Exactly!" said King George.

"Damn! And I was right there!" Gasped Chaloner.

"Yes, and if you had tried to nab him, you my dear Buddy, would be deader than four o'clock! He has a brutally effective staff protecting him around the clock!" Gus said.

"So, where'd he get the money to fund his doings?" Ogle asked.

"You'd better sit down for this one, Cal. Let me see that bottle!" beckoned the King.

"The goddamned Spanish are behind this, aren't they!" bellowed the Commander.

"Partially, 'yes' and somewhat, 'no'!" answered George.

"No?" questioned Commander Ogle.

"Chaloner, the Royal African Company went belly-up about ten years ago! The cause of this was mostly due to complacency and politics. Basically, the company reneged on its longstanding agreement to import the gold used to produce the British Crown's minted coins.

That fellow you interviewed, Hayes, was actually the little shrew who 'threw the switch' on his own countrymen! As it turned out, he was nothing more than an agent operating under von Sporck's hand." reported George Augustus.

The King flapped his fingers against his palm indicating he wanted the bottle of scotch again. After a pregnant moment he returned the empty crock to his friend and continued his discussion.

"With the use of his cousin's, the Duke of York, inheritance, Sporck was able to buy up the dilapidated R.A.C. building which had been Liverpool's headquarters for over fifty years. Incredibly, he did it without anyone but Mister Hayes knowing about it! What no one knew was, Sporck had absconded with the die-casts used to make the elephant and castle coins. About six years ago the counterfeited things began circulating around the cities contiguous to Liverpool. The only difference between the authentic gold ones and Sporck's phonies are the counterfeit pieces are made of tin and lead! The imitations are then finished off with a dip into a bath of gold paint!" explained the King of Britain.

"Gus, who is Sporck getting the gold from to plate these 'fake' coins?" asked the Commander.

"An outstanding question! Remind me to make you an Admiral one day!" responded Gus.

"Cal, Reverend Isaac Green created his own mint using the precious metals collected from pirates!" excitingly said George.

"Are you saying that Green melts the gold he gets from the pirates? How does he do that? I mean, they certainly don't just give it to him?" Ogle asked demonstratively.

"Commander Ogle, how Sporck does it clearly demonstrates his cleverness! Frankly, I rather admire his genius!

Our intelligence sources inform us he attracts his 'clients' with advertisement postings he has tacked onto every cathouse wall in the Caribbean! He promises fair appraisals on all 'estate settlements' and the payment in 'spendable' cash!" bluntly stated the King.

"So, this fellow Sporck, is running an international pawn and fencing operation is he?" cunningly questioned Chaloner Ogle.

"We're out of scotch, ole Boy!"

I'll get us another crock. Hang on, there is more to tell so don't go away!" said Gus.

While King George was rummaging around for more scotch, Ogle walked over to the 'Sporck Table'. He took particular interest in the drawings depicting the All Saints' Church.

"Good news! I also found some salami and two bottles of the nectar of the Gods! So, what do you think of the 'witch's hat'?" drunkenly asked the King.

"Very odd," remarked Cal.

"You don't know the half of it! 'The Bow Street Runners' report explained that the 'Thomas' along with three of England's best captains are already underway on their first leg to Africa!" demonstratively spouted Gus.

"The 'Thomas' is Jonn Kimber's ship isn't it?" asked Ogle.

"Yes, and William Bosman as well as James Stanfield are also onboard!" admiringly stated the King.

"Incredible! Gus, I know of all three of those men! They aren't the type to get hooked up with a crook!" exclaimed Ogle.

"We don't believe those men are aware of who they're actually working for! As far as they're concerned, it's just another fat R.A.C. job!

Just for your information, a Guineaman can earn up to a two pounds a head bonus for every living slave he delivers to an American block! The 'Thomas' will hold up to six-hundred slaves; you do the math!" said Gus.

"With all due respect, sir, I find it hard to believe that men of their caliber would even give Reverend Isaac Green the time of day!" spat Ogle.

"Unless they are prisoners!" said the near inebriated King.

Cal stood, he walked over to the bay window overlooking a well-manicured meadow. He mulled over the last hour's conversation with his old friend. With pure frustration in his voice he loudly spoke,

"King George, I believe that there is a glaringly ugly piece that apparently I am missing! Sure, this Sporck man is a slick operator but from what I've heard so far, he does not merit the level of attention that the King of England is giving to him!"

"And once again, you are spot on! There is more, much more to explain!" said George Augustus.

"Please continue," said Ogle with a respectful nod.

"I wouldn't even tell Caroline this but Ivan von Sporck is a scary guy! His diabolical nature concerns me greatly," gasped Gus.

"So, why don't you send some of your dagger toting Bow Street boys over to see Mister Green?" whispered the commander.

"I would have done it a long time ago if he weren't tied in with the Habsburgs!" briskly said the drunk King.

Chaloner got up again and walked back over to the window where he could see the meadow. He then turned toward his friend with a not so friendly expression this time and then staggered over to the fireplace. He became affixed on the crimson embers.

"King George, what's really going on here?" sternly asked Commander Chaloner Ogle.

George Augustus then lowered his head. He looked at Cal as if he were a stranger and then shyly joined his blood-brother at the fireplace. In a low whisper, the King came clean.

"'Deum, Diligite, Animalia, Diligentes' means 'Honoring God by Honoring His Creatures'. That is the motto used by the Order of St. Hubertus!"

Gus put a large piece of coal into the dying fire. He continued speaking.

"Forty-four years ago, Count Anton von Sporck brought together a moderate sized group of noblemen that were friendlies toward the Hapsburgs. To cloak its true purpose, von Sporck named his 'club' the Order of St. Hubertus.

The real Saint Hubertus was the patron saint of hunters and fishermen. Sporck's 'Order' however, has nothing to do with hunting or fishing at all. It is an attempt at conglomerating the string-pullers of this earth's wealth!

If he succeeds with his plan, a one Reverend Isaac Green will have corralled into his animal-headed syndrome approximately one third of

Europe's elite! A 'World-Order' is his ultimate objective of which, he intends to lead!"

Cal spun away from the heat given off by the purplish coal. He then suggested to the wobbly-kneed King that they go outside for a smoke.

Before the two men lit-up, it was suggested by Gus that they continue their lifelong game of "Steps"! Admittedly, George conceded his previous loss to Chaloner and therefore knew he had to fetch the bucket!

"Now that your tummy-tum-tum is full of his majesty's booze, it seems only fair that I allow you to call the 'step'! If my recollection serves me correctly, you took me by surprise the last time we played this game together." Gus said sardonically.

"Yes, and I can still whip your petunias any day of the week! Let's make it six steps down, toes on the edge of the porch, and there must be at least a shot's worth of piss in the bucket! Deal?" challenged Ogle.

"Before I commit to these parameters, what must I offer you in the case of my second loss to you?" the King asked.

"Promote me to Rear Admiral!" answered Ogle.

The most powerful man on earth turned toward his friend and laughed so hard he started to hiccup. With the grace of a sumo wrestler, King George II walked six steps down the front steps of his palace and set the piss-bucket in place.

Chaloner Ogle knew Gus had accepted the challenge when he saw him beginning to unbutton his britches. Neither man had peed within the past two hours!

The King now seeing by Cal's dancing in place, his friend was in dire need of relief! Being the fox he was, George Augustus decided to sweat him out a bit!

"Does this look about right, Cal?" taunted Augustus.

"Yea, yea, that'll be just fine! Go ahead and take your best shot!" impatiently said Ogle.

"Commander, I forgot to ask you a question." said the grinning ruler.

"Goddammit, Gus, help me untie this ridiculous cumber bun! Son, I have to pee!"

"My question is, 'what do I win if you are unable to hit your mark', my Friend?"

"I'll accept the mission you called me over here to take!" screamed the squatting Commander.

"Then go in peace, my child!" taunted the victorious King.

With the ring of one tiny silver bell, 'Baxter', Gus's butler entered the library and briskly returned to his awakening staff with the King's directory.

Still wearing a chiseled smile on his face, George Augustus suddenly turned toward the Commander and spoke in a very chilly tone.

"Chaloner, there is something I have not told you yet! I wasn't sure when the right time was but now seems as good as any!

By the way, before we get started, breakfast will be served to us within the hour! Have you gotten a taste for coffee yet?" consolingly asked George.

"Never have! I'm a tea and heavy cream man. You were saying, Sir?" questioned Chaloner.

"Intelligence has suggested that Sporck has even a far more sinister plan up his sleeve than simply embedding a couple of hundred good ole boys in America!" seriously said George.

"What do they suspect he might do?" asked Ogle.

"Annihilate America's ability to sustain itself!" bluntly retorted the King.

Baxter proudly walked over to the head of the dining table to announce that breakfast was soon to be served. He then bowed as he left the men.

"We know that Jonn Kimber is three days out. He is taking the 'Thomas' through its first leg. Sources guesstimate his ship will dock at Cote d'Ivoire in ten to fifteen days.

As Kimber will expect, the Royal African Company's representative will greet the Captain and his crew and show them to their quarters. After that, the counterpart of your friend Mister Charles Hayes, will inspect the 'Thomas'. Once assured the ship is stocked adequately for six hundred African natives and fifty-three crewmen to cross over, their second leg to the Caribbean Islands will begin!

Remember, Cal, Stanfield and William Bosman are also onboard the 'Thomas'! We don't know why Sporck picked those particular captains but for whatever reason, the outcome will certainly not be for anyone's benefit except for Sporck's!

SEA BUZZARDS

Our 'Gang' suspects that Reverend Green may have switched up his usual hodgepodge of breeders, bleeders and their niglets! For some odd reason he has chosen an all-male battalion of Sporckian trained Angolans to replace his usual haul!

The fifty 'animal heads' pretending to be Kimber's sea ready crew, are to be dropped off at the harbors closest to their plantations! You see, my friend, every single one of those crewmembers are in actuality very wealthy plantation owners trying to attain membership into Sporck's bloody hunt club! If I get half the chance…" Breakfast was served and the King became silent.

With a mouth half full of waffle, Commander Ogle leaned over to Gus and whispered some words which ended up with asking the King for a couple of favors.

"Gus, since what started off as the visiting of old friends and has now ended up as a briefing, I believe I should be granted two wishes!"

"And what might those be, sir?" asked George.

"Firstly, I would like to have another bottle of scotch and secondly, I hope to hear more about these trained 'animal heads'!" laughed Cal.

"Oh yea, and ole Sporck has done that one right too! European aristocrats grew up being a part of many clubs and fanfares so the International Order of St. Hubertus isn't that big of a deal to them.

On the other hand, the plantation classed Colonists having the ability to be associated with European noblemen is much akin to actually being one of the nobilities in the eyes of their local townsfolk! I mean, overnight they become celebrities! Some even tack on new titles to their names like, 'Duke' or 'Count'!

To earn that distinction, a candidate must submit an application to von Sporck along with an in-depth financial statement. Once approved, the appointee is then offered the opportunity to enroll in either the 'Sporckian School' in England or the one where the Angolans were trained, in Africa!

It is during these six weeks of 'special training' that these southern rich boys are placed into separate animal groupings and given a paper-made animal headpiece to wear during certain ceremonies. What the plantation heirs learn while enrolled in these schools deals mostly with the 'black arts,'" sharply stated the King.

"But still, Gus, I can't see how a few Angolans and some rich hicks could cause the 'annihilation of America'?" asked Ogle.

"Oh, they can't!" snapped Gus.

"Sir?" Ogle asked.

"Cal, Count Anton von Sporck has produced some kind of formula…," started the King when a distraction stopped him from speaking further.

A sneeze coming from behind the dining room curtains interrupted George's explanation of how the 'animal heads' were planning to destroy the colonies.

With a dagger drawn from his boot, George Augustus walked over to the draperies and slung them back! Behind them was an eleven-year-old boy. He was crying.

"And whom might you be?" The King semi seriously asked the lad.

No answer.

"Are you lost, Son?"

Still nothing.

With a kind gesture, Gus reached out to lift the apparently frightened child's chin. Expecting to see the typical sullen face of a mischievous youngster, the King's eyes met those of a determined assassin!

With lightning fast movements, the little killer pulled from behind his back a cocked pistol. Skillfully, he grasped both of his hands together, spread his legs apart, straightened his elbows and then took aim at the King's chest!

Realizing there was imminent danger, Commander Ogle withdrew his own pistol and shot the boy in the head! The palace guards stormed into the dining room and snatched the small body from off of the floor and then left as quickly as they had entered.

"As I was saying, Cal, Sporck has developed some kind of biological bomb that supposedly will spread the 'Black Death' throughout our American colonies! Our mole tells us the bacterial culture is to be used to cause the catastrophe!

When our scientists were asked to weigh in on our implant's story, they concurred. 'Yersinia pestis' they said, was the bacteria carried by fleas which tragically wiped out most of Europe three hundred years ago!" Preached George Augustus.

"How would Sporck possibly be able to introduce these bacteria onto a landmass as large as the Americas'? Since there are so many water sources and so few densely populated areas, I don't see how Sporck would be able to pull his scheme off!" argued Ogle.

"Commander, it is considered by our kingdom's brightest minds', Sporck will expose everyone on the 'Thomas' just before the plantation owners and the slave imposters are distributed onto their assigned properties. What's really sad, each and every one of those unfortunate passengers on the 'Thomas' will innocently be hosting an airborne strand of Bubonic plague!" prophetically stated Gus.

"Your Lordship, how do you propose we stop them?" questioned Cal.

"Commander, I wish I could tell you that one of my naval fleets would sail out this day in pursuit of the 'Thomas', cut them off halfway through her second leg and then blow the damn thing to smithereens! But I can't!

There is a plethora of reasons why that option is not available to me! The first being, the 'Thomas' flies under the British flag! The second reason and the third and so forth, are because England is at war with Spain and bracing for one with America!

Chaloner, can you imagine what the press would say if one inkling of such a deed were to ever make it back to land? I can read it now, 'King George Sinks His Own Ship; Kills 600 Slaves And 50 Americans!'" recited the very drunk King.

"Either way, you're going to have to take the 'Thomas' out! You know that don't you, sir?" alarmingly warned Cal.

"Commander Ogle, when you were a child did you ever dream of sailing the seven seas as a pirate? Were you not entranced by the swashbuckling tales of those Robin Hoods of the sea?" mused King George.

"Gus, are you wanting me to dress up like a pirate and fly the Jolly Roger whilst I dispose of the 'Thomas' and her infected passengers?

And where Sir, might I find a salty crew of actors with the skills necessary to make such an assault...?"

A loud knock on the dining room's door interrupted Commander Ogle's cross-acceptance speech.

The King stood up and approached the double doors. But before he could reach for the brass handle, Cal asked him an awkward question.

"Who was that boy back there?" dramatically asked Chaloner.

"That is why Sporck scares the shit out of me, Cal! He doesn't play within the bounds of civility! Example, 'dead boy'! Got it?" flatly stated George.

"Got it!" blurted the Commander.

When the King slid the dining room's mahogany doors open in stepped four Royal chevaliers. They were King George's elite guards.

With a quick wink given to his old buddy and another given to the detachment's major, King George Augustus ordered Commander Ogle to be placed under arrest and charged with 'High-Sea Piracy'! He then spoke directly to the arresting party.

"Take Commander Ogle to the Chichester facility. Make one of those London Gazette snoops pay a little bit for some 'leaked' information about your most recent prisoner! Tell them the King suspects 'Ogle' of consorting with the 'Gregory Gang' and will stand trial on the fifth of next month! Give them nothing else! Do you understand my orders, Major?" snapped Britain's King.

"Understood, sir!" said the Major.

"And one more thing, make sure you use the larger leg chains on my friend here! They make a lot of noise and they'll get the attention we need! Let the others know, their 'prison break' is set for 0300. Move to phase 'blue-dart' after that!" ordered King George.

"You know, Gus, I know you moved the bucket to step seven!" joked the chained commander.

"I did not! I put it at step eight!" laughed Gus.

Blanche had already taken precautions by gently sewing Charles Hayes's trouser cuffs together. To further insure her safety, she skillfully nailed his hand to the white pine flooring which of course woke the man up from his drunken unconsciousness.

"Fuck-Stick, you have shat upon yourself! You're quite disgusting, you know!" Blanche said from her position atop the rafters overlooking the Sub-Governor.

Because Charlie's right hand was stuck to the floor palm's-down, he couldn't look up at the wicked child staring down at him. He just laid there slamming his free hand on the rug like a referee counting the seconds until a 'pin' is called.

"Hey stupid! You down there, that's right, you with the nail in your hand!" yelled Blanche as she began peeing down upon the impaled Mister Hayes.

"Wake up you silly bastard! Ike wants to share a little prayer with you! It's about faith, I think!"

In a terrified manner, Charles Hayes turned his body so he could see the colorless wench through his peripheral vision. He tried to make a deal!

"Look! I've got a lot of money stashed away! Let me go and I'll give it to you, all of it!" pleaded Charles.

"Oh, my short-peckered Friend, are you talking about that measly bag of coins you stashed beneath your stove? My lord, Child, that wouldn't even match my travel allowance! Ike's very good to me, you know," mocked Blanche.

"You are the most despicable human being I have ever met! No wonder your mother sold you off! I'll even bet ole Ike paid double for you since he switched his interests from boys to sluts!" Seethed Charles Hayes.

With those remarks having been said, Blanche jumped down from the rafters. She then sashed from the R.A.C. office in order to fetch a one-hundred-foot coil of rope.

Upon her return, Ike's young lover firmly tied one end of the rope around Charlie's ankles. The other end of it was connected to the back of Blanche's donkey cart.

With the crack of a rawhide whip, Blanche headed back up the hill toward the All Saints' Church. She only stopped once and that was because she needed to light up a cigar.

First mate Henry Every had been on watch all night. He had decoded the semaphore messages which had come in during his time on duty. He personally delivered them to the 'Charles II's' Commander.

It had taken two days for the ship to get its communications! The most recent series of lights had 'said' struck Henry like the gong atop the Winchester Cathedral! The 'Charles II' had been ordered by the King himself to track down the 'Thomas' and sink her!

Seeing as how the 'Thomas' was a slaver, it seemed obvious to first mate Every that destroying her would be a total waste of money! Henry

Every was also aware that he along with the rest of the ship's crew had not been paid a single ounce of gold in more than eight months!

It is not too far of a stretch to understand why Every and several of his fellow crewmen made the decision to rechristen the 'Charles II' and rename her, the 'Fancy'! Obviously, this transition was not without a certain amount of bloodshed but all and all, the King's naval officers were treated with respect and let go on dry land!

Now flying the Jolly Roger and needing a goodly-sized bankroll, Every set out to strip the 'Charles' of its heavy upper works so she would sail more swiftly. Defenseless trading vessels were to be the 'Fancy's' first targets!

While resupplying in Togo, H+*+enry Every commissioned an army of painters to completely change the color of his attack ship to a two-tone gray.

With the stripped-down and nearly invisible 'Fancy' along with a wandering crew, all Every had to do was wait for the 'Thomas' to load up their newly purchased human cargo in Sierra-Leone, follow it to Guadalupe, switch over to a French flag and capture it! He would then either recruit or kill the slaver's crew members before he sold off the slaves at a bargain price!

Captain Every knew the pin-hookers dotted throughout the Caribbean shores would be his best bet! That way, there would be no taxes to worry with!

Henry was going to sell them off as quickly as possible, give two thirds of the bounty to his crew and then head off to some island where he could legally have a harem full of buxom virgins.

Benjamin Hornigold was sitting on the front porch of his bungalow throwing darts at the green flies. His targets were baited with a strip of bacon he had nailed to a mast.

Black flies brought ten points. The greens would get you fifty!

Ben and his next-door neighbor, Oliver were in a fierce dagger throwing competition when a light-skinned negro rode her bicycle across their firing line! She had in her basket a jar of pickled peaches.

"Gentlemen, I do apologize for the intrusion but I was wondering if you could point the way toward a Benjamin H. Augustus's address? All the road signs on this side of the island got blown down last month and I can't find squat over here! Could you help me find him please?" said the polished native girl.

Oliver LaBuse slowly lowered his yellow and black dart and carefully laid 'Stinger' back into her wooden box. He walked toward the little girl on the bicycle.

"Little Missy, maybe I can help you! Did you say, 'Augustus'?" gently asked Oliver.

"Yes, sir! The name I was given was, 'Benjamin H. Augustus'!" answered the girl.

"Now, sweetie, this is the home of a Mister Benjamin Hornigold. He and I are the only ones living down this road. My home is to the left of Ben's." politely responded LaBuse.

Mister Hornigold approached the interfacing two.

"I am Ben H. Augustus! I am afraid my neighbor wasn't aware of my formal name… how might I serve you, my Lady?" eloquently asked Hornigold.

"Well, then this jar of pickled peaches is for you! In it are some instructions.

If you do not accept the intricacies of this agreement, Mister Augustus, you are to return one hundred percent of the jar's contents to Woodes Rogers's Nassau office by noon tomorrow!

Ben, I suspect you and your buddy LaBuse are rum dummies therefore I am prepared to repeat myself if need be! So, should I go over it again or did you actually get it the first time?" sarcastically snarled the island girl.

Without saying another word, Hornigold broke off a thin branch from a nearby tree and began whipping the child's legs as she hurriedly peddled away!

"Benjamin, before we count the money let's read the message along with a nice bottle of rum?" suggested Oliver.

"You are hereby hired to perform an immeasurable service for the Royal African Company! The following will be required:

- You are to sail the 'Happy Return' and fifty of your best crewmen to Sierra-Leon within a spin of the clock.
- Captain William Bosman will be your contact. You are to hand over this document only to him. Bosman's course is to be set at Longitude<100° 15' 23" W…Latitude>25° 40' 36" N….

- You are to escort the 'Thomas' until she docks at Laguna Bay. At that point, you and your crew will receive five thousand two hundred and ninety-eight pounds. The three hundred and two pounds that were delivered with this message should be considered as your retainer. *You are to defend with your and your crew's lives the safety of the 'Thomas' and her entire payload from Sierra-Leon to Laguna Bay. Signed, Charles Hayes," read Hornigold.

Oliver LaBuse solemnly looked over at his friend and quietly began gathering his darts and other miscellaneous things around Ben's front porch. With the look of a man about ready to marry a woman for her money, Oliver grinned at Ben and muttered a few words as he stepped off the porch.

"Captain, this is the one we have been waiting for! Four o'clock 'onboard', okay with you, sir?" asked LaBuse.

"See you then, Oliver!" whispered Hornigold.

Chaloner Ogle sat in the back of King George's open carriage awaiting the arrival of his attorney. His shiny handcuffs caught the attention of couples who happened to be out for a midnight stroll at the front gate to Chichester Prison.

On the signal from the northernmost guard turret, Percy Fogg jumped up on the back of a flatbed wagon. He pulled out a megaphone from his large brown satchel along with a roll of red admission tickets.

Percy shoved the three-inch roll under his left foot so the wind wouldn't blow them away. He then raised the cone to his lips.

"Ladies and Gentlemen, what a surprise this is! Starting at eight o'clock in the morning, the public will be permitted to view the hanged body of Dick Turpin! Unfortunately, I will not be allowed to sell you folks tickets to see his gruesome corpse until sunrise!

But you know what, since ya'll are such a sophisticated bunch, I'll level with you, save your money! As terrible as Turpin was said to be, the treatment he received went way overboard if you ask me!

You see, good People, I saw the man when they cut him down! His head was hanging on by one little strand of flesh! I strongly suggest if you do decide to stick around till morning that only the men view Turpin's gory remains!

It's going to ultimately be your decision! If you do make that choice don't say that ole Percy Fogg here, didn't warn you!" barked Percy Fogg.

From the rear of the gathered onlookers a man's voice split the night's gossipy buzz.

"I thought they hanged Turpin in York! What are you trying to pull off here, Mister?" said the agitator in a high-pitched voice.

"King George himself has ordered that Turpin's body be displayed in front of every prison in Britain! He is sending out the message, "Piracy", whether it occurs on land or sea will be stopped permanently on his watch!

To let you in on a little secret, the very dead and soon to arrive Dick Turpin is just the first to be traipsed around the country! There are more than a dozen executions scheduled within the month!" animatedly exclaimed Percy.

"Is Commander Ogle one of them?" yelled the same man with the effeminate voice.

Percy deliberately slowed his movements down so the enlarging crowd would tip-toe closer to the cliff's edge. He knew that soon they would be hanging from it!

He took a long drink of whiskey, cleared his throat and pointed the megaphone directly at the girlish naysayer who was now hiding behind his obese wife.

"King George and let me say this again, will under no circumstance permit the unabated robberies of Englishmen any longer! When there is reason to suspect that such crimes have taken place no matter who or what class of people they are, your King will rid the menace as if they were rats!

In the case involving Chaloner Ogle, tomorrow morning he and a handful of his cronies are to have an arraignment hearing within those prison walls behind you! If they are found to be complicit in their wrongdoings then they too will be hanged just as Dick Turpin was!" loudly announced Percy Fogg.

The sound of a bugle shattered Fogg's instrumented somber air! A woman shrieked when four horsemen followed by a six-horse drawn hearse rumbled onto the prison grounds! Six dragoons all riding coal black stallions, closed in the casket baring procession as it came to a halt.

With the rat-a-tat of a single drum, the macabre parade braced for the Warden's command. The gigantic door opened into the prison grounds.

Cal Ogle's wagon was then escorted into the center of the penal facility. Another drumroll was heard as the entrance gate closed behind the King's detachment.

Hendrick Quintor paced back and forth in his cell. It wasn't the contrived jailbreak that had him so worried, it was the thought of riding a horse that made him start sweating bullets!

The Dutch-African sailor had never even sat on one of those animals before! This was mainly because he had not been on dry land for more than a day at a time during his whole life!

Quintor looked over his shoulder. His men were getting ready. He had drilled them on the coming maneuver many times but it was now show time! He could tell he needed to say something to his men.

"Gentlemen, take a knee! Alright fellows, this one's for real! It's going to be just like we practiced. We'll do just fine!

As soon as the sun comes up our man is going to begin selling tickets for the rights to lay eyes on a hanged man! While all of that commotion is going on, Dick Turpin's accompanying dragoons, our stand-in's, will enter our cell and commence to exchange their clothes for ours!

Commander Ogle will then fall in among us. We will then hop on the soldiers' horses and ride out of here as though we were the King's men themselves!

From our restaging position, we will split up into our three separate groups. The Reds will reach Dartford by way of a Gypsy caravan. Green group will launch a fishing boat up the Thames while the Blue's convert themselves into travelling Methodists.

We will converge at Allhallows in two days. After that, god only knows where we'll go. But wherever that place is, we will be there as very rich men and free ones at that!" said Quintor.

CHAPTER 3

MIDDLE PASSAGE

Jonn Kimber had to think about how many times he had resupplied in Senegal over the past decade. Nothing much had changed. The place still had the same smell. An ever-present stickiness always provoked a certain horniness within his bones.

Sabrina and he had four children together. They were working on another when a sharp rap disturbed the rush of tens of thousands of sperm cells into Sabrina's uterus.

A white boy of about ten years old stood on the front door of Jonn's home. His hands were clasped behind his back. His strawberry blond hair and crystal blue eyes made the impression he was from somewhere else. He had an Austrian accent.

Kimber had been expecting one of Sporck's child messengers so he asked Sabrina to open the door.

"Greetings from Reverend Green!" the little boy said as he clicked his heels together.

"Yes, young man, please step in out of the sun!" said Sabrina in a motherly tone.

"Mam, I don't have a lot of time to fuck around with this 'step in out of the sun' crap! I just need to speak to ole Jonnie Boy if you don't mind! So why don't you move that cute little ski-jump ass of yours and go fetch your squeeze for me, sweetie!" hissed the messenger.

Appalled by the boy's remarks, Sabrina shut the door to their relative mansion and began crying. With words squirting out between sobs, she quietly turned toward her sea-husband and uttered only one sentence.

"After you get what you need from that impudent little Sporckian outside, I want you to kill him for me! I'll enjoy feeding him to the sharks!"

Tickled by his woman's reaction, Jonn laughingly went out to greet the 'little turd'.

"I understand you have something for me!" boldly asked Kimber.

"Yes, sir, I certainly do but first you have to wish me a good morning!" Said the boy with an impudent smirk on his face.

No sooner had the smart mouthed kid finished that sentence when Jonn Kimber picked up a dried-up palm frond and began dancing with it as if he were a striptease artist! Immediately following his imaginary pole dance routine, Jonn removed his clothing!

The ten-year-old began to panic when he felt Jonn's tongue dart in and out of his ear! Jonn began playfully groping the young chap! "Let me go, Mister! If you don't stop, I'll tell the Constable!" screamed the boy.

The sobbing child pointed to the basket attached to the back of his bicycle seat. He sniveled through the explanation about the money in the pickled peaches jar and the message inside the cap of the peach container.

Just as he had done with the similar interaction he had experienced in Liverpool with the little blond bitch, Jonn walked over to the kid's bike, got the jar of peaches, picked up his feverishly discarded clothing and walked into his house without saying diddlysquat to the confounded youth!

Moments later, Sabrina offering no eye contact with the now bicycle mounted young man, immediately began setting up her shooting table! With her sand bag now comfortably hosting the stock of her rifle, Sabrina began dialing in a seventy-five-yard sighting.

Jonn Kimber then walked back out of his house with a naval captain's uniform on. He then ran over to the entrance of his driveway and drew a starting line across the sandy road leading back to town.

Kimber then motioned for the boy to put his bike's front tire on the starting mark. Jonn's instructions followed.

"Okay, Sport, here are your instructions so listen closely! When I blow this whistle, you are to ride your bicycle as fast as you can toward that clump of trees over there! They are exactly two hundred yards from here! While you're peddling for your life, ole Sabrina over there on the porch will begin loading her very fine snipers' rifle! You are to try to make your way up the road the best you can while my woman tries to shoot you in the head! Depending on how swiftly you can make it to those palms will determine how many rounds she can get off at you! I figure she'll pop you on the first one but if she doesn't, I'd expect two more to follow if I were you!" toyed Jonn.

"Oh please, Mister Kimber, I didn't mean to make you folks so mad! I was just being…" Jonn blew his whistle.

When the kid saw Sabrina tear off the tip of a powder pouch and cram it down the barrel with a ramrod, he started peddling his bike like his legs were on fire! Her first bullet blew off the lantern attached to his handlebars!

Sabrina spit down her smoking barrel just before she reloaded. She then winked confidently at Jonnathan before she clicked into place her set-trigger. The boy peddled even faster.

Just as the kid was about ready to reach the merciful group of trees in front of him, he became airborne! For only a split second, the little Sporckian saw his front tire explode into smithereens sending him sailing over the finish line!

The child victoriously picked himself up off the ground. He brushed himself off and then shot both Jonn and Sabrina the 'bird'. To his surprise, the boy noticed that his 'vulgar' finger was gone!

Knowing full well that Jonn would leave her half of whatever was in the jar of peaches, Sabrina wasted no time emptying its contents into the well bucket. She then proudly yelled out the door to her man that there were three hundred and two mint perfect coins now in their possession!

Jonn finished cleaning Sabrina's rifle and went inside to put it back over the mantle. He ignored the thirty stacks of coins on the kitchen table as he picked up the screw on cap to find out what Sporck's message had to say.

Once he had found his eyepiece, Kimber began reading out loud the words scrimshawed on the porcelain backed jar lid.

"Captain Kimber, you are to immediately travel by horseback to Sierra-Leon. There you will make contact with Benjamin Hornigold. His ship, 'Happy Return' has been contracted by the R.A.C. to accompany the 'Thomas' to Guadeloupe. Hornigold's mission is to protect the 'Thomas' at all costs. Convey to both Hornigold and Bosman to expect attacks from the pirates as well as the British. You are to install yourself aboard the 'Happy Return' as Hornigold's replacement should you need to dispatch him for his refusal to put fire on an English vessel. Upon your arrival to South Carolina, John Deas and his twin brother, David will distribute to you, Stanfield, and to Bosman the property deeds that you were promised. Remember, this is to look like any other middle passage run so particularly keep your eyes peeled for anything that might invite those looking for more than human cargo. C.H."

Sabrina's black eyes flashed with anger as she watched her man begin to meticulously roll up his things to stack in his overseas bag. She unclipped her raven hair and let it fall over her shoulders and then threw herself into Kimber's arms.

"Jonn, would you be honest with me if I asked you a question?"

"Of course! What's on your mind?" Jonn curiously responded.

"After this one, Jonn, are you coming back?" sniveled Sabrina.

"Sweetheart, as I promised you the last time we had this conversation, my intentions haven't budged one iota since then. I shall repeat myself again, I love you and have for the past ten years!

This trip will be in fact, be my last! After it is done, I shall return with only two questions that you must answer at that time!" Jonn intentionally did not continue his sentence because he wanted to playfully prod Sabrina's standard reaction.

Sabrina gently kneeled in front of Jonn and unbuttoned his pants. She inserted his uncircumcised penis into her mouth and commenced to bob her head up and down until Jonn was about to ejaculate. Paired with a firm squeeze, the bonze skinned native then asked Jonn a question of her own.

"And what two questions would you ask me?"

"Oh, Jesus Honey, finish and I'll tell you!" begged Jonn.

"Tell me now!" teased Jonn's sea wife.

"You are being quite the brat, Sabrina! But if you insist on spoiling your surprise, I'll go ahead and tell you… afterwards!" promised Jonn.

"You better, big boy!" said Sabrina before she lightly clinched her teeth around Jonn's flask and mischievously looked directly up into his watering eyes.

"I shall ask you to marry me in a Christian church and you and our children join me and my daughter in America!

So, there you have it, Sabrina. Those were to be my two questions," softly spoke Jonn.

Henry Every could hardly standup. He hadn't had a wink of sleep since the 'Fancy' had her makeover in Togo.

So far, the Shaman had been right, he would be blessed with 'good winds and good luck' for seven years! Henry remembered.

Although still dark, the adolescent captain could see the ebony silhouette of the woman he had picked from the 'Ganj-i-Sawai'. Talk about luck, Henry and his seventy-man crew of dilettante pirates after barely being out no more than a mile from the 'Fancy's' rebirthing dock, came upon a grounded-out Mughal trading vessel.

With his first shot, Every destroyed the 'Ganj-i-Sawai's' mainmast, and when one of the Indian ship's own cannons exploded, havoc reined on-deck! The fragments killed three or four of the gunners, and according to the woman that lay sleeping in his bed, 'the Captain panicked, taking refuge below, among a group of young Turkish women he had purchased to serve as his concubines'.

As a further confirmation about the 'luck thing', Captain Every found the Ganj-i-Sawai's crew put up little to no resistance, and a multi-day orgy followed! And again luckily, there were exactly the same number of 'broken-in' women as there were men in his unit!

Seventy men and seventy women! "What were the odds of that?" Henry mused as he laid down beside his new girlfriend. She smiled at her velvet-gloved captor before she comforted him off to sleep.

Meanwhile, outside of Every's quarters those couples sober enough to swing over to the 'Ganj-i-Sawai' joined in with the onboard 'strip-party' already underway! Once Every's crewmen finished 'stripping' the boat of its valuables, they all planked their way back over to the 'Fancy' before cutting the Indian ship away.

As was the custom, Every rewarded his crew with equal shares of the ill-gotten haul. Which incidentally came out to be roughly the amount of money each of them would have made on the 'Charles II' after twenty years of service to the Crown!

There should be no wonder as to the surprise the rowdy crew had when a lone man with a megaphone in his hand rowed up beside of the 'Fancy' and began speaking!

"Greetings! I come in peace! I have no weapons! Permission to board the 'Fancy'! My name is Governor Charles Hayes of the Royal African Company! I have an important message for Captain Henry Every!"

By this time, the frivolities of the late afternoon shifted to the starboard side of the 'Fancy' where the partygoers looked down at the funny man in the rowboat! Right off the bat, several of the wives began throwing pieces of cake and sea biscuits at the oddly clad Hayes.

Seagulls voraciously dove at the swatting R.A.C. man in hopes of snagging a morsel or two. With Charlie's usual style of panic, he stood up in the rowboat with one of his oars in hand and began swinging it at the diving birds!

A lot of splashing occurred especially when the novice boater attempted to retrieve the oar which had slipped out of his hands. When dusk arrives on the western coast of Africa and there is a pleasant exchange of tides, the predators awaken their senses and return to their favorite haunts. Splashes indicate their prey is near!

When a roasted chicken leg hit the surface of the water, the news went out to the local fishes. Two-and-three-foot dorsal fins cast passing shadows across Charles's blood drained face!

Realizing that this Governor fellow had called him by his name, Henry Every yelled down to the half-catatonic man.

"Don't worry, they're just sand sharks! I'm Every, how may I be of service to you this lovely evening, sir?"

"Oh please, Captain Every, come get me out of this boat!" screamed Charles Hayes.

"Just sit quietly, Mister Hayes! Did you say you had a message for me?" quizzed the sophomoric pirate.

"For god's sakes, man, did you see the size of that sonofabitch? Please, lift me out of here!" bloodily screamed the R.A.C. man.

"Yes, I saw him! Now, what do you wish to speak with me about, Mister Charles Hayes?" toyed Henry.

"That's a great white isn't it? Jesus in heaven, please save me!" Charles exclaimed.

Seeing as how it appeared that Charles Hayes was about ready to jump overboard and attempt to swim back to shore and given the fact that there was indeed the type of shark Charlie identified prowling beneath his rowboat, Henry gave the signal to send the rescue basket down to fetch the petrified sub-governor.

Two men had to climb down a rope ladder to lift Hayes's limp body along with his duffle bag onto the transport basket. Less than a minute after the rescuers had stepped off the oar-less rowboat, they looked down to see the empty dingy being bumped out to sea by 'ole whitey'.

The R.A.C. man was bent over with stomach cramps. His body trembled as if he were freezing to death. Charlie also had the dry heaves!

"Captain, I ain't never seen a man quite that scared before!" said Henry's drunk first mate.

"Oscar, what that man need is a good stiff drink! It isn't because of fear that Charles Hayes finds himself in a writhing fetal position! Our 'Governor' here, is suffering from the "monkeys"!" wisely stated Every.

"The what, sir?" asked Oscar.

"Alcohol withdrawal… go get this poor chap some brandy!" requested Henry.

A handful of the sea-wives volunteered to get Charlie cleaned up. Even though one could not understand what they were saying, be assured there was gossip spewing from their lips. They then whisked the babbling Charlie Hayes off to the gang showers giggling all the way.

Meanwhile, Henry and his girlfriend whom he had named 'Sara', took the R.A.C. representative's sea-bag to their quarters. Painstakingly they spread the bag's holdings onto the chart table much like one would do when preparing to start the construction of a jigsaw puzzle.

There were three odd yet identically sealed canisters setting on the chart table. They had been carefully rolled up into waxed bags.

A leather sack held more than a thousand gold coins in it! Other than a few items of clothing that was it. There was nothing else in Charlie's sea bag.

Four light taps on the Captain's door preempted the return of the presentable yet dazed, Charles Hayes. When he saw that his things had been pillaged through, Charlie abruptly shook off the supportive hands of the Turkish volunteers who had cleaned him up and began yelling at the 'Fancy's' Captain.

"What is the meaning of this, Captain Every? Do you normally ransack your guests' things in this manner? I sure as hell hope you haven't tampered with those tubes! Have you?"

Henry withdrew one of the four pistols he had tucked in his wide leather belt. He then jammed the barrel of his cocked sidearm into Charlie's mouth!

"Mister Hayes, I would like to remind you that you are aboard the 'Fancy', a genuine pirate's ship! I am sure you have heard of how we 'scoundrels of the sea' make unappreciative guests 'walk-the- plank'! Would that be true, Charles?" gruffly asked Captain Every.

Charlie nodded immediately to Henry's question.

"Am I to understand you have an important message for me?" threateningly asked Henry.

"No offense meant, Captain Every but I was just a little concerned when I saw the canisters laid out like that! They are crucial items with regard to the good tidings I bring you!" shakily apologized Charles Hayes.

"You have my attention… now, speak your piece, Mister Hayes!" said Every.

"Well, sir, I am the Sub Governor of the Royal African Company from Liverpool! My boss, Reverend Isaac Green wishes to employ your esteemed organization for a bit of clean-up work!" said Hayes. "Go on…!" pushed Henry.

"At this very moment, the 'Thomas' under the wheel of three captains Bosman, Kimber and Stanfield are preparing to set sail for Guadeloupe. They will be leaving West Africa with more than six hundred slaves onboard!

In addition to the worth of human cargo, there is also a 'hidden compartment' containing double the amount of plunder you got off the 'Ganj-i-Sawai'!" slyly remarked Hayes.

"Now wait a minute, Charles! How in the hell did you know about that?" surprisingly asked Every.

"Captain, the 'Thomas' along with its contents is Reverend Green's payment for your services! When you arrive in Guadeloupe you are to hand each of the 'Thomas's' captains one of those sealed containers! Once they have received their cannisters and safely put out on the island, the 'Thomas' is yours! Said Charles Hayes in a boastful manner.

"So what is to stop us from throwing you overboard and taking the whole kit and caboodle for ourselves, Charlie?" said Henry with a cajoling grin on his face.

"Two reasons!" sharply replied Hayes.

"Yea, well, what are they?" spat back Every.

"The first one, Captain Every, has to do with your notable integrity and the second concerns itself with the 'Happy Return'." calmly answered Charles.

"Hornigold's 'Happy Return'?" asked Every.

"The same," smugly answered Charles Hayes.

"What dog does he have in this fight?" snapped Henry Every. "The 'Happy Return' has also been hired to protect the 'Thomas'

during its Caribbean leg. After we reach our destination, I am to hand over to Captain Hornigold that bag of gold coins laying on your chart table!" bravely replied Charlie.

"And what would be the consequence should you not give Captain Benjamin Hornigold that extremely heavy bag of coins?" bluntly asked Every.

"Why ole Ben Hornigold would then take possession of the 'Thomas' as well as the 'Fancy', sir!" cockily replied Hayes.

"What's in the canasters?" asked Henry.

"Money, a plantation deed, and amnesty!" snapped Charles Hayes.

"Amnesty, under the protection of whom?" sarcastically asked Captain Henry Every.

"King George Augustus!" flatly answered Hayes.

"Mister Hayes, why in god's name would the King of Britain need to grant amnesty to those three slavers?" sharply asked the 'Fancy's' illegitimate captain.

Charles Hayes while staring directly into Every's eyes, wrenched the pistol out of the novice pirate's right hand, spun it one turn around and then handed it back to the young buccaneer butt first. At that point Charlie jumped up on top of the chart table and prepared to speak his "piece".

"The best way to take control over a people and control them is to take a little bit of their freedom at a time, to erode their rights by a thousand tiny and almost imperceptible reductions! In this way, the people will not see their freedoms being removed until past the point at which those changes cannot be reversed!" Wildly exclaimed Charlie Hayes.

From the expressions on the faces watching the previously seen as timorous man, might best be described by comparing it to looks on people's faces during a public hanging! It was a mixture of curiosity and perhaps even fear seen in their eyes. Mister Hayes's tantrum went on!

The unspoken consensus that zoomed around the captain's galley that night was that Charles Hayes was a madman! But then as if someone else was standing within Charlie's shoes, he dramatically switched his whole persona into an entirely different person and one with a Prussian accent at that!

With his arms spread out like he was grasping at falling money, Charlie or whomever in hell he thought he was, began speaking again. He was acting as if the sound coming from his mouth was actually being spoken by someone hiding within his own skin. A smile crept over Charles's face as he began his nonsensical jabber.

"Brother Sporckians, the sun is once again in the clutches of the lion, and the encircling season bids us to the forest... there to celebrate... the awful mysteries!"

Now on his knees as if bargaining with his executioner, Hayes called out to his audience a voice cracking plea!

"Sporckians come! Find home again in the place where worry and strife are whirled away from our lives... forever!"

At this juncture of Charles Hayes's performance, he returned to the top of the chart table with a vengeance! Hayes then began marching in place. His hobnailed boots offered the eerie effect of an army of demons hot on his tracks!

"Come out Sporckians! Come out and play, come with all the buoyant impetuous rush of youth!" Charlie yelled before he collapsed.

Thirty minutes later, Charles Hayes awakened due to a frog strangling wake which had splashed over the side of the 'Fancy's' emergency dinghy. He sat up only to see Captain Henry Every standing some thirty feet above his tethered craft!

"Oyez, oyez, oyez to you! This is your last chance to save yourself from being set adrift upon the angry sea beneath you! I shall check on you later to see if you are yet ready to remember what you came here to share with me!" yelled Every.

All of a sudden and much to no one's surprise, Charlie Hayes began squealing like a stuck pig. His consciousness returned and his spell had passed or so he proclaimed. It was midnight.

About two o'clock in the morning Henry was awakened by a loud clap of thunder. He then remembered he had left Charlie Hayes outside!

By the time Captain Every made his way aft to the rear deck, howling winds and whitecaps offered little hope to Every that he would be able to apologize to the madman for his terrible mistake! Visibility was zero.

Fearing the gnawing pain of guilty memories, Henry cupped his hands around his mouth and began yelling at where the towrope pointed down into the dark blur.

"Good Morning, Mister Hayes!" hollered Every.

"Good Morning, Mister Hayes!" henry repeated.

No answer.

"God damn it, Charlie, answer me!" desperately yelled the Captain.

No answer.

A lightning bolt magically offered a nanosecond of a glance at a man all balled up in the bow of the emergency dinghy. There was no body movement whatsoever.

Henry immediately sprang into action! Like a mechanical monkey slapping cymbals together, the Captain with blowing rain blinding him picked up the three pound clangor and commenced to beat the ship's bell as if it were a serpent's head!

In what seemed like molasses thick hours, everyone including the sea wives began pulling the rope connected to the waterfilled dinghy. Charlie offered no response.

"Henry, I don't have to tell you how close we came to killing that man!" whispered the former 'Charles II's' ship's physician, Doctor Stephen Garrison.

"There was no 'we' to it, Stephen! It was all 'me'!" humbly said Every.

"Well, the good news is, the boy's going to make it! It seems a good scotch continues to be his rallying elixir!" mumbled Doctor Garrison.

"When will I be able to speak with him?" asked the Captain. "Why not after breakfast? Speaking of which, when was the last time you had anything to eat, Captain Every?"

"I got your message, doc. I'll come back at noon. Thanks!" "You are welcome, Henry." said Doctor Garrison.

Once the signal from Chichester's Warden was acknowledged, Percy Fogg jumped back onto the bed of his parked flatbed. This commotion caught the attention of several loitering couples. That's when Percy grabbed his megaphone.

"Ladies and Gentlemen, in one hour, I am told the hearse containing the hanged and practically mutilated body of Dick Turpin will roll onto this very spot! It will stop just long enough for England's periodically-cognizant elite to examine the efficiency of our country's justice system!

Now, I must warn you of the gruesome sight you ticket holders are about to lay your fragile eyes upon! It may cause you nausea, feeble or faint out there! Remember, Mister Turpin's head was practically separated from the rest of his body when he dropped through the shoot at York!

For those of you who wish to see a man whose soul is burning in hell, then step right up these stairs here and place one guinea into the red box at the top of the steps! Unfortunately, I shall have to ask the squeamish to step back away from the wagon!" Chattered Percy Fogg.

On the third 'dong' echoing off of the Chichester's stone walls, the humongous gate opened like the parting of the Red Sea! Roaring out of the forty-foot passageway came a dozen dragoons all slapping the rumps of their military horses with merciless strikes of their riding crops!

Bullets began whizzing over the heads of those paid participant viewers atop Percy's flatbed. Thirteen horses and twelve unshaven men blew by the planned 'body-stop' like it was a roadside weed!

When the dust settled the discombobulated crowd realized that Percy Fogg was nowhere to be seen! The red box was gone also.

A dozen militiamen all dressed in their standard issue underwear, came running through the closing prison gate firing their muskets at their apparent fleeing prisoners! Not one single ball came within a meter of the escapees!

Count Anton von Sporck his hands clasped behind his back, gazed across Liverpool's horizon. He watched the tips of the high mast ships pass in and out of the faraway harbor.

Thomas Golightly hurriedly parked his carriage in front of the All Saints' Church. He didn't bother to tie his horse to the brass ringed hitching post. He was expected so there was no hassle given from Sporck's guards.

As soon as the elevator doors opened, Liverpool's mayor embraced Count Sporck in a much different manner than expected from two old school chums. Thomas whispered something into Sporck's ear which sparked some giggles from both!

But then, the study grew deathly silent as Mayor Golightly opened up the front page of the "St. James Chronicle". The headlines caused the lion head to have to sit down and put his head between his knees.

"Tom, they're on to us!" said Sporck.

"How could they be? There are only four people in the whole world who know about the vials?" clamored the Mayor.

"Did you read about Chaloner Ogle's fake allegations of collusion? And Mister Golightly, did you recognize any of the names of the escapees?" attacked Sporck.

"There weren't any! But, yes, I did read that part about the King's accusations." retorted Golightly.

"Exactly!" spat Sporck.

"What worries you so much about Chaloner Ogle, Isaac?" gently asked Thomas.

"For one thing, Ogle and King George are tighter than 'Dick's hatband'!" Snarled Sporck.

"They're friends?" asked Thomas.

"Hell, the goddamned King just promoted him to be the next Rear Admiral of his whole fucking navy! And they're going tell me that this same man was arrested for collusion with a bunch of pirates? Balderdash!" spouted Anton von Sporck.

"So, you think King George is in on this?" sheepishly asked Golightly.

"I'd bet my dick on it!" laughed Sporck.

Sporck walked over to the turret window that faced toward America. As if he were speaking to the outside world, he asked his official friend an odd question.

"Remind me again of the professor's name who put together our 'Colonial Cocktail' for us?"

"Sir, it's a very long name and it's French so let me get my notebook out and I'll even be able to tell you where he resides." whispered Tom.

While Thomas Golightly was searching through his briefcase for the address book, Anton von Sporck pensively stared across the Atlantic.

"Golightly, what proof do we have that this French chemist's concoction will do the job?" abruptly asked Sporck.

"Ike, you and I read the study's findings together, remember? The "Lesotho Experiment", does that ring a bell?" politely asked Golightly.

"Refresh my memory!" Anton responded.

"Here, I found him, 'Charles Francois de Cisternay du Fay'! He is the chief immunologist at the Royal Veterinary College in Hertfordshire.

That's the professor who injected a monkey full of 'our' serum and set it loose in the village of Lesotho!" excitedly stated Thomas. "And what were the results of Charles du Fay's 'Lesotho study', Mayor Golightly?" asked the back turned Sporck.

"Three months; zero survivors!" proudly reported Golightly.

"To your knowledge, Tom, did anyone come around asking any questions about the wiped-out African community?" questioned von Sporck.

"None that lived to tell about it!" bragged Tom. "What do you mean?" pried Sporck.

"Well, Ike, whatever that stuff is in those vials he sold to us, not only does it offer a fatal punch within the first week of exposure, Charles du Fay's aerial-effective agents continue to kill for up to three months!" said the grinning politician.

Sporck then turned toward his long-time business partner with a Cheshire cat's smile on his face. After a warm kiss goodbye, Ike walked Tom to the elevator doors. They shared one more kiss before Thomas Golightly stepped out into the dark abyss.

Jonn Kimber slapped 'Mildred's' backside with his reins as he continued on with his second day of travel toward Sierra-Leon! He would make it to Banjul by the next night if he kept up his pace. Timewise, he was cutting it awfully close!

He already had a saddle-sore the size of a doubloon on the inside of his right posterior cheek making the chances of a timely rendezvous an improbability. Jonn despised the land lubbers and he especially loathed their ways of getting around. Just the thought of having to plow a field made the lifelong seaman depressed.

As Jonn and Mildred rounded a curve in the wagon trail they came up on a boy carrying a fishing pole. He had a stringer full of croakers.

"That's a mighty nice mess of fish you have there, son!" said Kimber cheerfully.

"Look, Jonn, I don't mean to get us off on the wrong foot but I've been walking up and down this goddamned road for the past four hours waiting for you! Where in the hell have you been?" scolded the lad.

"I ought to beat your ass, you impudent little sonofabitch!" cursed Jonn.

"If you do, you'll miss the 'Happy Return's' launch by four hours! If that should happen well let's just say, ole Sporcky-baby will once again pick up another loved one and yall's 'redbones', and sell them off to the Turks!" laughingly said the lad.

Jonn Kimber sat on the wagon's bench as still as a busted whistle pig. He focused on Maggie's flipping of her tail while he reasoned with himself. 'If she got the fly, he would kill the kid but if Mildred missed it, he was going to shoot him anyway'. Which he did!

With the skill of a rancher, Kimber released the mare from the cart, turned the wagon over with the kid's body underneath it. He then set the staged wreck on fire and rode south faster than the 'word of god'!

The two-year-old dapple-gray seemed to laugh when Jonn provided her an opportunity to live on Madagascar! That was the promise Kimber made to Mildred!

Oliver LaBuse tapped on the door of Captain's Hornigold's quarters. He was troubled about something.

"Ben, our semaphores have informed me that a Captain Jonnathan Kimber will arrive here by noon today. He claims to have an important message for you!"

"But the peach lid said I was to meet up with a William Bosman, did it not?" asked Hornigold.

"It did, Sir; but Kimber states he was the first leg pilot up until the 'Thomas's' landing in Senegambia. His directive from the R.A.C. he claims, includes his boarding the 'Happy Return'!" explained LaBuse.

"I wonder if this R.A.C. man, Charles Hayes is playing us for fools? What do you think, Oliver?" queried Hornigold.

"Captain, so far… we're making money! Why don't we follow this string all the way to its end! Let's just see what happens." answered LaBuse.

"Very well but let me know when this Kimber fellow rides into town!" Benjamin Hornigold requested kindly.

"Aye-aye, Captain!" replied Oliver.

Blanche was ovulating. These were the times Sporck found it the most difficult to be in a committed relationship.

'Tink' the Chinese physician, had dropped by the church to give Reverend Green enough opium to get both him and Blanche through it again! The little yellow man left gleefully as he was paid his elephant headed due.

"Sweetheart, Tink brought over a little something to make you feel better! See if you can't sit up a bit so you can take a puff of this. It's probably the best we've had in quite some time! That's my girl!" consoled Sporck.

"Wow! That is good!" remarked Blanch.

"Blanche, I have a favor to ask of you." Cooed Ike.

"Sure, Honey, anything you want! Boy, am I feeling better! Thank you, Tink!" laughingly said Blanche.

"A professor Charles Francois de Cisternay du Fay needs to commit suicide!" coldly said Sporck.

"Not a problem, Ike! How about handing me that pipe, Sweetheart. Blanche said.

"Mister Hayes, the ship's doctor tells me you're going to be as good as new by the time we get to Guadeloupe! I understand the women on that island never wear clothing!

I also hear these same lusty nymphs search high and low for eligible men such as yourself! They do this because they want your babies, you know!" Teased Henry Every.

"Now, why in the world would a naked Caribbean want my babies?" mirthfully responded Charles Hayes.

"Governor Hayes, circumstances are the twisters of fate! We evolve only within the perimeters of what we are dealt!

Me, I left home because I had to; there was no love there and I was mistreated. You, well, have your own story!

The point I am making here, Charlie, is this, because of our individual circumstances we find each other during the performances of our separate roles! That's to say, you are acting as if you are an executive with money and I am learning to be a pirate!

Anyway, while we were acting out our circumstantially derived roles last night, I screwed up! Mister Hayes, while I was attempting to scare the 'bojesus' out of you in order to strip you of your last coin, I fell prey to the lures of wanton flesh and then I fell asleep!

Alarmingly, when I awoke and realized what I had inadvertently done to you, I fell on my knees and prayed. I promised to god that if you were still alive, I would not rob you but instead become your friend!" Sincerely exclaimed Every.

"As you said, Captain Every, we were just performing our reshaped roles! I also did some praying out there! I realized that I too had 'messed up'!" admitted Hayes.

"What do you mean, Charlie?" asked Henry.

"When the waves began white capping over your ship's rescue boat, I came to the realization that I was no longer afraid of dying! I have been a coward for…all my life!

It is time for me to stand on my own two feet! I will no longer hide in a dark office!

I shall no more utter the obsequious words of a common clerk! I want to be a pirate!" Loudly announced Charles Hayes.

"I am stunned! Charlie, what makes you think you are cut out for this line of dishonorable work?" Asked Every.

"For one thing, I have a remarkable memory and secondly, I know the names of every ship merchant who cross the Atlantic! I know where they're going and how much their cargos are worth! Helpful information no doubt, wouldn't you say, Henry?" gleefully stated Charlie.

"Do you want a job on the 'Fancy', Charlie?" asked Henry. "Indeed, I do, sir!" erupted Hayes.

"Very well then, let's see what you can do for us between now and the time we reach Guadalupe!" Stated Henry Every.

"Captain Every, you won't regret this, I assure you! I'll await your first order, sir!" said Charles Hayes.

Both Hendrick Quintor and Chaloner Ogle were dressed up as fat old gypsy women. They sat in the darkest part of a colorful wagon headed for Dartford.

A big festival was going on there. Sword swallowers and trapeze artists were the Shifflette's forte; but, they did it all! Edwin Shifflette, the grandfather along with being the wagon's driver, turned around just as a chicken flapped out of its overhead pen.

"Ladies, don't pay any mind to those goddamned chickens! We're in the middle of a bunch of 'marks' right now so keep your heads bowed in case one of them runs up for a 'peek-see'!" Edwin Shifflette said with a leer cutting across the lower half of his jaw.

There were four wagons all together of which most were occupied by real gypsies. But like with Shifflette's two imposters, the other three caravan wagons also had 'Red's' onboard.

Quintor got up from his bench seat and moved up behind Edwin Shifflette. He softly began speaking.

"Edwin, my men and I need to reach Allhallows by tomorrow night! How long do you think we will be detained here in Dartford?" politely asked Hendrick.

"Son, I've been working for the Crown for thirty some years now! When the 'kings' get into one of their cloak and dagger jags, I seem to get the same bloody impatient passengers every time!" complained the old gypsy.

From a very well-hidden sheath behind his back, Hendrick Quintor withdrew a dagger. He placed the tip of the stiletto into Edwin's ear opening and repeated his question in a more sadistic tone.

"When?" harshly whispered Quintor.

"If we only do one show we'll be out of here by sundown! You boys have plenty of time! Hell, Allhallows ain't but twenty miles south of here! I'll get you there, don't you worry, Fellows!" acquiesced Edwin.

"Mister Shifflette, I am afraid there has been a scheduling change! Today's show has been cancelled! Signal to the others we are not going to stop off at this town for even a minute!" briskly stated Quintor.

As though Edwin had glue running through his veins, the fossil like gypsy slowly rose from his seat. He lit a cigar with two stick matches and then sat back down.

Four seconds later, one caravan made up of four colorful gypsy wagons roared out of the sleepy borough of Dartford as if a pack of hellhounds were after it! An hour and a half later, all eight members of the Red Group were in position.

Mister Shifflette and his merry band of gypsies gladly departed. Behind, they left Chichester Prison's most recent escapees atop a hill overlooking the tiny port town of Allhallows.

Robert Maynard and Percy Fogg made up the entire Blue Group. With their Methodist ministers' garb humbly draped around their mortal bodies, the two men managed to make the entire journey without a single hitch. Everywhere they had gone, the townsfolk would welcome them with sacks of ham biscuits and bottles upon bottles of what the Maynard and Fogg duo called, 'repented-proof' wine.

When those two rode into town they had a real shtick going on for themselves! Percy Fogg usually kicked their ten-minute routine off by riding his horse through the front doors of the most heavily frequented drink house in whatever township they happen to be riding through that day.

This went on for their whole five-day trip! Sometimes they would knock-off as many as three taverns in one single day!

The way they did it was, Robert Maynard would ride through a village during a peak time searching out taverns having a reasonably high number of daytime imbibers. Once Bob determined whether a place was ripe enough for the picking, Reverends Fogg and Maynard would bust right into the establishment and jump up on some tables and start preaching the word of god!

Most of the time the patrons were so shocked by the audacity of the two ministers they barely had time to lodge a complaint before the Fogg and Bob show had captured their hearts! The bass voice of Preacher Bob always was the first to grab their attention!

"I know what you're thinking!" Robert Maynard would say.

"I know what you're thinking!" crooned the spotlighted Reverend Fogg.

"This is just another one of those hell-fire-and-damnation sermons. Ain't no way!" They would say as the duo opened up a new show.

Fogg would then cut in with a raunchy kind of bluesy sound echoing what his cohost had just said! When the bar crowd got good and mesmerized, Maynard would then throw Percy one of two white canes as both simultaneously jumped up on the bar.

What normally followed the cane routine probably will never be forgotten by the men who saw those two Methodists do their things! That's when the pair did a two-minute song and dance routine which would totally bring the house down!

When it ended and everybody was standing around all sweaty from their copulatory ideations, the whole 'congregation' started buying drinks for one another which made the establishment's owner quite happy!

Just as Bob and Percy were leaving, Percy Fogg would usually jump up on the table situated near the tavern's exit and begin preaching!

"I would like to quote the Bible if I may. What I am about to recite to you is indicative of the changing face of Christianity! Let us turn in our minds to JOHN 2:3-11."

'When the wine was gone, Jesus' mother said to him,

'They have no more wine'.

And then Jesus said, 'Woman, why do you involve me?'.

Mary then turned toward her servants, 'Do whatever he tells you.'.

Nearby stood six stone jars, the kind used by the Jews for ceremonial washing each holding from twenty to thirty gallons.

Jesus said to his mother's servants, 'Fill the jars with water'; so, they filled them to the brim. Then he said to them, 'Now draw some out and take it to the master of the banquet.'

After the servants did so and the master of the banquet tasted the water that had been turned into wine. He did not know where it had come from though the servants who had drawn the water knew.

Then, as the Bible says, the banquet's master called the bridegroom aside and said, 'Everyone brings out the choice wine first and then the cheaper wine after the guests have had too much to drink; but you have saved the best till now.'.

"My good people, what Jesus did that day in a tavern in Galilee much like this one, was to reveal his glory and to project a message for all 'Good Men' to hear!

What he was saying folks is this, Jesus does not deplore the imbibers, not at all! However, he does in fact despise the slovenly drunkard. He said this in Proverbs 20:1, 'Wine is a mocker and beer a brawler; whoever is led astray by them is not wise.'

And then Jesus repeated his message to us when he was quoted saying in Romans 13:13, 'Let us behave decently, as in the daytime, not in carousing and drunkenness, not in sexual immorality and debauchery, not in dissension and jealousy.'

And so there it is, Gentlemen, His message! God wants us to embrace the joys he has loaned to us! He enjoys watching the shepherds of his flock let their hair down once in a while!

So, you want proof of that? Well, hear this, it's from Psalm 104: 14-15! 'He makes grass grow for the cattle, and plants for people to cultivate- bringing forth food from the earth, wine that gladdens human hearts, oil to make their faces shine, and bread that sustains their hearts,'" proclaimed Fogg.

As Robert Maynard was struggling to make Reverend Fogg's descension a flawless one, Percy made his closing pitch on the way down.

"Christians! Listen well for these are God's words, not mine; 'If your brother or sister is distressed because of what you drink, you are no longer acting in love. Let us therefore make every effort to do what leads to peace and to mutual edification.

Do not destroy the work of God for the sake of drink!

Beverages made from the earth's bounty are clean, but it is wrong for a person to guzzle them that causes someone else to stumble.'

"Therefore, Jesus has provided us with a manner in which we can distinguish ourselves from what is normally associated with the dredges of our society. G.O.D.S. is an acronym used to describe a 'Jesus-Approved' society set up for the disciples way back then!

It was a way to certify the 'upper-crust' Christian drinkers as Gentlemen! What's so exciting about this ancient society is that it allows even we modern day Christians a chance to join this celestial group!

I'm sure Reverend Maynard will fill you in on the details in just a moment but before my brother Robert takes the floor, let me have one last word with you good people!

I was saved as a youngster, washed in the blood as a teenager, got my calling to spread the gospel in my early twenties and then I became a sovereign Christian! I was told just as I have shown you through the teachings of the gospel that becoming a member of the "Gentlemen Only Drinkers Society" is a level of which only blue-bloods of the highest order may be selected! To be a sovereign Chr...," screamed Percy Fogg.

"Hey there, Reverend Fogg! How about giving me the chance to spread the 'Good News'! I guess we all get a little carried away when we speak about the G.O.D.S.!

Let me share with you how you too can become a sovereign Christian! It is a very simple process. But before you enroll as a member of this sacred society, I feel it is my duty to alert you to this fact, once you have been brought into our realm of holiness, you will forevermore be under the watchful eyes of the G.O.D.S.!

As your new title of 'Deacon' is legally placed before your first name, it is most important that you uphold your own personal standards of moderate intoxication due to the coveted membership you are about to become a part of! Everyone will envy who you are so set a good example, please!

I have before me a papyrus scroll. I shall roll out about two feet of it so we may get the twenty signatures permitted for the Rainham Chapter's representation! And yes, I am aware there are thirty-three of you in this fine establishment; however, the rules are the rules!

You will also note, to the right of this Holy Sovereign Scroll is a purple box with a slot carved into the top of it. That box is for your lifetime pledge into the "Gentlemen Only Drinkers Society"!

If every one of you would please lineup in a single file, you will be able to sign up right here and now! All you need to do to gain immediate access into the celestial circle of Jesus's imbibing disciples is to sign your name on one of the blank lines on the papyrus scroll and drop one ounce of gold into the slotted purple box!" huffed Bob.

That's how it went for the two Methodist ministers for the entire six days after their springing from Chichester Prison. All the two had to do now was reach Allhallows by 1700 the next day.

Alex Selkirk, Rainbow Charley and a woman called Anne Bonny had already burned the boat they had stolen in Grays. They tried their best to blend into the populace of Allhallows but no matter what they did or who they spoke to, they always stood out like sore thumbs!

The village of Allhallows is probably the most boring spot on the planet to live. One can never quite reason why anyone would want to go there.

Of its fourteen hundred and twenty-three childless residents all of them wear grey coveralls. The buildings within the town's limits are not much more than wooden boxes stacked on top of one another.

Simply put, there is no color, no noise, no variety and definitely no booze! However, King George had already remedied that foreseen nuisance. He had arranged a civilized staging point for the Red, Green, and Blue groups to converge upon at a place where they would not be noticed.

Because of the King's forgiveness of some old tax arrearages, the Pympe family had generously provided for the Crown their spacious mansion. In it was a fully stocked bar, a deep-water harbor on Yantlet Creek and their absence!

Ironically, it was the very place where Anne Bonney, years ago, had lost her virginity!

In that she was vaguely familiar with the house's layout, the other two members of the 'Green group', Alex and Rainbow, unanimously voted her in as their 'Sunshine Chairman'!

This designation made her responsible for jimmying the lock open to the Pympe's front door.

Anne even commented on the illusory effects of time.

"This place is a lot smaller than when I use to come here for piano lessons! Everything seems spatially miniaturized!"

Rainbow Charlie was the last member of the Green group to enter the Pympe's house but was the first to raid the wine cellar!

"Holy Jesus! Ya'll come look at this!" yelled Rainbow.

Selkirk and Anne Bonney shuffled quickly across the kitchen's slate floor and down into a brick walled springhouse to see what Rainbow was so excited about.

"What'd you find, Charley?" asked Alex with a curious expression on his weather-beaten face.

"About the prettiest thing I ever seen, that's all! Look at these bottles! There's got to be a thousand of them!" exclaimed Rainbow Charlie.

"Well, I'd expect to run out and get some more if I were you! After the others get here, we'll go through that shit like cut bait!" laughingly chimed in Anne.

"I didn't see the ship, Anne, where do you think it is?" questioned Rainbow.

"Ogle will have to show us exactly where it is but I have the sneaky suspicion the bloody thing is hidden down there in Yantlet Creek somewhere!" surmised Anne Bonny as she pointed toward the west.

Jonn Kimber held Mildred's reins as he stood at the foot of the 'Happy Return's' gangplank. Oliver LaBuse rushed across the deck toward Captain Hornigold's cabin.

"Sir, he's here!"

"Well, ask the man to come aboard, Oliver," said Hornigold.

"Ben, he has a horse with him!" shrieked Oliver.

"Then turn it over to the cooks and we'll have it on our way to the Caribbean!" teased the Captain.

"Sir, Kimber insists on bringing the beast onboard! He claims he made a promise to 'Mildred'. That's his horse's name, Captain!" hissed LaBuse.

Sara had just finished setting out an arrangement of orchids on the table when she heard a tapping noise on the door. Thinking it was Henry and he had awakened from his nap, she unbuttoned her blouse so her cleavage was exposed. She then cracked the door open as if she were expecting a suitor.

"Yes, may I help you?" Sara embarrassingly asked.

"Mam, I am here to have dinner with Captain Every!" flatly stated Charles Hayes.

"Well Sir, I'm afraid he wasn't expecting anyone until eight," emurely explained Sara.

"Hey, don't I know you from somewhere? Hold on, it'll come to me! What time was I supposed to be here?" asked the boorish R.A.C. man.

"Eight o'clock, I believe." hollowly said Every's sea-wife.

"Hells bells, my watch stopped! Do you have the time? Liverpool, right?" rudely asked Hayes.

"Mister…?" asked Sara.

"Charles… Charlie Hayes!" answered Hayes.

"Well, Mister Hayes, it happens to be five thirty postmeridian and 'no', I have never had the pleasure of meeting you until now!" Charmingly said Sara.

"Lady, you're the spitting image of the wife of one of my employees! If you ain't her then your Pappy surely must have been a rounder, I'd say!" jeered Charles.

"Shall I remind the Captain of your eight o'clock arrival then?" politely asked the young woman.

"Yes, mam, do that for me! Did you ever know a Jonnathan Kimber?" loudly questioned Charlie.

"Good Evening, sir!" Every's sea-wife said as she slammed the cabin's door in Hayes's face.

There are a few things worth mentioning about a man's experiences while living more than a few years on Earth. One of those mentionable moments would most likely include seeing a Sierra-Leon sunset.

James Stanfield was admiring just that when the second leg's captain, William Bosman approached him from the stern side of the 'Thomas'.

"Good evening, Jim," greeted Bosman.

"How's it going, Captain?" asked Stanfield.

"So far, so good! It appears the weather will be in our favor for the next couple of days. I'm planning to set out at hightide. If the winds are kind to us, we should be under full sails by sunrise!" replied William.

"This is a remarkable journey we're about ready to make! I do hope that history will be kind to us, Bill," morosely commented Stanfield.

"I would guess, Jim, this particular trip like the hundreds of others we have made, will make no more of a dint in history any more than peeing in the ocean will affect its depth! But apparently you see it differently!" Cattily said Bosman.

"Not necessarily, but I am more than a little concerned about this Sporck fellow. He's a very bad man, Bill!" said Jim Stanfield.

"I agree but you have to admit this is the most profitable run of our lives, Jim!" laughed Bill.

"Indeed! But, Captain, one must ask, what are we really being paid so well… for?" bluntly questioned Stanfield.

Red Group's commander, Hendrick Quintor used a piece of reflector glass to signal their approach to the Pympe house. Chaloner Ogle peeled off from the others and headed down a rocky slope toward Yantlet Creek.

Alex Selkirk sat on the front porch of the Pympe house with his spyglass training on the movements behind the flickering light show happening from within the surrounding forest. He leaned back in his chair so the back locked against the house's wall. Alex then turned his head over his right shoulder and loudly announced Red Group's arrival.

At the very same time, a buckboard carrying two ministers came barreling up Yantlet Creek Road with two gaining horsemen hot on their trail! Quintor was the first to react.

With the speed of a panther, the tough-hand raced through a corner of the forest in an attempt at cutting off the pursuing riders. Once Maynard and Fogg had blown by, Hendrick stepped out into the center of the wagon path and held his right hand up high into the air!

Ten seconds later, two constables each wearing 'Bobbie' hats, rounded a curve which ended up running directly into Quintor's standing position! As anticipated, the policeman ignored the pedestrian's warning and rode by him as if he were a dead cat in the ditch.

Three more seconds later, both of the Bobbies' heads were laying on the Yantlet Creek Road. Their horses and riding torsos continued on a bit.

After three toots on a whistle, four of the Red Group team members appeared out of nowhere and tidied up the area. They cut the tale-telling garrote wire down, bagged the helmeted heads, cut the throats of the cops' horses and then set the whole mess on fire!

Commander Ogle sat at the end of the Pympe's banquet table enjoying the comraderies with King George's first official secret service unit. Everyone had their own bottle of something from the cellar and were engrossed in minor chitchat when Cal tapped the side of his goblet with his knife.

Oliver LaBuse stuck his head over the side railing on the 'Happy Return'! Jonn Kimber still had a smile on his face as he was waiting for permission to bring Mildred onboard.

"Captain Kimber, Captain Hornigold would like to welcome you aboard the 'Happy Return'! However, before you do, he suggests that you sell your horse to one of the livery stables located within a stone's throw of where you're standing!

The Captain has asked me to invite you to his quarters for dinner! You'll have plenty of time to shed your pony before then. May I have someone come down to get your things?" Loudly said LaBuse.

"Thank you, sir! But I would like to speak with Captain Benjamin Hornigold personally before I reject his hospitality! Tell him, I made a sailor's promise to an animal who saved my life! Monsieur LaBuse, your Captain will understand!" argued Kimber.

Henry Every commented to Sara about the colorful sunset they were having that evening, it meant clear sailing he said. His sea-wife did not respond. She looked away from him so Henry wouldn't see her tears.

Every approached Sara from behind and held her until the reason for her unusual behavior gushed out.

"Perhaps this is not the right time to say this and I am frightfully aware of the circumstances under which I find myself! And I know I am nothing more than another spoil from your fierce pirating adventures, but this time, you hooked onto a woman who has fallen in love with you!" sobbed Sara.

Henry spun the woman around and kissed her as the African sun sunk into the ocean. He then held Sara close to him and shared with her his innermost secret!

"Darling, let me be the first to begin this volley of truth-telling by saying that I also love you! I believe it only fair that I admit to you something well, actually two things!

You are the very first woman I ever made love to and I just became a pirate last month!" gushed Henry.

Sara then pulled herself away from his arms and sat down at the table she had placed the orchid arrangement upon. She smiled at Henry much in the way a cat would look at a squirrel.

"On both accounts, I knew that, Henry! I don't care! I fell in love the moment I laid eyes on you! But, sweetheart, I must tell you something I fear may negatively influence your affections toward me!" mumbled Sara.

"I doubt if it will do that but give it your best shot and then we'll see! I might have to throw you to the sharks afterwards if you tell me you no longer worship the ground I walk on!" said Every.

"Henry, that creepy little R.A.C. man, Mister Hayes recognized me today!" Sara said with a shaky voice.

"Why should that bother you, precious?" Every asked with a half-smile on his face.

"Because he knows my husband!" blurted Sara.

"Maybe I've had too much to drink, Sara, but I'm not following you! Start at the beginning; what husband?" pried Henry Every.

"We lived in Liverpool or I should say, my daughter and I existed there! My husband, Jonn Kimber worked for the Royal African Company! He is a captain on one of their slaver ships. The 'Thomas' was the last ship he captained as I remember." said Sara.

"So, what's the big stink over? You'll never see him again!" shouted Every.

"How can you be so sure of that, Henry?" asked Sara.

"For one reason, I know you want me to be your man and secondly, if the sonofabitch ever comes within a hundred miles of you, I'll kill him!" declared the inebriated 'Fancy's' captain.

There was a knock on the door.

"Ah, welcome Governor Hayes, Sara just mentioned to me you know her from Liverpool? Isn't it a small world!

Please, have a seat! Let's all have a nice chat, shall we?" requested Every.

Oliver LaBuse was cursing in French as he stormed through the ship's galley. He didn't apologize for overturning a stack of dishes on his way to Hornigold's cabin. He didn't bother to knock either!

"Ben, Kimber states that the dapple-gray saved his life and you would understand the meaning of a 'sailor's promise'!

Do you want me to make the guy scram?" asked the disturbed tough-hand.

"No, it appears our Mister Jonnathan Kimber is a man of principles! Just as you and I have always vowed to look out after one another, I'm guessing he made the same pact with his horse. A bad man won't do that! Let's make room for 'Mildred' in the storage space! Oliver, invite this modern day 'Noah' on board our 'Ark' please!" stated the Captain.

William Bosman watched the last bit of sunlight slip into the horizon's red line. The ship's chef had gone out of his way to prepare an okra gumbo in celebration of the morning's launch toward the Americas. Stanfield without comment, just sat at the Captain's table staring at the two or three shrimp floating in his bowl.

"Jim, are you still thinking about Sporck?" asked Bosman.

"I've got to admit that I am, Bill. It's not him so much as it is those Sporckian animal heads down below! Have you seen the way they're handling their so called, African constituents?" exclaimed Stanfield.

"Yes, I have and I keep reminding myself what we were paid to do by the Royal African Company! We're not only making in net cash ten times what we normally would earn in a year, we get our own plantation thrown in to boot!

Frankly, I don't give a 'tinker's damn' what those animal heads' issues are, I just want to get to Guadalupe, poke a few of their women, sit on the back porch of my mansion and pray for enough rain to quench my crops!" Said Bosman.

"But we're failing to answer the 'big' question here! Why would Anton von Sporck pay all of that money for something so regularly done as delivering a bunch of Africans to the Caribbean?

Why all the hullabaloo over secret drops, squads of slaves fighting for the Sporckian cause and not to mention the bombs bursting while witnessing a couple of horses go up in smoke? Does that really make any sense to you, Bill?" Stanfield strongly queried.

"If you put it that way, no it doesn't! So, what do you think is actually going on?" asked William Bosman.

"It is too early to know for sure but you can bet the ranch on one thing, ole Sporck has no intention of paying us anything! I believe he intends to kill us as soon as we reach the Spanish waters!

Furthermore, I am quite certain that Sporck is not operating in a vacuum! Powerful people perhaps even in conjunction with foreign countries, I believe, have a dog in this fight too!

America is a virgin land whose people are transplants. They also have an enormous appetite for land ownership and through what I have learned about the colonists, they're not a bit afraid to scrap over it!

Colonists think of wealth in terms of the numbers of acres they can gain possession! At the same time, they require slave labor in order to produce the needed number of agricultural products. With their profits the plantation czars acquire even more property!

My suspicions rest on the supposition that Sporck has devised a scheme to limit if not obliterate, his slave trading competitors! I believe he intends to use some diabolical method to gain full control of the world's slave transactions! The only problem is, I haven't yet figured out how he plans to do it!" Captain Stanfield boldly stated.

Bill Bosman resembled an unpainted statuette. He stood up and leaned across the table with his balled fists resting upon the embroidered tablecloth. The 'Thomas's' Captain then looked at Jim with the fury of a demon in his eyes!

"What do you propose we do, Jim? Should we fight our way out of this quagmire?" Bill hostilely queried.

"No, absolutely not! Those animal heads would be on us like white on rice if we delayed our departure! We'd never make it out of Sierra-Leon in one piece! Unfortunately, Bill, we're probably not going to be able to do much of anything until we reach the Caribbean. In the meantime, it would be prudent of us to subtly begin our preparations for our jumping ship!

It is my contention, those six hundred and thirty-three men down below us, feel pretty confident they have control of the 'Thomas' already! Why not let them continue to think that until the time is right for us to make our escape?" flatly commented Stanfield.

Chaloner Ogle rose from the Pympe's dusty dining room table. Behind him was a world map. With a fencing foil gripped in his hand, the Commander began an explanation of their assignment.

"Remarkable job! I am pleased to see we all made it here. I've got a lot to say and a very short time to brief you so let's get to it!

We are currently located here at Allhallows. In thirteen hours at sunrise tomorrow, we will take the 'Whydah'..." Ogle was saying.

Without any warning Anne Bonny slumped over in her chair!

Percy Fogg was the first to run to the woman's aid.

Quintor and Maynard like rabid wolves, ran through the seaside mansion checking every nook and cranny where an assailant could hide. They both shook their heads at Ogle indicating they had not found anything out of the ordinary.

Alex Selkirk with Rainbow Charlie raced out of the house and swiftly cleared the perimeter. Nothing seemed out of place.

Anne was regaining her consciousness just as Cal Ogle kneeled down beside of her. She wanted to say something.

"I'm so sorry Commander Ogle. I must have had too much of the Pympe's brandy!" muttered Bonnie.

"Anne, or should I say, Mary Hallett, as well as the rest of you, ya'll might as well come around the table so you can hear this! King George has assembled what he calls, "The Bow Street Runners" which is mostly made up of temporarily released prisoners. That's us!

The 'Whydah' as thought, never sank; instead, it was personally returned by Black Sam Bellamy to our beloved King as an olive branch! Sam Bellamy was retiring and he didn't want there to be any hard feelings between the two of them!

One couldn't say they were friends but there was a healthy respect for the other it seems! Bellamy presented George II with his favorite pirating ship in hopes it might be useful to him one day!

Being the fox he is, King George had the 'Whydah' setup to be one of his escape vehicles! In case he was ever overthrown or needed to leave the country in a hurry, Black Sam's ship would do the job!

Because of the absolutely dire situation facing the Colonies, our King provided us with this warship! I won't go into that now but let me just promise you this, the 'Whydah' can outshoot and outrun any ship on any of the seven seas!" Bellowed Ogle.

Even though her nose was still bleeding, Anne Bonnie rose from the floor and squared off with Commander Ogle. She looked at the man through the eyes of a mournful woman.

"Is Sam dead?" Anne reluctantly asked.

Out of the corner of his eye, Chaloner Ogle saw the familiar twitch on Quintor's face! Cal had seen before when something of a violent nature was about to happen!

Hendrick slid his way between Anne Bonnie and Commander Ogle. Like a hissing asp, Quintor verbally attacked the female pirate! "What do you mean by confronting our Captain in the manner in which you did, Ms. Bonnie? Do you feel that under these rather stressful circumstances, Commander Ogle should have had a consultation with you before he began his briefing with us?" sharply questioned Quintor.

"No, Sir; I do not," meekly answered Anne.

"Then, don't you think you owe our Commander an apology? And, if you act pretty, Anne Bonnie, I'll tell you exactly where ole Black Sam Bellamy is at this very moment! Now, do we understand each other, Mrs. Bellamy?" asked the grinning tough-hand.

With a flash of frustration ricocheting back at Quintor, Mary Bellamy (Anne Bonnie) curtsied to Ogle with a smile very much like that on the face of the "Mona Lisa".

"Sir, I beg your apology. I have no excuse for my unprofessional behavior, Commander Ogle," said Anne.

Chaloner Ogle turned toward the deflated woman with the demeanor of a wise old grandfather. He reached out with a warm beckoning for her to come into his arms. When she did, the whole story gushed out amongst all of the snot, spit, and tears!

"We were married, you know! It was a small gathering actually, just a witness, an organist, a minister, and a man and a woman very much in love!" wailed Anne.

Ogle's unit respectfully listened as Bellamy's estranged bride continued the tale of her lost lover. When Anne finally summed up her sorrows and regained her haughty demeanor, Hendrick Quintor stepped to the forefront so as to get on with the business at hand.

"Anne, your husband and I sailed together on countless tours at sea. Over the years we became the closest of friends.

After your wedding at your sister-in-law's tavern on Cape Cod and following the miniscule honeymoon the two of you shared in the upper loft of the Great Island Tavern, your hours old husband was sent out to sea on an emergency mission! That was the last time you ever heard from him, correct?" asked Hendrick Quintor.

Tears flooded out of Mary Bellamy's eyes as she nodded 'yes' to Quintor's question. But there was a big mystery still hanging in the destressed woman's mind that still Hendrick needed to address!

"Your husband is still alive, Mary! But he is in no way willing to allow visitors to see him! Samuel Bellamy was not lost in a gale as the rumors of his death purported!"

"He wasn't?" asked Mary timorously.

"Why, hell no! Sam would have called that little squall a summer's breeze! No, Mrs. Bellamy, your husband would have never died at the hands of a tricky sea! Your husband was rescued by the Indians! Sam was badly burned as a result of a boobytrap set by the former captain of the 'Whydah'! That explosion also cost Samuel most of his eyesight as well as the use of his legs!" explained Quintor.

"Who's taking care of him?" Segued Mary as Hendrick poured himself another drink.

"A few of our friends!" quickly answered Hendrick Quintor.

"May I ask you a personal question?" quizzically lashed Mary. "Sure, go ahead," reluctantly replied the black man.

"Have you and I ever met before, I mean like a long time ago?" asked Bellamy's wife.

"At your wedding! I was the best man, remember now?" gently prodded Quintor.

"Oh, my god! I thought you were a slave? You are the person who Commander Ogle was talking about, aren't you? Your name is 'Cato', right?" asked Mary.

"Yes, to all of your questions, Mrs. Bellamy." answered Cato.

Ogle slowly approached the reunited acquaintances with his arms spread wide open as if he were shooing away a gaggle of annoying geese.

He swallowed his last swig of ale and pointed his foil toward the Isle of Sheppey on the map.

"We will take the 'Whydah' south of 30 N latitude until we pick up the 'trades' in our favor. From that point onward and with good winds, we should make a sighting of the 'Thomas' within the week!" said Commander Ogle.

Alex Selkirk respectfully interrupted the Commander with a handwave. He nodded to the rest of the detachment before he addressed the 'Whydah's' captain.

"Sir, I might remind you of the dangers as dictated by the wisdom of our predecessors associated with the launching of a ship on a Friday; it's the day of Christ's crucifixion!

Not meaning to tamper with your authority, Commander, could we possibly set sail the day after tomorrow just for safety's sake?" politely requested Alexander.

Commander Ogle bowed his head for a moment and then looked over at Hendrick Quintor. He raised his chin so it was level with Alex's and began whispering not just to Selkirk but to the entire unit of specialists as well.

"Whether it is 'Friday' or not, we have not one second to waste! At this very moment there is a R.A.C. slaver, the 'Thomas', destined for the Caribbean. That heavily armed vessel will attempt to spread throughout the Americas one of the deadliest diseases known to man!

The King's intelligence reports reveal there are vials of an aerial-reactive concentrate intended to be opened upon the 'Thomas's' anchoring in Guadalupe! Our mission is to cut the 'Thomas' off before it enters the Caribbean waters. We are to destroy it along with its entire cargo!

We are not to bring on the survivors, English or not! And we are to purge the ship with fire once we have rendered it harmless. I regret to say this but King George has given us specific orders regarding the fates of the Thomas' perhaps innocent crew!" said Ogle.

Percy Fogg then took control of the floor by breaking out into an 'over-the-top' barrage of laughter! Percy then opened his arms out and made a three hundred and sixty degree turn as if he were trying to dry out a petticoat.

Once he had cleared out a good speaking space thus making him the intended center of attention, Percy jumped up on a nearby chair, stuck his right forefinger toward the heavens, opened his handy pocket-Bible, held it straight out in reconciliation with his presbyopia and began to read a purple-patched rendition of Psalms 23:4.

Halfway through it and beginning to sway now, Percy Fogg got to the part about 'fearing no evil', he fell confidently over backwards into his former Methodist accomplice's awaiting arms!

This lightened the dreary Pympe house up some! Cato and Selkirk then dragged the dining room table into a better location in order to catch the afternoon light. It was 1700.

Beginning at five o'clock on that Thursday evening and running through the time they were to board the 'Whydah' the next morning, thirteen of the world's most adapt mariners plotted and replotted their strategies aimed at the assassination of a ship's crew and the eradication of a ship named the 'Thomas'! In the backs of everyone's mind there was the nagging question as to the lengths at which Sporck had gone to protect his biologically infused plot!

Blanche had to use an alternate tree than the one she had originally picked to shoot from! Poison ivy had a tendency to spread like wildfire across her body. Ike didn't like to watch her dance when her flesh had blotchy marks on it!

She could see from her tree stand the professor had fallen asleep at his desk. Through her monocular, she looked for the hand flinches typical for a sleeping old man. There were none.

Fearing what she already suspected as being true, Blanche angrily jumped down from her inconspicuous position, rolled and then crouched within the shadows beneath Charles Francois de Cisternay du Fay's library window.

She pressed her ear to the wall hoping to hear the faint bass sound of a snore. Again, there were no emitted sounds linking the slumped over man to the living.

The now enraged assassin pulled from her camouflaged quiver a kaki green blow gun. She unbuttoned the breast pocket on her jacket and withdrew a small wooden box. Carefully, Blanch inserted from the mouthpiece end, a poison dart and with her little finger shoved the fur-backed missile into the breach of the barrel. Blanche then opened the professor's library door.

Charles du Fay's unmoved shoulders portrayed no reaction to the zebra colored dart sporting from between the back of his neck. There was a note tacked to the professor's sternum.

"Ike, I got the antidote! Shall we meet for a drink in Charlestown? Gus."

For nearly a minute, Blanche stared at the recognizable handwriting of King George!

After removing her dart and returning the impotent thing back into its box, Blanche leaned around and French kissed the dead man.

With a cynical grin on her face, she unscrewed the wick holder on the professor's desk lamp. Then Blanche poured the lamp oil on top of the scientist's head and the note addressed to Ike!

Following the study's sacking and after a few toasts over the corpse, Blanche lit a match. She waited around long enough to see the King's note turn a chocolate brown before comingling its fiery interests with the doctor's hair.

It was their little secret she thought as the deranged woman threw a jesting kiss back at the building while Charles du Fay's body burned to a crisp. Blanche would lie about the whole escapade when she got back home!

Realizing she had drawn blood from her incessant scratching, Blanche vowed to herself to punish the King for his arrogant message! She patted the box of darts in her breast pocket and then spun the rear tire of her bicycle on the sandy road leading away from the Royal Veterinary College.

Perhaps it was the moaning of a whale that awakened William Bosman or maybe it was the pelvic thrusting he was involved with in a dream but something made Captain Bosman sit up in his hammock. The same sound except closer this time, vibrated the floor beneath him!

The 'Thomas's' captain while still putting his boots on, grabbed his blunderbuss and cutlass before he rushed out of his cabin's door! To Bosman's relief, he ran into James Stanfield who was signaling 'silence' by placing his forefinger against his lips!

Both of the ship's captains tiptoed across the forward deck toward an air vent from where the noises of screaming men seemed to be coming from. When they looked down into the hold, they saw an encircled band of animal heads taunting a strapped down Angolan they were calling, "Jemmy"!

Bosman gently nudged Stanfield in his ribs! Bill kicked his head back indicating that the two men needed to speak where they could not be overheard! They then noiselessly walked to the Captains' wheelhouse together.

"Jim, those folks are getting out of hand down there!" said Bosman.

"I couldn't agree with you more, Bill! They act as if they're in some kind of a trance! As I am sure you have seen, during our formations those bloody animal heads perform as if they're in the damned jungle!" wildly exclaimed Stanfield.

"Jim, what do you think was going on with that Jemmy fellow strapped down on those transport boxes?" asked Bosman.

"Oh, that's their way of converting the slaves into Catholicism! They make them go through a modified crucifixion ritual which includes a couple of spear jabs and a sponge full of vinegar!" mockingly said Stanfield.

"My good Man, that seems terribly twisted to me!" Bosman said with his mouth agape.

Stanfield then faced William Bosman as if he were accusing him of cheating at a game of cards!

"Captain Bosman, sir, if you have any misconception about the plight we're in, please tell me now! From my perspective, we are sitting on top of a rumbling volcano! Just yesterday, Bill, I saw with my own two eyes those animal heads dangle a string of chained up Kongos just out of the water enough for their piss to bring in the sharks! That's way more than 'twisted', Captain! I don't know what Sporck did to them but you can bet on one thing, he did something! Also, Captain Bosman, I think they're planning on killing us!" grimly said Stanfield.

Count Anton von Sporck dialed in his tripod mounted telescope. He could see the dust billowing from behind Blanche's cart as she snapped her buggy whip at her donkey's ears! The rusty bicycle bounced about a foot into the air each time the cart's wheels approached an obstacle faster than it should.

With a piece of mirror Ike transmitted the firing signal for the cannoneers to commence with their training exercise! A new class had arrived day before yesterday and there was a lot for them to learn!

Perhaps one of the best lessons Kimber had ever learned, entailed discovering where a man falls on the 'food chain'! With Hornigold, Jonn figured he was about four rungs shy of being on the same plateau as 'the king of the pirates' was on!

Jonn Kimber answered the knock on his cabin door.

"Sir, I'm just checking to see if your quarters are acceptable!" said Oliver LaBuse with a disingenuous expression on his face.

"Indeed, they are, Captain LaBuse." said Kimber.

"Oh, monsieur, I am no 'captain', I'm just the tough-hand but thank you for the compliment, Captain Kimber!" said LaBuse.

"That certainly does surprise me, Oliver! A man of your caliber is mighty hard to find these days but I would guess Captain Hornigold has already told you that!" sincerely stated Jonn.

"Captain Hornigold and I have been crisscrossing the Caribbean together for near about thirty years I guess now! Thus far, we ain't grown gills yet so I reckon a man could say, 'we've been compatible'!" proudly said Oliver.

"Please thank the Captain for the very fine quarters he has offered to me! Kindly ask him for me, Mister LaBuse, if I might have the opportunity to meet with him tomorrow morning?" requested Jonn Kimber.

"Thank you for reminding me, Sir! Captain Hornigold would like you to join him for supper this evening! He said six would be fine!" stated Oliver LaBuse.

"Oliver, convey to the Captain, I would be delighted to join him!" responded Kimber.

Jonn looked around the ship. He could feel the power of the wind pugnaciously shoving the 'Happy Return' toward the open sea. 'Fear' was the only word that would describe his overall feeling.

There was the taste of copper in his mouth along with the sensation of having a brick setting inside his small intestines. Captain Kimber was constipated.

Benjamin Hornigold was reviewing his charts when Oliver LaBuse came into the wheelhouse.

"Captain, this Kimber chap doesn't seem to be anything like what I expected!" said Oliver.

"How's that?" asked Hornigold as he jotted down some numbers in his logbook.

"Uh, I don't really know but I can tell you one thing, he's not here to do us any harm!" muttered the tough-hand.

"LaBuse, have you forgotten the story of the Trojan horse? As you and I well know, the most poisonous snakes in the world are gorgeous to the eye!" Singsongingly stated Hornigold.

A knock interrupted the two friends' sharing their prophecies. "Captain Hornigold, your guest is standing outside of your quarters! Should I bring him up here?" Asked one of Ben's pirates.

"No, Tim, I'll leave the wheel in Oliver's capable hands and do the 'howdy do's' myself!" stiffly said Hornigold.

Jonn Kimber was astonished by the acrobatics of the dolphins as they raced the 'Happy Return' out of the port of Sierra-Leon. He listened as the ship's crew griped as they carried on with their chores.

Jonn smiled to himself, Hornigold's approach toward commanding a bunch of men was very similar to his own. He ruled by respect!

A surprisingly raspy voice broke into Kimber's pensive thoughts. "You know, Jonn, there is still time to turn back!" smoothly said Hornigold.

"Captain Benjamin Hornigold! My god, man, you startled me!" shrieked Jonn.

"I meant what I said, Mister Kimber, there is still little enough space between us and the land offering to you an opportunity to make a different choice!" said Ben.

"With all respect intended, Captain, why did you use the word, 'choice'?" aggressively asked Jonn Kimber.

"Look, Mister Kimber, or whoever in the hell you are, what in the devil's name am I to think when one of the King's loyal subjects and a veteran ships' captain at that, asks to come aboard my pirate ship?" snarled Hornigold.

"Sir, do you believe a man with the credentials you described would be so foolish as to ask to board such an infamous pirate's ship if he didn't have a damn good reason to do so, Captain Hornigold?" fired back Kimber.

"In that case, let's reduce the intensity of the moment by your whispering to me exactly why you are standing on the deck of the 'Happy Return'!" replied Benjamin.

"I am here to save your life!" matter-of-factly stated Jonnathan Kimber.

Hornigold was stunned by Jonn's audacious statement. He too began searching for something floating in the ocean.

The sea warriors knew there was a checkmate lurking somewhere close by so they both settled on a jug of rum in place of an olive branch.

Henry Every stared in amazement as Charles Hayes 'spilled the beans'! But just as ole Charlie was right in the middle of explaining how he embezzled a miniscule percentage of every R.A.C. shipment leaving its Liverpool harbor, he fell to the floor gripping his throat! Maybe it was just the 'mother' in her but Sara instantly kneeled down by the man's side attempting to revive him. Charles Hayes had stopped breathing.

Rigor mortis did not wait its customary four hours; instead, the hardening of Charley's muscles was practically instantaneous. Sara, a trained midwife, began a thorough exam of her first real cadaver.

What she found put a whole different lens on Every's contractor named Sporck! Bulging from Hayes's neck, what was thought to be a bubo turned out to be a peculiar ejection site.

Sara also discovered an enormous number of flea larvae wiggling about the dead man's hair follicles. Some of the hatchlings had already taken flight.

With a look of holy terror in her eyes, Sara turned toward her dashing young lover and muttered out some very frightening words.

"Henry, Sporck sent three vials with Charles Hayes is that correct? They were wax-dipped containers right? Well, I just found the lid to one of them in this poor sucker's pocket!" yelped Sara.

While James Stanfield was supervising the at-sea burial of six slaves, Bosman took the opportunity to reread what the two of them had word scripted about their plight upon the 'Thomas'. It was the combination of a historical synopsis and a 'Last Will and Testament'!

If there were enough time before the inevitable animal head putsch, the two had decided they would sink their 'final words' in hopes that one day the whole truth would be known! In the meantime, they were making preparations to escape the ship as soon as the very first opportunity presented itself!

Using the code name, 'Dicky Sam', Stanfield and Bosman devised a communication method they hoped would be picked up by Kimber. Both Bosman and Stanfield agreed, it was their only chance!

Cato marked out every ship's position as he could see from his vantage point. From the whereabouts of each craft, the tough-hand developed a hypothesis; he signaled his thoughts to the 'Whydah'.

"I suspect that Sporck under the guise of the R.A.C., contracted both the 'Fancy' and the 'Happy Return' to protect the 'Thomas' until its arrival to the Caribbean. Permission to communicate with the three ships requested."

Alex Selkirk felt the adrenalin rush through his body like hot acid. He cleared his throat before he read Cato's request to Ogle.

Selkirk then came to attention and mechanically if not coldly, assessed their position before Commander Ogle had a chance to respond.

"Commander, Cato's theory may very well be correct. Nevertheless, we need to weigh out our options! This very well may be a trick, sir!" warned Alex.

Ogle and Alex sketched out their optional strategies. Within ten minutes both seamen concluded that a frontal attack against three well-armed pirate ships was suicidal.

With that conclusion drawn, there were only two remaining alternates. The first being, to close off Fogo Pass and place the entire area under siege or to take a detachment of cannoneers up to where Cato was and pick off each ship one by one!

Neither option particularly enthused either one of the former pirate hunters. But then, another series of signals were sent down from Fogo Mountain!

Selkirk turned away from his telescope and excitedly broke the news of an interesting turn of events.

"Cato says the 'Thomas' has sent out a distress signal to the 'Happy Return'!"

"Ask Cato to repeat his message!" barked Ogle.

"I already have!" retorted Alex.

"Well?" snapped Cal.

"Cal, you're not going to believe this but the 'Thomas's' staff officers, two of them, have jumped overboard and are swimming toward the 'Happy Return'!" excitedly exclaimed Alexander Selkirk.

This latest bulletin caused Ogle to have to sit down. He just stared at Fogo Mountain in a state of total disbelief. Alex, toting two glasses and a jug of scotch, joined his old friend for some serious drinking.

Jim Stanfield and Bill Bosman would have swum all the way to the 'Happy Return' had it not been for an animal head named 'Jemmy'. It was three o'clock in the morning when the Angolan while relieving himself over the side of the 'Thomas, discovered a rope dangling into the water!

Having wrapped the important things in waxed cloth and inserting them into a tanned cow's bladder, the abandoning captains had fashioned a flotation device to be used for their escape. They were paddling their makeshift raft quite effectively until a flare was launched from the 'Thomas's' deck!

Jemmy gave the order to 'chum the water'! This seemed to bolster the self-ordained lion head's position in the minds of the six hundred or so Sporckian onlookers.

As though it had been practiced a thousand times before, Jemmy jumped on top of the nearest utility box with his sabre raised high into the air! Immolating Blackbeard, he lit a couple of candles and stuck them into the ears of the lion's head he was wearing! Thanks to a nearby zebra head who dosed a bucket of chum on Jemmy's flaming headgear, nothing was lost but the paper lion's left ear.

Despite the embarrassment, Jemmy stalwartly raised a megaphone to his lips and spoke to the 'Thomas's' goggling passengers.

"Do not shoot those cowards! Let our high finned friends of the sea do that work for us!

Take the buckets of waste from the galley and dump them overboard! I want to bring 'ole whitie' into the game!"

Cato had received the 'go-ahead' from Ogle but after viewing through his telescope the 'Thomas's' venal intent, his thoughts shifted toward a more final solution! It was clear the chum was being affective so he hurried to send another request to Commander Ogle.

Oliver LaBuse had already cocked his pistol by the time Kimber had taken three steps into the wheelhouse! Jonnathan glared at LaBuse out of the side of his eye as he approached Captain Hornigold.

"Captain, I need two jugs of coal oil, ten cork-grenades, four strong rowers, a hundred feet of rope and your dinghy in the water in five minutes! I have no time to explain the details but I have two shipmates out there about to be eaten alive!"

Hornigold nodded at LaBuse to accommodate Kimber's requests. He then reached his hand out to Jonn inviting him to grasp it as a token of respect.

Alex Selkirk looked at Ogle with a curious smile on his face.

"Cato suggests that you blow the 'Thomas' to smithereens!"

"Alex, would you care to raise the Jolly Roger?"

"I would be honored to do so, Sir! Shall I give the command to fire?"

"Absolutely," said Cal.

Reverend Isaac Green watched the workers lay the replacement shingles on Plumbs' Chapel's roof. Sporck was depressed.

The anxiety of not hearing from Charlie Hayes felt like fanged hookworms crawling through his stomach. That, coupled with the sad fact that Blanche was still alive had pushed the lion head to the brink of insanity! Consequently, he needed relief!

Tink was expected at any moment. Sporck had just enough time to make a visit to Kimberly's cell.

Henry Every felt like a caged tiger! He knew Rogers was right when he stated he needed to act more like a pirate should act! Therefore, he made the decision to attack the 'Whydah'!

Cato flashed the news to Ogle.

Ben Hornigold sent up two flares in order to give his cannoneers lighter. He ordered four shot canisters to be fired above the 'Thomas's' mast!

Reactively, the 'Thomas' viciously fired back at both the 'Whydah' and the 'Happy Return'!

Not wanting to be left out of his first foray, Every courageously moved the 'Fancy' in front of the targeted 'Thomas' so as to allow her protectant enough time to raise her sails and join him in their escape through the Fogo Pass! Henry then noticed Kimber's frantic efforts to rescue Bosman and Stanfield.

Cato scrambled to send out another urgent message! This time, he addressed the 'Happy Return'!

"In the name of the Crown you are to sink the 'Thomas'!" Blinked Cato.

"Who the hell are you?" messaged LaBuse.

"I am Cato. The 'Whydah' belongs to George II and has been ordered to destroy the 'Thomas'!" blinked Cato.

"For what reason?" surreptitiously signaled LaBuse.

"They are carrying vials of the 'Black Death' onboard!" replied Cato.

"Kindly repeat!" requested Oliver.

"Sporck has planned to wipe out the Colonies with the bubonic plague!" Answered Cato.

The 'Happy Return' did not respond.

Bosman kicked at the nose of a bull shark that had clamped onto the club he had been using to batter them off for the last few minutes! Stanfield's foot had been scraped or bitten! Jim warned Bill Bosman that he was bleeding!

Larger fins were joining into what seemed to be a macabre circle of shiny blades slicing through the water! Kimber was getting closer. Bullets starting whizzing above their heads!

The 'Fancy' then lurched forward thus creating a watery arena for the animal heads to see the carnage about to take place below! Jonnathan Kimber fired one of his muskets at the 'Fancy's' wheelhouse lantern. His shot was good!

Sara helped put the fire out her estranged husband had caused! The tiny burn she had received due to Jonn's marksmanship enraged her!

Sara Kimber burst out of the 'Fancy's' wheelhouse in hopes of taking a shot at her husband! A nanosecond after that, Sara was staring directly into the eyes of the man whom she had betrayed! Jonn cocked his pistol's hammer back and spoke to Sara.

"Where is Kimberly?" calmly asked Jonnathan Kimber.

"Sporck has her, Jonn! God I'm sorry…"

Jonn smiled as he pulled the trigger.

Jemmy now seizing an opportunity to utilize Every's naivety, swiftly lowered the 'Thomas's' rescue dingy and at gunpoint pulled both Bosman and Stanfield from the busy water!

By the time Henry Every discovered Sara's body on the ship's deck, the animal heads had already lashed the 'Thomas' to the 'Fancy'! Woodes Rogers had been tied to the main mast awaiting the blacksmith to fasten him to the anchor chain!

The harsh reality finally sunk into Henry's mind that the animal heads had not only overtaken the 'Thomas' but had done the same to the 'Fancy'! He had to make some quick choices. He could jump ship and try to catch the retreating Kimber or he could surrender to Jemmy's crew.

After killing two approaching hyena heads, Henry Every yelled out Jonn Kimber's name three times as loud as he could before he dove into the debris filled ocean below. Flames suddenly spread around him! Bullets thudded into the rolling waves engulfing him.

When the battle roars faded and replaced by the sounds of his drowning, a rope slapped into Every's face. Kimber was screaming at him as things went dark!

Jemmy's animal heads went through the 'Fancy' stripping it of anything of worth. Things like gun powder, maps, three vials of the 'Black Death', guns, whiskey and food were all moved over to the 'Thomas'!

When the animal heads were satisfied with their wall-to-wall plundering, they began drenching the deck with coal oil. Jemmy personally inspected the leg chains that had been hammered to the 'Fancy's' crewmen's ankles! They were lined up on the port side of the deck!

Woodes Rogers had been tied into a chair that set on the end of the 'Fancy's' fire-ram. The ship's anchor also clamped to the crewmen's chain, teetered on the ram's tip.

A four-foot span of rope connected to Roger's chair had been tied into the anchor's eye. Should either the anchor or Rogers fall into the water the entire crew would be dragged to their deaths! Cato transmitted a 'cease-fire' to both the 'Happy Return' and to the 'Whydah'.

Jemmy took the respite as an understanding. He ordered the sails of both ships, raised. The 'Fancy' and the 'Thomas' began their way toward the Fogo Pass.

CHAPTER 4

SLAVE REVOLTS

Blanche could feel the syrupy warmth of Tink's injection titillate her spinal cord. Things were better now. Even Ike's criticisms didn't make her feel so bad anymore.

She hoped there was an inkling of hope Sporck would forgive her. Since Tink's treatments were mainlined, a monkey had attached itself to Blanche's back!

That's how Sporck finally got to the truth about Charles Francois de Cisternay du Fay's murder. She even told him about the King's note, the fire, and the innocuous dart!

In Blanche's twisted mind, she searched for ways in which she might recapture Isaac's affections. One particular tidbit that struck her fancy came from a piece of newspaper which had been used to wrap a sandwich delivered to her in her cell.

Queen Caroline was coming to Oxfordshire! Caroline was to be present for the christening of Lord Frederick North.

Just the thought of a Royal sanction made Blanche moisten herself! With this brainstorm still dancing across her frontal lobe, she excitedly began banging her cup against the iron bars!

Henry Every sat in a chair watching a formation of albatrosses pass overhead. The 'Happy Return's' cook had removed what a shark had missed. Every's lower left leg was gone!

No matter what Kimber or Hornigold did nothing seemed to snap Every from his suicidal ideations. Even whiskey didn't work!

Finally, Oliver LaBuse managed to get a smile out of Henry when the Frenchman attempted to catch a terrified goose that had escaped from the galley. With the only movement seen from the man for over two weeks, Every pulled from behind his shirt collar a dagger and threw it at the honking bird!

Oliver appreciatively nodded as he retrieved the feathery lump from the 'Happy Return's' starboard deck. As LaBuse was handing over the dead goose to the same man who had amputated Every's foot, Henry looked up at Oliver and issued a challenge to the overheated first mate!

"Monsieur LaBuse, ask your Captain if he would care to receive a slight paddling at the hands of one of his prisoners! Tell him, Sir, that I will exchange some 'vial information' with him for my freedom! All he has to do is out-throw me in a single match of dagger-flies!" said Every.

It was dusk. At that time every day, Jemmy would offer a living sacrifice to the sea! The heavy hold covering slid open!

Bill Bosman had drawn the short straw! He was next!

On que, four ostrich heads climbed down into the 'Thomas's' hold. They ceremoniously cut Bosman's ankle-ring off of the all- connecting anchor chain and pulled him up to the main deck.

Dressed in full Sporckian regalia, more than a hundred animal heads were standing around a blazing fire! Jemmy wore the lion's head!

As soon as Bosman had been cleaned up and made to put on a white robe, he was taken to the side of the ship located closest to where Jemmy was seated. From his makeshift throne, the Angolan began his well-practiced sentencing speech!

"We once again stand before the great Aegir with yet another gift for him! Oh, thou wondrous god of the sea, we humbly pray for your continued kind countenance upon your loyal worshipers!"

William Bosman was then forced to walk up three steps while the white capped Atlantic rushed by beneath him. Bill knew his life held only seconds until it's end!

Percy Fogg received a message from the crow's ncst. Alex Selkirk who had just relieved Captain Ogle from his shift, had to call him back to the wheelhouse. Debris from the 'Fancy' had been spotted!

Anne Bellamy banged the clavicle sized hammer against the ship's bell so many times Rainbow Charlie had to come check on her! The thoughts of losing Sam again was unbearable. If he were hurt from Sporck's doings, Anne swore she would kill him herself!

Chaloner Ogle seeing that Anne was becoming hysterical, appointed her to get the lanterns filled. She also had to attach them to the clamps on the grappling sticks. It was dark outside.

Cato was the first to see it floating some eighty feet off of the starboard bow. An orange ball about the size of a cantaloupe was bobbing against the side of the 'Fancy's' floating mast.

By the color of the sphere and judging from where it was attached, Cato knew there was something inside of the cow's bladder worth seeing. He called for Anne's help to fish it out of the water.

Within the cow's bladder there was a single page of script! Chaloner Ogle carefully steamed off the wax that sealed the tiny scroll.

Anne cornered the table with four high-wicked lanterns as Ogle began to read the words written by Stanfield and Bosman.

"I, James Stanfield and William Bosman do hereby tell the truth about the happenings on the 'Thomas'. The Royal African Company contracted Jonn Kimber(escaped), James Stanfield and William Bosman to deliver 600(plus) slaves to the Caribbean along with 50 passengers of the Planters' Class.

We were deceived by the R.A.C. by them giving false claims as to our cargo. The 'Thomas' by Anton von Sporck's hand (same as, Rev. Isaac Greene) intends to destroy the Colonial coast with vials of flea eggs.

The spread of the Bubonic plague is to be the intended result of Sporck's attack on America. Beware of the 'Thomas's' lot fore they are the hosts!" wrote Bosman and Stanfield.

The 'Whydah' circled the bits of scorched materials for an hour. It was 0600.

As Tink excused himself from Kimberly's cell, he noticed Reverend Greene kneeling in front of Blanche's iron bars. Sporck must have been deep in prayer because when the oriental spoke with him the good Reverend acted as if he were startled.

"Good lord, man, you scared the bejewels out of me!" said Ike.

"So sorry, Reverend Green! I'm here at your wish, sir. Shall I visit Ms. Blanche now?" timorously stated Tink.

"Oh, not today, Tink. It appears that our little friend has elected to make this a day filled with tantalizing intrigue! She claims to have a secret gift for me; however, Blanche insists on having your company before mine!" innocently claimed Sporck.

Tink knew full well that Isaac Green was totally void of a conscience. If it weren't for the exorbitant fees he was paid, he wouldn't even chance it; but seeing as how Ike took disappointment, the doctor chose the obsequious route.

"Well, Reverend Green, I'll assure you that Blanche's interests as far as I am concerned, are limited to what I carry in my little leather satchel here! Anyway, you're looking mighty fit these days! Have you been taking the turmeric I gave you?" sidestepped the Chinese physician.

Just as Isaac was about ready to blushingly answer Tink's honey dipped question, Blanche kicked a chair out from under herself! The eleven second timeline of dying by strangulation had begun!

Dropping his bag to the floor to retrieve a scalpel, Tink loudly hollered at Ike to lift her up so he could stop the process of the Blanche's asphyxiation. Since the electrical thought pattern of most humans travel about two hundred miles per hour, it gave Blanche four seconds to spare! Using her time prudently, she swung her body over the top of the men's heads, shut them into her cell, locked the iron door with the key Ike had left in the keyhole, grabbed Tink's satchel and headed for the stairs! As Blanche was sweeping by Kimberly's cell, she noticed the little girl's smiling face.

"I'm glad you are getting away, Blanche! These people are so mean; don't let them catch you! Run, Blanche, run!" excitedly said Kimberly.

Sporck's key opened Kimberly's cell door! Without a single word spoken, the girls launched into a sprint up the spiral staircase leading to the All Saints' Church.

Bob Maynard and Percy Fogg were sitting on some barrels down in the 'Whydah's' galley's storage room. They were rolling bones and drinking rum when they heard a noise coming from behind a stack of cornmeal bags.

Percy clinched his dagger in his right fist while his extended arm held the lantern at the optimal length for exploring. Maynard jumped up on a stack of corn bags and then cocked his pistol.

Maynard aimed at Fogg's lantern expecting to pull the trigger on the first interruption of light surrounding the swinging wick-works.

Anne Bellamy and Commander Ogle with their hands held high above their heads, stood! Percy blew out his candle.

Woodes Rogers and Bill Bosman had decided it was Sunday! It was Bill's turn to recite the Nicaean Creed and check the crap traps. There had been high winds the night before so there would be plenty of debris to dry out for firewood.

When the 'Whydah' had fired its first volley of return fire at the 'Fancy', Rogers had been hit in the face with a lead ball. His jaw had been shattered and most of his teeth were scattered across the 'Fancy's' deck!

Because of his unconscious state, the animal heads cut him loose from the anchor chain and threw him overboard! Fortunately, Woodes was able to pull himself into the same emergency boat Charles Hayes had been in!

When Jemmy forced Bosman to jump into the water, it just so happened that Rogers was able to catch the back of Bill's shirt as the lifeboat swept by the sinking man! The two ended up on a rock and happy to be so! They were approximately five hundred miles from the Charlestown coast.

There was a festive spirit amongst the men aboard the 'Happy Return' that morning. Land had been spotted!

LaBuse had played up the 'dagger-flies' contest between Captain Hornigold and Henry Every to the hilt! There were flyers slapped on every flat surface of the ship's interior. They were advertising the noon bout between two former champions!

Jonn Kimber since he was still considered a 'neutral', was unanimously elected to be the holder of the booty. He was voted in as the 'Master of Ceremony' as well as being the contest's chief adjudicator. Jonn accepted his nomination with the understanding the whole thing was just for fun!

Oliver had gone to great pains setting up the 'official' throwing lane. The post which would hold the bait was to stand exactly seven feet high. Circumference wise, the target timber had to have less than a twenty-inch circuitous string-length in order to be aligned with LaBuse's 'official' rules!

Distance from the sitting thrower to the target was determined by the individual's height multiplied by three. Therefore, since Henry

Every standing on his good leg, was five feet and four inches tall, this meant that Henry would throw his ten daggers from sixteen feet away. A total pole miss meant immediate loss!

Arguably there are two types of fly-bait considered to be preferred by former 'dagger-flies' champions of past. Smoked bacon because of its aromatic appeal, has served on many occasions as the backstop for many a heart stopping tournaments!

However, cheese with a smear of honey on its surface provides a better target contrast! Plus, the honey's stickiness slows down the leg movements of the nibbling insects! Sometimes, just one little leg can make the difference between winning and not winning!

Finally, it was agreed upon by both contestants that the honey-cheese combination would suffice. Size although squabbled over, was finally established to not exceed a five-inch square. Any of the fly's detectable body part would be considered a hit!

At ten o'clock, Oliver LaBuse and four other men began setting up boxes in an amphitheater fashion. The throwing lane, sun to the throwers' backs, divided the spectators in half!

The blue-chip gamblers those with ten ounces of silver in the game, were seated less than a foot from the decisive slab of honey slathered cheese! All toll, Kimber's sea-chest which he was sitting on, contained a slight bit over a hundred ounces of French silver!

Those plugging for the guest contender Henry Every, sat on the left side of the range while the majority on the Captain's side were seated on the right. Both sets of rooters were able to see the tournament daggers which were proudly displayed on top of a barrel.

Two boxes of throwing knives had been laid out so there would be no question as to the integrity of the throwers. They were all the same except one set of the ten throwing daggers had a blued finish while the other had a pewter finish on them.

Which side got which set was to be determined by the simple toss of a coin! The winner of that toss would have to go first! It was twelve noon.

Just as Kimber's arched coin reached the highest point before its descent, the 'Fancy's' battering ram jabbed into the side of the 'Happy Return'! Chaos, fire and lead followed!

Hornigold cursed himself for allowing the crow's nest to go unattended! Furthermore, in his heart he knew he had made a life-costing blunder!

When Kimber got back on his feet he looked up at the 'Fancy's' wheelhouse. Chained to the wheel was James Stanfield who was screaming out a warning to those whom he had just rammed!

Jemmy was pointing a pistol at the back of Stanfield's neck! He had his lion's head on!

Jonn now realizing the 'Thomas's' remaining crew was in the same predicament as Stanfield, ran up to the 'Happy Return's' wheelhouse where he expected to see Hornigold.

Woodes Rogers's was in real trouble! The grapeshot or whatever it was that entered the left side of his face, had left a terrible mess upon its exit! Infection had no doubt set in because Rogers's head was swelling at a noticeable rate!

The wind was picking up but despite that, Jonn began diving for sea snails. Considering the moans coming from Woodes's, the prialt producing crustaceans would have to be his most immediate concern.

Hopefully, the snails' venom would at least bring him some relief, Bosman thought. Bill then made his fourth dive into the water surrounding their rock. So far, he had only found two.

He would have dived down for the fifth time but the current was becoming too dicey! What was going to be dangerous was holding Rogers down while forcing the snail's stinger to penetrate his nasal membrane!

Blanche quickly put her finger over her lips as the two girls made it to the last round of stairs. Voices were getting louder as they got closer to the exit door.

The sound of a key clicking inside the barrel of the lock sent a charge of fear surging through the girls' bodies. Kimberly squeezed Blanche's hand.

With a quick whisper, Blanche instructed Kimberly to begin beating on the door and claim that Ike and Tink had gone into convulsions! Blanche emphasized the importance of keeping the guard distracted.

"Help! Help!" screamed Kimberly as she banged on the iron casted door with her two balled fists! She had bloodied her own nose for more affect!

The evening guard was showing a new guy the ropes. It would be an understatement to say the retiring church employee was a little bit shocked when he saw a bloody faced girl frantically explaining Tink's and Sporck's conditions!

He actually shrieked louder than Kimberly did when he felt Blanche's two hands reach through the back of his thighs to grab his wrists. What followed the retiring guard's initial sound of surprise was dwarfed by the horrifying noise he made as he zoomed down the eye of the spiral stairway!

Realizing something was going very badly with his initial 'beat' tour, the fledgling watchman did what any red-blooded newbie with a bad conscience might do; he fell to his knees and began sobbingly asking for forgiveness!

With a kind face on show, Blanche reached down and gently raised the man's chin up so she could speak to him up close. She then softly made a kind remark to him.

"You have lovely blue eyes!" Blanche said a nanosecond before she sunk the skeleton key into the man's eye socket. The two girls then slid the body off the doorstep and let it drop to the same place where the old guard lay!

Alex Selkirk signaled that flashes of cannon fire had been spotted to the northwest! Three ships were involved. Cato rang the Captain's bell.

Chaloner Ogle spun the wheel of the 'Whydah' causing the repossessed pirate's ship to lurch some. He ordered Rainbow to pull the main sails up!

Also seeing the flashes of cannon fire on the horizon, Woodes Rogers attempted to make enough noise to wake up Bosman. The wind was blowing up a storm so hearing the calls from a man absent most of his tongue, created quite a challenge for Rogers. A rock solved the conundrum.

"Bill! Bill! There's cannon fire fifteen miles out at ten o'clock!" babbled Rogers.

Bosman instantaneously climbed to the top of the rock to strike up their driftwood collection! Bill had practiced a thousand times his plan to get the attention of a passing speck on the horizon! Fire, was what he had in mind.

Both men had grabbed out of the air anything that would serve as tinder. It was for the teepee like stacking of dried out ocean debris to be used for chances such as the one before them!

Bosman maniacally began spinning a stick between the palms of his hands. Hopefully, the friction would create enough heat to ignite the airborne scraps!

Amazingly, a fire did get lit but it only sent out a smidgen of light for less than a minute. Still, that was a very big deal for the two men.

In celebration of their accomplishment, they declared a night of total silence. They lay supine at a thirty-five-degree angle gazing at the stars and thinking about infinity.

Along with a fully cocked blunderbuss and four pistols in his belt, Jonn Kimber darted through the labyrinth of scattered boxes set up for the dagger-flies tournament. Bullets hissed by searching for flesh to penetrate!

When Kimber got within eyesight of the 'Happy Return's' wheelhouse, he could see the ship was engulfed in flames. But then Jonn noticed something quite odd. There were no white men among the attackers!

From Jonnathan Kimber's angle he saw more than a hundred black men crawling all over the 'Happy Return'! He heard Jim Stanfield calling his name!

Kimber could see the fury in Stanfield's eyes! Just as Jonn was preparing to swing over to the 'Fancy's' deck, three of Jemmy's men attacked him!

Brandishing machetes, the Angolans encircled Kimber! They then began to taunt Jonn much like wolves do before finishing off a large animal. But then almost comically, the mocking negros grew suddenly ashen faced and soon thereafter fell over dead!

Three daggers protruded from eye sockets belonging to the deceased slaves. Every motioned for Kimber to continue his mission to rescue Stanfield before sliding back into hiding.

Jonn Kimber was shocked by the barbarity inflicted upon the 'Thomas's' crew! Of those Jemmy had not already killed, the crazed lion head had hobbled those remaining. Additionally, every crippled man was chained to his particular duty station.

As they had done with the 'Fancy', Jemmy and his followers stripped the 'Happy Return' to its bare bones! Everything and anything of value including 'Mildred', were taken over to the 'Thomas'.

Jemmy then cut away the fire embroiled 'Fancy'! His animal heads cheered. The 'Thomas' then released a volley of cannon fire into the side of the 'Happy Return' as the 'Thomas' sped away.

James Stanfield broke into tears as he felt Kimber's hands touch his slit ankle tendons. Time was of the essence; both ships were sinking. Jonn did what he could to cut the others loose from their shackles but he knew he couldn't save them all.

The 'Whydah' was closing in on the 'Thomas'! Ogle ordered the 'Whydah' to 'run in the dark' which presented for Ogle's team the possibility of catching Jemmy by surprise.

After climbing down from the crow's nest, Cato made his way to Ogle's cabin. He needed to give him an update!

"Oh, please come in, Cato." lied Ben.

"Sir, the 'Thomas' slung the 'Fancy' into the side of the 'Happy Return'! Both ships are listing. There are survivors on the collided vessels!" reported Cato.

"Are we within firing range of the 'Thomas'?" calmly asked Hornigold.

"Captain, from what I observed there have been prisoners taken from both the 'Fancy' and the 'Happy Return'! I can't help but believe there has been a mutiny aboard the 'Thomas' as well!" excitedly stated Cato.

"What?" Asked the astonished Captain.

"Sir, the 'Thomas' it appears has been overtaken by the slaves or should I say, the 'hosts'! There is not a white face to be seen on the deck!" gasped Cato.

"I repeat, are we within range?" Hornigold exasperatedly asked.

"In thirty minutes, we will be, sir!" barked Cato.

"How much time before the ships go down?"

"Ten minutes at most!" answered Cato sardonically.

"We have no choice. Destroy the 'Thomas'!" commanded Hornigold.

Alex Selkirk did what he was supposed to do, he reported to the Captain's quarters for a briefing before his shift was to begin. He had heard only the tail end of Ben's last remarks to Cato.

"Reporting for duty, sir," said Selkirk.

"Ah, come in, Alex, we have somewhat of a crisis on our hands! Maybe you should weigh in with your thoughts on the matter!" gruffly muttered Captain Hornigold.

Alex glanced over his shoulder at Cato. After a quick read, Alexander Selkirk halfway formally approached Ogle. Their eyes interlocked.

"You have of course heard the story of Woodes Rogers rescuing me some years back, have you not?" baited Alex. Ogle nodded.

"Well, sir, Rogers was onboard the 'Charles II' before its disenchanted crew set-out their captain and his three loyalists on dry land! They then renamed the ship the 'Fancy'!

If Rogers is still alive, Captain Ogle, I'd consider it my duty to return the favor or at least give him a Christian burial!" courageously stated Selkirk.

"Very well done, Alex, you've made your point! Therefore, we shall suspend our pursuit of the 'Thomas' for now; however, we do not have the time to dawdle! We'll throw two hours of benevolence at the situation but after that time is spent, we must finish up what King George sent us out here to do! We cannot allow the 'Thomas' nor any of its passengers to reach the colonies whether they are alive or dead!" defiantly yelled Ogle.

Jemmy knew the 'Whydah' was a faster ship than the 'Thomas'. He was also aware of the glaring fact he had absolutely no knowledge of captaining a ship!

Still cursing himself for not checking who was to be sacrificed the previous night, he had inadvertently drowned one of the two men on the 'Thomas' who knew how to do it! He called for Stanfield to be cleaned up and brought to the wheelhouse at once!

Fifteen minutes later, a zebra head brought some disturbing news.

"Boss Lion, they say 'down-there' there ain't no Stanfield! What you want me to do, Boss Lion?" asked the frightened zebra head.

With his steely blue eyes, Jemmy glared through his lion's mask at the jittery slave for almost a minute. Then after gulping down a big swig of rum, Jemmy withdrew one of his four pistols from his belt and shot the zebra head between its striped eyes!

The first curious gawker busted through the wheelhouse door! Jemmy repeated his order; however, he supplemented this directive with a caveat.

"Listen to me you dumb sonofabitch, I want you and fifty others to go down into that hold and bring up every living creature to the main deck! While you're latching those white bastards to the anchor chain, I want ten more of you bloody niggers to go down there and kill anyone in hiding! Now go!" screamed Jemmy.

The Wroxton Abbey was bustling with excitement. Red coated horsemen patrolled the streets in and around Oxfordshire as if they were looking for small objects on the ground. Everything and everyone were checked either coming or going through the abbey's gates.

For security reasons, only family and the members of parliament were permitted to enter the Wroxton property. The well-wishers were shuffled off to the edge of town where there was a corded off area to accommodate them. Rows and rows of makeshift tables were being set up by those aiming to make some money selling food and memorabilia to commemorate Lord North's christening.

Bleachers were set up to offer seating for those who could afford it while another corded off space was created for those with shallower pockets. Both groups were hoping to get a glimpse of Queen Caroline!

Kimberly Kimber snapped the backside of the donkey's rump. The exhausted animal pulled their highjacked cart for a hair under thirty miles!

Blanche had disposed of the fishmonger's body some twenty miles back but not before stripping the rig's owner of all of his money!

The two girls sharply pulled the cart off of the clay packed road as a company of Royal cavalrymen rumbled by. It was time to visit Tink's satchel anyway!

It was midnight. There was a good strong wind coming out of the southeast. Jemmy had every right to celebrate the 'Thomas's' victory but instead, he was dealing with an inner panic which wouldn't go away!

Feeling trapped by his own ignorance, the lion head perused the two lines of shackled prisoners. He knew there had to be at least someone among the white devils who could get the 'Thomas' to Charlestown!

Things started to look up for Jemmy when one of the animal heads by the name of Jethro brought up one of the sea wives from the 'Fancy'. She couldn't speak very much English but she was naked which made an inquisition worthwhile.

SEA BUZZARDS

Jemmy in a deep throated voice, ordered Jethro out of the wheelhouse! He sauntered over to a locker and removed a crimson red jacket from its hangar.

After placing the jacket gently over the Turkish girl's shoulders, the "Thomas's" captain pulled up a chair so the two of them could have an up-close discussion of some sort. He poured her a mug of rum.

"What is your name?" Jemmy asked.

"Mira," the young woman said.

"Mira, that's a pretty name! Tell me, Mira, do you speak English?" questioned Jemmy.

"I can a little! Please do not kill me, sir!" pleaded the Turk.

As any decent human being would do to console another, Jemmy did exactly the opposite. He used her fear to get the answers he needed.

"Mira, I am afraid I cannot spare your life!" whispered Jemmy.

"But why? I have done no harm to you!" screamed Mira.

"Jethro mentioned to me there was something you wanted to tell me! Can you offer me anything that might cause me to change my mind? I had plans of appointing you our evening's sacrifice to the sea!" Jemmy said.

"Oh my god, I'll do anything! Just, please don't throw me into the ocean!" begged the brown skinned girl.

"Very well! Let's see just how much you want to stay dry, then! Where did the two captains of the 'Thomas' go? Are they still onboard?" interrogated the lion head.

"Sir, you sacrificed Captain Bosman two nights ago! Jim Stanfield was the one you made plow into the side of the 'Happy Return'.

I would assume he has drowned by now! Other than that, Captain Jemmy, I have no answers!" stuttered the frightened girl.

"Mira, I shall place a crown of flowers upon your head before you are offered to the sea tonight!" Jemmy loudly concluded.

"But there are other captains on the 'Thomas' at this very moment!" she answered in a squcaky kind of way.

Jethro hoisted the crimson clad woman back over his shoulder and was preparing to throw her into the Atlantic when Jemmy called out to Mira a one-last-chance opportunity to save her life!

"Hey, Mira, last offer! Give me the name of a ship captain currently aboard the 'Thomas'!"

"Captain Benjamin Hornigold" was all the time Mira had to say before Jethro had her in a mid-air trajectory into the water below! Jemmy felt like kicking himself for being so stupid. That was his favorite shirt! Jemmy put his lion's head on. He commanded Jethro to gather the 'Thomas's' all-white crew members together!

"At sunrise, we shall have us an auction! Let's see what the 'whites' bring on our block!" blurted Jemmy.

After the 'Thomas' left the African coast headed for the Caribbean, Jemmy figured out that the so-called Sporckians were not much more than a bunch of fat-assed rich kids acting like Robin Hood and his merry men! It didn't take very much to overtake them; after all, the blacks outnumbered the whites ten to one!

After a vision, Jemmy was convinced he was the negro version of "Spartacus"! The Angolan slave felt he had been appointed by Jesus to lead the slaves out of their chains! They were destined to move into the plantation owners' big houses living on the Colonial coast!

To do this, he planned to take his men and get up with some folks he was related to in Charlestown! He would rebel-raise the incarcerated slaves, take over the plantations and live happily in peace after that!

Jemmy figured that by the time he had finished with Charlestown, the remainder of the Colonial plantation owners would abandon their properties and flee to the west somewhere! They would be afraid of their women being raped by mythically hung blacks, Jemmy surmised.

All of these things were running through Jemmy's mind when Jethro presented him with a stark reminder as to the need for someone to navigate the ship! Lights had been spotted two miles behind them.

The golden strip of sun light offered absolutely no help in spotting the survivors. Cato and Rainbow Charlie had taken the lifeboat out a mile from the 'Whydah' just to avoid the swirling suck-hole created when a ship goes down. Rainbow sent up a flare!

Henry Every and Oliver LaBuse were sharing a floating box, Stanfield and Kimber were lying on a piece of the 'Happy Return's' mainmast while six other survivors clung to various life preservers of their choosing. Each one of them were wounded in some way or another.

Anne was at the wheel while Maynard, Ogle and Cato prepared to debrief the survivors as soon as they were lifted to safety. What had happened on the 'Thomas' and the whereabouts of its lost men were the two questions requiring immediate answers!

Alexander Selkirk was the first to speak to the shivering survivors. Hypothermia was the main worry but Alex felt he couldn't wait to question them! He leaned down into Every's face.

"Henry, do you know where Woodes Rogers is?" sharply asked Selkirk.

Every speaking with a weak voice, answered.

"The R.A.C. hired us to protect the 'Thomas' to the Caribbean. Its cargo of slaves took over that ship before I realized it was too late to stop them! They tricked us... and I lost my 'Fancy' to them!"

"What happened to Rogers?" pressed Alex.

Ogle stepped into the questioning and pressed Henry Every even harder!

"Son, is it possible that Woodes Rogers is still alive?" Ogle asked.

Every looked up at the 'Whydah's' captain with a grim smile running across his jaw.

"Well, sir, considering that he was hit in the face by only one musket ball, I'd say he might still be alive! But I'm telling you right now, those machete wielding slaves moved on us like lightning!"

Jonnathan Kimber attempted to stand but found his legs were like rubber and therefore couldn't do it. As an alternative, Kimber loudly yelled out a question to his friend who was also a survivor, James Stanfield!

"Hey Jim, what happened to Bosman?" yelled Jonn.

"Jemmy offered him to the sea as a sacrifice!" Stanfield answered.

"Didn't the Sporckians resist?" requisitioned Kimber.

"No, Jemmy killed most of them right off the bat!" said James Stanfield.

Chaloner Ogle glanced over at Cato and then over to Selkirk. He tried to read their thoughts and somehow come up with some sort of conclusion to the fragmented scenario. Cal then turned back to Cato.

"Cato, grab the chart from off the table. Let's figure out where those lights came from!" Ogle anxiously said.

By the time Blanche and Kimberly had reached the outskirts of Oxfordshire, the orchestra had just completed a tune with a bunch of horns in it! This made Kimberly believe the christening hadn't started yet. That was good news, because Blanche was nowhere close to finishing the pinwheel she had started to make.

Kimberly pointed out a spot near a tiny brook where they could maybe get a chance to see Blanche's uncle go by! She had promised her that the Earl of Sandwich would most probably take them to his castle if they could catch his attention!

Blanche worked diligently making the inside of her pinwheel stick as smooth as possible. It was to become a blowgun!

She had used some canvas and a tack to fashion the spinning wheel but that was only a ruse to disguise its real purpose! Blanche was intending to shoot Queen Caroline with it!

Jemmy and his insurrectionists began frisking the men and women who were chained to the 'Thomas's' outside deck railing. They were looking for the man Mira called "Benjamin Hornigold".

Jemmy had promised a mock auction to the slaves. The preparation of each block contestant would offer an opportune time for him to do some profiling!

He grabbed the ship's megaphone to announce his directive to the joyously onlooking Africans. The prisoners groaned.

"In preparation of today's auction, these lively young white folks are to be washed from head to toe! You are to pamper them with care! Treat them as if they were in preparation for our evening's sacrificial ceremony!

Once they are bathed and oiled, we shall then proceed to place a value on them! Those with any age will bring the highest fee provided they have at least some useful skill about them!

For those found to be combative, kindly remove their heads and throw their chatting noggins into the sea! Now, about the women…

I understand their value! But remember, any that you do purchase must be disposed of before we get to shore!" harped Jemmy.

Bill Bosman had seen flashes of light toward the northwest at some time during the night! It was an impervious happening of no more significance than a guppy washed up on shore, he said to himself.

Woodes's face had enlarged to the size of a moon melon with about the same color of one too. What had once been a goatee encircled mouth was now an unhinged gaping opening!

His breathing was coupled with a bubbling sound with each of his exhalations. Time was running out for both of them!

Blanche sat in the shadow of an elm tree watching the landing patterns of the green flies. They were assaulting the remnants of mackerel in the corners of the fish mongers' truck.

She was particularly interested in the rotted pieces the insects ignored. Those were the deadly ones!

The effects of scombroid poisoning once it entered Caroline's blood stream, would go unnoticed for at least as long as it would take to get her back to the palace! What a delightful scare this would give old George, Blanche thought.

The gates of the Wroxton Abbey burst open as a detachment of twenty red coated cavalry men galloped out! They forced the encroaching crowd to make way for the entourage about to follow!

Blanche inserted her needle tipped garden pea into the breach of her spinning pinwheel. She gently poked Kimberly in the ribs to pump up her excitement!

With a sisterly hug, Blanche drew her little friend closer to her so she could whisper something in her ear! The crowd was very noisy.

"Now Kimberly, if we're going to ever get Uncle Earl's attention, you're going to have to do something to slow their carriages down! I was thinking if you were to allow the Queen's wagon to run over your leg, it would give me enough time to reacquaint myself with my Uncle Sandwich!

Honey, I'd do it myself but given the merciful fact you haven't grown tits yet, they'll take more pity on you and therefore be more inclined to stop the Royal caravan! It's a big sacrifice to make but when you think how nice it will be to live in a real castle and be fed grapes by servants, it makes it a superb proposition in my mind!

And besides, Kim, just think about how proud your father will be when he discovers his own flesh and blood is comingling with the Royalty of our country! I'll bet he'll even come for you after he learns of your good fortune!" instructed Blanche.

Jethro and his assistant named Braden, stood at the end of the line of the freshly scrubbed captives. They had been oiled down just as the negroes would have been if they were to be sold on a Charlestown block.

Braden was wearing a pair of slacks which pretty much fit him around his waist but they had an inseam at least a foot longer than needed. After stuffing the excess material into his oversized boots, Braden picked up a rope handled bucket containing a sponge, a gallon of sea water and a meat cleaver! He was proud to be one of the inspectors!

Jethro was the first to examine the 'Happy Return's' captives. He was followed by Jemmy.

Only Jemmy knew whom he was really looking for; however, in order to make it appear as if he were doing a pre-block going over, the lion head licked the foreheads of each of the prisoners chained to the railing. As Jemmy explained to Jethro, 'sick peoples sweat always tastes like vinegar'.

Probably because Jemmy wanted to set an example, he ordered Braden to decapitate the third man the inspection team came up on! When that time had come and Braden was about to bring his meat cleaver down upon the back of LaBuse's neck, Ben Hornigold yelled out!

"You do know the 'Whydah' is preparing to sink the 'Thomas', don't you? Sir, before you kill the only man on this ship who can save us, I would suggest that we abandon this mock auction of yours and get on with our 'Last Rights' communion service!"

Jemmy was caught off guard by Hornigold's outburst. He signaled Braden to cease his intent!

The blue-eyed negro spun away from the three-man inspection team. He then made a beeline straight to where Ben was standing!

"Did you say something to me, Boy?" Snarled Jemmy.

"Indeed, sir!" said Hornigold as if he were offering the time of day.

"What I said, Captain, was, 'if you keep moving this ship in circles, your adversary, Rear Admiral Chaloner Ogle of his Majesty's Royal Navy will soon be on you within the day! That's what I said, sir!" explained Hornigold.

"Well maybe you can do it better than me?" Jemmy asked in a surly manner.

"No sir, I can't, but Captain Oliver can!" calmly said Ben.

"How much time will it take us to get to Charlestown if we can outrun the 'Whydah'? asked Jemmy.

"You'll have to see Captain Oliver about that! I'm just one of his tough-hands but since you asked me a question in a gentlemanly manner, I'll give you my thoughts on the matter if you would like, sir!" meekly stated Hornigold.

Jemmy motioned for Braden to bring him the bucket. He then slid the three-gallon pail over the top of Hornigold's head so the bucket's edging firmly sat on the real captain's shoulders.

With an exceedingly swift movement, Jemmy whipped the meat cleaver around the pail's lip causing the entire circumference of Ben's neck to begin leaking blood. He then began speaking to the inside of the inverted bucket!

"I shall finish the job I started and throw your head into the Atlantic if what you say displeases me in any way! Do you understand what I'm saying?" Jemmy said.

The bucket nodded.

"I repeat! How long will it take for us to reach Charlestown if we are unencumbered by this so-called Ogle fellow?" snarled Jemmy as he asked his question.

"Four days under full sails!" said Hornigold.

"And how long will it take if we attack the 'Whydah'?" inquired Jemmy.

"Never!" answered the three-gallon bucket.

While Kimberly was making her way through the tall legs of British onlookers, Blanche had doubled back to the cart. In a quiet spot in the back of the fish monger's storage space the 'jonesing' girl opened Tink's box and began her preparation.

The music had stopped. Blanche could tell from her position that the anticipatory crowd's conversations had diminished. The Abbey's gates opened.

As expected, high pitched screams perforated the applauses from the well-wishers! Kimberly had made her move!

The prearranged accident had brought more of the Queen's attention than previously supposed. Blanche came up with a new plan!

Wading through the colored marsh in her mind, she elected to abandon the infected dart idea. She opted simplicity instead.

Loaded with one of Tink's syringes full of Oxfordshire air, Blanche palmed it in her left fist. Her thumb rested on the plunger!

Screaming like a long-lost sister, Blanche rushed through the celebratory citizens stealing a child's rag-doll along the way! She elbowed her way to the real-time accident site. There she saw Kimberly laying in the arms of the Queen of England!

Faster than the protective guards' reflexes could muster, Blanche climbed over a lady changing her child's diaper and then fell on the Queen like a sack of wet grain! Amidst Kimberly's shrieks of pain and Caroline's reaction to Tink's bamboo needle, Blanche was able to slither through the ankles of those darkened by the shadows cast by Wroxton Abbey!

Bill Bosman had seen the flashes of meaningless light at some point during the night. Roger's face had swollen into an unrecognizable state. Time had become a nuisance!

Alex Selkirk wept as he and Cato lifted Woodes's body onto the 'Whydah's' lifeboat. Anne and Percy tried their best to convince Bosman that they weren't part of Jemmy's animal heads.

Jemmy didn't want to lose the confidence he had already instilled with his followers. Because he had blue-eyed-Jemmy had his men convinced he was actually a white man who had been directly appointed by Jesus to rid America of its slave owners!

For this reason, Jemmy had to be very cautious about displaying his lack of boat-driving ability. His solution to that conundrum was solved by distracting his followers by turning the auctioneers, Jethro and Braden, loose on the women chained to the starboard side of the 'Thomas'!

Jemmy then ordered Captain LaBuse and his tough-hand, 'Mister Bucket Head' to be taken up to the 'Thomas's' wheelhouse. He threatened the assigned transporters with certain death if one bone of either of his 'special prisoners' were injured!

Reverend Isaac Green had his tripoded telescope perfectly focused onto the crossroads about a mile from the All Saints' Church. He was anxious to hear what his hired sleuth had to say.

Finally, after three agonizing hours, Sporck saw what he was hoping to see. A jockey sized Spaniard by the name of Joseph Cinquez was slowly making his way up to the church's campus on the back of a potbellied donkey. Ike hurried down to meet him.

"Hello there, fellow Christian." Isaac said piously.

"Greetings, Reverend!" answered the innocuous looking detective.

"I trust you had a safe and productive journey, Joseph?" asked Isaac Green.

"To tell you the truth, Reverend Green, I believe it would only be fair to return half the money you gave me to track your daughters down! Oh, I had no trouble from them or anything like that, it was just that everywhere those two girls went they left a swath of death behind them!" grimly stated the gumshoe.

With a look of utter shock on his face, Sporck approached Cinquez and closed in the distance between them rather quickly.

"What the hell do you mean, 'they left a swath of death behind them'? Those damn ladies wouldn't hurt a fly!" screeched Sporck.

"Unfortunately, Reverend, you are sorely incorrect about that, Sir! To take this to a higher level of scrutiny would be counterproductive simply because to do so would implicate your daughters in the murder of Queen Caroline!"

Countered Joseph.

"For god's sake, Man, are you saying that my girls killed King George's wife?" Asked Reverend Green in a high-pitched voice.

The Spaniard then turned away from the lion head and sauntered over to his donkey to fetch some proof for the disenchanted man of the cloth. He returned with Tink's empty cherry wood satchel.

By the lighting of a cigar, Sporck signaled to the shooter in the bell tower that Joseph Cinquez was ready to leave the earth! A single bullet then passed through the Spaniard's brain.

Sporck then stepping on his newly lit cigar. That action cued an immediate response from the church's busy cleanup crew.

Cato's hands moved like trained tarantulas across the 'Whydah's' wheel. He kept a close watch for the signals being sent to him from the dinghy that was poling for shoals in front of him.

The fog's viscosity resembled that of blackstrap molasses. Any normally advantageous sunlight was nonplussed by an unbroken whiteness.

Blunted echoes were about all Cato could depend on for guidance. There was zero wind.

Captain Ogle glanced into Cato's eyes. Noting a smile on Cato's face, Cal interrupted the pirate with a personal question which hopefully would slake his curiosity.

"Ah, the mark of a professional is one who finds levity within danger! What say you about that, Cato?" Ogle said furtively.

Cato grinned as he quickly turned the 'Whydah's' rudder to the right. Looking over his shoulder, he returned Cal's serve.

"Captain, I am rejoicing!"

"How so?" asked Ogle.

"Because there is no such thing as a rambunctious slave being capable of alluding catastrophe through this labyrinth!" laughed Cato.

"So, you think Hornigold is still alive?" queried Ogle with a glitter in his eye.

"I'd bet on it!" said Cato through clinched teeth.

King George was exhausted. His wrist muscles ached from the ten thousand or more mourners' hands he had shaken over the past week! A deep depression was coming on.

Gus found himself going over Caroline's faults in his mind; it kept him from thinking about his. All in all, he concluded, he had been a pretty bad husband to her!

Yes, it was true they had nine children together but in hindsight, he wouldn't have sired those if he hadn't been so confined! The King's thoughts shifted toward Ogle and then to Sporck.

For quite some time George Augustus had looked for an excuse to leave the throne! War was the only face-saving way to escape his responsibilities.

It wasn't god's disenchantment with him that bothered him so much, he didn't buy into that reasoning anyway, it was history that made him quake in his boots! He didn't want it to be kinder to his father than it would be toward him!

But now he had the perfect alibi and he planned to cash in on it! His scheme would be to use Sporck's venal actions as the fuse to ignite a long overdue clash with the Austrians! This in turn, would provide the King a ticket out of England and away from the ticking time bomb of political disfavor!

Just from the abbreviated conversations he had with Jonnathan Kimber, Hornigold knew the 'Whydah's' intention was to obliterate the bubonic carrying 'Thomas'! Ben also was aware of Jemmy's composite disposition which resembled that of a rabid dog's!

LaBuse's lack of ability to perform the expected tasks that real captains did was the chink in their theatrical armor! Jemmy was certainly ignorant when it came to oceanic matters but he was by no means a stupid man, thought Benjamin.

Should Oliver slip up at the wrong time and if the lion head were to catch wind of their duplicity, neither Hornigold nor LaBuse would ever step foot on land again! These were the things weighing heavy on Benjamin's mind as he swung his lantern to the right three times indicating to "Captain" Oliver to turn the wheel three degrees to the right!

A fully loaded blunderbuss had been tied to the back of LaBuse's chair in such a way that if the Frenchman even leaned forward one least little bit, the scrap metal payload would disintegrate his spinal cord.

Three times the 'Thomas's' hull skidded across sandbars! Each time it happened Jemmy's attention would quickly switch over to the big mouthed scattergun!

To make matters worse and because of the white-out they were enduring outside, Jemmy had become very seasick. Vomit had made the wheelhouse's floor as slick as glass!

Oliver LaBuse could see from his unstable position that Ben was moving his lantern straight up and down. This meant in landlubbers' lingo, the 'Thomas' had smooth sailing in front of her for the next quarter of a mile!

LaBuse took Jemmy's surfeited affliction as an opportunity to do some exploration into the blue-eyed Angolan's mind. So, with the demeanor of a grave digger, Oliver began his cretaceous journey.

"Captain, I have cured many a crewmember of mine of the very same spell as the one you have had cast upon you! I would help you if I could but you haven't built up enough trust in me yet!" said the stone-faced LaBuse.

"Whitey, don't fuck with me! I'll kill you dead, I will!" threatened Jemmy.

"Oh, no, sir, I wasn't trying to antagonize you, not at all! It probably wouldn't work on you anyway!" baited LaBusc.

"Why, because I'm a slave?" contested the negro with a greenish pallor.

"Well, not exactly," rebutted Oliver with a pensive stare out toward Hornigold's direction.

"If that's not the reason then why can't you help me?" curiously prodded Jemmy.

Oliver pretended like he was thinking about some ethereal complexity! He had noticed the silver cross Jemmy wore around his neck. So LaBuse did what any smart gambler would do when he has nothing left to lose, he bluffed!

"Sir, my ancient remedy can only help those who have been baptized as a believer in Jesus! I am sorry but that decision belongs in the Lord's hands, not mine!" said Oliver.

"I happened to be a devout Catholic!" answered Jemmy as if he had won a raffle.

"Then you're in luck! I can get you feeling like your old self in about thirty minutes!" said LaBuse with a haughty tone.

"I'm going to make you a promise, a genuine and truthful one, Captain! I will allow you and your tough-hand out there to remain onboard once we get to Charlestown!

I shall grant you your lives if you can do what you say you can do to help me! However, if you cannot then you will join the rest of your crew on the sea floor!" said Jemmy.

Oliver angrily whipped around after hearing about the murdering of his crewmates but then he heard the mechanical sounds of the firing lanyard tightening on the blunderbuss's trigger housing! With that hardwired recognition in mind, Oliver LaBuse changed his tune.

"Sir, I am quite aware of our current roles. Furthermore, it is my belief that the two of us Christian 'captains' need to come together and ask Jesus to intervene so we might be able to move forward with our lives! When this test is over, we survive it, it is my soulful wish that we can at least say the two of us even though we're enemy's, acted as Jesus would have wanted us to do! In that vein, Captain Jemmy, I would like to rid you of the evil spell which has fallen upon you!" proclaimed Oliver LaBuse.

With that being so heart wrenchingly said, Jemmy began weeping like a bloody-nosed school kid! He immediately fell at the base of LaBuse's hair triggered chair and spoke.

"Oh please, Captain LaBuse, do whatever you must do! I am so goddamned sick! I give you my word on Mother Mary's grave, I will do everything I can to honor my commitment to you and Mister Hornigold, I swear I will! Just help me get off this boat!" pleaded Jemmy.

"Very well, Captain, I shall extend my good faith in view of the sincere oath you have made with Jesus's mother and me! For safety's sake and because of the 'Silver-Ball Ritual', I will kindly ask that you cut away these deadly bindings of mine while I administer the 'Rite of Degrees'! I shall also need a Bible and a thermometer!" ordered Oliver.

Amidst his dry heaves, Jemmy on his hands and knees crawled over to his duffle bag and pulled out of it a tattered Bible. He then withdrew his boot knife and proceeded to cut the silk strand that was looped around the blunderbuss's trigger.

But then with a desperate look on his face, Jemmy looked up at Oliver with the belief that LaBuse was his Uncle Asberry!

"Where can I find a thermometer?" Jemmy painfully queried.

"There is one on the wall closest to the door," said Oliver.

Seeing exactly what his "uncle" was talking about, Jemmy begrudgingly made his on-all-fours journey to fetch it for him. When he was praised sufficiently for his effort, Oliver began the 'Silver-Ball Ritual'!

"Please turn in your Bible to Proverbs twenty-three: verse thirty-four. There you will see a question that has been posed to you by Jesus himself! Kindly read God's words out loud." 'Uncle Asberry' stated with an omnipotent flair.

"Reeling and seasick, drunk as a sailor?" Jemmy read with conviction.

"Take the thermometer and place it in those holy pages as if it were a bookmark! Now close the good-book and repeat after me, 'Avast you demon serpent of the belly!

I trust that the Lord will deliver me from this awful grip!'" roared LaBuse.

Jemmy verbatim repeated what LaBuse had said.

"Then Jemmy, take that Bible you have in your mortal hands and slam that book on the floor of this damnable ship! And then stand like a man of God and stamp on it as if it were filled with pestilence!" preached Oliver LaBuse.

Jemmy did that too.

"Carefully open your Bible back to where the thermometer was placed beside of the question the Lord asked you. You will see there are tiny silver balls rolling in between the pages. You are to allow those silver balls to roll down into your plagued belly so they may do God's work. Do this at once!" ordered Oliver.

Jemmy swallowed the quicksilver.

Blanche knew that Kimberly was a pretty tough cookie as they say, but no one is bigger than the monkey riding on their back! After all, Sporck had them both strung-out for more than a month.

This left Blanche with two pipers to pay! The first and most important dilemma she had to solve was the monkey thing. Her second obstacle was to escape the watchful eyes of anyone who could identify her!

King George had plastered posters of a complimentary drawing of her on anything that stood perpendicular to the earth's surface! Blanche chuckled to herself when she calculated that her body was worth more than a house! Blanche was a wanted woman.

Unbeknownst to anyone else but Blanche, whenever she was faced with anything she had to really think about, she always climbed a tall tree! Once up there, the young woman could most always get a fresh perspective on whatever it was perplexing her.

Blanche picked out a hemlock with plenty of low hanging branches near the bottom of its trunk.

At sixty feet above ground level, Blanche could see the happenings going on around Oxfordshire. Her prospects of escape appeared to be somewhere between slim and none; however, a whiff of peanut oil offered her a miniscule glimmer of hope!

When night finally fell over the site of the Queen's assignation, she made her way through the maze of checkpoints set up by the King's soldiers. Blanche ended up in the middle of Chinatown! From there things got a whole lot easier.

The very first thing Blanche did when she reached an establishment, she felt comfortable with was to get a fix. She enjoyed her rush alongside a fat man lying in the cot next to hers.

As expected, Blanche's coquette antics landed her a place to hole up for a while. Sporck's henchmen were the searchers she was most concerned about. Unlike the King's massive police force, Ike's people although fewer in numbers, would go to any lengths to find their quarry!

Blanche felt as if she was reasonably safe hidden away in a three hundred square foot flat belonging to one of the town's many junkies. In that she still had plenty of the fishmonger's money left and was pretty confident the animal heads would not expect her to remain at the scene of her crime for so long, Blanche figured a week would just about chill her trail!

Chaloner Ogle stared out at a blood red line across the empty horizon. The 'Thomas' had out commandeered him!

Anger and embarrassment were the fueling agents pressing Cal into the decision to return to his old ways of killing human beings! With a death wish the size of China looming in the darkest pits of his mind, the humiliated war dog made the decision to bring that very bad part of him back out into the open!

After Ogle rang the Captains' bell, he looked over the conglomeration of fighters sitting before him! All were veterans and all were as deadly as a nest of rattlers.

When Cal finished the last bit of jerky he was chewing, he wiped his mouth with his sleeve and prepared to speak. His audience was exhilarated.

"Consider us a bunch of stray dogs circumstantially packed up on a strange ship if you want to but the way I see it, that's what we were born to do anyway! No matter who we are or where we came from or even the reason why we are here, none of us can escape the fact that we know the right thing to do!

Anne and Gentlemen, it is true the 'Thomas' double backed on us! And yes, she slipped right by us without a single sound; however, do not despair, we still have another day to catch them and 'catch' them we will!

I realize we are a mixed bag of adversaries but when you consider the magnitude of what Anton von Sporck is attempting to do, it diminishes our previous commitments into a fraction of nothing! In less than two days, the 'Thomas' will be within landing range of Charlestown.

When and if Sporck's plan unfolds, the entire city will be infested with flea larvae hatchlings! From there, the Black-Death will spread like wildfire! America will perish!" stated Commander Ogle.

Sporck had studied the city of Oxfordshire's street map for three consecutive hours. He also knew Blanche pretty well.

The woman would need what Tink had given her! Being in a place where there were no contacts meant that Blanche would no doubt turn to the people who were known to readily sell it!

The fishmonger probably had some money! Sporck reasoned. Therefore, the odds were, Blanche was hiding out in Oxfordshire's Chinatown!

With three quick pulls on the butlers' chain, Ike ordered his carriage to be readied by sunrise. His new 'fancy boy', David was to travel with him on his journey.

They were to appear as a father and his son taking a three-day holiday together. Lin, Tink's niece had prepared a special kit for Sporck to use on Blanche when he located her. She had also put together a rather ornate starter-set for David and of course a hefty supply for him to enjoy along the way as well.

Jemmy began writhing on the floor! All LaBuse could do was to encourage him as he was enduring the convulsive effects of an exorcism!

"God is chasing out the demons!" Oliver kept saying.

LaBuse figured Jemmy would die within the hour so he began the rigorous activity of knot-gnawing. He had to free himself before the slaves realize their leader was dead.

But then something quite unexpected happened, Jemmy sat up as straight as a board! He had an expression on his face which was a cross between a thousand-yard stare and a man achieving a long overdue bowl movement.

"The divine intervention has now concluded! You may walk among the living!" babbled the reality riveted Oliver.

Without saying a word, Jemmy rose to his feet. Just his steely stare alone would have wounded a small animal. He staggered toward Oliver like a fabled cyclops.

LaBuse intentionally tried to recall his childhood as he was waiting for the sting of Jemmy's blade. Instead, the now grinning Angolan began slicing through Oliver's bindings while joyously conversing with the piss-wet Frenchman.

"You are the true son of God, aren't you?" quizzingly praised Jemmy.

"Indeed." Responded the now saved but still crafty Oliver LaBuse.

"You have delivered me from the jaws of Hell!" cried Jemmy. "Of course, my child! Isn't that what you asked our mother to do?" Lightly scolded LaBuse.

"Our mother?" rebounded Jemmy.

Fearing that he might be losing his grip on the hoax, the now ambulatory pseudo-captain chose the correct lifeline and quickly rebounded by covering up any blunders with a question!

"Do you not recognize me, Jemmy? Was I not with you back yonder at Uncle Asberry's front porch? Don't you realize, my Lamb, I am your brother from days long gone?"

Jemmy just watched the words melodically float from Oliver's mouth. He said nothing.

"Jemmy, it has taken this event to finally reunite us! Praise the Lord!" said Oliver as his turtle tears fell like rain.

But then Jemmy broke away from their embrace and walked over to the wheelhouse window as if he were gazing out at the horizon.

He spun quickly around with a chillingly serious look on his face before he spoke.

"I have always known this! Take me to Charlestown! Let them know of my coming!" prophetically 'spaketh' Jemmy.

At that, Jemmy left the wheelhouse in a tither. He said he was retiring to his quarters in order to prepare for his inaugural sermon!

This left Oliver LaBuse at the wheel trying to signal Hornigold while at the same time doing his best to absorb the reality of Jemmy's madness! The slaves would be curious and come peeking through the windows if they became uneasy with their leader's competency!

After six minutes of charade like body movements and a lantern show that would pale a comet, Hornigold caught on to what was going on inside of the 'Thomas's' wheelhouse! LaBuse would need a decoy before he jumped overboard!

There was no time to waste! In Hornigold's dinghy were a set of oars, one lantern and a fifty-foot pole. What Oliver took with him would be all the men would have to survive in the unruly Atlantic. They were thirty miles from land.

It would be easier to make their getaway when the possibility of grounding out the 'Thomas' was more probable, Oliver thought. He drew out a cunningly brilliant map which would wrongly guide the animal heads to Dewees Island instead of Charlestown!

As for an onboard diversion during his escape, LaBuse chose a pound of black powder coupled with a ten-minute fuse. With these items expertly placed inside of an empty barrel, it should draw the focus of the slaves to the rear of the ship once it detonated some hundred yards behind the 'Thomas's' wake!

This might just give them enough of a head start to get far enough away so that the slaves' small arms fire wouldn't be affective! That would force Jemmy to use his cannons. Then hopefully, the 'Whydah' would find them! It was broad daylight.

King George had pictured this moment a thousand times over in his mind. He had prepared for this day and it was finally here! He took a deep breath and looked all around him for what he hoped would be the very last time!

Gus deeply hoped no one would find out he was leaving London. Under the guise of a gravedigger was the King's plan! George Augustus even went so far as to print business cards boasting of his superlative skills as a sexton!

He had decided to handle Sporck on his own! The political backwash following a military action against anyone related to an Austrian would have a devastating effect on the diplomacy efforts being put forth to prevent their succession from the British Empire! Anyway, George just wanted to kill Sporck; period, end of story!

It felt wonderful Gus thought, to be riding through the countryside without being surrounded by sheep dressed in wolves' clothing! Even his generals were cowards!

The Royal gravedigger pulled his black utility wagon into the entranceway of Liverpool's finest hotel, The Royal Clarence. A nice young man helped the King from his utility wagon.

Vinibal, the hotel's bartender nodded as the incognito traveler ordered a bottle of scotch and some high-priced conversation!

"Welcome to the Royal Clarence! May I have our chefs fix you a sandwich or something?" congenially asked Vinibal.

"No thanks, I just need to clean some dust out of my throat! It's been a long day." answered Gus.

"Did you come in from the north? An earlier customer mentioned something about it blowing up a storm up there! Shall I bill this to your room, sir?" Blandly asked Vinibal.

"My key has the number '21' on it; will that suffice?" asked King George.

"Absolutely, Sir." answered the bartender.

"Hey, Vinibal, before you get too busy, I was wondering if I might get a message sent over to the stable?" George said with a toothy grin.

"Would you care to send that message by your own pen, Sir? Every person employed by the Clarence is literate, Sir!" boasted Vinibal.

"As a matter of fact, I would! Could you fetch me a pad and pencil, my good Man?" King George said with too much 'blue-blood' exuding from his lips.

"There you go, Sir! Shall I wait to carry the post myself?" patiently asked Vinibal.

King George looked up at the Clarence's bartender with a twitch of a smile jumping from the corners of his mouth and then made a couple of interesting remarks to him.

"Vinibal, I do not know whether you are aware of this or not but you are about ready to become an incredibly wealthy man! Now I know that sounds like a far-fetched pile of malarkey coming from a common gravedigger. Although, I happened to be on a quest at the wishes of a benefactor offering to pay a whale of a handsome sum for some information!

But before we continue this discussion further, let me ask you if the word 'Sporckian' has any meaning to you? If not, my employer thanks you and I shall leave a pound for your troubles! If yes, then we will meet later tonight! Your thoughts, Mister Baggott?" Asked Gus.

Vinibal Baggott's professional staunchness was exchanged for an icy stare! He snapped back up his pad and pencil from Gus's table, clicked his heels together, filled the King's glass up to the brim and left for the stables with a blank piece of paper folded up into his jacket pocket!

From over his shoulder, Vinibal nodded with a pleasant look of contentment on his face as he exited the lounge. Robert Barbara saw the whole thing!

The King of England propped his feet up on the bench setting on the other side of the booth he was sitting in. His third glass of scotch had delivered it's promised buzz! That all changed when Gus read the note Vinibal had scribbled on the back of his drink coaster!

"Meet me at the gazebo on the south lawn at midnight"

Glancing at the huge clock mounted midway up the hotel's fireplace chimney, George realized he had just enough time to take a hot bath and to catch a quick catnap.

In that no one was left in the bar, Gus left a couple of shillings for the young busboy bracing against the kitchen wall. The boy was anxious to cleanup it seemed.

Blanche could smell the acrid smell of excrement coming from 'Mister Warthog's' side of his one room flat. She had named him that because the man resembled what she thought one of those animals must behave like. He was a pig!

Since there was no window to look out of, Blanche made her way to the flimsy door which opened directly onto River Street. She was investigating the sounds she heard of many scraping feet against a cobblestoned surface!

About a hundred yards from the 'Warthog's' barely opened door, Blanche spotted a horrifying sight. Reverend Isaac Green with the help of his tight-assed little helper, were distributing printed drawings of her along with a wordy description of a kidnapped orphan girl named 'Blanche'.

Jolts of adrenalin sent the hunted woman into a fast flurry of evasive action! Without a second of hesitation, Blanche retreated back into Mister Warthog's flat and found with her hands the only lantern possessed by the sleeping swine.

She unscrewed the lantern's fuel top and sprinkled the contents over the comatose addict's body! Blanche filled her pipe with tobacco and then proceeded to wake the slob up with some exciting news!

"Good Morning! Wake up, sleepyhead! There is a man and his son standing on the back of a wagon just outside our door! They have come for you!

It is my understanding they wish to take you back to their farm way out in the country where you will be paid lots of money to look after their sheep! Oh please, take me with you! Don't leave me here alone!" pleaded the sociopathic young woman.

Slowly "Mister Warthog" arose from his soiled mattress and managed to stand up on his own two feet. He turned toward Blanche with honest tears rolling down his stubbled cheeks and delivered a short proclamation.

"Little one, since the minute I laid my eyes on you my life changed! Your kindness coupled with your loving touch has made me a new man! I would never leave you nor would I ever tender in my imagination anything close to forsaking you! I see this wonderful thing you describe standing outside as an omen, a message if you will, from heaven! It is a confirmation of God's grace upon us! With this grand opportunity gifted to us, let us rejoice! Hand in hand the couple we are, must now give thanks in unison to this great benefactor; please come with me. Let us experience as one, the rebirthing of our lives together!" sobbed Mister Warthog.

Blanche rushed into the slob's arms. She kissed him ever so sweetly on his kerosene sprinkled cheek while gently inserting the corncob pipe between his liver colored lips.

With a motherly kind of push, similar to that of a 'first day at school' nudge, Blanche softly whispered something consoling to the fat junkie just as she spun him around and playfully patted his behind. She then set Mister Warthog on fire!

Cato was the first to run toward the wheelhouse window when a flash followed by a faint boom, interrupted Captain Ogle's call to action meeting! He quickly multiplied in his head the number of seconds between the time he saw the flash and heard the explosion's report.

With a grim face, Cato turned to the 'Whydah's' captain and reverently bowed his head. With a building grin which erupted into laughter, Cato looked into Cal's eyes and joyfully exclaimed.

"Captain, the 'Thomas' is three miles away! Sir, may I remind you our guns must be within a half mile to be fully affective!" exclaimed Cato.

With that said, Ogle looked at his war hardened crew with a smile. He turned toward the direction Cato had pointed out. After a long pause, Chaloner Ogle walked back over to the meeting table and stopped.

Like a squared-off bulldog, the 'Whydah's' captain leaned forward with his fists balancing his entire torso on the table and spoke.

"We shall approach them head-on until we are within range! We'll unleash twenty cannons from our starboard side and then zigzag after our initial pass and finish the 'Thomas' off with our port guns! Cato will coordinate the munitions along with Selkirk and Maynard. Rainbow and Anne will set up in the crow's nest and pepper the 'Thomas' with sniper fire. Percy, you and Stanfield will man the mortar; use incinerating charges only! Kimber and Every will stay with me; they will serve as my runners and copilots. That's it, now let's get busy! We have less than two hours to sink the 'Thomas'!"

Ike's fancy-boy was the first to see the man on fire! He looked up at the Reverend who was busy speaking with the good folks of Oxfordshire or at least those who thought they had 'seen' Blanche within the last couple of days!

With a loud shrill, David, Sporck's fancy-boy yelled out a frightful warning that someone on fire was rushing toward their wagon! The blazing man was screaming out Sporck's name!

Ike grabbed a nearby blanket and snuffed out the flames by knocking the man to the ground and rolling him around like a hot potato. Realizing the blaze had scorched the addict's lungs, the lion head knew there was little time to pull out what he needed to know!

Blanche no doubt, was behind the dramatic diversion, Sporck reasoned. If the man died before he learned anything, the only option left would be to trace back to where Blanche had lit him up!

"Sir! Sir! You are now in the arms of a priest! I wish to pray for your soul! Is there anything you would like to get off of your chest before you meet your maker?" asked Reverend Isaac Green.

With shortening gasps, Blanche's victim looked up into Isaac's eyes and began speaking to the man of god as if nothing whatsoever had just happened to him! It sounded more like a child asking his father's permission to do something than a man answering the prompts offered by a 'priest' administering his last rites.

"So, when do I get to meet the sheep I'll be tending?" asked the burned man.

"And what sheep do you speak of, my Child?" probed Sporck. "The ones 'Little one' told me you wanted me to look after!"

Mister Warthog clearly said.

"Does this drawing look like 'Little one'?" Sporck shrieked.

"Yes! We're getting married as soon as we move onto your farm out in the wide-open spaces!" said the dying fat man.

"Where is your lovely bride-to-be at this very moment?" needled Ike.

"She's back at our flat packing of course!" weakly said Mister Warthog.

"Can you point to where you live?" harshly asked Sporck.

With a silly grin on his face, the lung gurgling man stood for only seconds before he collapsed back down to the ground. He then died.

Anton von Sporck had picked up Blanche's trail! There was no reason to go to where she had been holed up in because she'd be gone from there. Anyway, Ike planned to bushwhack his lover on her way toward the only place in the world she could go!

Benjamin Hornigold about jumped out of his skin when LaBuse's diversionary charge exploded a couple of hundred feet behind the 'Thomas'! Oliver grinned at his old captain when he noticed the shocked look on his face!

Their escape dinghy bobbed up and down from the explosion's rippling affect! Oliver LaBuse then explained to Hornigold exactly what he had done.

"Captain, I tampered with the charts enough so that Jemmy will groundout near Dewees Island! Hopefully, he will believe he has landed in Charlestown! Maybe we'll have enough time to get there first before the 'Whydah' strikes again!"

"Oh my god, Oliver, take a look behind you!" screamed Ben.

Jemmy glared at the two men feverishly trying to out race the 'Thomas' in the ship's emergency dinghy. His rage was apparent by the way he motioned to the slaves below him!

With the lion head fully in place and his crimson and purple robe blowing in the wind behind him, the angry Angolan raised his arms above his frizzy mane and began swearing in what sounded like Afrikaner. But no matter what language he was using, its message was quite clear all the same!

Jemmy intended on killing his last two prisoners even if it meant the total destruction of his own ship and everyone on it! Although the 'Whydah' was clearly in an attack mode and only a mile out, the lion head insisted his fellow Africans do whatever they could to dispatch the escaping 'white devils' before they made it to land!

Three aspiring young men each claiming they were good swimmers, approached the lion head timidly. Jemmy took off his head gear in order to hear what they were trying to say. There was a great deal of clamor being created by the pandemonium caused by the natives jumping around in the background!

"And how pray tell, can you boys help us get to those white rats out there?" queried Jemmy.

"My leader, if you will raise only the main sail and steer the 'Thomas' so that we can jump into the dinghy, we believe our knives will stop them! If we can't do it then we'll certainly die trying, sir!" said the tallest of the three boys.

Jemmy was stunned by the three slaves' extraordinary show of bravery. Their exemplary behavior seemed as though it brought the lion head back to the realization that he and every other living thing on board the 'Thomas' was about to die!

George Augustus was awakened by a light tap on his hotel room's door. He lit the lantern on his nightstand, adjusted his monocle to fit his good eye, cocked both of his pistols and placed his ear so as to detect any telltale sounds coming from the hallway.

Gus had definitely determined someone was standing outside of his room. They were waiting for him to open his door!

With a lightning fast movement, the British King tiptoed over to the window facing the Clarence's impressive entranceway and jumped two stories down into the hotel's rose garden. After an awkward but injury free landing, he scrambled to his feet and burst through the Clarence Hotel's front door in his bare feet and sprinted back up to his room's hallway!

An icepick protruded just a little to the left of Vinibal Baggott's spinal cord! He was still breathing but the breaths he did take were hard fought for!

Little bubbles popped up around the weapon's handle! Vinibal's lungs were filling with each articular pump. Every word the bartender tried to speak came at the cost of lessening his lifespan by a second!

"I should have seen it coming! Sporck uses children to do his venal work! Leave this place now! Go back to London and protect your family! He is coming for them!"

Gus shut Vinibal's eyes with his fore and middle fingers. He had seen a lot of men die during his lifetime but this one got to him!

The powerful man sat that night in the middle of the hallway holding a dead Englander! That internal rage had reignited. Only spilled blood would extinguish its blaze!

Blanche's tears offered her only seconds of relief as a northwesterly breeze swept through the grove of trees she was camped up in! From her lofty angle of sight, she could watch the roads.

The last of the 'warthog's' opium was gone. The gnawing effects of withdrawal had begun!

With serious care, the wicked teen started braiding cutout stripes of her britches and fashioned them into a rope. She had concluded that running was useless!

After tying one end of her four-foot strand to a sturdy branch above her and the other end around her neck, Blanche settled into the last crook of an elm tree. She then slit her wrist with the piece of glass she had used to make her noose.

With the first big spurt seen shooting from her left arm, Blanche went into shock! When she became unconscious, she surmised. Her fall would snap her neck!

It would be a remarkable suicide and one people would talk about for years, Blanche thought as her weakening state caused an unexpected drowsiness to overtake her. She fell asleep!

James Stanfield flashed a signal to Anne Bellamy who in turn relayed the message to the 'Whydah's' wheelhouse. Ogle then nodded to Cato who saluted the ship's captain before he climbed down into the gun room where Selkirk and Maynard were waiting.

The 'Whydah' shook when their first volley of starboard cannons sent out across a quarter of a mile of ocean a barrage of hot lead calibrated to splinter the 'Thomas' upon contact! Four additional sets of launches followed.

Ben Hornigold knew what the 'Whydah' must do! He had only a few seconds to say what he needed to say before his long overdue life was snuffed out!

Benjamin stopped rowing and stood straight up in the middle of the 'Thomas's' rescue dinghy and saluted Oliver LaBuse! What he was going to tell his old shipmate will never be known!

Jemmy could not believe what he was seeing! The 'Thomas' was engulfed in fire! The fifteen knot winds fanned the flames which had spread to the ship's unfurled sails. His crew had already jumped overboard.

Sniper fire prevented any form of defensive response from the 'Thomas'! Cannon balls kept passing through the ship's outer skin and exploding within its interior! Finally, the slaver began listing! The 'Thomas' was going down! Hightide was nearing.

On their ride back to Liverpool, David had learned a whole lot about America from the tales spun by Reverend Green! He was mostly interested in the stories about naked Indians, the ones with painted faces and bird feathers stuck in their hair!

Ike had promised his fancy boy a trip to the Colonies as soon as the lad passed his loyalty examinations! Those mentioned tests mainly focused upon David's ability to accomplish various missions designed to gage the child's intestinal fortitude!

The back and forth catapulting between his duty to England and the bitter revenge he intended to personally execute upon Sporck had exhausted him. Gus needed some time to think things out!

After putting some distance between him and the Clarence Hotel, King George drove his gravedigger's wagon to an old friend's place. He had not seen his school chum since their days back in Hanover.

Much of Thomas Newcomen's wealth had come from his father's mining interests but his notoriety among certain nefarious groups was earned through weaponry engineering! His brilliance was unmatched by any other military analyst in the world which was why the King was compelled to dig up some old roots!

"Well, aren't you a sight for sore eyes! How in the world are you, Gus?" softly exclaimed the frizzy-headed genius.

After embracing, Thomas waved to a girl sitting on his front steps and quietly whispered a request for her to move his friend's rig into the bunker behind the house! Obediently, she did as he asked.

"Tom, I'm a little concerned with your being able to help that little lady with her homework given the fact today's primary schools are teaching algebra to their young upstarts!" Gus said kiddingly as the two friends shuffled into Newcomen's underground abode.

"George, here I was sitting right there in the same place you are right now when one day about three months ago I guess, that precious little stray rode up here on her bicycle! I haven't the heart to turn her back onto the streets!

Besides, she's wonderful company and one hell of a good cook!" sheepishly said Thomas after winking at the King.

"Thomas, I am here on matters of grave importance to Britain! I desperately need your help!" pleaded Gus.

"Good god, George, what's wrong?" said the disturbed host.

"How long would it take you to pack up some things and come with me to London?" asked the regally toned King.

"Oh, two or three days, I guess." answered the confused scientist.

"Is it possible for you to leave now?" pushed George.

Due to a flicker of light or maybe due to Vinibal's dying words, George reacted as he did when he noticed Tom's adopted ragamuffin had a dagger hidden behind the pot of tea she was about to serve! He simply stood up from his chair withdrew his pistol and shot the little squatter right between her eyes!

When Thomas Newcomen saw the dropped dagger sticking up in the floor, he looked over at his old schoolmate with humbled resignation. Then with an adrenalin charged movement, Tom began throwing his belongings into a suitcase!

A few minutes later, George and Tom rolled down the driveway leaving behind a lit fuse connected to more than three hundred pounds of black powder! Needless to say, there was nothing evidentiary left behind.

CHAPTER 5

CHARLESTOWN

Major John Boone was abruptly awakened by the sound of his house servant's sharp knock on his bedroom's door. Ezekiel's voice was strained.

"Major, a message was just received from a ship about a mile out from our harbor!"

"Who aboard that ship sent the signal, Ezekiel?" sleepily asked John Boone.

"Sir, the sender did not identify himself with a name but he did sign-off his request to port with three numbers; seven, two, and six!"

"In that case, respond to the 'Whydah' with this being said, 'Enter the passageway between the Bull and Capers Islands. Pinckney Cove awaits. Will contact. Six-two-one.'"

Reverend Isaac Green snapped the reins on the backs of the horses pulling their covered wagon up Kempston Road's steepest grade. When they reached the summit, Isaac pulled his rig off at a spot often favored by Liverpool's sap full youth.

From the top of the hill the locals called "Prescote Mountain", Isaac was able to point out to David the astounding dock operations lining the city's chance at the Mersey River. While the lad was busy counting the number of ships docked a half mile below them, Sporck was glassing the smoldering pit which once supported the home belonging to Thomas Newcomen!

Ike had seen enough. With a sharp two-banger rap on top of David's crown and a reprimand for his dawdling, Reverend Green tied a rope around David's waist and forced the boy to run behind the wagon for the remaining six miles back to the All Saints' Church.

No sooner had Sporck jumped from his wagon and preparing to untie David when out of seemingly nowhere came a bloodcurdling scream followed by a loud thump! Looking up toward the window near the top of the church's turret, Isaac could see a blueish strand slapping upside the sandstone blocks.

Isaac walked to the edge of the rose garden which practically surrounded the All Saints' newly built alcove. He discovered at the end of a hemp rope the body of his chief security officer! The man had been gutted and then dropped from his study's window!

Sporck could hardly contain his fear! His security guards were nowhere to be seen. Someone was waiting for him inside, he suspected!

Sporting a grandfatherly smile, the panicking Reverend hurriedly untied David and swooped the lad up and onto the back of his wagon. They were about eye to eye when Sporck reached out and hugged David and began whispering his praises of him.

"David, you are so close now to becoming the youngest Sporckian to have ever lived! You have but one last test to fulfill before the little lion's head is mounted upon your shoulders! Are you ready, my Child?"

Jemmy and several others within sight had taken advantage of the shore directed currents and bits of the 'Thomas's' debris. Except for an occasional renegade shark, only fatigue offered a diminishment to the slaves' hopes.

A distant grove of trees offered a chance for them to make it to land on their flotation devices. None of them could swim because of the dangers learned from their mothers' mouths. Anacondas and crocodiles get a bunch of babies along the river banks in Africa!

When Jemmy's men could touch the bottom with their feet they mustered up enough gumption to walk ashore. Thirty-two of them had survived.

Bentley Connery was the district of Oxfordshire's warden. He had been tipped off by some nearby farmers there had been a lot of afterhours poaching going on in the King's forest. There was a full moon that night.

While Warden Connery was setting up the furry decoy intended to be the star of that evening's sting operation, he noticed a woman's body hanging from the top of a tree! Racing to the base of that tree, the King's steward frantically began climbing to the branch where Blanche's cloth rope was attached! Her face was blue.

By tying a bowline under Blanche's arm pits and throwing the other end of his rope over a higher limp, Bentley was able to cut the taught noose with his knife. He then lowered the tiny woman's body to the ground.

Because of the looks of things, there wasn't much point in hurrying the warden thought. He leaned over to see if he could hear any kind of heartbeat. He did!

With incredible endurance, the official swept Blanche up in his arms and carried her to Doctor Thomas Carter's residence. Luckily, he was at home.

"Doc, I cut this girl out of the top of a tree back over near the old Swift's place! I didn't think she was alive until I felt she had a pulse! Do you think you can help her?" asked the stressed warden.

Suddenly, Doctor Carter changed into anything but the mild-mannered gentleman he was reputed to be. The physician jerked Blanche out of Warden Connery's arms and threw her onto his kitchen table and began violently pounding on the young woman's chest!

With still no sign of life, the lone surgeon reached over to his butchers' block and unstuck a meat cleaver. After one sternum splitting whack, Thomas Carter had Blanche's heart in his hands! A minute later, it started beating!

Mary Read hid in Sporck's study's fireplace! Her crossbow was cocked and ready for Ike's appearance. Three extra bolts were by the assassin's side!

When David crept into her weapon's peep sight, Mary released a deadly arrow! Curiously she approached the downed lad with catlike movements. Read now had dead bait!

George Whitefield stood against a lamppost located at the western entrance of the St. Michael's Churchyard. He lit a long white pipe filled with tobacco. He let the fire from his stick match begin to burn his fingers before he blew it out. It was a signal.

Standing at the entranceway to the "George and Vulture Tavern" was a stocky gentleman who too lit a similar pipe and also tempted a finger burn before blowing out his flame. His name was Captain George Anson.

After an unheard swap of hand signals, the two indiscreetly dressed gentlemen entered the tavern as though they were already pretty deep into their cups. Whitefield was the first to blurt out a typically drunken remark.

"Who in bloody hell do I talk to about shutting that goddamned bird up?" sloppily yelled the British agent.

"Sir, that depends on whether you like your carrion aged or on the half shell?" retorted the bartender.

Captain Anson stepped forward and put both of his elbows on the bar while balancing a boiled egg between his two forefingers. The ship captain then looked up at the burley looking barkeep and answered his question.

"I have the buzzard egg!"

The tavern doors and windows were then slammed shut! The establishment's lighting was snuffed out!

Not a sound could be heard from the outside street! It was as though the place had closed for the night.

A single candle was placed on the center of a small table. Both Anson and Whitefield were seated so close to the flame it made it impossible to see the group of men facing them. The gruff voice of an older man broke the silence.

"'Operation Cricket' has begun! The 'Centurion' will sail in seventy-two hours!

Needless to say, Gentlemen, you must give no indication of your leaving either in body or spirit! No wills are to be written nor are you to deliver any farewell addresses to those of whom you know!

Should this mission be compromised our lives along with hundreds of others will abruptly cease! The Sporckians have launched a biological attack on the Colonies!

We in turn have sent one of our own ships after them! We must wait to hear of the outcome. Hopefully we'll get good news by summer's end.

Before we part, let me say just how proud I am to have you brave men stand beside of me! Although our acts will never be registered in the history books, England's next generation will stand in silent testament of your courageous deeds! Thank you," proclaimed the mysterious voice.

With the meeting now over, the lights came back on, the doors and windows reopened and the caged vulture began squawking again. The two Georges', Anson and Whitefield, pretended to stagger as they confusedly navigated down Cornhill Avenue.

In a very low grunt, Captain Anson bid George Whitefield a pleasant evening before turning down his apartment's street. Whitefield then stopped to help a boy with the kickstand on his bicycle!

George Whitefield was shocked when the King stopped his gravedigger's truck in the middle of Cornhill Avenue and shot the young cyclist in the back of his head! King George then offered a comforting smile to Reverend Whitefield as he rode off.

Whitefield an evangelical minister, fell upon his knees beside the very dead boy! An out of place whistling sound echoed off of St. Michael's cathedral walls reminding the holy man of the realities at hand. He then disappeared into the night.

Jemmy was awakened by the feel of little hands going through his pockets! After checking out the size of his intruder's bare feet, the slave leader rolled over and began chasing the Gullah boy on his hands and knees while growling like a rabid bear!

The entire village of tree-dwellers assisted the remainder of Jemmy's men from the beach and hid them from the slave snatcher's telescopes. Since the Gullahs were runaways themselves, there was no need for additional information. Skin color did that anyway!

After firing one of the two pistols David had been instructed to use, Mary placed a couple of pillows in one of Sporck's highbacked chairs so the dead boy would appear to be standing by the study's window! Agent four-two-eight began communicating with Sporck as if David were the triumphant orator.

"Ike, I got him!" said Mary using her best childlike voice.

"Was there more than one of them?" asked the suspicious lion head.

"No, sir, just the one who was waiting for you but I surprised him! He wasn't expecting a kid! That's when I shot the guy!" hoorayed Mary.

Sporck never answered.

Dressed as a nun, Mary left the All Saints' Church. The British agent left her calling card clinched within David's jaws! It was Queen Caroline's wedding ring!

David and John Deas had heard from some of the county's plantation owners there was some trouble brewing amongst the slaves just north of Charlestown. Rumor had it, the Gullahs were holing up Jemmy's 'exacerbators' on Bull Island!

Talk of an uprising choked out the usual gossip circulation which typically traveled daily up and down the southern coastline. Rather than the normal chattering swapped within the local taverns, conversations shifted to discussions involving words such as 'fences' and 'handguns'! The whites were frightened!

The Deas brothers wasted no time in getting the latest scoop to one of their best customers, Major John Boone. Their wagon almost skidded into a washed-out ditch as the twins hammered the backs of their horse team between the stone pillars ensconcing the entranceway into the Boone Hall Plantation.

From Jemmy's perspective, the Boone place would offer the ideal headquarters for him and his warriors! Plus, the 'Whydah' once overtaken, would make for a sweet escape vehicle as well as the perfect invasion craft for what was to come!

The bamboo wind chimes rattled like a forgotten cadaver! It was almost dark and seven hundred pounds of corn had to be moved into the storage bin before the squalls began!

Already the Stono River had dropped its depth by three feet. Tidal waves would surely come as a result of the Atlantic's windup. If that happened thought Sandra Hutchinson, the bonfires would be drowned out!

So many good people had died as a result of what the local authorities were calling a "grippe" epidemic. It wasn't that at all!

Sandra knew it was a full-blown outbreak of the bubonic plague!

So many of the dead had to be burned!

Just as widow Hutchison and her son Tad, were latching down their storm shutters a man rode up to their front porch. He was the gentleman living two farms south of them.

Maxwell McRae practically jumped off of his stallion before the sweaty animal even had time to slow up! Tad ran up to his neighbor in order to help him with his sweat slickened horse. The fourteen- year-old boy was taken back by the unusual abruptness in which Mister McRae greeted him!

"Here, son, take these damn reins! Keep your mind on what you're doing or that devil will get away from you! Where is your mother? I need to speak with her at once!"

Feeling something was dreadfully wrong, Sandra stepped down from the porch and rushed towards her son and the out of breath McRae.

"Why hello there, Max! What brings you way out here on this stormy Saturday night?" said the widow.

"Sandra, as much as I wish this was a social call, I am afraid I have some very bad news! There has been an uprising!" exclaimed Maxwell McRae.

"An uprising, Mister McRae?" calmly queried Tad's mother.

"The Sheriff tells me that close to a hundred of those Gullahs have already overrun a couple of plantations up the Awendaw way! We don't know to what extent the families have been affected. My guess is that being harvest time and all, those niggers will have wiped out about all the Marions living up there by now!" huffed McRae.

"What do you recommend we do, Maxwell?" asked Sandra Hutchins.

"I'd say it'd be best for you and Tad to come with me to Boone Hall! The Major is pulling together a bunch of men; that is, if he can find enough that ain't sick!" muttered Mister McRae.

Sandra didn't make a sound as McRae remounted his freshly watered mount.

"Your boy looks to me like he's stout enough to shoot a musket! He could be a big help, Mrs. Hutchinson!

It won't take more than a half hour to pack ya'll up and I'd be honored to escort you there myself!" said Maxwell.

"Thank you just the same, Mister McRae! I believe we'll be safe for the time being. I wouldn't expect anyone with half a brain to be out pillaging on a night like this one!

Kindly inform Major Boone that Tad and I will ride over there after church tomorrow. Tell Kitty I'll bring the drapery materials she ordered last June. They just came in on Thursday!" said Sandra.

Elizabeth Boone and her husband John, were renowned for their 'fist to cuff' altercations! Considering her house was turned upside down due to Charlestown's recent misfortunes and the fact that armed men were coming in and out of her plantation like red ants, "Kitty" felt justified in slapping her husband upside his head with a good-sized piece of firewood!

In that the Deas brothers were still seated at their dinner table when all of that happened, Major Boone restrained himself from decking her! Wisely, he ignored his wife's abreaction by continuing his comments regarding the use of those proficient at shooting a rifle!

But when the Boone's grandsons, John's and Edward's names were 'thrown into the hat' to stand guard at the fort, all hell broke loose! It took both the Deas brothers to stop Kitty Boone from setting her own house on fire!

Hearing that her grandchildren might be exposed danger was apparently what pushed the woman to the brink of psychosis. In less than a minute, the petite aristocrat had managed to break every piece of glass including the lanterns in the dining room with the same piece of kindling she used on her husband!

After the better part of an hour and a good rope, the men were able to subdue Elizabeth enough to get her down to Miss Cyrus's shanty! The old slave woman had been part of the plantation since the turn of the century.

Miss Cyrus was a dyed in the wool medicine woman. Taking Mrs. Boone down to see her made all the sense in the world!

Maxwell McRae turned toward the Deas boys and Major Boone with shear panic brimming from his eyes! Despite his hiccups, he struggled to say what needed to be said.

"Gentlemen, from my count, we have near about twenty able men including the four of us, to stop this goddamned 'revolt' from spreading! With most of the roads flooded, our options are limited! If what the Sheriff heard was accurate, the Marions' out on Bull's Pointe were hit by a band of Gullahs last night! It is believed their only weapons were primitive one's at best! I feel that now is the time to attack them! We can't afford for those jackals to get their hands on some guns!" roared McRae.

Doctor Thomas Carter had not slept much over the past few days! Blanche's chest incision had become infected. But that wasn't what had caused him to lose sleep!

His ruminations were partially prompted by the conclusions drawn from his examination of her! Yes, the girl's needle-tracks were of some concern but Thomas's ultimate worry stemmed from Blanche's ambivalence regarding her condition!

The girl didn't seem to care about much of anything! Her reaction to pain was never evident and she neither laughed nor cried! Blanche was emotionally flatlined concluded Doctor Carter.

Warden Connery also had some difficulty sleeping but not because of medical concerns. The girl he had cut down from the tree was a 'dead-ringer' of the person depicted as being Caroline's murderer! The similarities were beyond the scope of coincidence!

Due to those uncanny similarities, the Warden decided to drive over to Doctor Carter's house to arrest Blanche. Taking with him the Constable and two of his deputies, they arrived at the physician's home just before sunrise. Bentley knocked on the doctor's door.

"Good morning, Bent! What brings you out here in the country this rainy day?" greeted Doctor Carter.

"Well, sir, I'm afraid I must pick that girl we rescued up for questioning! She fits the posters the King has scattered throughout England. Personally doc, I'm pretty damn sure that young woman is the person wanted for killing the Queen!" said Warden Connery.

"I regret to break the bad news to you, Warden, but that poor little thing died not long after you brought her by! I'm afraid that for whatever reason, her desire to die overpowered her will to live! Because of some findings discovered during her postmortem examination, I deemed it necessary to incinerate her body! It is possible the woman had chickenpox; therefore, it seemed prudent to purge her remains! I shall file my medical report with the Coroner's office as soon as this rain eases up! With this gloomy weather we've been having, I have unfortunately had my hands full! Bent, have you been feeling rather peeked lately? Why don't you step into my office for a little bit! Let's get you inoculated right away!" said Thomas Carter.

"Inoculated?" asked the Warden.

"It's a precautionary step administered to ensure your continued good health, Mister Connery! Although quite painful, the measurable effects of the 'shot' have proven quite successful in thwarting the chicken pox from breaking out among the herds of beef cattle already tested!" lied the doctor.

"Wait a minute, Doctor Carter, ain't that inoculator shot thing for farm animals?" fearfully asked Connery.

"Well, yes, but it's better to be safe than sorry. don't you agree, Mister Connery?" toyed Carter.

All of a sudden, the Warden was reminded of a pressing matter awaiting him back in the city! He and his three cohorts wasted no more time with idle chitchat. They rode off with the confidence that once again, justice had prevailed!

Once Warden Connery, Constable Higgins and his two deputies had departed, Thomas Carter returned to the room where Blanche had been so hurriedly stashed. Blanche was gone and so were his pain medications!

Seven days had passed and still no word of Jemmy or his men! It was hoped they had contracted the black-death!

Sometime after two-thirty in the morning, Captain Ogle entered the crews' sleeping quarters and awakened them with slight nudges.

"Cato just received a signal from Major Boone. It is a call for help! It appears our old friend Jemmy made it to land!

Boone reports that about thirty of the local Gullahs joined in with Jemmy's gang and attacked a settlement about six miles north of here! No word yet on the number of deaths!

We are to join up with the Major within the hour! This will be a ground action so pack accordingly. There'll be plenty of rain so make sure your loads are water tight. We'll depart in thirty minutes." Cooley said Ogle.

Tad had just latched the barn doors together when he heard his mother call for him. He knew something was wrong! Pretending as if he did not hear her, he reopened the barn doors as if he were going back inside.

As soon as Tad got to the spot where he could watch his house without anyone seeing him do it, he carefully peeked out at his home's windows. What he could see despite the heavy sheets of rain were the torsos of negroes torching the inside of his living room!

Caught in a schism that no boy should ever be exposed to, Tad had to make that proverbial 'fight or flight' decision! Remembering McRae's summation of the uprising around Bull Island, he figured his mom was already dead!

Next, they would come to the barn and then to the store. They'd be after guns, powder and liquor, he figured. Attempting to burn the place down before they got to it would be utterly suicidal.

Tad had only seconds to conquer the anathema. He then grabbed a pitchfork before mounting the store's delivery horse and charged out of the Hutchinson barn holding the farm tool as if it were a lance!

Jemmy and two others noticed the movement and ran outside to prevent the horseman's escape! Tad jabbed one of them in the neck but lost his weapon in the melee, divvying out to him one last option!

With all of the strength left in his body, the Hutchinson boy held on to the neck of his panicked animal and then drove the beast into his attackers! Tad intended on the beast's crushing hooves to open up a pathway to freedom! Fate sadly construed the variables differently.

Jemmy had seen that maneuver before! With the alacrity of a puma, the lion head reared back and released his spear at the distancing rider! His throw was good!

Not quite sure of exactly what had happened, Tad's reaction was to ignore the flapping spear handle! Two hundred feet later, the kid fell off of the delivery animal. He lived long enough to witness his horse's unencumbered escape into the stormy abyss.

All Sporck had going for him was money! His cover had been blown, Blanche had seen to that! His only choice was to leave Britain!

His goal was to reach America undetected. In order to do that Anton von Sporck would have to take on someone else's identity!

Drawing from his knowledge of human nature, Ike searched for someone who had a burning desire to fulfill some celestially inspired quest! This person would have to be an individual without the means to carry out his lust for that badly needed fame! Sporck had to locate a person willing to exchange his soul for it!

Anton Sporck disguised as a blindman, set out to find an evangelist who believed in the miraculous power of prayer! Such a person purported to fit Ike's twisted profile did exist and happened to be concluding a weeklong 'tent meeting' in Liverpool the very next day!

A dense fog had crept in off the Mersey River overnight. This made Sporck's wardrobe selection an almost effortless task to fulfil.

There was nothing more to it than coming up behind a man of about his size, slipping a wire strand around the unsuspecting fellow's neck and then dragging his body off the sidewalk!

By eight o'clock the now 'Mr. Smith', had transformed himself into a pitiful looking vagabond. Using the bundle of pencils, he had found in the pocket of his victim, Sporck proceeded to immolate a blind pencil salesman!

Setting himself up just a stone's throw from the revival tent's entrance offered an immense number of opportunities for the entering Christians to show their real colors.

Ike found a box to sit on and a jar to hold his wares in. He waited for their arrival.

Written on a colorfully backgrounded piece of slate, the name John Wesley appeared about six inches above his sermon's title, 'Of Evil Angels'. When Sporck saw there was a cost for admission, he knew he had found his mark!

Maybe it was Wesley's tone of voice or perhaps it was in his vivacious mannerisms captivating the congregation's attention but nonetheless, mass swooning became commonplace! No doubt about it, there was "Hell" and "Damnations" being laid down that morning up on Beacon Hill!

Wearing a soot covered pair of spectacles and smacking a red- tipped cane in front of him, Sporck made his way through the congregation toward the arm swinging preacher! As the blind beggar passed by, folks whispered to one another in hopes some self- described dignity might be gained by the use of consensual scorn!

Just as the sweat drenched evangelist was summing up his well plotted remarks, he noticed a shabbily dressed man standing directly below his pulpit! After calling for his staff officer to remove the derelict from the premises, John Wesley happened to notice the disheveled vagrant was trying to hand him a note!

With an air of condescension, the silver tonged reverend grabbed the message from Sporck's hand. After a quick scan and then followed by a much closer read, the Methodist raised his arms high into the air! God, he thought, had finally answered his prayers!

Wesley's musicians were given the que to fire up the revivalists!

They needed to know that a miracle was about to happen!

Pretending he had been jolted by an epiphany, John Wesley sprang to his feet in such a manner it caused a few of the kids in the audience to pee in their britches! It was surely something to witness!

The minister shifted his demeanor to one of a 'meek lamb of God'. He held the Bible to his forehead and began reciting a verse which would lead up to his introduction of the sightless "Mister Smith"!

"'We wrestle not against flesh and blood, but against principalities, against powers, against the rulers of the darkness of this world, against wicked spirits in heavenly places.' But I must ask you this my brothers and sisters, how can we save those of us who have dropped below our such lofty standards?

How can we as pedigree Christians, turn our backs to even the wretch whom lost his way? Even the recidivists, those that have basked in sin for years, realize that there is a time to apologize! A time to be forgiven....

I say to each of you, listen to such a Man! Pay close attention to the message he brings to you; fore, he was afflicted by those wicked spirits, those curvy harlots along with all of the temptations coming from down under! Hear how God punished him for his iniquities!

Folks, please welcome into our canvas sanctuary one who admittedly has broken every single Commandment handed down to Moses! A fool who paid with his sight, just to lay eyes on the "Devil" himself! I present to you, "Mister Smith!"

It took several able-bodied men to help Sporck up to the pulpit. The only props he carried up there with him were his red tipped cane, his sooty glasses and a clay jar with some unsold pencils sticking out of it.

By jutting his chin out a little up and slightly to the left, the lion head indelibly branded in the minds of his onlookers that he was indeed a fallen angel! Next, he intended to further hoodwink them by performing a little magic show!

But before that, Ike needed to disarm his audience with a good slathering of guilt! After fumbling around a bit while pretending to have difficulties finding a place to put his cane, he began.

"This morning I completed my pilgrimage to this place known as, 'The Beacon'! It has been a long journey, my Friends!

But before I say what I so deeply feel in my heart, I would like to say thank you for the kindnesses shown to me! Your generosities are but a mere reflection of your inner goodness but I cannot accept your gifts of gold!

All I want from you is your forgiveness! I shall return your offerings when I am done! Could we bow our heads please?" smoothly said Ike.

John Wesley was beginning to get a little antsy. Mister Smith's appearance was not turning toward the direction in which it was supposed to be headed! After all, Sporck's note had promised a tenfold return while at the same time, the penniless blindman had vowed to return a nonexistent offering back to a group of people of which had purchased not one single pencil from him!

Wesley stood and then walked up behind the blind orator and gently tapped him on his shoulder!

"Mister Smith, there seems to be a misunderst…" whispered John.

Angrily snapping his glasses off of his face, Sporck wheeled around and put his mouth a gnat's wing away from Wesley's ear. He whispered.

"Listen, Son, you've been pole-vaulting over 'pounds for pennies' long enough! Unless you intend on remaining a two-bit Bible thumper, I would suggest you piously return your ass back down to your chair and watch a real master do his work!" screeched Mister Smith.

Sporck began to pray.

"I lay bare before you the darkest areas of my life! I give you the things which I have done wrong and the areas where I have failed to act as I should! I never wish to live that way again!

Right now, I have chosen to turn away from everything I know to be wrong about my life! I ask for your forgiveness!

As I kneel before you in adoration, I pray that you will pluck the stinger from my sin ravaged flesh and suave the pain caused by my shameful wickedness! Amen.

To those of you that accepted me and the righteous ones who embraced me with your offerings, allow me to return to you an even more valuable gift! For you see, unbeknownst to you, I, but for a shadow of a second have entered into the body of the retched blindman introduced to you as, "Mister Smith"! I am not whom I appear to be!

Therefore, as my Father has empowered me to do, I shall return your alms to the degree that could only reflect God's love and the countenance he so greatly has bestowed upon you! So, in his words I say unto you, 'he that have rendered unto the poor, shall receive a great prize'!" explosively stated Ike.

It was astonishing to watch the audience's collective eyes as Sporck turned upside down his pencil jar and twelve 'doubloons' clattered onto the stage floor! Gasps could be heard throughout the canvas walls!

John Wesley then joined the loudly clapping congregation! The drums started tapping, the tent flaps were shut and candles were cheerfully doled out!

Sporck then prepared to set his hook. He again spoke.

"I shall now spread these earthly goods before you! For any man, woman, or child who 'gave to me', let that person pass by and collect their due! If you did not, well then, maybe the Lord is giving you a second chance to do the right thing!" harped the imposter.

As the last congregate was leaving the revival tent, John Wesley looked over at Mister Smith with an admiring grin on his face. Pole-vaulting was on his mind.

Sporck smiled back at the fidgety young minister thus blowing his blindman charade. Then with the coolness of a victorious matador, he separated with his bare toe that Sunday morning's take.

After the dozens of Spork's elephant headed coins were moved to the side, what remained took Wesley's breath away! In less than fifteen minutes, Mister Smith had amassed in two equal piles, more money than the entire revival had levied over the whole week!

Below, a cacophony of the city's church bells announced the noon hour. Ike and Wesley loaded the last of the stage boxes onto the back of John's wagon. A pair of mules were harnessed and waiting.

This was the moment Sporck had been waiting for. Time was now of the essence!

"Mister Wesley, I am sure that you were handpicked by God to do something prolific! I mean that, John.

Here's what I'm getting at, Son, you're wasting your time on this side of the pond!" said Sporck in a fatherly fashion.

"What's wrong with England? They're plenty of sinners here!" teasingly mused John.

"Because what you're selling over here ain't being bought!" said Sporck with an air of arrogance in his silky voice.

"That's preposterous! You saw the crowd of folks I brought in, didn't you?" cried Wesley.

"Yes, John, I saw all twenty-three of them!" Mockingly commented Anton.

"Please then, tell me why my meetings aren't in fashion?" Squealed John Wesley.

"First and foremost, you aren't preaching the Anglican message! Secondly, the messages you do send out to your 'following' are counterintuitive of the norm! They are revolutionary in tone, Sir!

And finally, if you'll move your roadshow to America, I can assure you you'd be able to brand your name into the minds of every man, woman and child from New York down to Savannah! I'll even pay for it!" hollered Ike.

John Wesley seemed to freeze in place when he heard Mister Smith's grandiose offer! The young minister then pushed the bill of his hat back so no shadow would interfere with the eye contact between he and Sporck.

John smiled as he removed his work gloves. After a brotherly hug, John stepped back to an arms-length's distance and meekly whispered.

"Mister Smith, it is ironic that twice this week someone has offered to pay for my ministry's relocation to America! Why all of a sudden, do you suppose my little tent game as you would call it, has become so worthy of these grand proposals?" said Wesley.

Anxious to know who the other benefactor was but at the same time not wanting to tip John off about his curiosity, Sporck playfully grinned, scratched the road with his counting toe and looked up at the exiting minister and softly spoke.

"Who, other than I, could offer you more?"

"The King of England!" answered John.

"Well, you got me there, Mister Wesley! I suspect that ole King George must have attended one of your revivals then?" Responded the still reeling Mister Smith.

"No, actually my partner, George Whitefield landed that whale for us! Oh, it's not a permanent thing, just a three-month gig that's all! It seems you aren't the only one who believes the Colonies are ripe for saving, Mister Smith!" remarked John.

John Wesley had driven his wagon about a hundred feet up the road when he realized Sporck was running after him at a breakneck speed!

"Hey, Reverend, you forgot your gloves! You'll need them where you're going!" yelled Ike.

"Thanks! But I understand we're going to be mostly ministering to the plantation owners! Hopefully, the heaviest thing we'll be lifting is a Communion chalice!" said Wesley.

"Are you leaving midsummer?" asked Sporck.

"Mister Smith, I'll be at sea in three days!" John said as he waved a hardy farewell.

James Wolfe had rubbed salt all over the boiled egg he was attempting to hold between his two fingers. He would need to master that miniature skill in short order. He'd be doing it for real in the next little while!

The tavern's barmaid without even being asked, refilled the marine's empty mug for the third time. On several occasions she attempted to pull the recuperating young man out of his funk. She peppered him with nun-choking jokes but it never seemed to brighten him up in the least little bit.

A cannon recoil had shattered his left elbow leaving him in a place he despised being, land! The training accident had also cost him a shot at a big opportunity!

Instead of him commanding the 'Centurion', Anson got the job! It really meant King George would more than likely promote George Anson to an Admirals' ranking before him! That's why he was drinking.

As the night drummed onward and the ale began slipping into his gullet like sweet tea, Wolfe noticed a remarkably well-dressed woman staring at him. The mishap with the smashed elbow didn't seem quite so important anymore!

After an agonizing five minutes of playing the 'talking eyes' game, James finally mustered up enough courage to approach his pheromone emitting admirer. It would be erroneous to assume however that James's introduction to Blanche went flawlessly well; because, it did not!

The inebriated sailor hadn't gotten more than three steps into his approach toward the woman when his legs buckled beneath him! Vomiting followed.

Seeing her suitor's predicament, Blanche leaped from her stool and ran over to the naval officer. With soothing words like those coming from a caring human being, she got the boy to finally open up his eyes!

"Well, aren't you a mess! Somebody's not taking very good care of you! Let's see if a real woman can't do a better job!" whispered Blanche.

"You remind me of an angel! What is your name?" asked the sputum faced Wolfe.

"I am the lady you have been searching for your whole life! My last name I hope will soon be the same as yours, but you can call me 'Blanche'!" stated the smiling protagonist as she motioned for the barmaid to have the man taken to her room!

Blanche had learned that lightning-fast strikes were far more effective than the schmoozing approach! Take her room acquisition for an example, Mister and Mrs. Limerick had checked into their hotel suite two days ago, died the next day, which now provided her with a perfect place to operate from!

The drunken soldier represented in Blanche's mind passage to America! How she got there was now dependent on Mister Wolfe's tolerance of Doctor Carter's medications!

Mister and Mrs. Limerick had developed an unpleasant smell! Even though the two were set up in chairs way out on the suite's veranda, their odor was unmistakably that of a dead person's!

She hadn't planned for Captain Wolfe's arrival; otherwise, she would have already had their bodies long gone. For now, she would just have to leave them out there on the porch appearing to be playing cribbage. She'd be gone by the morning anyway!

John Deas had spent an enormous amount of time chopping his way into the front door! A live oak's roots had been loosened by the recent flood currents and then blown over onto his and his brother's office. A lot of their business records were soaked!

The black armbands worn by the masked city workers signified they were the 'Body Collectors'. Four of them had stopped their wagon directly in front of a neighbor's home. Sadly, everyone knew why!

Out of respect for the Twiggs family's misfortune, David walked over to the city's rubbish truck to get the latest fatality numbers.

"Three hundred and fifty-one so far!" said one of the collectors.

Suddenly, John called for help! Fooling around with downed trees can be a most dangerous undertaking.

When David got to his brother it was too late! Jemmy and his band of forty or so painted up natives had already beheaded John! Their evil work continued.

Mary Read had watched the whole thing. She was even a little awestruck by Sporck's blindman performance! Mary sort of admired him in a twisted sort of way.

She elected to stay on his tail instead of killing him right off! With the overheard comments between him and John Wesley, it made better sense to stick with this unfurling mystery than it did to kill the main character before finding out who the real villains were!

Before Mary left for London, she stopped off at the local constable's office to send an encrypted message to King George. Addressed to the "Whittingham Haberdashery", the agent stated that she would catch up with them in Charlestown.

"It will be on the King's desk by morning!" swore the official carrier.

"Thank you, Sheriff! What you have in that pouch, Sir, are two rubies which were thought to have been forever lost! They were jiggled out of the Queen's crown during her murder! King George will be grateful for their return!" spoke the pan faced woman.

John Boone was sitting at the head of the empty dining table when a knock on the front door made him dive to the floor! He immediately blew out the lantern, cocked his blunderbuss and then waited in silence for the 'coded' response.

"The Sea Buzzards have arrived!" said Cato from outside on the porch.

Major John Boone opened the reinforced door allowing the 'Whydah's' crew to file into his massive dining room! Commander Ogle lit a candle and softly began speaking.

"'Operation Cricket' has now passed through its first phase! The 'Centurion' will arrive in fifteen days. Phase two will then commence!

For now, we're going to have to clean up this Jemmy mess! He's quite the cagey one and a dangerous force to reckon with no doubt about it but I am sure with Major Boone's guidance, we can exterminate Jemmy and his boys in quick order! Your thoughts, Major?" stated Ogle.

Still under the dim effect of Ogle's single candle, Boone briskly unfolded a hand drawn map of the Charlestown coastline. With his forefinger he pointed to the spot where he suspected the negroes had last attacked, the Hutchinson's store! Cato then asked a question.

"John, have they been able to get their hands on any guns?"

"None that I know of except for those they might have gotten from the Marion raids. And maybe three or four rifles from the Hutchinson's but it's hard to say for sure." Said Major Boone.

"So, how much time passed between Jemmy's raid on the Marion properties and the supposed attack at the Hutchinson's store?" Cato pressed.

"I would guess, no more than a day and a half!" Responded John.

Cato glanced over at Chaloner Ogle with a sneer on his face. He then turned back toward Major Boone and asked him one more question.

"How many horses do you have in your stables?"

"About thirty, why?" asked the confused Major.

"Because Jemmy and his animal heads more than likely have already surrounded us! Commander Ogle, I suggest we exit with a two directional assault at once!"

Without waiting for Ogle's response, Major Boone loudly called for Ezekiel to saddle up the horses. The servant did not answer.

Then as if their clothes were on fire, each person in the Boone's dining room that night charged out of the house waving their readied weapons and screaming like wild men! Jemmy's soldiers weren't out there.

Gratefully, Ezekiel had already managed to have most of the saddles situated by the time everyone had regrouped in front of the stables. Commander Ogle's orders were as parsimonious as they could be!

There were to be no prisoners! Jonn Kimber's group was to advance northward while Cato's team was to seal off the bottom half of the city! None were to return to Boone Hall defeated; it was just that simple!

At the southern tip of the thirty acres of London's docking network there is a rather inconspicuous canal connecting the Wapping Basin to the Thames River. It was there that the second phase of operation 'Cricket' was to get underway.

The 'Centurion' appeared to lurch as sharp easterly winds offered to push the warship out to sea! Tobacco Dock was to be the spot where the King's specialists would depart from but it would take another day to load up their supplies.

Gus nervously rolled a boiled egg between his left hand's thumb and forefinger. He was tempted to take a couple of swigs from the jug beneath his wagon's seat.

After a miniscule inner argument, the King elected to settle his internal debate by ladling only one gulp down his throat. It seemed like a fair compromise to him.

Augustus knew he was all alone on this operation! England's political climate was a cesspool!

France, Spain, Portugal and Austria all wanted a piece of the Colonial pie! Twisted contracts, miswritten peace agreements, hired assassins every bit of which were nothing more than symptoms of those countries' greed!

Handshakes, nods of acceptance, or even an honest answer were becoming artifacts of days gone by! These were the cynicisms scraping through the King's mind as he waited for his last chance to do something to thwart the world's collision course!

'Operation Cricket' was the Earth's opportunity to save itself! America, because of its virginity would be the most ideal spot on the planet to set up the headquarters for his governmental operation! World order would be its objective!

But first, America needed to become a level playing field! That was why this particular mission had to be! It would purge the Colonies of any metastasizing influences which had seeped into the fledgling nation's governmental formation!

Tomorrow, George thought, would begin the largest 'brain drain' in European history! The 'Centurion's' passengers would find their 'gifts' well received in a land where the people were hungry for what the 'scientists' had to teach them!

In Gus's new world, tradition would take a backseat to new inventions! It was to be the perfect incubator for the hatching of an international renaissance!

This was the once in a millennium's opportunity for the world to resynchronize itself! When wisdom did take hold and learning new ways to solve problems found eager minds awaiting, then and only then would mankind survive!

Gus was jarred awake by a clap of thunder! He had either kicked over his jug of scotch or he had drunk it, he didn't remember. But one thing for sure, whether it was a dream or not, he was bloody positive about his commitment to ensure the future of the planet! Tomorrow had come.

Blanche had fashioned a teaspoon into a heating dish. The silver utensil was bent into an 's' shape so it would stand up a little above the candle's flame. A gram of Doctor Carter's water-dissolved poppy powder began to bubble!

After sucking up the tepid fluid through a tiny ball of cotton, Blanche injected three quarters of the syringe's contents into her thigh. Captain Wolfe got the remainder.

Both had reached that certain point in which their insides had become warm. When their minds began whirling around, Blanche went to work on him!

Twice, there had been complaints about the noise coming from the 'Limerick's' room. Loud moans of promised allegiance even matrimony, bellowed down the hallways!

Acrid smells of which were a cross between soured milk and burning pine needles, escaped into other rooms! People began to talk and then they surmised.

Even the folks from across the street started to wonder how the Limerick's could play a board game without light! Torches were lit when curiosity got the best of them! A mob formed.

Having learned of where the King would be, Blanche very gently untied Captain Wolfe's legs and his good arm from the bed posts. After a thorough looking over, Blanche gathered the hotel room's oil lamps and placed them beside the odorous Limerick's ankles!

An oil drenched bed sheet was then thrown over the card playing duo! A match was struck! Blanche and Wolfe left for Tobacco Dock! Jemmy now had nine rifles and plenty of ammunition! He knew the crew aboard the 'Whydah' would join up with the other whites at Boone Hall!

Because Jemmy wasn't sure where he and his men actually were, the Angolan led his warriors up toward the mouth of the Stono River. That was the right decision to make for two reasons.

The first being, it was thirty miles away from Boone Hall and the other was, Jemmy and his surviving crew were closer to the Floridian border. There, the Spanish harbored runaways!

Cato and Major Boone followed the blue-tick's wails through a misty swamp until the dog's timbre switched over to a high-pitched bark. 'Sara' was back on the animal heads' trail again!

Armed to the teeth and camouflaged, Jonn Kimber, Ogle and ten others began their sweep northward. A passing shower quieted their footsteps as they slipped through the marshy terrain.

When Kimber's team ran across their first patch of debris, it became obvious that what was to come next would not be pretty! As it turned out, that assumption was correct; however, there was one survivor!

A machete had been used on the boy. His collarbone incorrectly jutted away from his neck! He had lost a lot of blood. Ogle knelt beside him.

"Son, we're going to get you out of here! You've got a pretty evil cut to your shoulder but you're going to make it!" Cal said using his best bedside mannerisms.

"I'm not going anywhere without my brother!" sputtered the injured boy.

Ogle then leaned closer to the frightened lad's face and softly spoke.

"What's your brother's name?"

"Francis!" answered the pale adolescent.

"I don't see anyone else but you around! Is he hiding somewhere?" Ogle asked.

"Mister, if you don't hold up in the air a white handkerchief within the next five seconds, you're going to be shot!" Threatened the injured youth.

Chaloner did as he was advised. A few seconds later, Francis Marion stepped out from behind a nearby live oak. The eight-year-old uncocked his rifle and then ran over to his wounded brother's side.

"Job, these are Boone's people. We're safe now!" said Francis Marion.

Job looked up at Francis's face for reassurance and then into Commander Ogle's eyes before he spoke.

"About fifty of them hit our uncle's farm three nights ago! Only one of his slaves were able to warn us; the others joined up with them!

My sisters and ma hightailed it to Charlestown. Dad went to ambush them before they got to us!"

Jonn Kimber turned toward the boys. After a military salute fit for the highest of ranking generals, he slowly bowed his head and spoke to Francis and Job as though they were seasoned marines.

"Until I met you fellows, I thought I had seen some tough soldiers in my time! But I have to tell you both, you guys are two of the bravest young men I've ever run across!

When all of these blow over, I shall personally see to it that King George recognizes your demonstrated valor! It wouldn't be surprising to me at all, if 'ole Gus' himself knighted himself once he hears of you men's fortitudes!

Unfortunately, though, we will have to postpone those festivities until after we attend to this uprising! Job, those two characters standing over there, the ones dressed as bushes, are going to carry you down to Boone Hall! They'll get that shoulder fixed up for you!

Francis, do you think you could show us where your uncle lives?

If so, would you be so kind as to lead the way, Son?"

Mary Read watched Sporck as he paddled beneath a cluster of wharf pilings. Minutes later he emerged as a cane toting man of the gospel. He walked into the Willingham Mercantile Company as if he were the owner of it!

"Good morning, Reverend, how can we serve you today?" spoke the perky clerk.

"And thanks to god it is, Sir! But I have a situation I am afraid if I cannot fix, I shall catch the wrath of several of my district's congregations!" lied Sporck.

"How could our shipping company be of any assistance to these upset folks you speak of, Bishop?" asked the befuddled Mister Willingham.

Sporck bowed his head, mumbled a prayer, and then hobbled over to the store's owner close enough that Reverend Green could tell there had been a nip or two taken from the jug beneath the service counter! With tears the size of corn kernels rolling down the sides of his cheeks, Ike whispered to the tipsy clerk.

"Because I made a dreadful mistake!" gasped Anton.

"Oh, things can't be that bad! What's happened that has gotten you so upset?" asked Willingham.

"Over the past six months my congregation along with three others from the Manchester Conference, have collected Bibles! It was my responsibility to see that they were properly shipped to America!" stated Sporck.

"Did you ship them to the wrong place?" asked the empathetic storekeeper.

"No, worse than that!" answered the snare setting lion head.

"Now listen, Reverend, if I'm going to be of any help to you and your benevolent congregates, I'll need some details! Where are your Bibles at this time?" pressed the shopkeeper.

This time Sporck really laid it on thick! He dropped his walking cane and crumbled to Willingham's feet! First came the admonition and then the plea!

"America's moral compass will in part be determined by the delivery of my parish's Bibles! Mister Willingham, did you know that America buys and sells human beings?

To combat that sinful activity, Christians throughout England are amassing in impressive numbers to put a stop to slavery! I probably should not say anything further for security reasons but let me just say, right now on this very dock there are about a hundred missionaries boarding the 'Centurion'! I was late getting their desperately needed Bibles! They have already pulled up their loading ramps!

Frankly, it was the weakness of my flesh, my love of the taste of rum that made me neglectful of my duties! And even though I am embarrassingly wealthy, I am now unable to carry through with my good intentions!

Oh, please instruct me as to my possible options, kind Sir! I will pay you a handsome fee if you could help me recover from my terrible mistake!" gushed Ike.

Mister Willingham's altruistic spirit seemed to heighten when the pleading Reverend Green handed him a heavy bag of coins. Curiously he opened the leather pouch.

Obviously elated by his rapid calculations, the clerk assisted the defrocked holy man to his feet! Eye to eye and with a comforting hand on Sporck's shoulders, Willingham shared some words of hope!

"To whom do you wish to address your shipment?"

Mary Read lowered her telescope when her target emerged from the Willingham Mercantile Company. She watched Sporck return to his well-hidden boat and disappear beneath the vast network of poles supporting the acres of docks above them.

Jemmy had come to the realization he had overestimated the willingness and maybe even the ability of his men to fight for their freedom! Of his twenty-three followers, only two of them had ever held a rifle!

After building a fire, Jemmy gathered the Gullahs together for a meeting. Following the new ranking awards along with appointing a parade marshal, he lined up the men into a single file. The Angolan then instructed them as to how they were to march through the community of Stono Creek!

Jethro and he were to hold back so the parade participants would be protected by their marksmanship. After painting a sign spelling, "Liberty", the slaves began their peaceful protest. Not one single one of the parade's participants had a weapon of any sort!

Nathaniel, the leading parade marshal as well as being the acting lion head, had mustered up a little marching tune which ended up having the word, 'liberty' at the end of all five of its stanzas. Nevertheless, they were awfully loud!

It just so happened on that very morning, Lieutenant Governor William Bull was on a hunting trip with some of his relatives at Stono Creek. When they heard the men singing from about a half mile away, Bull made the determination that 'now' was not the best time to release his foxhounds!

Instead, he blew on his hunting horn! Bull then rallied his horse backed cronies together before heading toward Boone Hall for help!

The disrupted foxhunters hadn't ridden any more than a mile when they ran into Major Boone and nineteen other very serious men! Shortly following the story of the singing renegades, Ogle ordered his men to draw their sabers. John Boone asked the same of his neighbors.

From four different directions came the screaming horsemen! Only two negroes were unaccounted for!

The upriser's heads were perched on sharpened stakes which had been spaced fifty feet apart alongside the town's main thoroughfare! No one could doubt the message's intention!

Jemmy and Jethro riding some stolen horses, crossed the Stono River in order to seek refuge in a nearby swamp. They were armed to the teeth!

Their intention was to cut a swath of fire all the way to the Floridian border! The Spanish harbored runaways!

It took three days and the skill of a Chickasaw tracker to catch up with the agitators. When they did, only Jethro's body ended up in a bonfire blaze! The Angolan had again evaded their grasp!

Blanche wore a highly starched nursing cap along with a burgundy cape which was being blown by the wind. She wheeled Wolfe up to the check-in station where Captain Anson was standing!

"Well, aren't you a sight for sore eyes? I was so sorry to hear about your accident, old Chum! It looks like you'll be back on your feet in no time! Say, aren't you supposed to be on furlough?" chirped Anson.

Blanche with a sickening grin stretched across her jaws, motioned for Captain Anson to lean forward as if to share a grim secret with him! Expecting to hear a dim diagnosis, Captain Anson leaned forward in a conciliating way.

A fine stream of turpentine jettisoned into the Captain's eyes!

Squeals of agony followed!

Wolfe's wheelchair began rolling backwards down the gangplank! Blanche of course, disappeared within the bowels of the 'Centurion'!

Shocked by what she saw from the opposite of Tobacco Dock, Mary Read had to put down her telescope! It wasn't so much she was disturbed by Blanche's cunningness, her bloodline explained that, it was the fact of who the young woman actually was!

Without dwelling too long on the good times of past nor going back to a place not too far back in time, Mary tried her best to think of something else. But that 'something else' always slipped back into her mind!

It was a decade old story about a man and a woman very much in love! From that torrid romance, they conceived a daughter! Yes, they were pirates for sure but not bad ones!

"Calico Jack" Rodman and she should have made it all the way to the end of their days together! They would have continued to run their little shop and simply been a normal family, but, another woman came into the picture and that was that!

Mary Read was quickly snapped out of her reminiscence as a wagon with the name of "Willingham Mercantile Company" painted on its sideboards stopped in front of the 'Centurion's' loading dock. There was a wooden box setting in the back of the wagon's bed.

As he always did, Sir Robert Walpole walked to the tiny sanctuary located just three blocks down from his Downing Street address. It was eleven o'clock.

Except this particular morning's objective was not destined for prayerful retribution; not at all, today's exercise was all about saving his own skin! There had been a second attempt on his life just the day before!

Costumed as a monk, King George Augustus was waiting for Walpole's arrival. Everything was still on schedule.

Confident that the chapel was empty, Robert sat down beside his longtime friend. Beginning with a quiet nod and a smile, the Prime Minister started whispering.

"Gus, I had to kill a boy yesterday; it's eating me up inside! I mean, my god, Man, what's this world coming to?" huffed Walpole. "It's not the world, Bob, it's the Austrians!" the King complained.

"Do you mean Sporck?" calmly questioned Walpole.

"Sporck's simply a renegade puppet! But, yes, he's the one sending out the children to do his sanctions! Incredible, isn't it?" Snorted the King.

"So, why does he do it? If the goddamned Austrians want control of the African commerce why don't they do what we do; that is, just take it over and then fight to defend it? Why would they stoop to such despicable levels?"

Whined the Prime Minister.

The King looked over at his kneeling friend. With a disparaging tone, Gus answered Walpole's question.

"Because he's figured out what we're up to!" said George Augustus.

"Are you saying, Sporck is aware of "Cricket"?" questioned Walpole.

"…And more!" answered the King.

"Gus, you're scaring me now! How do you know this?"

"Because Sporck has attempted to kill out the population of Charlestown with Bubonic hosting fleas! It is possible he has already accomplished that dastardly deed!" bellowed George.

"Why?" asked the panicking Prime Minister.

"To undermine our attempts to cripple America's military expansion and receive the royalty fees for every slave exported to the Colonies from the African continent!" concluded George.

For a little while both men kneeled quietly side by side. But then, Walpole shrieked an alarmingly loud yelp resulting from an epiphany he had just experienced!

"Well, so what! It will make no difference in the long run! Our Cambridge boys have already done the math!

Once those viral bucks over there get done with their unabated fornications, the Colonial militias won't have the manpower to put down the revolts that will follow! They'll be so many of those niggers running around they'll overrun the plantations and spread like locust beyond them!" said Walpole.

"Which is exactly why the sonofabitch sent Professor du Fay's flea larvae to Charlestown! He intends to 'checkmate' their exponential growth by killing them off before they overpopulate themselves!

After that, he plans to band the Spaniards, African-Americans, and the Austrians together and take control of the whole bloody continent! To complicate matters even further, the Spanish and Austrian war chests are bottomless and if you think about it, their standing slave army is already imbedded with more being shipped in daily!" blurted out the angry King.

"Gus, I wouldn't underestimate Chaloner Ogle's capabilities in the least! He and that prison-plucked crew of buccaneers would be a tough match to contend with no matter whose navy was up against them! They just might have stopped the 'Fancy' from delivering them!" said Robert Walpole measuredly.

Augustus George felt the muscles tighten in the back of his neck. He had found the leak! The flea eggs were supposed to be onboard the 'Thomas'!

Walpole was Sporck's conduit; that's how Ike had second-guessed his every move. That would end now! Thought Gus.

Pretending he had to rush off to another meeting, King George II rose to his feet and embraced the statesman in a farewell manner. As they made their departing handshake, Gus's ring pricked Walpole's palm! Both men politely said goodbye.

Sporck had lost count of the hours since he had last seen sunlight. Dried fruit, several pounds of gold coins, Lebanese sausage and six pints of water was all he had in the box destined for Charlestown!

Sound was the only stimuli preventing madness. Time without light likened itself to a swimmer in the middle of the ocean. There was no end to it!

Even the ship's rats became the highlight of a period of time thought to be a day! Their voracious hunger made him feel powerful and maybe even liked.

They would come around the airholes whenever an inviting smell seeped from the Bible box. Occasionally one of the ship's cats would set up an ambush site close to Sporck's hideaway so whenever an unsuspecting rodent came scampering along, it was almost always taken away by the cat!

Blanche slid closer to the spot where she was almost positive that she heard a man mumbling! It could have been dolphins although most of them she presumed, didn't use curse words!

For the past few hours, the sea had been quite rough. Even she was beginning to feel green around the gills.

Blanche knew if someone else were hiding in the shipping hold, they too would become seasick. She was correct!

Even with his own hands, Ike could not prevent the contents of his stomach jettisoning from his mouth! Noisy heaves followed.

Telltale smells along with some more sounds had Blanche honed onto Sporck's position within his second "goddamn it"! She laid beside his box listening to him breathe.

With the use of her teeth, she began fashioning stoppers out of a raw potato she had found on the floor. One by one, Blanche silently started plugging up Sporck's airholes!

It wasn't until the very last breathing hole was practically sealed when Reverend Green began speaking.

"Blanche, of all of my many acquaintances you by far, were my favorite!"

There was no answer.

"I was rough on you, my Love, for a very good reason! I wanted to be assured in my own mind if you were worthy enough to bare our children!" schmoozed Ike.

Nothing.

"You know, Darling, as a couple, we are an unstoppable duo! Let us once again enjoin out strengths! Together as man and wife, we shall rule the 'New World'!" swore Ike.

Blanche inserted the last potato plug! She rejoiced at the thought of hearing Sporck's feet kicking on the inside of the transport box!

"Okay, okay, what do you want from me? Come on, let's let bygones be bygones! What's it going to take, Blanche?" bartered Sporck.

"Just one tiny little thing, my Love!" toyed Blanche.

"And what might that be, my Princess?" squeaked Ike.

"Your foreskin!" answered Blanche.

Jemmy had laid submerged within the muck compiled within an outhouse for over a day! A reed supplied his main feed of oxygen. Twice the trackers had fired bullets from above the hole but both times they had missed him.

After carefully exiting through the outhouse's door, the Angolan headed in the opposite direction of his earlier decided upon escape route! Boone's men would be covering the southern bound waterways as well as the roads!

He made his way to Goose Creek by following a lesser used trading path. From that point onward however, it was unclear exactly how Jemmy got to where he did! One will never know the truth but most people believe he joined up with the Chichanee who guided him northwest into the Carolinas' interior!

But what makes Jemmy's saga so incredible was the time in which it took for him to reach New York! Unfortunately, all that is known about his trip was after he evaded Boone's men at the Hanahan Plantation, he showed up on the outskirts of Manhattan a month later!

Mary Read was lifted to her feet. The blindfolded woman was then taken to Captain Anson's quarters.

"It is my understanding that after two days at sea, you approached my cabin in hopes of having a private conference with me! That's a little irregular, don't you think, Ms. Read?" questioned the Captain.

"As I said to your brutes when I made my request, 'I have some very important information to share with you and you only, Captain!'" impudently said Mary.

"Then tell me who in the hell you are and why you have taken it upon yourself to illegally board my ship and then to have the audacity to ask for a meeting with me? Who gives you the right to act in such a bodacious way?" spat the 'Centurion's' Captain.

"Would you happen to have a "buzzard egg" on you, Captain Anson?" whispered Read.

"Speak to me!" yelled Anson.

"I shall, but I would appreciate your taking this blindfold off first!" Demanded Mary Read.

The 'Centurion's' captain did as the King's agent requested.

"I am four-two-eight! My orders were to sanction Sporck! I believe he is stowed away on your ship, Sir!" said the Bow Street Runner.

"How in the hell did he do that?" angrily retorted Captain Anson.

"In a Bible box!" chortled Mary.

"In a what?"

"Right after the mishap with Captain Wolfe's "nurse", a large wooden container was delivered by the "Willingham Mercantile Company" to the Tobacco Dock. While your officers were busy fishing Captain Wolfe out of the Thames and you were flushing out your eyes, four heavily bribed dock workers loaded Anton von Sporck onto your ship!

And now for the bad news, Wolfe's helper, the girl who spit that stuff into your eyes, also is in hiding! I am not sure the two incidences are connected; but you know what 'they' say about coincidences!" angrily commented Mary.

Captain Anson jumped to his feet and called for Read's chains to be removed! He then summonsed James Wolfe to be brought to his quarters.

"I'm sorry to be so abrupt, James, but I need to know exactly the relationship you shared with the woman who spit the turpentine into my eyes! Miss Read over here, she's one of us, seems to believe the woman has hidden herself away on our ship! What are your thoughts on this matter, Sir?" questioned Captain Anson.

James Wolfe told them everything! He mentioned his dim recollections of a dead couple playing a board game, needles that multiplied the legs on people, abnormal sex and even the hotel fire! After that, he slipped back off to sleep.

The two agents spoke after Wolfe had been returned to the sickbay.

"Captain, I'm afraid we'll have to assume that Sporck and the girl are together! Perhaps it would be best if we rooted them out ourselves instead of alarming our King's precious cargo.

I don't think their academic minds could stand the strain of knowing that a mass murderer was hiding in their midst! Why don't you go about the business of taking this boat to wherever your taking it while I give the 'Centurion' a good midnight scrubbing! I'll be as quiet as a mouse!" promised Mary Read.

Without any further discussion, Anson walked over to his chifforobe and pulled from out of its top drawer a box containing two miniature pistols. Along with a pouch of an adequate amount of black powder and a few lead balls, Captain Anson offered the specialist a respectful salute. She then quietly left.

Lieutenant Governor William Bull was furious! He knew as everyone else did that the Stono River revolt would be the catalyst for more insurrections to come. Their drums were already chatting up and down the rivers. The natives were indeed becoming restless!

As a show of his power, the Lieutenant Governor jumped up on a stack of milled corn bags and prepared to say something to the hundred or so men who had helped to put down Jemmy's revolt. The mood of those tired men was anything but festive; nevertheless, they all gathered in closer to hear what Governor Bull had to say.

"Boys, I fear this event that we thankfully squashed, is merely the tip of a gigantic iceberg! I am afraid that incidences such as this particular one will become commonplace!

But while you brave men were rustling up those damn renegades, it occurred to me that we never ran into these kinds of problems in the past! So, I had to ask myself a question, 'what is the cause of this uneasiness'? My conclusion might surprise you!

Since the English began meddling in the affairs of our commerce, we have experienced a multitude of hardships! Every landowner all along our coast can attest to their being victimized at the hands of corrupt British officials!

They hide behind the hypocritical vail of humanity and fairness to human beings of every color! And yet, these same red coated devils are the first to hold their hands out beneath the table for a percentage of something they're not entitled to!

England for the most part has been good to us! However, that does not give them the right to tamper with our livelihoods! Nor does George have our permissions to interfere with our ways of making them! Using human labor to build our civilization is a necessary thing!

To mistreat that labor force would be foolish. We understand that! But, to say that slavery is not a Christian endeavor is preposterous!

Maybe it's time to send a message back to England! Perhaps their welcome has begun to smell like rotting fish!

If I may be so bold as to assume you gentry agree with what I have said, I put forth an idea to you! Return our guests from the 'Whydah' back to England!

Further, let us send with them a well scripted document outlining our dissatisfactions! Maybe then, they'll understand!" preached Bull.

Chaloner Ogle then stood! He and his crew moved to the front of the aroused southerners! Ogle jumped up on the corn bags.

"My fellow Englishmen, before we lambaste our King too much let me share with you the very reason why he sent us here! And by the way, Governor Bull, any funny business going on around the docks were most likely spawned by your fellow Americans!

Six months ago, a diabolical plot was uncovered by British Intelligence! An Austrian fused biological attack was discovered in the making!

Our agents were able to determine what slave ship was to be the carrier of several vials containing unhatched flea larvae! Charlestown was to be its destination!

We were dispatched out of London to sink the 'Thomas'! Along the way, we were attacked by a pair of the 'Thomas's' escorts! After several failed efforts, my crew finally saw to it that all three of the Austrian invaders were destroyed!

Due to a dense fog, some of the slaves managed to make it to some islands about fifteen miles north of Charlestown. We made every attempt possible to prevent them from escaping which ultimately was the reason we ended up here!

We came to warn you but we were obviously too late!

Their leader, Jemmy will most likely attempt to enter Florida by land. It would be a good idea...."

A pistol shot suddenly exploded within the confines of Major Boone's barn! Everyone seemed frozen with shock from the surprise of the blast. Elizabeth Boone held the smoking gun!

She made her way to the speakers' bags and with some gentlemanly assistance, found herself standing in front of more than a hundred angry men! Beth cleared her throat and then purified it with a deep swallow of Irish whiskey. She spoke through a megaphone.

"I reckon ya'll remember when we were little ones, we use to play with the same darkies that we today are huddling in our homes over! We liked them and they liked us back then!

But as Governor Bull so aptly stated, 'England has no right to interfere with our ways of supporting our families!' We, all landowners, have the inherent duty to produce enough for our families' subsistence. In order to do that, we need our old friends' help!

So now you say, 'the slaves are communicating', that may be true but let me tell you this, Commander Ogle, there isn't one single negro on our farms who wouldn't come to us if there was a problem! Don't you see, Man, these slaves as you call them, are like family to us!

What has happened here has become a very unnatural thing! Someone from somewhere has shot a bunch of malarkeys to those folks and that someone ain't from around here!

So, my suggestion is that you good 'Samaritans' pack your bags up, get back on your ship and finish up the goddamned job you started out to do! Go catch that blue-eyed devil and skin him alive if you want to but remember this, from here on out, we'll manage our own matters!

You go tell King George to his face that Elizabeth Patey-Boone said she would personally shoot the next Englishman to walk on her property offering to do anything but moving on! We don't need you people anyway; now, get off my land!" screamed the southern lady.

With their heads bowed, Chaloner Ogle's crew humbly left the Boone barn. In a single file, nine men and one woman without a word being spoken among them, boarded the 'Whydah'. An hour later they were at sea.

Kimberly Kimber had gained a little weight since King George last saw her. A little over a month ago she couldn't even walk but now Kimberly was practically running! The physicians had done an excellent job.

From what was gleaned by Gus's best interrogators, the girl's mother was married to a Captain Jonnathan Kimber. Evidence clearly pointed toward the fact that Sporck and Mrs. Kimber conspired to hold Jonnathan's daughter hostage in order to force him to captain the 'Thomas' to Charlestown! Apparently, the mother levied a heap of cash from the deal. In essence, Kimberly was clean.

Kimberly Kimber and King George Augustus sat on a wooden bench with a big lion painted on the back of it! They were fishing.

Just as the King had promised if she got well, 'they would catch a whale together'. Kimberly started crying.

"I feel so bad inside! What happened to your pretty wife was mostly my fault, you know! Blanche told me that her Uncle Sandwich would help us! I am so sorry; I wish I would just die!" sobbingly said Kimberly.

King George put his arm around the little girl's shoulder and started singing a deliriously funny song about a duck and a kitten trying to get across a mudpuddle. The vocal part was terrible but the end result was successful.

After an hour of 'drawing-time' together, Britain's king had a nearly perfect layout of Sporck's All Saints' Church. George also realized he had sent Ogle out to kill Kimberly's father!

Captain Anson prayed that Mary would dispatch the stowaways! Otherwise, his entire crew could lose their lives! The King had warned them about infiltrators and now he had two of them onboard the 'Centurion'!

To give the appearance that all was well upon the 'Centurion', George Anson rang the Captain's Bell signifying it was time for vespers. Both George Whitefield and John Wesley would administer the thirty-minute service.

As planned, when Whitfield opened the service with the "Nicaean Creed", Mary began her search for Sporck! From top to bottom, she scoured through every space a person could possibly hide. Even the crow's nest was checked.

Mary shook her head as a subtle signal to Captain Anson. She had not located Sporck yet. Her message did however indicate that the upper deck had been sanitized! Next, were the lower compartments.

Musical instruments and heavy foot stomping offered a welcomed diversion on the one hand; however, on the other, it made it impossible to hear little scurrying's escapees often make!

When John Wesley began his prayer of Benediction, Mary held her ear to the storage compartment's floor. The Postlude was seconds away!

The British agent could sense she was not alone in the shipping hold! There was a smell of garlic faintly drifting in the slow-moving currents of air. With no light, Mary was forced to use her hands to blaze her way through the labyrinth of crates.

Read heard what she thought to be a muffled sneeze! With an unfortunate move born from the excitement of what was thought to be enemy contact, four-two-eight allowed her boot knife to scrape against the base of a shovel!

It clanged as it's handle hit the storage room's floor. Her invisible presence was now compromised!

Mary laid motionless but then through the stillness of the darkness, Blanche began speaking to agent Read!

"You are still as beautiful as I remember you," said Blanche.

Mary remained quiet.

"There have been some times when I could have used a mother! Maybe one day you can explain to me why you abandoned me!" angrily seethed Blanche.

"Because I was in prison goddamn it!" explained Read.

"You could have at least tried to find me." cattily remarked Blanche.

"Where is Sporck?" fired Mary.

"I'm sitting on him!" cackled Blanche.

"Is he dead?" Mary Read asked.

"No, Mam, not yet!" impudently responded Blanche.

"Blanche, I came here after Sporck! Are you tied in with him?" calmly asked Mary.

"Well, Mom, that depends on your answer to a question I would like to ask you!" Blanche arrogantly said.

"Alright, what do you wish to ask me?"

"If I turn Sporck over to you, what…"

With a table lantern tucked within his sling and a cocked blunderbuss extended from his good arm, Captain James Wolfe marched directly over to Blanche and placed the ballooned barrel on her forehead! He spoke through clinched teeth.

"I want you to slowly crawl down from that box!" said the captain.

Wolfe held the scattergun no less than an inch from her face while she climbed to the floor. He then motioned for her to lay down on her stomach and put her hands together in the small of her back.

Using a woven bamboo tube, Captain Wolfe plugged both of Blanche's thumbs into the opposing ends! The Chinese handcuffs would make an escape attempt remarkably difficult.

James then placed the glass lantern over one of the unplugged airholes on top of the crate that Blanche had been sitting on. While he was leaning down to assist her to her feet, Sporck took aim at the base of the oil lamp.

With more than a pint of lamp oil now splattered all over the storage compartment and a fire the size of a grand piano in search of things to burn, Wolfe had no choice but to leave the scene and call for help! The blaze had spread to the 'Centurion's' walls!

"The Lord bless and keep you; the Lord make …" Was as far as George Whitefield got before he heard Wolfe's fire call! Black smoke welcomed those foolish enough to try and stop the fire's voracious birth!

Then with a couple of acts of rarely observed decency, Blanche pried off the top of Sporck's Bible box and led both him and four- two-eight out of the hold's hellish inferno! No one noticed the three laying on the 'Centurion's' deck taking in the priceless sea air!

At gun point, while the ship's crew was chaining hundreds of buckets down to the frontline firefighters, Sporck and Blanche forced Mary Read to jump overboard! Along with a bag of anything they could grab before their escape, the amazingly swift duo then shimmied down into the ship's lifeboat! Mary's pleas were ignored as their dinghy slipped by her!

Samuel Fraunces cracked open a freshly laid duck egg into his mug. He then poured an ounce of vinegar and a shot of gin into the small crock along with a dash of salt before gulping the whole mess down.

Thus, a new day had begun and one which promised the beginning of a successful career! He was to pick up the sign for his new tavern at eight o'clock!

'The Queen's Head Tavern' said it all, at least in a tongue and cheek sort of way. After all, Caroline was already dead Samuel mused as he swatted the back end of his mule. It was a ten-minute wagon ride into town.

King George had gotten himself quite drunk. He had become fond of his evening fireside chats with himself. The enjoyment he received while toasting his toes before a roaring fire became indescribable. Gus always worked things out that way!

The scotch and his subconscious found the answers from the dancing flames! His depression worsened as each day regretfully arrived.

Despite the dim lighting, George Augustus could clearly read the investigators' report. Kimberly's diagram had made the raid fruitful!

There were some alarming discoveries which had turned the sweet nectar of the successful caper into a bitter pill for the King to swallow! Sporck was no longer an agent of the Hapsburgs. He had gone rogue!

No longer was Sporck to be an instrument of the Austrians! He was now an 'on the loose' menace! There was no longer a creed for him to follow; instead, chaos and mayhem were to be the charred remains from the tail of his overhead passing!

But the real burr still sticking in Gus's crawl was the current whereabouts of Sporck himself! He had abandoned the All Saints' Church! Everything had been cleaned out, wall to wall! It appeared as if Sporck had ever lived there!

Robert Crommelin hid in the bushes surrounding the schoolhouse until he saw the lights come on from the next-door rectory. Even though Reverend Murray was in his sixties, Robert intended to beat the hell out of him!

Twice he had been promised payment for the work he had done on the church's new addition and twice he had been dismissed due to the rector's 'very-busy' schedule! But on that night, Crommelin knew the squirrelly minister and he would have all the time in the world to work out their differences!

Crommelin tapped a three-sided spike into the rector's front doorjamb! No one responded from the inside. Robert then started yelling the reasons why he was nailing the man into captivity!

"For almost a month now, you have been promising me you would pay me for the six weeks of labor I provided! You either hand over the ten pounds you owe me or so help me god, I'll tear out every goddamned board I put up in your school!

And when I finish doing that, I'll nail every one of the sonofabitches over your windows so you'll never step foot on green grass again! I'll entomb your ass!"

A clinking leather bag slipped through the kitchen window! Robert Crommelin then rode away leaving the spike in the rector's front door! He was in a hurry to get to a meeting that night!

Jemmy had amalgamated into obscurity. By positioning himself as a field worker on the Staats's plantation, he pretended to be a contented young freeman who had an unquenchable thirst for learning!

In order for him to perfect his schtick, Jemmy needed to be discovered! The scheme he came up with so as to catch the eyes of the whites, was remarkable! He held himself out to be a genius.

Never before had an African ever come to those parts with the acumen that this one demonstrated! The grapevine said he might even be a black prophet!

By claiming his inability to read, people became profoundly curious as to how he learned so many things which only an educated European would know about! Jemmy had even convinced his critics he had learned the English language during his transport to Charlestown. He said he had listened to the slavers talk and from there, he just started speaking it.

Jemmy went about the daily chores required to receive his weekly pay but after work, he could always be found loitering around a newly met friend's house. As a matter of fact, it was Jemmy who helped his buddy hang the sign advertising the opening of his new tavern.

Samuel Fraunces and he had become fast friends. Both men had white fathers, they had blue eyes, each had an entrepreneurial spirit and neither of them liked white people! It was no wonder when Jemmy was under Samuel's fulltime employ!

Within a month, the Queen's Head Tavern had become the place to go to! It was an establishment where the elite could strut their stuff!

Soon it was the bedrock for those in the know who wished to enhance their thoughts of themselves by simply crushing those who might one day cast a shadow upon them!

But mostly, the Queen's Head Tavern was an establishment where gentlemen would go for a drink and an occasional hoochy coochie show! In actuality, it had become the brokerage hub for intellectual trading!

The tavern's hottest commodities were secrets! Big ones, little ones, or any size in between, it made no difference! If a customer wanted to know something about someone or something and they had the money to pay for it, all they had to do was talk with Jemmy! A day later, that customer would get his money's worth!

Jonn was absolutely exhausted. He hadn't slept for days.

Unfortunately, he had to go on duty in an hour!

Kimber had been thinking about his daughter a whole lot lately. How he wished he could go back and change things. If only he could start all over again, he would be a real father to her!

These disturbances were what was on Jonn's mind as he saluted James Stanfield. Jim had been at the helm all night and Jonn was there to relieve him.

"You're looking about like I feel, Jim, how's it been going?" said Jonn.

"As far as I can tell, the weather should hold up for you. We are on course!

Fortunately, we picked up a good wind during the night so you should expect smooth sailing. It looks like it's going to be a royal day!" Stanfield said cheerfully.

Kimber took the wheel after double checking the charts. He really wanted to talk to Stanfield. Jonn Kimber was deeply depressed.

As the relieved captain was leaving the wheelhouse, he turned toward Captain Kimber. Jim reached into his breast pocket and pulled out a sealed envelope. He handed it to Jonn. It was from Commander Ogle!

"Jonn, after reading this note, I ask that you burn it! We have a mole aboard our ship! Whomever it is, left a coded message beneath a coil of rope back at the Boone place!

Therefore, you are to gradually adjust your headings toward the northeast! Tomorrow morning, I shall announce our return to London but in fact we'll be making a beeline straight toward New York!"

George Anson knew he couldn't stand on his feet much longer! The sea was almost glasslike so he wasn't too worried about his relief officer taking over the wheel for the night.

His bed seemed to envelop him just like a cloud would do. George enjoyed the warm sensation of drifting into a quiet darkness but then the dreams came!

The fire had killed four men two of which were officers! Wolfe was out of commission! Agent four-two-eight was missing and Sporck and that turpentine spitting she-devil had escaped!

General Abraham Staats was frustrated! His arthritis made it very difficult to grip a boiled egg with his forefingers. Even salt didn't help!

Further agitation came as a result of one Mister Robert Crommelin's tardiness! If it were to ever get back to King George and it would, that the Cricket Club's first meeting was delayed by a drunk redbone, he would become the laughingstock of New York!

Following a tear drawing ride down Montgomerie's Avenue, Crommelin delivered the Cricket Club's chairman to the entrance gate of the Queen's Head Tavern with three minutes to spare! A top hatted black man helped the general from Robert's wagon.

"Welcome, General Staats, if you would be so kind as to follow me, Sir! My name's 'Sonny', anything you need while visiting the Queen's Head all you gotta do is click me!"

"Click you, Sonny?" asked Staats.

"Oh, I'm sorry, General, I forgot to give you a clicker! That little seashell looking device you have in your hand there, is a 'clicker'! It's supposed to sound like a cricket! To make it 'click' you simply press the metal backing thusly, 'Click-click-click', see what I mean, Sir?" instructed Sonny.

"That's very interesting but for what purpose is this clicker used for?" asked Abraham.

"General, with that thing you won't need to do the egg maneuver!" jokingly said Sonny.

Reverend Harold P. Murray had packed most of his things in boxes! They would probably pick them up in a day or two. He didn't care!

Ten years earlier, his wife and their two-year-old daughter rented a little house in lower Manhattan on account of Abraham Staats's generous gift of a five-acre plot of land! The property was to be used for one purpose and one purpose only, to educate the slaves who demonstrated a proclivity for learning!

General Staats had commissioned Harold a recent graduate of Oxford, to take the reins of the massive undertaking and to build for the exponentially expanding slave population, an educational institution. The general's only dictates were that the negroes be taught three things: civility, reverence, and humility!

As Reverend Murray had understood it, the reason for those mandates were due to the General's belief that the black race would eventually snuff themselves out because of their inherent stupidity! His favorite example of that had to do with swimming!

On more than one occasion, Harold had heard the General speak of the high rate of infant drownings of those living along the banks of the Congo River. And yet, he would say, "all those kids wouldn't die if their parents knew how to swim"!

His theory hinged on the supposition that once a negro was a little bit educated, he would be less likely to burden his holder with the undue financial loss caused by the death of an ignorant laborer. The Trinity Schoolhouse therefore, was conceptually founded to better socialize the slaves so they would become a more amenable bunch to manage over the long haul!

But now, his wife and child had gone back home! The locals abhorred the idea of teaching their coloreds to count money. And worst of all, General Staats had fired him!

Sure, a new school would replace the one he attempted to build! Reverend Murray knew in his heart he had failed. In essence, it was over!

With these thoughts pounding in his brain, Reverend Harold Murray walked out to the wellhouse, cut the bucket and four feet of rope off from the cranking line, fashioned a noose from the freshly sliced end and jumped! Harold's note was never read because an afternoon breeze blew it away!

When Sporck and Blanche escaped from the 'Centurion' and stole its lifeboat, they left the emergency dinghy's connection line dragging behind the mothership. It was this umbilical replicant that saved agent four-two-eight's life!

Right after Blanche and Sporck had rowed out of sight, Mary swam close to a mile in pursuit of the distancing 'Centurion'. Luckily but mostly due to the storage room fire, the 'Centurion' made a complete circle offering Read another shot at the swiftly moving line.

After hours of exposure, she was lifted into the bowels of the ship. Mary Read died that night.

Hypothermia had outraced her drowning! The Atlantic got a good one that time!

Jemmy knew there were over thirty men having a meeting in the Queen's Head's basement! Even his boss Samuel Fraunces, was a participant in it.

The intrigue of cricket sounding devices stoked the Angolan's curiosity. He knew when people substituted words with replicated sounds, they were almost always up to something secretive!

When the bar's trafficking had settled into a temporary lull, Jemmy disappeared into the tavern's dry storage room. Behind a stack of peanut bags was a space just big enough for a man to lay down and put his ear to the floor where a predrilled listening hole awaited.

"…and that Gentlemen, is all we know to date. When the 'Centurion' arrives, the school's new faculty will be dispersed to your assigned homes. Construction should be completed no later than the first of the year, so, they'll be out of your hair in less than a couple of months!" Jemmy thought General Staats had spoken.

With that valuable piece of eavesdropped information, the old lion head went back to his bartending duties. Already, he figured he had about a thousand pounds worth of memorized soundbites. Now, he had to find a buyer!

If someone were to ever say that 'god looks after even the evil doers', you could certainly say there is proof of such an assertion! Because in less than a day's worth of oar-smacking hell, Sporck and Blanche were rescued by a Spanish warship headed toward their Floridian colony.

Under the circumstance they mutually shared, Sporck used about ninety percent of his stored-up charm to win Blanche's miniscule heart back! After all, their new roles were that of a castaway physician and his assistant who had survived an attack by the English warship named the 'Centurion'!

"They had been simply protected by the Lord", was the mantra they went by whenever the two of them were questioned about their recent plight. Their ship the 'Thomas' they said, was on a relief effort from Portugal. Its mission was to assist the escaped slaves with their medical needs.

While enjoying a fine dinner together, the ship's captain, Hernando Felipe was made aware of a secret that Doctor Anton von Sporck and his loyal assistant, nurse Blanchard shared. With that discovery unveiled, Captain Felipe decided to pry a little more deeply into exactly where Calico Jack's famous treasure was hidden. Rum was then served.

"Now, how is it that a physician and his nurse came upon such a map?" questioned the Spaniard.

"There's no map, Captain Felipe! Nurse Blanchard knows precisely where it is!" nonchalantly stated the pretending medical man.

"I don't mean to sound confrontational, Doctor Sporck, but pray tell, how could a young lady ever get tied up with such a scoundrel as Calico Jack?"

"Because he was my father!" chimed in Blanche.

Poor ole Captain Felipe almost sucked an oyster down his windpipe! He swiftly stood as a precautionary measure.

After a minute or two of coughing, the 'Bartholomew's' captain sat back down to the dining table. With a stare that would kill a small animal, Captain Felipe pulled from his belt a pistol and pointed it directly at Sporck's temple!

Then motioning for Blanche to slide her chair over to Doctor Sporck's side, the red-faced Spaniard stepped behind the two suspected tricksters so they could not see his face! After pulling out a second weapon and cocking them both, Hernando Felipe began frightfully whispering.

"When I reach my hand out to help the less fortunate, I like to believe that god smiles at me! And when I open my arms to a friend, I expect them to embrace my provisions with reverence and respect! But when I find that my deeds fall into a sty with pigs who then crunch up my pearls of graciousness, I begin to question my role as a Christian! Sometimes, I feel closer to the devil under those circumstances! Such is the occasion at this moment! I am caught in a quagmire, my friends;

I cannot determine whether you are swine or saints!" harshly said the captain.

Blanche casually glanced over at Sporck and then with a slight smile on her face turned around in her chair and looked the Captain square in his eyes! She then eased her chair back enough for her to stand before she spoke.

"Captain Felipe, I want you to put those terrible pistols of yours on the table and take my hands! Let us pray together! I believe as we entwine our faiths together you will see as I do, that god will enlighten…"

The 'Bartholomew's' captain lay dead on the floor! Sporck was still holding his smoking weapon! He winked at Blanche just before he leveled the unfired gun at her forehead but then shoved the cocked pistol into his belt after a brief odd weighing within his mind.

With the speed of a pair of field mice, they rolled Hernando's body up in the cabin's rug. Both ends of the Turkish carpet roll were lifted and then thrown into the ocean!

After that, the two returned to the Captain's quarters and immediately began setting up an emergency triage station. Saws and an array of other carpentry tools were hurriedly scattered out as if they were the instruments seen only by surgical professionals. Blanche even turned down the light's wick so the room's affect would take on a more subdued patina. Sporck began ringing the Captain's Bell.

From the ship's galley an assortment of instruments was displayed on a bedsheet covered table which had been set up on the main deck. Blanche and Sporck had put on surgical masks; both wore leather gloves. A sterilization fire was started!

Soon, the 'Bartholomew's' entire crew had gathered in front of the boiling pot of "medical water"! Blanche was using a pedal driven honing wheel to sharpen a meat cleaver. Every sailor watched her do so.

At that exact moment, Doctor Sporck walked forward to make an important announcement. He painstakingly removed his mask.

"Less than one hour ago, my new friend and your Captain chose to end his own life! He did this for your benefits! Nurse Blanchard will read to you the note he left behind! I believe you will understand the reasons for his benevolent sacrifice once you hear the message he left for all of you to hear!"

Blanche stood with the aura of a matador, she carefully unfolded the fictitious suicide note, placed a pair of inane spectacles on the bridge of her nose and prepared to read it. All ears were peeled.

"To my men: One year ago, I contracted the fatal disease known as, 'Squamous Epithelioid Arachnus'! This morning when I awakened, I realized that the unthinkable had happened! Tiny spiders had begun crawling from my ears! I killed all that I could find; but I knew more were to come!

Finally, I accepted my plight and painfully realized my options were limited to only one. I eliminated the probability of my whole crew's demise by drowning the carrier!

I would have suffered a thousand deaths to prevent my men from having to undergo the immense hell of which I have endured! Therefore, I have entrusted the honorable Doctor Anton von Sporck and his able assistant, Nurse Blanchard to render all safety measures necessary to stop these microscopic arachnids from biting my men!

Therefore, it is my last will and testimony that my entire holdings be equally dispersed among those crewmen present at the time of its distribution! Additionally, I propose that my plantation in New York be sold at auction from which the proceeds be likewise divided among those attending the said auction!

As a last wish, I would like to see to it that each of my loyal crew members undergo a voluntary examination for preventative reasons, and that if anyone who discovers they have contracted my same illness, it is expected they do the noble thing as well! I bid you farewell. Hernando Felipe"

Not surprisingly, there were no curious souls. The majority of the crew crossed their hearts to their commitment to fling themselves overboard if faced with the same malady as their captain had been! But until that dreadful moment arrived, they were content with extending their voyage to New York in hopes for the best to happen!

George took a deep breath of snow smattered air. He had to get back to London.

The Prime Minister had taken ill. Spencer Compton and he were scheduled to discuss Walpole's successor should Sir Robert not pull through.

A coaxing hand prevented the King from dressing right away. Cassandra had the touch that only older men could appreciate.

Samuel Johnson and Robert Crommelin crossed Wall Street hurriedly. Traffic it seemed had passed the nuisance stage and was nipping at the heels of unbearable! Also, it had rained, making it impossible to fully accomplish what Samuel needed to do.

'Sam' as he liked to be called, was about at the end of his rope. His inheritance was nearly gone and his only hope of landing the Dean's position hanged himself in a well! Professor Johnson was going for broke!

Crommelin knew everything there was to know about Samuel Johnson. He was acutely aware of the nearly diminished fortune that the doctor of philosophy had squandered. Sam Johnson was a gambler.

Robert Crommelin had a big one on the line! Jemmy was paying these days upwards in the twenty-percentile range for a freshly delivered 'mullet'! Robert figured that'd be close to a pound for a pound seeing as the professor would weigh out a bit over a hundred of them.

Sam had approached Crommelin two days earlier. It was when they had scheduled their meeting. Here's how it went:

"Well, top of the morning to you, Mister Crommelin! How long do you figure this rain will hold out?" cheerfully greeted Sam.

"Oh, I'd say it'll burn off by two," answered the mulatto.

"So, this is where the wall is going to be built?" asked Samuel Johnson.

"Yes, Sir, starting from right over there to that elm tree close to those bushes and then to the right and all the way back to the East River. It'll run for five acres total!" said Crommelin as he drew the directive with his walking cane in the air in front of Sam.

"That's going to cost a pretty penny!" exclaimed the nervous professor.

"Yea, but there are some mighty deep pockets funding the college!" cast Robert.

"Who?" weakly asked Samuel Johnson.

"Professor Johnson, I'm just the guy that'll be tearing the old church down! And, I certainly would be telling you a lie if I said I wouldn't jump at the chance to build the new schoolhouse; but, that kind of decision is way out of my prayer range. If you know what I mean!" said Crommelin.

"How could I find out where the money is coming from? I would be interested in knowing who controls the purse strings, Robert," puffed the professor.

Crommelin could plainly see his strike indicator was fully underwater but he decided to hold off on setting the hook just yet! A full swallow was the objective!

"I'd expect the only person on this entire island who would know the answer to that question would be an acquaintance of mine; but the price one would have to pay for that sort of information would I imagine, be cost prohibitive!" tightened Robert.

"How much do you think the tab would be?" Samuel hesitantly asked.

"I would be afraid to say, Professor," said the cagey fisherman.

"Would you accept twenty pounds for your effort in establishing a meeting with this individual?" Pressed the wannabe headmaster.

"Absolutely not!" fired back the rod holder.

"Why not?" queried the puzzled professor.

"Because, I don't charge my friends for favors! I'll see what I can do and it will cost you nothing! Let's meet again around four o'clock!"

"Where?" asked Johnson.

"The Queen's Head Tavern." Answered Robert as he jerked his "line" tight.

Chaloner couldn't stop thinking about Elizabeth Boone's acidic remarks! It frightened him to imagine a war with America.

He had heard those familiar utterances before. Sounds exclaimed by victorious warriors who had never lived through an authentic battle. It's one thing to snuff out the lives of a couple of dozen unarmed slaves but quite another to face a thousand glaring bayonets, Ogle thought.

The fire Chaloner saw in those southerners' eyes, the stinging glances that screamed for idealistic justice were clearly signs of the dangers ahead! Men carrying flags were like the rattles on the tip end of a serpent's tail.

But, unfortunately, that's what they were doing! He would put that in his report.

As his orders had stated, he was to destroy the 'Thomas'! He had done that! Secondly, he had been instructed to personally see to it that every member of Sporck's slaver ship were dead before returning to England! There were to be no survivors, friend or foe!

In that none of the 'Thomas's' original crew who were still alive exhibited any sign of the plague. But Walpole's orders were crystal clear: "Other than your dozen criminal crew members, you are to extinguish the lives of any and all collateral collected along the way"!

Cal opened up a bottle of his favorite scotch. After placing a pair of matching goblets side by side, he filled both to the brim.

On the left side of the commander's table he slid over to its edge one of the vessels of scotch and then named that half of the table, 'Red Dog'. On the opposite side, he did exactly the same thing except that side he named, 'Blue Dog'.

Red Dog represented the King, his own unabbreviated career coupled with six broken matrimonial engagements and bloody ole England in general! Blue Dog stood for quite something else. Dreams, hopes, a squaw and a shot at a brand-new start!

The Colonies offered a chance for anybody to do whatever they wanted to do! All one had to do was work for it and it was yours lock, stock, and barrel!

A man had a chance to be anything he desired to be no matter his 'pedigree'! The Blue side would hopefully end up the winner, Ogle daydreamed.

Still alone and getting drunker by the minute, Chaloner Ogle began his opening argument. This time, he deliberated on Gus's behalf.

This went on for most of the night! One ship's captain a hundred miles from his destination, desperately attempting to unravel a very tangled anathema! By early the following morning, Ogle had figured out that a lie would solve it all!

CHAPTER 6

NEW YORK

Hercules Mulligan was in big trouble, maybe! He wasn't sure if Mrs. Caruthers had recognized him or not. If she did, he was in for more than a tongue lashing this time!

On three previous occasions, some busybody had mentioned to his father that "Hercules" had been seen leaving the Queen's Head Tavern. I each case, the fourteen-year-old denied it! But this time, he might have really been nailed!

As firsts go, Master Mulligan had struck gold! She was his same age, experienced and beautiful!

Secretly, the prostitute and he were engaged! Their wedding would occur right after his graduation.

But as they had agreed, the couple would keep their plans under wraps until that day came. In the meantime, he would still have to pay her normal fee just to keep up appearances!

What had happened to arouse the East Ward's constable's wife's suspicion was due to jealousy! Margaret Caruthers was expecting to catch her husband again creeping down the tavern's back stairs leading on to Queen Street. She was hiding in the bushes!

Instead of smacking her husband square in the back with a garden hoe, she hit Hercules! Upon realizing her error, she profusely began her apologies to her not so innocent victim. It was dark so making a correct identification was going to be a tossup!

Sixteen feet from the rear corner of his mother's and father's house, there was a massive elm tree. A year before, Hercules had hammered a number of spikes into its trunk so he could take hold of a leg sized branch. It stretched out above his room's upstairs' window. It was four o'clock in the morning.

In one more hour Hercules projected, his mother would be waking him up to tend to his daily chores! That at least was what the lad was expecting the morning to foldout like; but it didn't turn out that way!

The first clue that his evening's caper had gone askew, was when he realized his climbing spikes had been removed from the elm tree! The second was when his father and Major James Wolfe walked out from behind that elm tree!

Major Wolfe approached Hercules! He motioned for the boy to step away with him so the two of them could speak out of his father's earshot.

"Son, I'm going to tell you something that if you ever repeat what I said, I'll deny it! I wouldn't give a rat's-ass for a young man who hadn't the taste for 'poontang'; I sort of like the stuff myself! But, Hercules, you lacked the necessary skills of evasion and consequently you got caught! Now, let me explain to you your options at this juncture in your life. Mister Mulligan, your father had asked you to cease your visits to the Queen's Head Tavern did he not?" snapped Major Wolfe.

"Well, sir, not exactly! My father "claimed" that someone had seen me "near" The Queen's Head Tavern!" calmly responded young Mister Mulligan.

"On how many occasions has this supposed subterfuge been brought to your father's attention?" asked the Major

"I'm not sure. You mentioned options, sir?" interjected Hercules.

"Son, I'll repeat…" Wolfe was saying.

"This will be the 'fourth' in a string of coincidences!" blurted Hercules.

"I see! So now, all we have left to discuss are the remaining consequences, would that be correct, Mister Hercules McMullen?" asked Wolfe.

"Whatever you say, Major!" smartly quipped Hercules.

"Very well! You may go directly to the docks and sign onboard as a crewman on any ship of your choice; another option would be to join the Continental Army!" said the pan faced James Wolfe.

"That's it, I have only two?" asked the stunned youth.

"Actually, there is a third, Hercules; however, I am afraid you may not qualify for that one!" baited the Major.

"And what lofty and unreasonably difficult 'height' must I reach in order to obtain this dangling prize in which you believe I am too short to grasp, Mister Wolfe?" impudently retorted Mulligan.

"Manhood," whispered James Wolfe.

With that demoralizing response coming from the British Army officer, Hercules had no choice but to bow-up like a prizefighter. Somehow Hercules had to regain his destabilized dignity; therefore, he did what so many young men do, he fabricated an alibi!

"Let me see if I understand your perspectives on this particular scenario, Major! Here we have a British officer and my obviously disturbed father, lurking amongst the shadows awaiting the return of a thought-to-be charlatanic teen when in fact, there is nothing more here than a boy putting in a good fartlek before beginning his morning duties!

And speaking of consequences of which I have been offered only two and not eligible for a third because of height constraints, where is the proof of my alleged whore *houndishness*? How could a tiny number of casual remarks or unsubstantiated gossip lead to such an erroneous conclusion?" gallantly said the 'slippery' teen.

Suddenly, a woman's voice cut through the crisp morning air!

"That's a lying little sonofabitch right there, Major! Take a look at his goddamned back! I popped his ass with a hoe when I caught him coming down the back stairs of the Queen's Head Tavern!" shrieked Mrs. Caruthers.

Hercules smiled as he began the witnesses' cross-examination.

"Correct! That happened! No doubt about it! But why? Why would I receive such a blow from Mrs. Caruthers's hoe?

I was in fact attempting to prevent our beloved Constable's murder!

Major Wolfe, there is the criminal, not me! Fortunately, I was jogging by or I am quite sure this conversation would be taking place somewhere else than in front of an innocent kid's home!" said Hercules as he closed his remarks.

James Wolfe could hardly contain himself. The Mulligan boy had the right stuff to become whatever he wanted to be! He was that rare type of individual who had the capability of becoming a cadet!

Wolfe glanced over at Hercules's timid father and then over to the venomous Mrs. Caruthers! James put himself into the brilliant young man's 'shoes' and decided to change his tactics.

"Son, straight out, do you want to leave your home?" asked the softened Major.

Hercules welled up. He tried to turn his face but it did him no good. The tears came anyway.

Then with a burst of new-found strength, he looked directly in between Major Wolfe's eyes. Intrepidly the boy stepped three steps backward and folded his hands behind his back before he spoke.

"Yes!" barked Hercules.

"Would you be willing to offer your life's work for the benefit of your country?" politely asked Major Wolfe.

"And which country is that, sir?" toyed Hercules.

It was Wolfe's turn to step back from the shock of Mulligan's response. He quickly shot back with another sharp-edged answer.

"The one you would leave the security of your home for!" said James Wolfe.

"In that case, either one will do, sir!" flatly answered Hercules.

"When could you get your things over to King's College?" asked Wolfe.

"Right now!" answered the boy.

And that is exactly how Hercules Mulligan became enrolled in America's first breeding ground for British military officers. Hercules's trajectory was indelibly elevated when Major James Wolfe drove him out of the Mulligan's driveway!

It took almost sixty days of working around the clock to complete the chapel's facelift but Blanche, Sporck, and twenty negroes did it! They were now ready to begin their operation!

Odds were the both of them had convinced the local farmers of their legitimacy enough so that Reverend Green and his trusty sidekick, nurse Blanche could pretty much count on filling the pews every Sunday morning! Since the last minister they had hanged himself, a lot of effort was spent assuring the old congregation of their minister's stability!

On the first day of the church's grand debut, the relocated Trinity Church invited every negro freed or not, to take part in the ceremonious affair! There was music, wine, fried fish and words of faith shared throughout the whole shebang!

By sundown, Blanche and Sporck had grossed nearly a hundred pounds of cash along with a bag full of tendered promissory notes! Commitments had been made from landowners with deep pockets full of decades' old money!

They plantation owners adored the concept of 'inclusion'! Worshiping with their slaves seemed to anesthetize many of the Biblical schisms. The badness of it all was absolved that way!

As a show of appreciation to their gentry classed congregates, Ike and Blanche announced that beginning the day after the coming Sabbath, a medical clinic would open for the explicit care of all negroes! It would specialize in keeping them fertile and healthy!

Another tantalizing caveat which should be mentioned, would be the secret offerings made to certain plantation owners! Some of the Trinity Church's major donors were chosen to be "Upper- Room" members!

To those few, the clinic would provide a "selective breeding program" which guaranteed an exponential increase in their holdings' populations!

Since sentiments were running high regarding the taxation levied on human imports, it behooved the slaveholders to produce their own! The main problem however with letting the 'Toms' pick out their own mates was that more often than not, the 'bucks' would want to pair off with only one 'broom-jumping' wife!

What was needed and what the Trinity Church Clinic provided, was a fool-proof system that matched the needs of the plantation! 'Upper-Room' members were privileged to borrow certain breeders loaned out from the clinic at no charge!

That is, if a particular plantation owner living on the northern edge of Manhattan Island was short on 'lackeys' for housework and such, the church would send out a small framed 'redbone' for a week or two! 'Selectivity' and 'adaptability' were the operative words at play here; simply, the owner would state his need to the church and the clinic would match that need with the properly selected donor!

In the cases where certain enterprising landowners wished to farm out a few of their 'picaninny bleeders', the church offered a feeless brokerage service connected with the Queen's Head Tavern. Once sired, the midwifing was on the house!

It wasn't very long, six weeks or so, before scads of black folk started hanging around the churchyard. Knowing full well the effects of devilish idleness, Sporck put them to work. He never even needed a whip.

Soon, a wall would be built and everybody would get their own house! That is, as long as the negroes worked where they were needed!

At night the men would gather for drinks, a little music and a whole lot of insurrection talk! Jemmy was usually present.

Mary Burton flashed her pocket mirror at the clock tower atop College Hall. When she received the returned signal, Mary walked across Wall Street and directly through the entranceway of King's College. Number one-two-seven pretended to be looking for someone.

After three pulls on the school's door ringer, a very pleasant older woman welcomed 'Miss Burton' into the guest seating area. A red coated butler approached the young lady with a tray full of cookies and a steaming pot of hot chocolate.

Mary could hear the receptionist whispering the announcement of her arrival.

Finally after eating half of a cookie and setting aside a cup of undrunk coco, she heard the footsteps of the college's president. Mary Burton stood as Professor Samuel Johnson approached her.

"Mrs. Woodhull mentioned to me you were trying to locate a friend of yours?" politely questioned the headmaster.

"Yes, Sir!" answered Mary.

"And what name might this fortunately sought after young man go by?" playfully asked the professor.

"Well actually, Sir, it's a 'she'!" Mary said.

"Her name?" pushed Samuel.

"Mrs. Elanor Cricket," answered the King's agent.

"Do you have an address for Mrs. Cricket?

"One-two-seven Wall Street is all that I have," stuttered Miss Burton.

"I believe Mrs. Woodhull will be able to escort you to where you need to go!" concluded the headmaster as he quietly returned to his office.

Chaloner Ogle glared at the outline of Manhattan Island against its blazing backdrop of the burning walls of Fort George! He called for Cato.

"Reporting, Sir!" said the out of breath agent.

"Cato, listen very carefully, we must do some serious reconnaissance work and we must do it at once! From the appearance of things, I believe it would be prudent of us to examine the circumstances before we tie-down to a fiery dock!

You and Maynard get out there and find out what's happening on the streets! Have Anne put on her lowest cut blouse and let's get our party boy, Captain Every to escort her into the city's underground! This might give us a peek at what's really going on in this town!" calmly commanded Ogle.

"Will you be staying onboard, Commander?" snapped Cato.

"No, I intend on paying General Abraham Staats a little visit! I may even have him shot for treason!" Ogle snapped.

"Say again, Sir?" Cato asked.

"Cato, did King George give you private orders to message him regarding our departure from Boone Hall?" struck Ogle.

"Yes, Sir!" whispered Cato.

"Then why did you turn that 'secret' message over to me as if we had an imposter on board?" re-struck Ogle.

"May I speak candidly, Sir?" asked Cato.

"Of course! Say what you want to say, my Friend!"

Cato unbraced his stance and casually walked over to the table where he pulled out a couple of chairs. He poured two glasses of rum and motioned for the 'Whydah's' captain to share in a toast with him!

"Here's to all the fools who braved the wild Atlantic upon the good ship 'Whydah'! We, the jokers, who have been played like a well-tuned harp! May we go down in history as being entranced by the sweetest 'lullaby' ever sung by a king! Here's to perhaps the greatest warbler of melodies of all time, ole 'Gus'!" loudly said Cato.

Chaloner stared at Cato for an uncomfortable length of time! After standing, Ogle reached out and placed his hand upon Cato's shoulder. Then with sort of a grimace on his cheeks, he leaned over and whispered into Cato's gold-ringed ear.

"I agree! Now, find out where Jemmy is and kill him!"

Alex Hamilton was going on guard duty in fifteen minutes. His boots glistened as he did an about-face in front of the full length mirror. He spat on the palm of his glove so he would never drop his sabre again! The last time that happened, he had to sleep with the bloody thing for a week!

His roommate, Hercules Mulligan and he were bottling that night. Passes into the city were scheduled for noon on Sunday but that was only if 'Company B' won the inspection.

That's why getting the homebrew into sellable containers was so infinitely important! Getting drunk and oiling down every piece of wood in the dormitory just went together! It was the true elixir for champions!

Close to four inches of snow had covered the walkways leading in and out of College Hall. Tracks in fallen snow offered only a glimpse of its recent use. Therefore, it made good sense for Hercules to step into the frozen impressions previously made by Hamilton's marching boots!

Making it to the school's maintenance shed undetected was the least of Hercules's problem. Returning back to the dorm's third floor would pose the greatest obstacle. Thirty-six jars had to reach Bravo Company within the hour! The Commandant was on campus!

"The Ghost", as Major James Wolfe had been coined was known to bust up a many of the cadets' ploys by the utilization of stealth! His successes at doing such were largely due to the fact that no one knew where the man was at any given time of the day or night!

This conundrum was solved by Bravo Company's bribing of the Headmaster's assistant's eight year old grandson, Sam.

Samuel Woodhull was the kind of kid anyone would like to have as a little brother. He was smart, resourceful, cunning and a born thrill seeker!

Sam's job was to keep a watchful eye on the Commandant of Cadets when it was necessary to know where he happened to be at a particular time! Window lanterns systematically switched around accomplished that end!

At eighteen hundred hours and without provocation, Jemmy and ten other animal headed men fired a cannonball through King's College's front door! No attack followed.

Mary Burton tried her best to escape the area before a perimeter was set up around the college! Fortunately, little Sam Woodhull saw the woman jump into the rain barrel located just below his window sill!

He then blinked out the warning signal to Hercules who had just delivered his last case of homebrew to the awaiting boys on Bravo's hall. Thinking that Major Wolfe was going to be on their floor at any moment, all thirty cadets threw their precious jars out of the dorm's windows! Despite a small snowdrift, most of them broke upon impact.

Much to the shock of the entire corps of cadets, two masked commandos sealed off the campus's quarters! Major James Wolfe along with every cadet was blindfolded and shackled!

All were made to lay facedown on the floor. Absolute silence was their only requirement!

Soon, the sounds of a sopping wet prisoner echoed from the end of the dormitory's long hallway! Smells of burning flesh coupled with high pitched screams made the whole scene frighteningly real! Five minutes later, the hooded invaders were gone!

Chaloner Ogle could see through the front window that General Staats was eating alone! He was sitting by his fireplace finishing up a turkey leg. It was almost dark.

Just after Abraham had lit his pipe and Ogle had cocked his pistols, a deep voice coming from behind shattered Cal's immediate intentions.

"Commander Ogle, we have a prisoner! Perhaps you should delay your visit with the General until another day!

Maynard already has the woman onboard; I felt as if she might be able to clear up some of the mysteries surrounding ole Gus for the both of us! I had a hunch you'd want to be the first to question her," said Cato.

Henry Every and Anne were pretending to be admiring the sunset when a wagon load of half-drunk negroes came barreling down Queen Street! One of them still had a zebra head bouncing on top of his shoulders!

After offloading their buckboard and entering the rear entrance into the Queen's Head Tavern, the rowdy bunch disappeared into the tavern's basement by way of its spring cellar's door. Jemmy then returned to his bartending duties.

Following a 'heads or tails' flip of a doubloon, Anne Bellamy elected to stick with Jemmy until Ogle's orders to the contrary were cut! Every agreed to run to the ship to secure the 'go-ahead' but promised to return within the hour!

Much to Anne's dislike, having to wait for permission to kill someone seemed ludicrous to her! Since Jemmy was their target in the first place, she felt plumb stupid standing in front of the tavern's front window with her 'mark' less than a knife's throw away!

Mary Burton had been searched from head to toe! Percy Fogg had seen to that! Selkirk was at the wheel waiting for Ogle's command. Things were getting rough on land according to Cato but now with Jemmy being located, a decision had to be made!

The King's orders had clearly specified that once the 'Whydah' had successfully achieved her mission, Ogle and his team of 'pirates' were to return to England! Upon the ship's return as promised, King George Augustus II would offer a blanket pardon to Cal's crew as well as a promotion for him.

To disobey those semi-friendly orders would ruin his career and consequently mar his legacy! Forever, the name, 'Ogle', would get mingled up with 'traitor' or worse, 'coward' when he was referred to in historical print! Chaloner knew he couldn't live with that!

As much as he yearned to remain in America, Chaloner had to leave it! Ogle would return to Britain. He would deny ever having met Every, Stanfield, Bosman or even Jonnathan Kimber for that matter!

Commander Ogle could see no point in questioning the prisoner, he already knew her answers anyway! It was true, King George was tampering with America's fate! And positively, he had no business fooling with that den of serpents!

A knock on his cabin door jolted Ogle from within the quarry of his thoughts! It was Cato. They were ready for him to meet Mary Burton!

When Chaloner Ogle's eyes met those of Mary's, the Commander's aura became electrified! She was perfect and everything he had always wanted in a woman! Not only was she beautiful but dignified as well! Cal struggled for words.

"I understand you were found hiding in a rain barrel over at King's College earlier this evening?" asked Ogle.

"I was, answered Mary.

"Were you aware that we are nearing the end of November, Mrs. Burton?" gleefully prodded Chaloner.

"It is 'Miss' Burton and 'yes', I am aware of the month!" quipped the svelte Misses.

"...And so, you jumped into a rain barrel for what reason?" questioned Cal.

"Because the college was under attack!" sharply retorted Mary.

"Whom are you employed by, Miss Burton?" strategically pressed the Commander.

"We share exactly the same employer, Commander Ogle!" spat Mary.

"Well just for 'shucks and grins', tell me who that might be, Mary?" pressed Ogle.

"King George the Second!" sarcastically answered Miss Burton.

Making every attempt possible to cover up his reaction to Mary's response, Commander Ogle withdrew his pistol he had stuffed into his waist sash. After cocking the hand weapon, he placed the barrel squarely against the back of Miss Burton's skull before he asked her another question!

"Assuming what you say is factual then precisely explain to me your duties under the Crown's employ?" asked Ogle.

"In short, I am a spy!" belligerently answered Burton.

Still reeling from the woman's response, Ogle returned his pistol to its original place within his sash and pulled up a chair so he could look at the 'spy's' face when she answered his next question!

"Mary, I shall…" Cato knocked and then entered the Commander's quarters.

"Commander, we have a positive on our target! Your call, Sir?"

Ogle abruptly stood and then approached Cato with a spring in his step! As if oddly making a proposal to the seven foot mulatto, Cal dropped to one knee, grabbed Cato's right hand and kissed his ring finger as though the tough-hand were a Cardinal!

With a snicker trying to escape his lips, Ogle looked up at Cato. Now in a full blown state of hyperphrenic glee, the Commander spoke!

"Bring the bastard's head to me on a silver platter as soon as possible! We will be leaving New York at dawn! We'll take it back to London with us. It will make a splendid Christmas gift for ole Gus, don't you think, Cato?"

"Indeed I do, Sir! Shall I wake the two of you upon my return to the ship, Sir?" asked Cato kiddingly.

"Absolutely!" answered Cal.

Once Cato had left the room, Commander Ogle returned to his seat setting across from Mary's chair. Her arms and legs were still securely fastened to it. He continued his play-like questions as she did with her coquette answers!

"Now where were we? Ah yes, you had said you were a spy…" asked Ogle.

"And, you had started to say, 'Mary, I shall…' and then that man you call 'Cato' interrupted you. You were saying?" Chimed in the perky redhead.

"It was just that your vocation surprised me, that's all," replied Cal sheepishly.

"And what would you really like to know about me, Commander?" Teased Mary.

"I would like to know why you are in New York." Soberly requested Ogle.

"You know, Chaloner, we would get along a lot better if you would remove these ridiculous bindings!" whined the naked woman.

"Why were you sent here, Mary?" stabbed the Commander. "I was inspecting King's College. That's why!" Mary snapped.

Ogle quickly stood and walked toward his desk. From the third drawer down on the left side of his mahogany study, he withdrew a footlong piece of fuse cord.

He then wove the black powdered strand between the toes on Mary's right foot and lit the fuse's end closest to her pinky. Nothing but the truth followed!

Rasmussen Smyth was by far the fastest negro on General Staats's plantation and maybe on the whole island! The kid could run a mile in less than five minutes and could do it even faster than that if the money was right! Such was the case that very night!

As soon as Professor Samuel Johnson and the Commandant of Cadets, Captain Wolfe had finished telling General Staats about the animal heads destroying the college's entrance door and the woman in the rain barrel and of course the commando invasion, Staats asked that Rasmussen come see him! A minute later, the lad was standing on the General's back porch.

"Son, come on in the house! You're going to catch the grippe if you don't get warmed up! Could I fix you a cup of hot broth, Rasmussen?" questioned General Staats.

"No, Sir, I've already eaten today! Mister Eddy said you was calling for me?" asked Rasmussen.

"How far and how fast could you run for one solid ounce of gold, young Mister Smyth?" coyly asked the General.

"I speck I could make it to Spain and back before dawn for it, Sir!" exclaimed Rasmussen.

"Do you think if I drew you a map, you could deliver an important message to a friend of mine?" condescendingly asked Abraham.

"I'll do my best but General Staats, how 'fast' depends on how far apart this friend of yours is from right here! When were you wanting me to do it, Sir?" bravely spoke the slave.

"Do you know where the Queen's Head Tavern is, Mister Smyth?" respectfully asked Staats.

The boy nodded.

"I want you to take this egg to the owner of that tavern. His name is, Samuel Fraunces. Give him that 'cackle-berry' and say the word, 'Cricket' and then leave! Do you understand, Rasmussen?" pushed the retired British General.

"Do I still get the ounce of gold, Sir?" pressed back the young negro.

"Certainly, Son, as soon as you return!" sternly said Abraham.

No sooner had Rasmussen left the kitchen when the General ordered up his best horse to be saddled. From above his mantle he removed his sabre and attached it to his belt's frog shaped swivel. He then slung over his shoulder a leather bag filled with powder and bullets.

Temperatures had dropped into the low teens. The docks had become so slippery that loading personnel would be treacherous if not impossible! Ogle could hear what he thought to be gunfire but he wasn't sure.

The 'Whydah's' mooring ropes had to be chipped free of ice before they could be pulled onboard. They were like frozen snakes!

A rapidly moving fog bank rolled down the Hudson leaving within its tracks an ice glazed warning of its devilish passing. Petrified movement would best describe the situation through Ogle's eyes.

Only hearing but not seeing the explosion taking place made Chaloner's skin crawl. He knew what was coming next!

As expected, a mortar round whizzed over the top of the 'Whydah's' mainmast! On the ball's downhill arch it exploded about three feet off the river's surface. Shrapnel bits clinked against the other metal things it impacted while softer surfaced objects quietly took the hit. Luckily, the shell had missed the ship!

Commander Ogle had to get out of the gauntlet he was facing! A half mile of hostile gunfire left him and his three remaining crewmen in a perilous situation!

Mary Burton had told him all about 'Operation Cricket', the Queen's murder and King George's plan to infiltrate the Colonial government with his own men! He had also learned that King's College was to be Gus's headquarters as soon as New York was secured!

King George's, not Britain's, legislative body had long range plans to weaken England's grip on the Colonies! He planned to do this by embedding every firebrand he could get his hands on, washing them through his war college and then positioning them throughout the provinces to enact their prescribed agitations!

Once accomplished, Gus was going to sweep into his little home away from home and take charge of his already established government! Then, he would combine the military strengths of North America along with those of the British Empire and finish off the rest of the Europeans once and for all!

Bullets started popping against the side of the 'Whydah'! Muzzle blasts could be detected coming from both sides of the Hudson River! Flares lit the harbor as if it were noon!

Ogle could see a mob of people shaking their fists at the ship as it slowly sailed by. Sniper fire was becoming exceedingly more accurate!

The chances of the 'Whydah' making it to open water made it superfluous to think of anything else but the imminence of death! But then a miracle happened!

General Abraham Staats with his sabre drawn but standing by his horse because of the slipperiness, gave a command to Major Wolfe to move his cadets forward. From a roof top, Cato's silhouette could be seen against a swirl of roaring flames! He was pointing toward the clusters of trouble spots within the torch carrying crowd below!

Mixed within the protesters were a handful of blacks led by Jemmy! His men turned out to be the only ones shooting at the 'Whydah'! Upon that realization, Cato lit a hand grenade and dropped it down into their midst!

With the sight of six or seven darkies being blown into the air, Major Wolfe commanded all but Delta Company to fire upon the dozen shell-shocked negros still on their feet! While they were reloading, Delta made a 'V' shaped bayonet charge! They killed them all off!

General Staats then mounted his horse and began ordering the bystanders to leave the wharf area! Cato saluted the 'Whydah' as it slipped out of harm's way.

Sporck smiled at Blanche as they tossed the last dead negro onto the back of the clinic's ambulance! Jemmy's headless carcass was on the top of the heap! It would soon be time for their burials.

As the two had agreed, Sunday would be the most optimal day for digging. The freezing temperatures would keep the bodies from thawing.

She hadn't told Ike yet that she was pregnant! Ruby, Blanche's servant, had told her she was expecting a son. It seemed like the best time to bring that subject up since they had a five-mile haul back to the Trinity Church's new graveyard.

Sharp winds and the sleet made it extremely difficult for Cato to receive Ogle's signals. Fog had crept in thus blocking Cato's returned transmissions. But this is what Cato managed to write down, "To England…Back with force in May…." And then the sight of the 'Whydah' was lost!

It was three o'clock in the morning when the battalion of 'Buzzards' as the King's College cadet corps liked to call themselves, reached the front steps of Judge Daniel Horsmanden's city home. Leading them was Major James Wolfe!

Three men, General Staats, Professor Johnson and Lieutenant Governor George Clarke approached the Judge's door. After only one knock, the three callers were invited into the Judge's library for what turned out to be an 'all-nighter', as they say!

A little after sunrise, General Abraham Staats ordered Wolfe to move the King's College's cadets to Fort George! They would stand in reserve should the fort come under another attack!

Already several new fires had sprung up throughout the island! Brigades of women passed along endless buckets of water to the men attempting to drown out the spewing column of homes leading toward the city. Slick conditions stifled all but those attempting their escapes from Manhattan Island. The temperature was in single digits and there was some wind.

Cato blocked out the light from his lantern four times which messaged to the others he had found a place for them to hide! Beneath the 'Hoboken Ironworks Foundry' was a bricked-up storage basement with no windows and an unlocked door. Fortunately, there was a fireplace and about three hours-worth of coal.

Anne and Bob Maynard immediately began the process of starting a fire. Stanfield and Bosman commenced a serious exploration of the inside of the building; they were looking for anything that might help the marooned crew's escape from the island.

The footsteps of soldiers patrolling the streets began to pick up their repetitiveness as it got lighter outside! Every and Cato were to go on watch within the hour. Stanfield and Kimber had to get some sleep if not for but just a little while.

At six minutes until nine o'clock, a ring of keys clanked against the Foundry's front door. Cato woke everyone up. Someone was entering the upstairs building!

Oliver Thimbles was the company's business manager. He was the man you went to when something big was broken or it needed to be made. Also, Mister Thimbles was whom you spoke with concerning the cost of such matters.

It was Monday morning and as customary for the day to begin, Oliver always put on the stove a fresh pot of tea. But, when he realized the stovepipe was warm, he made the fatal error of entering the storage basement looking for the cause!

It was then discovered that the Hoboken Foundry was scheduled to deliver four truckloads of iron barring to Fort George that very morning! A crew of six were expected to load at ten. A detachment of cavalrymen would be escorting the shipment to the fort!

Oliver Thimbles was a big man and he didn't take kindly to being tied to his own desk chair. He was not sparing with his derogatory remarks in which he aimed toward his captors; however, Anne Bonnie's slap to the back of his head considerably readjusted his explicative laden vernacular! Anne then got Oliver to pay attention to what she had to say!

"Mister Thimbles, your life and the lives of several innocent men are about to come to an unnecessary end! I suggest that you listen to what Cato is about to explain to you and then decide if you wish to see your family again!"

Cato then pulled up a chair close enough that he could smell the leeks on Thimble's breath. With a broad smile, Cato leaned forward and began speaking.

"Oliver, we are here in America at the direction of our King, George Augustus II! We were separated from our ship last night during the riots. We broke into your basement here in order to survive the night air. We intended to bring you no harm but under the circumstances, that may be an unavoidable tragedy!

Our purpose for being here on this island was to extinguish the lives of the perpetrators who created the very mayhem that you New Yorkers have been under! We followed the renegade slaves all the way from Charlestown to here before we killed their ringleader!

Because of the obvious reception the King's ship received last night and coupled with the traveling difficulties that befell all of us, we basically missed our ride home! Yet, here we are with only my story and we have no identification nor proof of its authenticity.

As exemplified by the attack on his majesty's ship, I do not feel my men would fare well under the conclusions drawn by an American militiaman should we happen to walk up on one of them! I'm afraid they would not believe the same tale I just spun for you!

In short, we need to gain an untethered entry into Fort George before we ask for their asylum! Do you understand our predicament, Oliver?" Cato asked.

Thimbles's eyes told Cato he was willing to talk this time with a civil tongue in his head! Anne removed his gag.

"First, I want to tell you, Mister Cato, I am an Englander at heart! I have been no part of the sentiments that you speak of!" squealed Oliver.

Anne walked up behind the now weeping Mister Thimbles and pressed the razor-sharp edge of her knife against his Adam's apple. Cato again spoke!

"Will you assist us, Oliver?"

"Yes!" answered the petrified man. Suddenly the Foundry's front door was splintered by the impact of a battering-ram! Five pike holding vagabonds dressed as dragoons, swiftly surrounded the inside of

Mister Thimble's office a moment before their commanding officer, "Lieutenant" Alex Selkirk entered it!

With the ostentatious swagger of a British general, Alex walked over to the bound man's chair while he withdrew his sheath knife! Then with a move resembling that of a cat's paw, Selkirk cut Oliver Thimble's windpipe wide open!

Alex motioned for his imposters to do what they were paid to do! Immediately they began dowsing the foundry's walls with lamp oil!

While the bowery boys were getting ready to torch the place, Selkirk turned toward his awestruck fellow crewman almost as if he were at his mother's funeral. With a forlorn demeanor about the seaman, he motioned for them to huddle around him. He had to verbally give them Ogle's last order!

"You have proved yourselves worthy of your country's highest honors; however, the circumstances concerning your indictments leave your futures somewhat in question. I therefore command that Cato and Maynard return with Selkirk to our ship! To the others, all the best!" Alex said.

As Selkirk finished reciting Ogle's directory, he noticed Cato approaching him. With the offering of a brotherly hug, Cato embraced Selkirk but then abruptly stepped away. He cleared the sadness from his throat and then whispered the response he wished to have returned to Commander Ogle!

"With the exception of you, I am no longer enambured with the British! I shall become an American now! Godspeed, my Friend."

Selkirk nodded in acknowledgment at Cato then turned toward Maynard with a questioning stare. Militantly, Alex straightened his back in wait of the pirate's response to his silent question.

"Alex, kindly bid Commander Ogle my farewell! I too, would like a fresh start!"

Selkirk put his finger over his lips to signify the importance of the sheet of paper he was handing to them. With a low toned voice, Alex explained their exit plan. The light cast from the inflamed foundry made it easy to make out the scribblings Ogle had penned out on the map.

Rasmussen watched the fire starters load up into the back of a stolen ice truck! His little brother, Thomas was to go back to the Staats place and update the General on the new events that had just taken place! Thomas was also supposed to suggest to General Staats that another ounce of gold would ensure the reporting's accuracy!

Anne smacked the backside of the single Clydesdale pulling the ice wagon. Selkirk had already disappeared into the many rows of buildings built on the island's western coastline. Ogle's map promised refuge in the bottom half of a dilapidated warehouse on Duck Street!

Just as the "East Ward Ice Company's" horse wagon was about done with its right turn onto Bridge Avenue, Cato threw the wagon's loading door open and then tackled Rasmussen who was chasing them down the street in his bare feet! Ten minutes later, the wagon changed its direction and turned toward the Staat's place!

Blanche and Sporck were on the outs again! The vibrations from the rough road had caused two s of the clinic's wagon. Ike was refusing to go back after them on account of Ruby's soothsaying!

As Sporck had said, "this was no time to be bogged down with a baby!" and if it turned out they had a son, "he would bring a pretty penny on the block!" But that alone was not the reason they were squabbling!

Blanche insisted the thirty some blacks be stacked onto the back of the clinic's ambulance with their heads pointed toward the driver's side while Sporck chose to just throw them into the back of the wagon in a helter-skelter fashion! The end result was exactly what Blanche was reiterating before Ivan von Sporck knocked her out of their moving wagon!

Had there been a loaded pistol close by, Sporck would have most certainly been shot by it! Instead, Blanche simply followed the corpse filled wagon for close to a mile before Sporck allowed her to rejoin him on the cart's bench seat!

Foolishly believing a turtle-teared apology would suffice, Ike made the suggestion that the two of them pull off to the side of the road for a nice injection together! The result of that decision proved to be a radical misjudgment on Sporck's part!

No sooner than both had completed their fixes and were in their after-glow stage of euphoria, Blanche jabbed a nail into Sporck's right ear hole. Writhing in absolute agony, Ivan rolled out of the rolling wagon and onto the rocky road!

With Blanche now in the wagon's driver's seat, she proceeded to circle the horse drawn wagon around and begin chasing Sporck across an open field! Three more bodies were lost during that incident!

The entire altercation ended with both of them walking hand-in-hand back to the Trinity Church! Since the wagon's axel had broken and twenty percent of the bodies had bounced off the ambulance's bed anyway, they decided to make amends by shooting the horse and burning the whole kit and caboodle right there where all the trouble had started in the first place!

In their minds, not having to deal with the rigmarole of digging a mass grave and putting up with the pomp and circumstance of a typical negro funeral, their mutual decision was indeed the first-step toward a more compatible relationship. Concerning the phantom pregnancy, both agreed that selling the child was the best solution given the economic conditions at that time!

Samuel Fraunces was beside himself with frustration when he learned of Jemmy's abuse of his property! Frankly, the man's death saved him the unnerving responsibility of terminating him!

There was now a gaping hole in the management of the girls upstairs as well as the verdant favor brokering business! Jemmy would be a hard man to replace.

As fate would have it, that afternoon while Samuel was restocking his bar with a new barrel of ale, he met Cato and his fully cocked blunderbuss! Rasmussen furnished the formal introduction!

"Mister Fraunces, I was very sorry to hear about the death of your bartender. But it seems there is a replacement for him standing in the wings! His name is Cato and I sure hope and pray you will offer him the opportunity to take Jemmy's place!" said Rasmussen.

Samuel looked down at the frightened young lad with a comforting look upon his face. He then walked over to his cash box and withdrew one silver coin along with a small pistol which he cleverly hid in his coat sleeve!

When the tavern's owner handed Rasmussen the silver piece and began ushering the fast-footed boy from the building, he whipped the pistol from his woolen sleeve and pressed the weapon against Cato's temple! Surprisingly, Samuel Fraunces then uncocked his gun and winked at Cato as if it had all been a joke!

He then sent Rasmussen home with the agreement that none of what had transpired would ever be spoken of again! Once the boy had left through the tavern's backdoor, Samuel turned toward Cato and spoke.

"Am I to understand that you, Sir, are looking for a job?" questioned Samuel.

Cato broke into a roaring belly laugh and then responded to Fraunces's question.

"Only if you have a need for a half dozen good buzzard eggs!"

"Well in that case, may I ask if you had a number in mind?" queried Samuel.

"Seven-two-six." quickly snapped Cato.

"And the others?" fished the tavern owner.

"As yet, unnumbered!"

"Have these men ever rolled an egg?" Sam asked.

"One woman, four men, all pirates!" stiffly reported Cato.

"Oh, that's comforting!" sarcastically responded Fraunces.

Cato turned toward Samuel in a brotherly way but then walked toward a table where there were no chairs surrounding it. Skittishly he requested a bottle of whiskey, two glasses and a world map!

After a fairly long talk, Samuel Fraunces understood the how's and why's of Cato's presence. He also realized two more mind boggling things!

First, the King of England, George Augustus was making preparations to steal America from Britain and to make himself the ruler of it! Secondly, more than likely, Cato and he were brothers which meant that Black Sam Bellamy was their father!

This incubated trust! Therefore, the remaining obstacle was to protect Bellamy's betrothal of his holdings for the American war chest!

Chaloner Ogle dabbed a cool cloth into the empty socket in his lower left jaw! That and several other medical issues had to be attended to before he met with Walpole! Fortunately for Cal, the prime minister was recovering from an illness so his scheduled debriefing was delayed a week.

Much had changed in London since the Commander's absence. The people seemed to be more stilted than before. Even their steps reflected a dower aura suitable for wakes. They "felt" like pouting children, Cal thought.

It had been four days since the 'Whydah's' landing. Enough time to put it all behind him; but, he couldn't!

The killings were still vivid but that wasn't the nagger, it was the look in the eyes of the Americans! He had seen it before! It was the same glare given by the sailors on a defeated ship, one of anger mixed with righteousness!

And what was so strikingly ironic about it, Ogle understood their point of view! Truth be told, he was quietly rooting for them!

His main hope was, he would never have to launch an invasion against them! Cal pushed his way into the Black Dog Tavern.

In the rear of the tavern two men were arm-wrestling between numbers of candles serving as motivational stimulants for either weakening competitor! There was a lot of money riding in the back of the bar so the choice of seats upfront were wide open. Cal chose a booth. He felt like drinking alone.

After ordering a bottle of scotch and a clean glass, Commander Ogle pulled from his breast pocket a pencil and a folded piece of paper. He was attempting to construct a timeline for Walpole's report. The whiskey helped him to forget some of the superfluous details.

From the short yelp and some loudly rustling feet, Cal guessed that the contest going on in the back was over. To Ogle's surprise, one pair of those passing noisy boots belonged to Sir Robert Walpole!

Disguised as a wigless pedestrian, the British prime minister plopped down in the seat across from the commander and proceeded to fill up the glass he brought with him with Chaloner's scotch. Then with a guilty wink, Walpole ordered another bottle from the buxom barmaid he had summoned to the booth.

As Cal was preparing to offer a respectful stand, Robert Walpole reached over and grabbed his wrist so as to indicate not to draw attention to themselves! As if leaning over to tell Ogle a discolored joke, Robert told him why he was there!

"Commander, as your friend, I have come to warn you about some boobytraps which have been set for you! I regret having to say this, Chaloner, but the King has become quite suspicious of just about everyone these days! I believe the word 'paranoid' would befit his general mood," whispered Walpole.

Ogle tried to look shocked. He was unsure of Walpole's motives so he asked him pointblank, 'why he thought the King's mental state had gone askew?'.

"Because the bloody bastard tried to kill me!" spat Sir Robert Walpole.

Inwardly, Cal knew that the prime minister was probably correct about his assumption; however, for appearances sake, he gave Sir Walpole his best 'astounded' face! Once Ogle was sure that Walpole had bought in to his look, he proceeded with the other part of his act and exclaimed!

"King George tried to kill you? How can you be so sure of this, Sir?"

"Let me be clear with you, Commander, I may be a drunkard but I most certainly am no fool! Have you any doubt of the intentions of those in your past who have attempted to do you in, Chaloner?" cunningly queried the politician.

"No, Sir!" answered Commander Ogle.

"Then don't question my intuitiveness again!" Hissed Robert. "My apologies, Mister Prime Minister!"

"Cal, I followed you here in order to arm you with some critical information before you go traipsing into the parliamentary jaws awaiting you! They want to make a full investigation of the King's secret mission which involved the surreptitious releasing of the world's most dangerous pirates some of which were scheduled for execution!"

"Sir, as you are aware, I am not at liberty to speak with anyone regarding my orders and that includes members of the Parliament!" fired back Ogle.

"That may be so but the group I speak of have much further stretching tentacles than just needed for our empire! 'They' being faceless people of bottomless wealth, have assembled because of what appears to be a breach in their tightly managed establishment of the world's 'rules'!

Consequently, they are not happy with our mutual friend Gus! Soon, these men will come looking for you and they're going to want the truth about your mission's authenticities!

These folks mean business and my assumption is they will go to any lengths to obtain whatever it is they are looking for! If I were you, I'd cooperate with them and tell them what they want to know!" Gasped the heavily breathing prime minister.

"Sir, I can grasp in my mind 'who' these people are but what I can't understand is, what they could possibly glean from my latest catch and destroy mission! It was just not that big of a deal!" expounded the Commander.

"Did you find it odd, George's crew selection?" curtly questioned Walpole.

"Not particularly, Sir. There were others in past of similar scope!" said Cal flippantly.

"But how many of 'those' trips entailed the dropping off of three of the planet's most infamous pirates on the shores of New York?" venomously asked the Prime Minister.

Stunned, the commander helplessly looked into Robert Walpole's eyes. After a deep swallow of scotch, he answered the question.

"Because they jumped ship!"

"Cato too?" softly prodded Walpole.

"Especially him, Sir! Both he and Maynard didn't trust Britain's promise of freeing them! It's as simple as that, Robert!"

"What about Anne Bonnie?" bluntly questioned Walpole.

"She stayed back there with them! Curiously asking, Sir, why did you ask about her?" questioned Ogle.

"Oh my god, Man, you really don't know, do you?" spritely spouted Walpole.

"Know what!" angrily fired back Chaloner.

"Cal, have you ever heard of a pirate named, 'Black Sam'?" baited Walpole.

"Black Sam Bellamy! Of course I have!" Cal answered.

"Well, did you know the reason that Miss Bonnie was not hanged last spring was because the woman knew where Black Sam's money was hidden?"

Trying his best to recover from Walpole's bombshell of a question, Ogle did what most good commanders do when they are under a frontal assault, he attacked!

"Sir Walpole, I am but one of the swords used against the enemies of Britain! I do not question my orders nor do I examine the politics of them, Sir!"

"Does that exonerate you from your conscience, Cal?" venomously snarled Walpole.

"No!" flatly responded the Commander.

"Then by your coy recalcitrance, I gather that you are either protecting your friend the King, or you are ignorant as a stone of his doings! Which might it be, Commander Ogle?" stabbed Walpole.

"Sir, what in the bloody hell does 'Black Sam' have to do with any of these matters?" asked Ogle.

The Prime Minister examined the Commander's eyes looking for inklings of jocularity. He found none therefore he whispered his true thoughts!

"Because that goddamned 'pirate' is the financier of America's succession from England!"

"Well, they certainly are ready for war from what I saw over there! Jemmy's animal heads tried to burn Fort George down to the ground at New York after attempting a biological attack on Charlestown!

Yes, I'd say the Colonists are quite ready to shed Britain's chains given the agitations we have purposely or inadvertently cast upon them! I'm afraid we've fallen from our previously enjoyed 'big brother' status! Today, the Americans see us as a rabid pet!" Ogle said somewhat in agreement with Walpole's theory.

"And you really didn't know of Black Sam's involvement in this, Chaloner?" asked the pugnacious Prime Minister.

"Why should I, Sir? The man's been dead for years now! He was killed off of Nantucket, I believe!" quibbled Cal.

"Commander Ogle, do you know the name of the ship that 'Black Sam' died upon?" Innocently questioned Robert.

"No, Sir, I don't!" responded Ogle.

"It was the 'Whydah'!" lashed out Robert Walpole.

Daring not to stand for fear of toppling over, Cal felt the blood rush toward the center of his body! He just learned he had been sent by his friend on an innocuous mission for the sake of whacking the proverbial beehive!

George had ordered him to eradicate all who could have witnessed his misdoings! Cato no doubt, was to kill him and then make his way to New York where he would join up with the rest of the King's cohorts to make ready for America's new King, George Augustus II!

After gathering his senses, Chaloner Ogle then leaned forward across the table with his hands spread on the tabletop and began speaking.

"Then why didn't Cato and the others kill me? They certainly had the opportunities to do so!" blurted Ogle.

"Because they were double agents all working for the same cause and the same man!" responded Walpole.

"So, you're saying my entire crew were all the while actually American spies?" asked the befuddled Commander.

"As were Every and Hornigold! All recruited by the wealthiest human being on earth, Samuel Bellamy!" laughed Robert.

"What about Kimber, Stanfield and Bosman?" Ogle asked. "Just collateral! They were simply slavers hired to do a job." bluntly answered Walpole.

"Who the hell is Sporck and where does he fit into the game, Sir?" Ogle asked pointedly.

The British prime minister switched his demeanor to one of a man speaking of a licentious gravedigger. His teeth clenched when he spoke Sporck's formal name.

"Count Franz Anton von Sporck, founder of the International Order of St. Hubertus. This so called 'order' is in all actuality, nothing more than a sham!

He mostly entices the restless sons of plantation owners to join so they will become members of the "world's most prestigious hunting club"! Of course, Sporck's real intention is to soak his members along with their daddies' dry of whatever he can get from them!

Anton von Sporck is one of the bastard Hapsburg children tossed out of the empire to protect their fathers' names! Probably the Archduke of Austria was the sperm donor in Sporck's case! Either way, as long as Anton never sets foot in Hungary again, he will forever more be on their payroll!

But, Commander Ogle, that's not all! There is an interesting twist to this story one in which I believe will help you unwind the entanglement within your mind!

Sporck's sexual interests fall along a broad spectrum of preferences; i.e., sometimes he likes boys and sometimes he likes girls! There is one lover however who brings this whole thing into focus.

'Blanche' is her name!

Intelligence reports indicate the young woman is the daughter of the late Mary Hallett who by the way happened to be King George's paramour as well as one of his favorite special agents. As it turns out, Commander, Blanche's father is none other than, Black Sam Bellamy!"

Ogle stared at Walpole's mouth as he listened to the close of the Prime Minister's last sentence. He was utterly in shock!

Kindly, Samuel Walpole extended his outstretched arm so that his hand fell on Ogle's shoulder. Then with a comforting pat, Robert cleared his throat indicating he had more to say.

"Chaloner, since Caroline's murder, Gus has become affixed on war! Just during the time between your departure and return, our King has evaded any opportunity put before him which could lead to some peaceful solutions! Instead, he provokes his enemies into even greater confrontations!

It is my belief, Cal, our old buddy is plotting to embroil the planet in an all-out world war! I am practically sure he intends on making America his operations' headquarters once he spills all the British blood he needs to take ownership of it!" Bellowed Walpole.

"So that is why he is after Black Sam's legendary wealth!" Interrupted Ogle.

"That is partly correct, Commander, but, don't forget that Sporck too is after Sam's treasure!" corrected Robert Walpole.

"Just how much 'wealth' does it take for the king of the most powerful country in the world to turn against his own people? I can understand Sporck's reasoning but Gus's, never!" cried Ogle.

"Oh, Chaloner, this is not about money! It's about one-upmanship!" spouted Robert.

"One-upsmanship, Sir?" questioned Chaloner Ogle.

"You see, Cal, Augustus along with his dear mother were severely abused by George I, Gus's father! At one time or another the old man had both of them thrown into jail over some simple family squabbles!

I'm afraid that anger has worn away our King's temperament and left only the exposed nerves belonging to his father's irreparable abuse! Additionally you should know, Samuel Bellamy and Gus's father were for over a decade, business partners and very good friends!

I would expect you are beginning to get the picture, Commander! But let's not forget why I'm here! I came to warn you of those whom I believe would want to know the whereabouts of ole Black Sam's treasure!

I, like you, have no idea where it might be! But I do know that Black Sam Bellamy is very much alive and he was the instrumental cause of overturning the King's latest attempt at infiltrating the Colonial government!

'Operation Cricket' failed due to Bellamy's high jacking of our agents and his converting them into Americans!" lectured Robert Walpole.

"What do you recommend I do, Robert?" asked the frightened Commander.

"I suggest you do as I am doing; that is, leave England at once!" coldly stated Walpole.

At four-thirty and on schedule, Robert Crommelin drove a delivery wagon from 'The Island Lumber Company' and backed his load onto the delivery dock located at the rear of the Queen's Head Tavern. On the bed of that two horse wagon were twenty-four slabs of tongue and groove lumber.

Once succinctly docked, Crommelin leaped from the delivery wagon's seat and rapidly entered the service entrance's door. Ten minutes later, that same driver snapped the rumps of his horses and skillfully guided his rig into a northerly direction. This time, Robert was hauling a much heavier load!

Within the box fitted together with numbered pieces of lumber, were Samuel Fraunces, Cato and his fellow pirates!

They believed they were on their way to General Staats's plantation but in actuality they were headed into the heart of the Iroquois Confederacy! That's where Black Sam Bellamy lived!

Alex Selkirk knew how to bide his time. He had been a prisoner before. At least back then he had sunlight, Alex thought.

They had nabbed him soon after he disembarked the 'Whydah'! Just as he was within a stone's throw of his villa, two men jumped out from behind some overgrown hedges while another goon crowned him with a wooden mallet! He was tightly bound, bagged, and then delivered to wherever he was at that moment.

Selkirk suspected he was in a cellar of some type. The sweet smell of machine oil supported that notion. Tools of all sorts had been orderly arranged across the four imprisoning walls. Hand drawn numbers with decimal points were meticulously labeled beneath each implement.

All Alex could do was gaze out from his chair and wonder who had done this to him. "What do they want?" Was the pressing question on his mind. There was no sound nor an escape option!

Descriptively, Alex Selkirk was a man strapped in an oak armchair who had been deprived of much sensory worth for five days! His tongue had swollen to the point that breathing was done only through his nose! The room's temperature was thirty-eight degrees Fahrenheit.

On day six, Alex was awakened by the sound of a key rattling in a door from the next floor above him! Then came the recognizable sounds of a one-legged man making his way down a flight of wooden steps. The unmistakable echoing of a brass tipped peg instantaneously told Selkirk who had shanghaied him!

"Alex, it seems as though the years have been good to you despite the complications normally following a reasonably long prison stent! Buccaneering can be awfully tenuous at times! One just never knows who their enemy is in that game! Wouldn't you agree, Alex?" tauntingly questioned Captain Thomas Stradling.

Unable to speak because of his swollen tongue, Alex just glared at his capturer! Stradling had expected nothing less from his former sailing master therefore he opened a cannister filled with chicken broth after he had pulled up a chair and situated it directly in front of where Alex was buckled into. Stradling then offered Selkirk a spoonful of the aromatic soup!

"It was your choice to leave the 'Cinque Ports', Alex, not mine! Captain William Dampier your commanding officer, was the one who insisted that you have your way!" coldly stated Thomas Stradling.

Alex continued accepting the mouthfuls of broth he was being spoon-fed. Defiantly he offered nothing to Stradling's comments except a slight nod of appreciation for the sustenance. His former commander continued with further remarks.

"Because you lambasted Captain Dampier in front of his entire crew, he had no choice but to allow you to remain on Juan Fernandez Island. What you said I shall repeat, 'Dampier, I would prefer a musket, a hatchet, a knife, a cooking pot, a Bible and some clothes to another hour on this waterlogged ship!'

I was there, Selkirk, and I'll never forget it! No, you brought that one upon yourself, old boy! I had nothing to do with it!

But, that does bring us to a matter at present so I'll get right to the point! Before we begin however, let me inform you that I nor anyone else will be entering my foundry again until my return next summer! That means when you get down to the 'short-hairs' of it, Alex, this will become your tomb if you do not accurately answer my questions! Am I clear on that?" slyly summed up Commander Stradling.

Selkirk nodded.

"Given that your tongue is swollen and in bad need of relief, I shall provide you a hefty spoonful of this delicious broth for each 'yes' or 'no' answer you give me to the series of questions I have instore for you! Should you provide me with a falsehood, Alex, then I shall simply close up shop and leave you as Dampier did! Understood?"

Again, Alex nodded.

"Excellent, here is my initial question, 'Were you on the 'Whydah' along with Commander Ogle recently?" sharply questioned Stradling.

Selkirk's face turned blue! His head thrashed forward and backward as he struggled for a breath of air! Alex's tongue had apparently closed off his windpipe!

In an effort to save his captive's life, Stradling grabbed the suffocating man's jaw with his left hand while pressing the spoon down on Selkirk's massive tongue blade in order to allow for some oxygen intake! This proved to be a fatal mistake on Commander Stradling's part.

At the speed of a snapping turtle's head, Selkirk locked his teeth into the base of the spoon and jabbed the handle into Stradling's eye! Without so much as a flinch, Selkirk's former commander dropped to the floor like a sack of potatoes!

By dawn of day seven, Alex had successfully chewed through Thomas's jacket pocket and retrieved his reading spectacles consequently providing after its lenses were shattered, a right nifty cutting tool! It was enough at least for Selkirk to escape into London's abysmal underground!

William Burnet had ridden his granddaughter's pony around the entire perimeter of his estate. There wasn't a single thing wrong with the animal as his granddaughter had claimed! The retiring governor knew two things practically better than anybody else on the planet! Governor Burnet was an expert horseman and he knew people!

'Will' as his friends called him, was aware his favorite grandchild 'Misty', had fallen in love with a feisty two year old appaloosa the Mohawks had dropped off for him to sell for them. The governor connected the dots and immediately realized that Misty's pony had contracted a mild case of 'coveting thy neighbor's horse'!

The problem with giving her the Indians' appaloosa was not because of the price, it was cheap enough. The real reason was due to the fact that the animal had been stolen from a Canadian rancher! A brand on its rump attested to that!

So as these things were mulling about in Governor Burnet's mind, it is no wonder that he did not notice the subtle changes in the barn which had gone on while he was taking Misty's pony for a test ride. As Will was hanging up his granddaughter's bridle on its regular wooden peg, he heard the caustic sound of a hammer being cocked into place.

Suddenly the tack room's lantern was extinguished leaving the Governor with only his sense of hearing! A nonthreatening voice broke the icy silence.

"Good morning to you, Governor! Please forgive our boorish introduction, Sir, but a 'buzzard' needs to be careful these days! General Staats sends his best! He has brought you a half dozen eggs!" said Robert Crommelin.

"Bob, you scared the shit out of me! You were supposed to be here day before yesterday! What the hell happened?" vociferously spat Will.

"We had to burn our way out of town! Ogle and Selkirk returned to England leaving Cato and five of his men or I should say, four men and one woman behind! They were the crew that foiled Sporck's onslaught and killed Jemmy!" summed up Crommelin.

"I would like to shake their hands and I would if I could see them!" quipped Burnet.

Cato lit the still smoking wick illuminating the faces of the infamous pirates Robert Crommelin had hauled up from Manhattan! The Governor's jaw flew open with amazement when he compared their actual personas with the one's he had pictured in his mind!

Although the amber flicker masked most of his facial features, William Burnet could not hide the disappointment on his face! He solemnly began speaking.

"The Iroquois along with a smattering of French mercenaries have been raiding our villages recently! Throughout the German Flatts area have come reports of families completely disappearing without a sign of a struggle being left behind. According to a few witnessing survivors, they believe the young women and children are being taken into Canada!

Tanacharison their leader, has made it impossible for anyone to pass through his so-called Mingo territory. There have been more than a couple of attempts to strike a peace accord with him but his response has always been the same. He beheads the olive branch bearers!" Said Burnet.

"Why haven't the soldiers from Forts Herkimer squashed this, Governor?" anxiously segued Cato.

"Because King George does not wish to antagonize the French! They've got their hands full with the Spanish at the moment and therefore can't afford to spread themselves out too thin!" rebutted Will Burnet.

"Sir, how might you suggest we reach Sam Bellamy's property?" impatiently asked Cato.

The Governor then straightened his back and took two steps forward so he was a nose length away from Cato's face. He then spoke his mind.

"Number seven-two-six, and the rest of you hoodlums, hear me well on this, we were doing just fine with the Indians and the bloody French until your previous bosses began meddling in our affairs! Because of it, we are left with the burden of smoothing out your King's entanglements!

For your information, we have lost close to three hundred people due to Britain's insistence on Colonial separatism! Hell, man, we live beside these people! They have been our friends for more than a century so now we're at war with our neighbors simply because ole 'Gus' says we are? I don't think so!" preached the Governor.

"Governor Burnet, may I also remind you that the reason we are here is to bolster the Colonial cause! In other words, Sir, we are on the same mission as you; after all, we too are Americans!" softly stated Cato.

With Cato's eloquent retort, Will's bristled demeanor seemed to melt away. The elderly statesman lowered his head and then offered an apologetic smile to his tack room visitors. He then indirectly answered Cato's original question but replaced it with a new one.

"Have you ever heard of the military term, 'Trojan horse'?" questioned Burnet.

Everyone in the smoky room nodded to the positive.

"In five days there will be a full eclipse of the sun! In two days, Abraham Staats will arrive with a hundred and eighty of King's College's strapping young men along with as many militia as he can conger up!

We're going to make those goddamned Mingo bastards beg us to pass through their territory! I'm tired of pussyfooting around with those lowdown dogs anyway!"

"Governor, how can we be of service to what seems like an already well planned attack?" seriously questioned Cato.

"Oh, we're not going to attack anyone! We are just going to scare the living daylights out of the red rascals!

To answer your question, Cato, if all goes as expected, we're going to use you and your men as decoys! Miss Bonnie will be the bait!" chortled the Governor.

Blanche was in no mood to entertain guests! The spasms had returned to mostly her back muscles and she didn't feel up to the challenge of pretending to be Anton von Sporck's happy little expectant bride!

Ike had gotten a message which stated that within the week and probably as soon as the coming Sunday, Pietro Ottoboni's personal chef would be paying the Trinity Church a visit! Blanche knew it was a smokescreen or more accurately, a payoff!

She knew that Sporck had secretly been meeting with some of the Catholic missionaries passing in and out of the city harbors. Something had happened or it was about to; otherwise, a clandestine tinged rendezvous wouldn't be necessary! Blanche's suspicions leaned toward Ike's obsession with the undermining of King George's rein!

Since her pregnancy admission, Ike had very little to do with her! There was absolutely no substantive conversation taking place between the two unless it was a complaint of some sort regarding her weight gain or her insatiable appetite! In short, Blanche was miserable!

Justified or not, Blanche started to hate Sporck! She had resolved that once her son was born, she would find her father. He would take care of both of them!

Alex Selkirk knew if he attempted to retrace any of his past's footsteps his antagonists would nab him for sure! His adrenalin pumps were forcing him toward the edge of panic. He had no friends but he did have the money he had gotten off of Stradling's body!

Maybe the sea was the safest place, he thought, but then again they would expect him to think that way! Alex decided his best alternative was to leave London and join back up with Cato in New York!

In order to do that he would need some help from a few unsavory characters. Liverpool would be his next stop!

Red Squirrel proudly stood on top of the only mountain that one could see most of the German Flatts area which included Fort Herkimer. His single eagle feather jutted out just over his right shoulder. He touched it frequently just to make sure it was still there!

It represented his greatest accomplishment to date! He had become the youngest boy in his family to reach 'Brave' status before growing pubic hair!

On his third day of his assigned ten day watch, Red Squirrel noticed high plumes of black smoke coming from the town of German Flatts some fifteen miles away! Not only were there signs of fire but also the sounds of distant cannon shots!

From his naked eyes, it appeared as though there were hundreds of horsemen surrounding the British fort but there was too much smoke to distinguish who they were! Red Squirrel needed to report the turn of events immediately!

Thirty minutes later and after a ten mile ride, Red Squirrel reported his sightings to Tanacharison. Following that, the entire Iroquois Confederacy was alerted to battle readiness! Smoke and drums were the methods used to spread the news of the coming conflict.

Seven councilmen were appointed by Tanacharison to surveil the reported activity. They were to signal back their findings by sundown!

If indeed there was an expressed intent against his people, he would unleash his warriors upon the German Flatts' population! And just for spite, he'd have his warriors wipe out the Fort Herkimer's soldiers once and for all!

Color Guardsmen, Hercules Mulligan and Alexander Hamilton along with the drummer boy, Samuel Woodhull stood at attention as General Staats waited for the remainder of the cadets to fall into their proper positions! It was four o'clock so the fort's shadow would prevent the Mingo's from seeing their formation.

Finally after an antagonizing length of time, maybe ten minutes, and after his own militiamen had fallen in behind the cadets, Abraham Staats laid out the plans which were to take place over the next twelve hours. It would prove to be one of the greatest ruses ever performed on American soil!

"Alright men, this is the way we're going to get this wagonload of the King's men through Tanacharison's warriors! We'll use their own superstition to gain access to Samuel Bellamy's citadel!" Said General Staats confidently.

James Wolfe rode his horse up to the rear of the battalion's formation. Knowing full well that the one hundred and eighty one cadets he was leading were frightened, he dismounted and began walking amongst their ranks and informally chatting with each one of the jittery lads.

Tensions eased a bit when General Staats brought up two wagons complete with a cooking staff and a half dozen freshly killed piglets. Immediately the moods of everyone noticeably lightened as Staat's kitchen crew began their preparations for supper. One hour remained until sundown.

More wagons, about six of them in all, were pulled up onto the clearing surrounding Fort Herkimer! Three of the trucks were packed tight with what looked like boxes of candelabras, the kind used to hang on church ceilings. The other wagons had been stacked up to their sideboards' edges with yards of black cloth.

Soon after the cadets from King's College and General Staat's two hundred or so men had finished their dinners, everyone noticed some torch lights approaching the fort! Governor Burnet, General Staats and Cato immediately mounted their horses and rode off to meet what appeared to be an Iroquois war party!

Strangely, all wearing unbuttoned British officers' topcoats, seven of Tanacharison's elders closed in on the Governor's representatives as if they were in an attack mode! General Staats was the first to make a comment on the rapidly oncoming warriors.

"Steady boys, they are just trying to test our fortitude! With all of the smoke they can't count the number of soldiers we have behind us. They just want to slake their curiosities, that's all!"

Four of the Iroquois horsemen split off from the others and rode in a quarter mile half circle in order to buffer the white men's rear thus protecting their three senior councilmen from the fort's sniper fire. They boxed in the Governor and his entourage!

Black Beaver lightly kicked the rump of his horse so he would establish himself as the Mingo spokesperson! Governor Burnet followed suit.

Both elderly men bore into the other's eyes. Each of them were searching for tell-tale dilations!

Without a single word being spoken, Will Burnet carefully pulled from his fur lined overcoat a copy of the most recently published, "The New York Gazette". Will then unrolled the three page newspaper and at a turtle's pace, handed it over to Black Beaver.

The broad shouldered councilman took the Governor's offering and blankly stared at the misaligned print. He then dropped the Gazette's copy to the ground making sure his horse's hooves trampled it!

Black Beaver drove his painted mare in between Cato and William Burnet so he and the Governor's face were no more than a foot apart! Black Beaver spoke.

"The only thing I distrust more than the white man's tongue is his quill! Why have you brought so many soldiers to our border?" angrily asked Black Beaver.

"Chief Black Beaver, we bring only the last wishes from the Holy Roman Emperor, Charles VI! Before his resurrection into heaven, he spiritually summonsed his many Colonial priests to carry out his final edict!

In his dying words, he asked that the "Princess of the Darkness" be sacrificed on behalf of the people he admired the most during his lifetime! Right or wrong, the Holy Emperor believed that the Iroquois Nation were God's chosen people; he felt that it would be on your land that Jesus's second coming would occur!

By sacrificing the 'Princess of the Darkness' at the mouth of the Mohawk River, Pope Charles VI was under the belief that Tanacharison's people would forever remain an impregnable nation and therefore the safest place for our Savior's return to this Earth!" stated Governor Burnet.

"Then why did you bring those armed militia with you? Or, did you think we dumb savages don't have the sense to see beyond your deceptive tactics?" incipiently spoke Black Beaver.

"Exactly the reason why I brought you the Gazette's announcement of the Emperor's death! And, as for the militia, I brought them here for your protection!" burnet excitedly said.

"For our protection?" laughingly quizzed the Chief Councilman.

"Indeed!" smugly stated Burnet.

"From whom?" fired back Black Beaver.

"God!" yelled the Governor.

In the light of the 'Super moon' one could see plainly the consternation within Black Beaver's eyes. He became as pale as a ghost.

Even though he was obviously at a loss of words, the Chief did his best to offer a quickly put together rebuttal.

"And what will this 'god' do to my people if I do not cooperate with your morose wishes, Governor William Burnet?" snapped Black Beaver.

"He will steal the light from the sky!" curtly answered Will. "That is absolute hogwash! You may not pass through our land!"

calmly stated Black Beaver.

With that finality having been so ineloquently stated, the four rear positioned councilmen backed their horses up and then began whooping and hollering as if they were in preparation of an attack!

Just as all seven of the Iroquois representatives had regathered into what appeared to be a war party, the moon began to darken!

Presenting a look of utter panic and mixed with the body language of a terrified human being, Black Beaver started screaming the names of the six others who had ridden with him! He ordered them to follow him back to Tanacharison's position which of course they did!

This left the Governor, Cato and General Staats staring across a darkening span of land with only the lessening images of their seven Iroquois visitors lost in a cloud of kicked up snow. Cato was the first to speak.

"General Staats, may I make a suggestion, Sir?"

"By all means, Cato. What are your thoughts?" said Abraham Staats.

"While Black Beaver is conferring with Tanacharison why not set our plan into motion? Let's get Anne Bonnie dressed and into the back of the wagon and start the procession before he returns!

"That's a pretty risky proposition you're talking about there, Cato! I've grown up beside these Indians and have gotten along with them for pretty close to forty years now; but, recently they have come under the influence of the French!

My guess is, Tanacharison's people feel like they are being pressed between three separate countries! And, they are right about that!

They very well know, sooner or later there will be nothing left of any of their five nations at the conclusion of the many wars to come! I'd guess I would be ornery too if I were in their shoes!

But be that as it may, I agree with you, Cato, but please understand this, the odds of your crew making it to the mouth of the Mohawk River are mighty thin! The ten miles that lay ahead puts you on the edge of the Iroquois's sacred burial grounds!

They are not as civil as even the fellows you were just introduced to! As a matter of probable interest, the Algonquin meaning for the word "Mohawk", is "flesh-eater" so keep that in mind as you get closer to the headwaters! Do not underestimate their treachery, Cato!" spoke the Governor in a fatherly manner.

As the Earth's shadow had halfway eclipsed the giant moon, one hundred and eighty one barefooted cadets clad in hooded priests' costumes and each carrying a fully lit two pound candelabra, headed out across a mile long stretch of snow covered road! They were in a single file formation and being led by the also barefooted Cato and his crew!

Anne was tied to a 'T' shaped structure that had been secured in the center of their ceremonial wagon. The outside temperature was below the freezing mark.

From Tanacharison's telescopic perspective, it appeared that a long and fiery snake was weaving its way toward his village! He was impatiently waiting for Black Beaver's explanation.

Finally, the Chief Councilman raced his horse up to Logstown Rock where he knew the six nation chief was waiting. Black Beaver was a little bit embarrassed with the authentic circumstances surrounding the story he was about to spin; therefore, he decided to embellish it some!

"King Tanacharison, according to Governor Burnet's words, Pope Charles VI has died! Supposedly on the Pope's deathbed, he called for the "Princess of the Darkness" to be sacrificed at the mouth of the Mohawk River so 'our' nations would forever be protected from our foes!

General Abraham Staats asked if his soldiers could escort the ceremonial procession but I forbid him to encroach another step onto our property! I pray that my decisiveness pleases you, your highness!" meekly said the Chief.

"So who exactly is this 'Princess of the Darkness', Black Beaver?" demanded the Iroquois king.

"Your majesty, she is a gift to you as I understand! Once her body has been cast into the river, we shall be empowered to climatically thwart any offenses to our people! As you can plainly see, King Tanacharison, with her presence she has caused the moon to darken!" Black Beaver said in a high pitched voice.

"I don't put much stock in the words of white men! But if they are unarmed and all they want to do is sacrifice a princess and fling her ashes into the Mohawk River, I can see no harm in that!

Acts of goodwill shown toward our friendly neighbors will benefit us immensely but let me very clear on this point, should there be any other intention shown by our visitors other than the ones described, I want you and War Eagle to incinerate the whole bunch of them!

In that you gave them permission to pass through to the Mohawk's headwaters, I shall appoint you as their overseer! I don't want a single one of those bloody priests to be left to wander any further north than their requested destination!

I suggest that you have War Eagle's braves flank the mourners all the way to their destination! Once they satiate their ridiculously primitive ritual, you are to return to me with the guarantee that those that entered our territory are escorted off of it by morning's light!" bristly stated Tanacharison.

After Black Beaver's departure, the Iroquois leader placed his telescope to his right eye and began counting the number of candelabras passing below him. He wrote the number, '189' on his pant leg!

Blanche rolled her eyes when she heard the insincere remarks being exchanged between Sporck and Cardinal Pietro Ottoboni's chef! It was a collection call!

"How in the world are you doing, Piero?" Greeted Sporck.

"The sea was rough and the wagon ride was even tougher on this old man but considering that, I am doing well, my Friend! I must say, this Colonial living has seemingly done well for you; you're as fit as a fiddle!" obsequiously spoke Chef Columbo.

"I received the message you sent over a month ago regarding your arrival to Philadelphia. You have warmed my heart by your gracious journey to New York, Sir!

Tell me, Piero, for what occasion do we need to celebrate regarding your visit to America?" Anton von Sporck curiously asked.

A smile grew across Piero's face which signaled to Sporck that Ottoboni's presence had to do with much more than a visit from a childhood friend. Something that Ike was unaware of had happened!

Sporck had about a moment's notice to ask the obvious suspense breaking questions but then Piero Columbo pulled out of his leather satchel a folded copy of "The New York Gazette".

There on the second page of the monthly newspaper's publication dated December of 1740, was an announcement of Charles VI's death! The headlines written by J.P. Zenger read, 'Death of the Holy Roman emperor ends the Habsburg's lineage!'

As Sporck read onward he too smiled! His excitement was exemplified by his planting a big kiss on the visiting Chef's mouth. But then Sporck quickly turned toward his old chum with an enormously pressing question to ask you.

"What about his daughter, Maria Theresa? Surely, she will be under consideration to fill his shoes!"

"Not a chance, Ike! You know the family better than I do! There is no way a Hapsburg would allow a woman to 'man' such a large empire as theirs! No, I am sure the Austrians will select my former employer, Cardinal Pietro Ottoboni as the next Emperor!" said Piero defensively!

"Did you say, 'former employer', Piero? Were you caught?" sharply questioned Ike.

"I don't think so but I certainly didn't meander through the streets of Vienna for very long after the Pope's collapse! My accomplices all of which have departed this earth, arranged my passage to America! I was the galley master on a damned cargo ship for eight miserable weeks!" whined Columbo.

"How did you do it, my Friend?" gasped Sporck.

"With a rotted oyster!" answered the possibly infamous chef.

"Was Ottoboni instrumental in these doings?" queried Ike.

"Of course!" condescended Piero.

"Then why did you feel you had to flee from your home? You always loved the Fatherland, Piero?" responded Sporck in a bullying manner.

"Because I am the only man except for you, who knows of Cardinal Ottoboni's aspirations! I was hoping to land some kind of a position on the island and lay low for a while just in case ole Pietro decided to 'erase' the only track left on the trail!

I might even make New York my permanent home! What are your thoughts of that, Ike?" mildly asked Piero.

"That may not be the best decision, my Friend! This is pretty rough country up here or at least it has been for me! The weather is cantankerous and most of the Colonists are as rough as corncobs!

You'd need a fairly large grubstake to get started and if you're hoping to meet a lady in these parts, there aren't any!" said Sporck.

"I don't know about that, Ike! I met a woman just last night that indeed met my fancy!

After we docked yesterday, I got a room at the Dartmouth Inn.

As soon as I got settled, I walked across the street over to the Queen's Head Tavern for a pint. That's when I met her!" Recalled the Chef.

"Since you have already entwined with the woman of your dreams, that part seems to be taken care of! It seems the only remaining issue is 'money' right?

My dear Boy, might I assume that you have come to pay your respects to an old friend and wishing to receive his promised payment? Am I correct about that, Piero?"

Columbo embarrassingly nodded.

"After we hoist a few brews together I'll have my assistant take you down to show you an ideal spot for your new home! You'll make a delightful neighbor, you will!" Said Sporck.

"That's mighty generous of you, Ike, but I'm going to look around for a bit before I decide whether I prefer the city or the country! Who knows, I might even take up farming!

If it's all the same to you, I'd just as soon be paid in gold, Sir," edgily stated Colombo.

"Then in that case, Piero, come inside and let's get a hot meal in you! You can leave your buggy tied up out front. My stable boy will come along directly and he'll give her a bag of oats," reassuringly stated Sporck.

The two men walked down the slate covered pathway leading toward the rectory's front door. As soon as they entered, the smells of an opium based concoction shockingly greeted them! Blanche bulgingly naked, was standing over the cooking stove!

"Good morning, Gentlemen! After a three night span of sleeplessness coupled with a few hundred roundhouse kicks from the rambunctious little bastard laying in my belly, I elected to take a holiday away from this misery! Please excuse my appearance but mommy needed a little helper today!

If you boys would have yourselves a seat, I'll get the jug and a couple of those French goblets! Mister Columbo, what did you think of the Queen's Head Tavern?" Coiled Blanche.

Stumbling for words and purposely trying to keep his eyes off of Blanche's humongous breasts, Piero turned toward his old friend, Sporck using his movement as a respectful alibi, and began answering her question as delicately as Blanche had asked it.

"I liked it a lot! It's as clean as a whistle but when I was there, the place was pretty much empty! Most of the usual's I was told, were up in the Iroquois lands helping some of the King's men through to the Canadian border!

'Misty', the woman I met, told me that on normal nights the place was generally packed to the walls but apparently something sort of earth shattering was going on! I believe she said they took the cadets from a nearby college with them!" rattled on the chef.

Sporck abruptly stood and then briskly walked around to the back of Piero's chair, stopped, withdrew a pistol from his jacket pocket, cocked it and stuck the muzzle into the Columbo's ear! Sporck then softly spoke like they were back yonder in the 'good old days'.

"It is very important that you clear your murky memory, Piero, or I am afraid your visit to New York will end badly for you, my Friend! Please go back in your mind and tell me everything you can possibly recall about your experience at the Queen's Head Tavern! I want the names of the folks whom you may have overheard being spoken of and especially those that sweet "Misty" may have gossiped about!

I shall now ask my chubby little spouse to fasten you into your chair! This way you won't be distracted during those anticipated spells of amnesia! But, Piero, there is a silver lining at the end of this story if in fact your hindsight is on the mark! Do you understand, Mister Columbo?"

The now blindfolded chef nodded but it was obvious he was as angry as a hornet! This caused a certain degree of consternation for Blanche for in her mind, his behavior was disturbing her state of ecstasy!

To remedy her angst, Blanche prepared one syringe for Chef Columbo's acceptable remembrances and another one for his forgetfulness! The first contained the 'smack'. Blanche's second syringe held a few drops of lye. She playfully began questioning Piero.

"Say three names of people whom you may have heard mentioned during your time spent at or near the tavern!" giggled Blanche.

"I'll have you both arrested for this! Let me go!" screamed Piero. "What were some names?" coldly asked Blanche.

Columbo said nothing.

Blanche inserted the lye squirting needle into Piero's neck which instantaneously made the man start convulsing. She repeated her last question.

"Staats! Cato! King George and who ever in hell else there was… lady, I swear there were no others I can recall!

Please let me go! I'll forget about the hundred pounds!" screamed Columbo.

"Now, mommy's going to make her baby happy!" said Blanche as she nodded to Sporck to pull his pistol's trigger.

They then flipped a coin for the cleanup duty! Blanche lost the toss.

Chaloner Ogle pulled up the thick wool collar of his pea coat's lapels and pinched them together as tightly as they could get. Forty knot winds were turning the sheets of falling sleet into a blinding foe.

A sudden blast of wind shifted the air currents enough so that Ogle got a whiff of tobacco smoke! Using the sides of buildings and peek-through louvered shutters, Cal was able to negotiate his way toward what he hoped would be an oasis.

The sign over the establishment's entranceway read, "The Spot". Six feet of an ice covered bannister dishonestly steadied Ogle's descent down the stairs.

An oak door with a heavy lock on the front of it was all that greeted Chaloner.

The basement's alcove he was attempting to stand in offered very little light but he was fairly sure there was a message painted on the door's front.

He struck a match so he could read it. When he did, he caught an instantaneous glimpse of Alexander Selkirk!

"Commander Ogle, I'm going to ask you to raise your hands into the air! Do not reach for your weapons! Just answer my questions!

Why were you following me?" demanded Alex.

"Alex, thank god, you're alright!" proclaimed Ogle.

"Answer my question, Commander!" sternly pressed Selkirk.

As the burning matchstick was nearly at Ogle's fingertips, he flipped it backwards and into Selkirk's face! With a sharp stomp onto the top of Alex's left foot followed by a knee driven into his crotch and taking under consideration the glass-slick surface they were tussling on, the seasoned warriors ended up flat on their backs! Both men began laughing!

From their supine positions the men only for a fleeting second, chose to ignore reality; rather, they pretended to order an imaginary dinner. Alex selected the proper wine while Chaloner carefully matched it with a smoked pheasant. But then came the 'clip-clop' sounds of the local constable's wagon!

"And what might you two ruffians be doing loitering around down there? You blokes don't have larceny on your minds do you? Say!" demanded the policeman.

"Constable, I'm very grateful you came along! I was taking a leisurely stroll home from tipping a few when this bloody idiot tried to rob me!" Selkirk excitedly explained.

"Now, that's a bloody dog's assed lie, if I ever heard one, Sir! This eel has been peeking into my windows trying to steal a gander at my wife! I had just caught up with him about the time you showed up! I was getting ready to tan his hide, I was!" rebutted Cal.

"In that case, how about the two of you getting your asses up here right this minute! If I have to come down there after you, you'll rue the day you met ole John Sampler's ugly stick!" yelled Constable Sampler.

The orange glimmer cast from Constable Sampler's carriage lamp offered just enough light for Selkirk to catch Ogle's signal. A decision to spare a fellow countryman's life would have to be made if they were able to provoke the lawman into their trap. But that was a longshot!

John Sampler was nobody's fool! He looked like he had been a cop for a long time!

"Alright! Get up here, pronto!" demanded the hot tempered policeman.

No sound came from The Spot's alcove.

"This is your last chance! Come out of there right now!" Yelled Sampler.

John could hear the men snickering. He carefully climbed out of his ice crusted carriage with a lead filled 'Billy' clinched in his meaty fist.

Constable Sampler stood at the top of the slick flight of steps. Because of the alcove's darkness and the step's condition, he attempted to appeal to the men's common sense.

"It is cold out here, Guys! You've had your fun! Just come on out of there and we'll forget about the whole thing! Now, come on damnit!" said the agitated law officer.

More snickers.

Like a wild bear, John lumbered down the rock staircase missing all but the first and last step of the decline! By the time he caught some semblance of balance, Ogle and Selkirk had the man hog tied and ready for loading!

With a whole lot of effort and not much conversation, Commander Ogle, Alexander Selkirk and John Sampler drove out of that strange part of London and on to another section of the city where there was a higher elevation! Soon it would be Mister Sampler's turn to make a life or death decision!

"Alex, it is absolutely unbelievable the coincidence of our ending up at The Spot at the same time and under the circumstances we are currently experiencing! It's almost as if it were a preplanned meeting, don't you think?" lightly questioned Ogle.

"There was no 'preplanning' on my part, Cal, I'll assure you of that! I ended up in the hands of an old captain of mine! The bastard's name was Thomas Stradling!

Commander, there was nothing political about his intentions at all! He wanted to know about Black Sam's treasures' whereabouts!

Even though Constable Sampler was gagged and tied upright in the back seat of his police wagon, he was still trying to make loud noises in order to alert the others of his predicament! Anyway, a whap on the side of his head kept him quiet long enough for them to reach the top of Westerham Heights. Screaming was acceptable there!

Ogle handed Alex the reins connected to the constable's horse once he had silenced the lawman. He sat back down into his wagon's seat and answered Selkirk's conspiracy question.

"I met with Walpole! In short, he said our King was a megalomaniac and is planning a full-scale attack on the Colonies once he gets the Spanish under wraps! Apparently the Prime Minister believes as I do, America is to become the headquarters for George Augustus's new world order!

Robert Walpole also mentioned Black Sam Bellamy's part in ruining the King's 'Operation Cricket'! It was the King's intention to imbed his future cabinet members within the already congealing American government!

Surprisingly as you already know, Black Sam did exactly the same thing to us! Somehow, Mister Bellamy turned most of our crew into expatriates as well!" Ogle said.

"Cal, do you think Black Sam is doing all of his magical stuff because of money?" queried Alex.

"No, I don't! I am sure it's the idea of 'freedom'!" stated Ogle. "Freedom from what?" quizzed Selkirk.

"I'm not sure, Alex. Maybe it's just the concept of it that is so alluring! But, I do know one thing, men like Cato, Every, Maynard and even Anne Bonnie, can't be bought for any price!

No, Captain Selkirk, those people weren't swayed by Black Sam's gold! They had previously experienced the loss of freedom if you will remember. I would expect their stints in prison made that commodity, 'freedom', quite priceless!" said Cal.

"Commander, shouldn't we go directly to King George about this? I mean, goddamn it, you grew up with the man, surely he can't say we did anything disloyal to the Crown! We accomplished our mission, didn't we?" whined Alex.

"That is true except for one thing! We were supposed to kill everyone on the 'Thomas' along with any other witnesses of our crime!" yelled Ogle.

"We were following orders, Commander Ogle! We committed no crimes!" argued Selkirk.

"But we didn't explicitly follow the King's 'orders'! We chose to rescue them instead and then to top it all off, they defected!" spat Ogle.

"We did the right thing, Sir! No decent man alive would have allowed those valorous people to be at the hands of the likes of Jemmy! They risked their lives for us; therefore, they deserved the same conciliation!" angrily remarked Alex.

"Maybe now, you can see those pirates' reasonings for declaring their independence from the British! They lost their trust of the kingdom and truthfully, I don't blame them! I'm thinking about doing the same thing myself!" harshly said Ogle.

As the horse strained to crest the top of Westerham Heights, John Sampler became the object of focus. Selkirk parked the police wagon and then scotched the wheels with monkey head sized rocks. Ogle pulled the constable out of his seat and threw him on the ground as if he were a sack of potatoes!

The two seamen lifted the bound man to his feet and marched him to the edge of a hundred and twenty foot drop-off! John's boot toes loosened some gravel measuring in real time the distance below London's highest peak! Alex removed the handkerchief that Ogle had stuffed into his mouth!

"Go ahead and jump if you want to! We won't stop you!" jeered Chaloner.

Sampler had already wet his pants before he was jerked out of the carriage's back seat. His knees were shaking!

John's bowls then gave away on him! He had probably developed diarrhea from all of the stress he was under.

"An old sailor once told me a tale about a British naval commander pulling a pirate that had attempted to rob him out of the sea! Later on that evening after the gratefully acting buccaneer had recuperated, that evil pretender slit the captain's throat in his sleep! He took the ship's rescue dinghy and then set the boat that had saved his life on fire!" prophetically said Ogle.

John Sampler said nothing.

"And what might you guess the moral to that story is, Constable Sampler?" gently asked Cal.

"That you're going to push me off this cliff!" cried John.

"Commander, do you want me to push him off?" blurted Selkirk.

"Not yet, Captain, ole John here will have to make that decision but get ready to do it in case the Constable gives me another mouthful of backtalk!" barked Ogle.

"Alright, alright, what do you want me to do?" pleaded Sampler.

"I want you to forget that we ever met and for you to erase the names and events that took place forever from your mind! My suggestion would be that you return to your office as if you were just beginning another day!

Tell the newspapers that someone stole your police rig and one day you may spellbound your grandchildren with your fascinating story!" sarcastically said Commander Ogle.

"And what if I put together a little hunting party and track you boys down like a menstruating fox? You'll end up hanging anyway!

Hey, untie me, don't leave me like this, you bastards! Come back here! You sons of a bitches are under arrest!" threatened the tightly bound policeman.

"And where in the hell do you think you're going, Blanche?" asked the inebriated Anton von Sporck.

"Oh honey, you really don't want to know the answer to your ridiculous question! But if you insist, I'll tell you; but, you'll become jealous when I mention to you how well he's hung!" slyly teased Blanche.

"Seriously, why are you putting on your jacket? I'll take Piero off after dark! Come on, sweetheart, come have a drink with old papa here!" begged Sporck.

"I'm about ready to go out of my mind, Ike! Perhaps I'll feel better after a good long ride! I might even lose this goddamned baby along the way!" complained Blanche.

Seven miles from the New York side of Lake Erie, there is a mountain which looms more than a hundred feet above the surface of the border lake. Within this massive rock are hundreds of tunnels honeycombing throughout the entire insides of the mountain.

There were three reasons why the Mississauga Mountain's interior had been carved into an almost impervious citadel. The first one had to do with the glaciers that had ground through the area centuries ago. The second set of masons were the ancient Seneca's who had turned the sandstone monolith into a thousand-year-old burial vault.

But the third cause of Mississauga Mountain's evolvement was due to the extraordinary skills of a couple of hundred Iroquois Indians and several bags of Black Sam's gold! They had even built a rail system by which the believed to be Shaman, could transport himself throughout his dwelling. He vigilantly looked after their dead!

Samuel Bellamy pulled himself along the narrow corridor leading to the eastern lookout window. The freshly greased wheels beneath his seat hummed as he coasted to the railed overlook.

After lighting the wicks to the row of lanterns just above his head, Bellamy returned his response to Tanacharison by way of the semaphores their French friends had shared with them. By moving certain sets of light-blocking sheets of wood, Black Sam, was able to transmit his permission for the sacrificial procession to enter the Mohawk burial grounds!

Bellamy smiled as he snuffed out his semaphore transmission flames. "Princess of Darkness", he bellowed along with a boisterous laugh as he rolled his chair back into the slot which returned him to his study. Sam knew his past had finally caught up with him!

Red Squirrel could hardly contain himself! Just the sight of white people coming onto their sacred grounds made him sick to his stomach! It was obvious to him as well as to most of the council members, that Red Jacket was correct in his assessment of the white man!

"Their blue eyes may smile and their tongues may even attract the bee but mind you, the white man's intent is our extinction! Even now, it is difficult to throw a blanket out without overlapping your brother's!

We would be prudent not to befriend any of them! While we still have the wherewithal to stop their further spread, it is my vote that we strike now! We should exterminate those that are already here and then stand at the beaches in readiness to kill any of them that step out of their big boats and onto our continent again!"

Perhaps it was because of the slugs of whiskey he had swallowed but whatever it was that caused Red Squirrel to do what he did was what got him killed! Red Squirrel charged the 'Princess of the Darkness' with the intention of running her through with his lance. Cato shot him!

Kimberly Kimber slid the piece of paper she had written a secret note on. If she got caught messaging another inmate, she would get a week in isolation! That meant bread and water and no interaction with the other girls!

Mrs. Olivia Covington had been the headmaster at the "Covington Institute for Wayward Girls" for more than three decades! It had been named after her father, the late Howard G. Covington who had bequeathed an enormous amount of money to the school for mostly expectant mothers and young women who had run up against the wrong side of the law!

It was rumored that "warden" Covington had never been married but used the 'Mrs.' in front of her name to disguise the sad truth that there had never been a single man who had ever shown her any attention! That was because of the fact, Olivia was most probably the ugliest female to have ever been born to homo sapiens!

Because the warden was just as awful on her insides as her appearance outwardly proclaimed, Kimberly took extra care in hiding her lead pencil after she had swallowed her cell mate's encrypted note! The Covington Institute was not a fun place to be! Fortunately, she only had eight more months to go before she was up for her first parole hearing. Kimberly wanted to finish it out 'easy'.

In that she was a parentless minor, she was sentenced to 'time served' plus one year! So far, the only trouble she had run into was from Mrs. Covington but experience had taught her how to blend into the crowd so most of the time that did the trick!

Mrs. Covington was terribly harsh on the girls who made spectacles of themselves! She would use a bamboo cane on the lewdest of them and a sock full of sand for the bellicose others!

Commander Ogle and Captain Selkirk had just about climbed every tree surrounding the Covington women's prison! They were attempting to spot the matchup to the portrait of Jonnathan's daughter which he had with him on the 'Whydah'!

All of the inmates were required to wear bonnets whenever they were allowed out in the yard. This made it difficult to pick Kimberly out.

About four o'clock in the afternoon, Alex Selkirk happened to notice a heap of old military jackets mixed up in a mound of rubbish. It was about six heaps away from where he and Ogle had constructed a lean-to out of a discarded barndoor. They were camped in the middle of London's city dump.

After selecting various uniform parts none of which matched, they were able to put together a reasonably believable outfit which would more than likely suit their purposes. Alex was to be the arresting officer. Chaloner Ogle was to pass as the driver because he had the only hat they could find.

At six o'clock the bell above the Institute's chapel began faintly ringing. Apparently the bell's clapper had rusted and thus gave off a halfway normal clang but it was enough for the two 'policemen' to know that in forty five minutes, Kimberly Kimber would be among the dismissed worshipers!

Once Father McGrath had completed the last lines of his benediction something like fifty young women poured out of the chapel and broke out into small groups. As Mrs. Covington had promised, the girls were obliged with fifteen minutes of fraternization and allowed to smoke if they had anything to do it with.

As the last bunch of inmates were breaking up, one very young girl maybe ten years old, hobbled down the chapel's stairs with the help of Reverend McGrath's arm! Even from Ogle's position, he could clearly read on the minister's face that he was put out by the child's sloth like movements! That's when Selkirk started blowing his whistle!

To the very brim of his lungs' capacity, Alex blared out Father McGrath's name and announced that he was being arrested for harboring a fugitive by the name of "Kimberly Kimber"! Within seconds the ectomorphic holy man had Kimberly sitting in the front seat of the police wagon while he ran back toward the chapel with his arms waving in the air like there was a swarm of bees after him! It was that simple!

Chaloner looked over at Kimberly with a comforting look upon his face. As if he were the child's grandfather, Cal reached over and gently pulled her chin up so he could see the child's eyes. He then softly spoke.

"Kimberly, would you like to drive this wagon? The horse's name is 'Millie' so all you have to do is just hold these reins and tell her where you want to go!"

"To tell you the truth, Sir, I don't like to criticize a man's driving but if I were holding those reins, I'd be a hell of a lot further down the road than we are right now! Let's get out of here and fast! They'll come after us, I'll assure you!

By the way, who are you people? I know you aren't cops and it isn't that I'm not grateful for your help but I sure would like to know the men's names who rescued me from that pit!" Said the audacious girl.

"Kimberly, your father was forced to take a group of very bad men to America! That was the reason Anton von Sporck or you may know him as "Reverend Greene", took you away from your mother and held you in a cell for so long. That was…" Alex was saying.

"Correction there, Alex, my mother sold me to 'Ike' for a bag of gold! I saw her do it!" Matter-of-factly said Kimberly.

"I see! I am saddened to hear that, Sweetheart! Would you like to go with us to visit your father?

I know he wants to see you again! He even told me that you learned to read before you could walk! Is that really true or was ole Jonnathan pulling my leg about you? Fathers do that from time to time, you know!" said Alex.

Ogle then chimed in with another timely remark but before he could finish it, Kimberly peppered 'Millie's' backside by flicking the reins with both of her wrists. For close to thirty minutes both Selkirk and Ogle had themselves a white knuckled ride!

"Jonn was afraid you might not want to see him! He suspected that your mother had said bad things about him, untrue things!

Kimberly, if you really do wish to join back up with the person who believes the sun rises and sets upon your head, we would very much like for you to come with us! All we need to do now is find a ship to take us there!" said Ogle.

With the introductions being made and the understanding that the circumstances were not ideal, the three of them turned back toward the city. Once they ditched the police wagon, they planned to make their way to Liverpool. Selkirk knew where he could get a ship!

Red Squirrel laid motionless in the snow. Even in the darkness one could see the gaping hole in the back of the brave's head! The torch holding escorts had dowsed their flaming sticks before disappearing into the surrounding forest. Cato sent out the word that the cadets needed to prepare for an attack!

War Eagle furiously rode up to where he knew Tanacharison was waiting. He wasted no time getting right to the point.

"King Tanacharison, Red Squirrel was murdered by one of the priests!"

"How could that happen, War Eagle? My orders were quite specific! I said, 'no one was to attack the 'Princess of the Darkness's' procession! Was Red Squirrel provoked or did he act on his own, War Eagle?" pushed the confederate chief.

"Sir, he deliberately attacked the sacrificial wagon with his lance unsheathed!" War Eagle admitted.

"In that case, those young warriors of yours have learned a valuable lesson! 'You are not to attack the white man's procession unless a command is issued directly from me', is what I said, did I not, War Eagle?" asked Tanacharison.

"Your message is crystal clear, Sir!" begrudgingly answered the Iroquois battle commander.

"I would suggest you reappoint another few men as the "Princess's" escorts but then take the mass of your warriors to the procession's rear and block off any attempt made by the Americans to assist the Pope's mourners. I am sure those soldiers back at Fort Herkimer heard Red Squirrel's killing shot!" Tanacharison said.

Governor Burnet punched General Staats's shoulder letting him know a single horseback rider was approaching their formation! The General then raised his right arm signaling his regiment to a halt. A pregnant woman obviously was in need of some help!

CHAPTER 7

BLACK SAM AND THE INDIANS

George Augustus heard the evening's butler drop another bundle of letters into the wooden box just outside of his quarter's front door. After many hours of perusing its structural diagram, the northernmost turret of Kensington Palace was his final selection. He could be alone up there.

Since Caroline's death there was no one he could confide in anymore! All that seemed to matter was staying warm and having a dark place to ruminate from wall to wall in.

The turret's thick walls provided a delicate quietness which Gus so desperately needed. His depression returned and it was really bad this time!

His issues floundered between his feelings of inadequacy ignited by his bombastic father's criticisms over to the deep hatred of his mother in which he for years, tried to hide from the rest of the world! It never worked out for him!

No matter what George attempted to accomplish and though most of the time he was successful at his endeavors, Gus was never praised! Not even one simple pat on the head did he ever receive!

Gus knew the world was in trouble! After all, that was why 'Timothy' had become his friend! It was also in part the reason why the King of England had chosen to move his headquarters to where he did. People back in London were disturbed by his 'live' conversations with 'Timothy'.

Usually Augustus's visits from 'Tim' occurred when no one else was around. He would appear when things got all tangled up in his mind!

Tim was very patient but a little hesitant to offer advice. Timothy was Gus's only friend.

Their latest conversations had centered around Maria Theresa the author of "The Pragmatic Sanction". Charles VI was the Hapsburg's last male. The Holy Emperor's last wishes enabled his daughter Maria to succeed him after the extinction of the male line of the House of Hapsburg!

This "woman" being seated dug up quite a few not yet rotted bones within the Netherlands's provinces! Austria was so offended by it they succeeded from whatever flimsy relationships it had had with the current powers at hand! Spain followed suit!

Timothy seemed to believe that all of the world's happenings were due to the alignment of the stars! This was quite a boom for George Augustus because they were currently aligned just as they were for Caesar in his rein!

If there was any truth to Tim's alignment theory, Gus had been granted the insight to take the planet to new heights! Tim promised he would be with him for the long-haul!

Just as the King and Timothy were crafting a penned note of support to Empress Maria Theresa, a loud knock interrupted their tweaking. George spoke out.

"Who is it?"

There was no response coming from the other side of the iron enforced door.

"What do you want? I am not to be disturbed at this time!" yelled King George.

Again, no one answered.

After cocking his two pistols, George Augustus crossed ten feet of the stone floor and flung the heavy door open! When it slammed against the turret's wall the force chipped off a piece of rock about the size of a child's hand!

Sir Robert Walpole was standing in front of him with a bottle of scotch and two pewter cups in his hands!

"Greetings, Gus! I thought to myself this morning when I awakened, 'I need to talk with my old friend George today'! It is discomforting to be separated from our closest of confidants for too long!" slurred Robert.

"I'm in no mood for reminiscing today, Prime Minister! With the parliamentary hearings around the corner, I would have figured that you would have distanced yourself from me after the 'Jenkins' Ear' ordeal! So, why are you here?" angrily asked Gus.

"I am here because I truly fear you have gone out of your mind! Look at yourself, Man! Imagine, the great King George hiding up here in this godforsaken tower and talking to your imaginary friend, 'Timothy'!

Maybe I should be asking you the same question you asked me, 'why are You here?', Gus! Do you not think your humble servants the ones who empty your chamber pot and bring you your meals, go home to eager ears awaiting the animated tales of the mad King?

Are you aware of the thousands upon thousands of your loyal subjects who happen to believe you are right up there with the heavenly ghosts? At least for the sake of them and our country's reputation, get a hold of yourself!" calmly stated Walpole.

"How did you know about 'Timothy', Robert?" innocently asked the crying King.

"Gus, there is no 'Timothy'! And furthermore, if I ever hear you say his name again, I'll have you put under lock and key in a place that would make these living quarters of yours, look like the Taj Mahal!

It is absolutely preposterous that a man, a real man of your stature would allow the arrows of reality to slay his pride! Every living man on earth faces the onslaught of fate! Why should you be an exception, George?

Kings of countries are not given the luxury of having nervous breakdowns! Therefore, I shall consider this visit a friendly preemptive one; however, tomorrow at this same noon hour I shall expect a full report as to the whereabouts of my Commanders! I will want to know where and why their ships were dispatched!" warned the Secretary of War.

With Walpole's piece having been so bluntly said, he had no other alternative but to walk out of the turret's door as contentiously as he could. The King got the point!

Gus watched Walpole's carriage disappear over the horizon. 'Timothy's' attitude was reflected in the tone of his voice. He was very upset with Gus!

"My lord, George, do you really believe that Carolyn's secret lover has an inkling of understanding of the traumas you have undergone? How could Walpole even fathom the pressures you bare upon your shoulders?

And to think, the poor bastard had the audacity to prance up here and threaten you with some contrived timeline! Why don't you have him arrested and show him who the boss is around this place!" said 'Timothy' in the king's mind.

"But what if he's right, Tim?" questioned the confused King.

"I'm afraid you still need lots of rest, George! Revisit this conundrum in a couple of days. You'll feel so much better after a night or two of good sleep!

No, wait a minute, I have a better idea! Why don't you and I have one of those good old-fashioned drinking bouts! It'll put Walpole's scotch to a more palatable use!" concluded 'Tim'.

As history is concerned, it will more than likely tell a different version of what happened next but the real truth is, King George took 'Timothy's' advice over Walpole's and ended up going on a ten-day binge! All of which came to a screeching halt when the naked King of Britain was found wandering around the palace's gardens with a belt full of loaded pistols!

George claimed he intended to rid Kensington of the pesky hares known to feast there in the morning hours! The physicians soon joined in with the King's efforts but convinced him that there was better hunting in the clover fields behind the castle's medical facility!

Two weeks after that, King George was his old self again. He fired Sir Robert Walpole, repossessed his house on Downing Street, replaced him with Spencer Compton but furnished the defrocked Secretary of War with a retirement bonus and the innocuous title as the Earl of Orford and that was that!

Without Walpole's resistance and experiencing the free-flight syndrome initially felt by sobriety, George perceived that now was the time to strike out at his enemies! His plan, and 'Timothy' concurred, would be to bait his nemeses onto a battlefield or body of ocean and fight them till their deaths! The Americas would be his lure!

"Oh, please help me, Gentlemen! There was supposed to be a group of men waiting for me! I paid them to take me to the Samuel Bellamy estate! How could they have done this to me?" pleadingly questioned Blanche.

"Mam, hold on a moment! Slow up please! Kindly tell us who you are and what you're upset about." Gently spoke Governor Burnet.

Blanche dismounted her horse as clumsily as it could be done. She pretended as though the pangs of her labor pains were only seconds apart!

Looks of confusion and helplessness spread through the militiamen's ranks. Blanche of course fainted, forcing the men to gather around her as if they were peering at a net full of dead fish! It was then that Blanche lit the fuse of a grenade!

General Staats's horse reared up when it sensed the panic among the men. Everyone reacted with tissue tearing movements all in an effort to escape the kill zone's radius!

Governor Burnet had unfortunately fallen and broken his collarbone which left his mount's reins just a little shy of Blanche's easy reach!

With the swiftness of an alley cat the pregnant woman sprang onto the appaloosa's back, kicked the warhorse into it's attack mode and then made the terrified beast trample over the backs of several of the fleeing soldiers!

Because the grenade had such a long fuse, its explosion caused no harm to any of those who witnessed the clever assault. Blanche was a mile away when it went off.

The General and his men looked at one another in utter disbelief! Probably not one single one of them would speak of that experience ever again!

Cato did his best to keep the cadets from panicking. He requested that Anne Bonnie begin singing anything she knew. She didn't so Bob Maynard began teaching the boys a raunchy drinking song!

Henry Every and James Stanfield took it upon themselves to relight the cadets' candelabras while Bosman and Kimber got the procession moving again. Eight horse riding Indians followed behind.

James Penny had changed his jacket three different times before he was satisfied with the 'right' look. After all, Mayor Golightly in his absence, had asked him to represent the City of Liverpool during the visit by several of the parliamentary members!

Penny was practicing his speech while modeling his attire in front of his bedroom's full-length mirror.

"And furthermore, the slave trading industry has produced in tax revenues alone more than three..." Recited James Penny until he saw Captain Selkirk's pistol muzzle stealing some space from him in the mirror's reflection!

You would have thought the man would crumble at any moment!

Mister Penny had heard that Selkirk was dead!

Alex Selkirk wasted no time in getting to the point as to why he, Ogle and Kimberly Kimber were there. Alex pressed the muzzle of his pistol onto the back of Penny's neck and slowly spoke.

"I am going to mention three names to you! It will be your responsibility to put those three words into a meaningful story: 'Sporck', 'Golightly', 'Thomas'! Speak you bloody squid or I'm going to send a pellet of lead through the center of your brain!" grumbled Selkirk.

"Sporck and Golightly are on the outs! Ike most likely killed him! I was just an investor..." Penny said until he stopped because he felt Selkirk cock his pistol.

"I need to hear a happy ending, James! Think more futuristically! We do not wish to listen for an instant more of the happenings of past! I want to discover what the heroes of your wonderful tale were sailing off into the sunset for! What was the actual purpose of the 'Thomas's' sailing, Mister Soontobeacorps?" Selkirk asked.

"Jesus, Alex, what the hell did I ever do to you?" screamed Golightly's bitch.

"The three of you pin-hooked the 'Thomas's' contract from the Royal African Company and misrepresented the 'out of ordinary cargo' that we agreed to transport to America for you bloody bastards! A lot of good men died because of your greed and for that reason alone, I shall enjoy seeing you gasp for your last breath!" seethed Alex.

"Then take the 'Kitty's Amelia'! I'll not report it gone until after the sabbath! For god's sakes, Captain Selkirk, just take the goddamned ship and we'll be square, I give you my word, Sir!" wailed James.

"Where is it?" politely asked Alexander.

"It is moored at the Midland Dock! It's just your typical slaver, the ship is relatively new so just take it! Please don't kill me, Alex, please!" Pleaded Mister Penny.

"Then write me a 'Bill of Sale' for it, James!"

James Penny did exactly as he was asked to do. He was then tied-up and placed upside down into his broom closet! Upon the threesome's departure from James Penny's bedroom, Alex Selkirk left with a parting message!

"James, if we should ever lay eyes on one another again, you should know and I give you my word on this, I will drop you dead in your tracks!"

When Blanche's grenade exploded, War Eagle immediately signaled for Black Beaver to flank his horsemen toward the southeast while his fighters came in from the northwest. They would converge a mile out from the fort, on the border!

Each of the warriors had two French naval pistols, a lance, a tomahawk and was mounted on someone's stolen horse! There were over three hundred of Tanacharison's soldiers, all disciplined and well-armed, braced to attack the militiamen the second they stepped foot onto Iroquois land!

From their correct staging positions, the 'no attack' signals by way of bird sounds, were exchanged between War Eagle and responded to by Black Beaver! The only thing that had crossed their property line was one rider traveling as if her horse's tail were on fire!

"And their original properties were doubtless the same with those of the holy angels! There is no absurdity in supposing Satan their chief, otherwise styled, 'son of the morning' to have been one of the first Archangels. Like the other sons of…" John Wesley's Bible along with some substantive notes, flew over his left shoulder causing the evangelist to cease the conclusion of his message!

George Whitfield sprang up from his seat and leaped toward the eight-year-old boy who had somehow discharged his grandfather's shotgun! While his grandparents were up and clapping and generally feeling the spirit of the Lord, little Willie Perkins out of sheer boredom no doubt, began fidgeting with his grandpa's double- barreled rabbit gun. The accident afterwards, brought the collection numbers up substantially!

Like all the rest of those swooped up in King George's visions of a place where academic freedoms would rein and a country whose people would welcome their ideas, found themselves having to scratch out a living by the use of their own imaginations! Take for instance the cases of John Wesley and George Whitfield, they, instead of getting teaching posts on the King's College's campus, found themselves once again hustling up congregations for another one of their Sunday morning tent shows!

Even the scientists who had believed that their 'break-throughs' would automatically print their names in some book about great innovators, considered themselves fortunate to land a job of any sort! At that point, survival replaced pride.

'Operation Cricket' had been a flop. Samuel Johnson, the college's president was a blooming idiot. All the students were "away on exercises", and people had been killed or apprehended on the school's grounds and the locals hated the British! Even men such as Wolfe and Anson didn't flinch an iota when something derogatory was said about their motherland.

To hear the folks talk, one would have thought they viewed King George and his cronies in the same light as they would have seen a bunch of pirates!

"All they (England) do is tax anything of ours that is of value to both of our countries and yet they provide nothing of a benefit for us in return!" was the mantra spoken from a church pew to the backend of a plow mule! Dissention filled the air.

America wanted out from under Britain's control! That was the message, plain and simple!

The people of means, Americans who employed others, found themselves towing the rope for the King's defense of their wavy territorial boundary lines on both extremes of North America's eastern coast!

The French were beginning to ebb their way out of Canada and into the headwaters of America's most navigable rivers. Spain encroached its Catholic self upon the major ports where these same French 'polluted' rivers made their exits into the sea.

Anyone could see the powder keg affect which certainly influenced the parliamentary body's decision to have the Colonies take up some of the economic slack caused by the military defense costs associated with the trespassers! Not only did the Brits ask for remarkable tax increases, they also insisted the Colonist's form their own military factions to help them fight off the French to the north and the Spanish in Florida!

These were the circumstances facing King George's "brain trust" immigrants! In the few open discussions among the 'Centurion's' former passengers, it was pretty much the consensus that until King George arrived in New York, they would have to fin for themselves!

Considering that Frederick, the King's oldest son, had returned from Germany, it made total sense for George to follow through with the 'operation'! In the meantime, they would lay low and only chum around with the Loyalists because if they didn't, there would be hell to pay! King George II was known to decapitate his betrayers!

Because they felt as if they were leagues above the pedestrians who worked with their hands, the professors of this or that had a most difficult time fitting in with those outside of their overblown bubble! Basically, they did things such as correcting the minister's grammar during his sermon or explaining one of Newton's theories to a street corner apple vender!

People would steer clear of them for fear of an explanation of their greeting! But while some members of the island's community found "those" King's College professors a nuisance, others recognized their intrinsic value!

So, there is no stretch to the imagination as to 'why' the group drew the interests of some men with more money than scruples. People for instance, who might be interested in getting rid of a few thousand Indians through the use of some manufactured chemical compounds!

Therefore, it was not surprising when a long black carriage pulled by six black stallions pulled up to the professors' dormitory all to deliver an invitation to a banquet being held in their collective honor! Each scholar would be paid a stipend for their attendance as well as given the opportunity to put their names in the hat for an employment opportunity at the new munitions' factory being built at that very moment!

Anton von Sporck along with the help of ten broad strapped negroes, completely cleared out the church's clinic to the walls sending a gaggle of expectant mothers grappling for someplace to go! All of the midwifery implements were either boxed up or thrown out on the church's ever smoking trash dump.

Just as Sporck had ordered, the Trinity Church's sign was taken down and reprinted. It now read, "The European Institute of Defense Research". After forty hours of frenetic effort, the place really looked like an institute of higher learning which of course was of huge importance in Sporck's scheme.

With Blanche's dead weight off of his shoulders, Ike was unencumbered. He could now reinvent himself!

Anton would become King George's North American chief research scientist. From there on out, everything that was to go on within the 'Institute's' gates would be considered the deepest of secrets!

The employable blacks who had seen fit to squat on the Trinity Church's grounds, immediately found themselves clad in uniforms. It had to remind the professors of Europe!

Trinity Church's rather spacious sanctuary had been transformed into a maze of work stations. Cubicles of various sizes and all with running water, appeared to beckon the scientifically minded ones the most.

A large lecture room had been established to accommodate those academics who leaned more toward the psychological warfare end of the spectrum. Mock battle plans hung on every wall!

It should not be forgotten that Sporck had very deep pockets at that time and therefore one would not be surprised at the ease in which he stole King's College's entire faculty! Sporck even had an attorney present during their introductory visit who helped the lion's share of them submit their letters of resignation to the school's president, Professor Samuel Johnson!

With the exceptions of Captains' Anson and Wolfe, Sporck got them all! By dawn of the morning following the professors' lavish banquet, Ike had their worldly possessions trucked over to his place!

Where Sporck would store their things or for that matter, where they would sleep, was a horse of a different color! Sporck just sold them on the outlandish idea that their inconveniences were all part of King George's manifesto!

Their job, the work done by the brave and pioneering professors from that time forward, would be on behalf of Great Britain! With collaborative thinking, those few great minds would forever preserve the safety of England along with her colonies forever more!

Thusly, Sporck divided his newly employed scientists into two groups, Group A and Group B. Each held an equal balance of chemists, mathematicians, and biologists.

The A Group would act as the aggressors; i.e., they would imagine ways in which an enemy might devastate if not annihilate, a country's inhabitants! There were no strategies barred.

A Group could "use" anything or any way to eradicate their target. Drugs, disease, explosives, poisons or anything else that would conceivably render their opponent helpless, was fair game!

B Group's task was to come up with ways to combat Group A's creative assaults. They too could use any means necessary to neutralize or destroy their aggressor. Both groups were given separate but uniforme jumpsuits to wear, A Group wore orange suits while B Group was issued green ones.

The orange team won the toss; therefore, they had twenty-four hours to mount their theoretical attack and to diagram their plot on the side of the church's rear wall!

Having been recently painted a snow white, the back wall was like a huge mocked up battlefield! Orange arrows replicated the points of attack while green zeroes would represent the defense's efforts to thwart the affront!

As Ike explained, their first hypothetical situation would be kept on a smaller scale so as to smooth out any kinks that might inadvertently occur during their initial exposure to this type of scientific approach! For simplicity's sake, Sporck drew out in black paint the outline of Tanacharison's village. Ironically, they were less than a hundred miles away!

"It was just a model," Sporck said.

By the next morning even before the sun came up, the aggressors (A Group) had painted in for Sporck their 'make believe' proposal. They had chosen a biological approach, one that would insure at least ninety-percent of the by Spring!

Incensed but now clued-in, the B Group (the defenders) took their twenty-four hours to research the methods in which the Indians might be able to repel their exposure to small pox! Antidotes all the way to smoke treatments were the first problems addressed by the defending scientists. A Group collectively snickered as they left the green circle makers in a quandary!

Sir Jeffery Amherst was A Group's leader. At four o'clock on the dot, the immunologist awakened due to some inner calamity caused by a bad dream. To resolve his concern of not being able to return to a peaceful sleep, Professor Amherst decided to take a stroll around the research compound's campus.

It was minus three degrees outside and the wind was stirring about ten miles an hour. At first, Jeffery's intention was to briskly walk all the way to the main gate and back but when he saw Sporck standing on his front porch, he wandered over to get a little brown-nosing done instead.

Not much time had passed before Sporck and Jeffery found themselves having drinks beside a roaring fire and talking about A Group's approach concerning the Iroquois' susceptibility to small pox! The professor vociferously expressed his frustrations to his newly discovered lover.

"Anton, if such a plan were to be enacted for real, I mean, the only problem I could fathom would be the manner in which the virus was introduced to the Indians!

They have two rivers running through their territory, the Mohawk and Ohio, and a million springs and streams in between! Therefore, using water as the delivery agent is out of the question.

My team members and I have even discussed the use of hot air balloons that would drop tainted candy or toys. But given the dangers of shifting winds, we've sort of canned that idea for the time being! I'll be anxious to hear what B Group's ideas are regarding their defense of our infectious onslaught," whispered Jeffrey.

"It sounds like you've put a lot of thought into this! My compliments to you, Sir! But, tell me, where are you going to get live cultures way up here?" softly questioned Sporck.

"Most of we chemists, on both sides, keep all sorts of scary things in our bags! Don't forget, King George sent us here to do the same things that you are intending for us to do!" sharply answered Jeffrey.

"I'm sorry, I really didn't mean to offend you. Did I?" recanted Ike.

"It was just that I desperately wanted you to feel that I am smart enough to back up my theories! Can't you see the emotional seesaw one is put through when that one person only wants to make his master proud of him?" cried Jeffrey Amherst.

With a comforting pat and a tiny nip to Jeffrey's ear, Sporck gave the sobbing professor a promise.

"After B Group's presentation this morning, I shall return here to my quarters with the hopes the rest of them believe I am in contemplation of the markings the two groups will receive. While in actuality, my decision is already made!

I am quite positive that small pox is the perfect solution to the Indian problem! More importantly, I am in love with the man who thought it up!" admitted Sporck.

Jeffrey Amherst blushed as he was leaving Ike's cozy cottage. Just as he was closing the front door, Sporck spoke out in a high-pitched voice!

"Be thinking as to how we can make our secret plan work in the dead of winter! It's my understanding, insects don't fare very well this time of year!"

With Jeffrey's head cocked in such a way, Sporck knew his 'boy's' farewell remark would be self-righteously fueled! He also was aware of Jeff's fragile ego. Perhaps, he thought, another ingratiating comment before Amherst's final comment, would remove the stinger from it.

"Ah yes, Professor, before you scat off, let me say on King George's behalf, how very proud we are to have you onboard with us!" schmoozed Ike.

"Weather nor sucrose statements will ever influence my scientific values! I can tell you this, if we were shooting real bullets under this scenario, I promise you without a doubt in my mind, there wouldn't be a single two-legged survivor within a hundred-mile radius surrounding Tanacharison's hut!" hissed the scientist upon his hasty exit.

George Augustus had made a vow the night before! Attesting to his claim of 'here on out sobriety', Gus had written out using his drunken scribble, a promise to the great people of the world, he would be a better leader! He had signed the document with his own blood!

King George had not intentionally drawn his own blood. As a matter for the record, when you got right down to it, the mighty King was rather squeamish! What had happened was when Gus had made his commitment to give up the sauce, he threw his next to the last bottle of scotch into the smoldering coals in the fireplace!

Anyway, the jug did not end up where it was supposed to go; instead, it ricocheted off of the teakwood mantel and bounced back onto the bridge of Gus's nose! Although blaming 'Timothy' for his poor throw, the two finally laughed it off as 'just an accident' and toasted away the last bottle in the name of posterity.

That's when they made a good use of Gus's nosebleed! There came an unexpected knock on the door!

"I made the specific request that I am not to be disturbed until Monday! What do you want?" roared the King of England.

"Sir, Commanders Ogle and Selkirk have kidnapped the Kimber girl! The three of them showed up at James Penny's home in Liverpool! They tied him up and then made him sign a bill of sale for he and Golightly's newest slaver, the 'Kitty's Amelia'! Penny suspects they are taking the ship to America, your Majesty!" yelled the nervous messenger.

"Have you alerted Walpole about this?" squealed the King.

"Sir, you removed him from office last week! Shall I contact Cromwell?" asked the nervous servant.

"Well, find him! Tell the bastard that he has his old job back! Have him report to my office in the palace tomorrow morning at ten o'clock!

Also, alert Captain Dorce to these matters! I want the 'Rebecca' manned and ready to sail by Friday! Is that understood, whoever you are?" commanded the sobering King.

"Understood, Sir!" said the messenger and then there was silence. General Staats had no more of an intention of retreating from the Iroquois than flying to the moon! He was pulling a faint; that is, he was permitting the Indians to only see his "frazzled" troops noisily hightailing it back to the fort! But in fact, what the general had done was having his men jump off of their horses and regroup as an infantry division or better described as a guerilla unit!

Immediately upon dismounting their horses each soldier reversed their uniform jackets. The side now exposed, made their parade jackets into a camouflaged ghillie covering which offered to the enemy a much more difficult target to spot!

Then as if choreographed, the crack New York militiamen began crawling toward the now celebrating and therefore unsuspecting warriors! Black Beaver's men began mimicking the fleeting whites to the benefit of War Eagle's jocularity!

They had Blanche tied down with her face down on the back of the cavalry mount she had taken from Governor Burnet! War Eagle's men, not wanting to be upstaged by the other mimickers, responded to their joint capture by riding around in a circle while each of War Eagle's braves from their horses' backs, urinated on the potty-mouthed pregnant girl! The Indians had no idea that Staats's guerillas had surrounded them!

There are many things concerning human behavior which seem to change over time but one thing that will not, are the numbers of able-bodied men hanging around dock pubs looking for a boat ride out of town! That makes the price for crewmen shift from hard currency to a promise!

Of course, Selkirk and Ogle knew this, which is why when they got to Liverpool, they headed straight for the place best known for brokering paperless understandings, the 'Three-legged Dog Tavern'! The owner's dim-witted son had just opened. It was 0600.

"A pleasant good morning to you, Governor! How about whipping us up some eggs and sausages, three glasses, and a bottle of your best scotch, my Man! Oh yes, and a pail of milk for my granddaughter!" greeted Ogle.

"I haven't started a fire yet!" responded the boy behind the bar.

"No matter, how about the scotch and milk?" pleasantly asked Chaloner.

"What about them?" innocently quizzed the idiot.

Seeing there was a problem incubating, Kimberly stepped forward on her good leg while propping her crutches against the edge of the bar's padded lip. With a gesture she probably learned from Blanche, the girl leaned over the bar so as to expose her baron chest to the nitwit who was goggling at her with his mouth agape.

She motioned for him to come closer as if she had a secret to share!

"You know, big Boy, if you play your cards right, I might just have a special tip for you! Why don't you make my Grandpa and Uncle happy and I'll see what I can do to make it worth your trouble!" whispered the coquet acting ten-year-old.

The very slow boy with a 'just screwed a chicken' expression on his face, speedily pulled from his shelf a gallon of scotch and three drinking glasses. He put the items across the bar's top as if they were the objects used in a magic trick! Then the dumb boy excused himself while he went looking for some fresh milk and a deck of cards!

Blanche picked up rather quickly that Black Beaver despised War Eagle! Although she was in no position to drive a deeper wedge between the two, it at least gave her a glimmer of hope! Provided she were given the opportunity, she intended to utilize that knowledge.

As soon as all one hundred or so of War Eagle's testosterone ignited warriors had finished their fluid releasing follies, Blanche overheard Black Beaver mimicking War Eagle's accent! It sounded like he was doing his mockery for her benefit! That was the edge Blanche had hoped she would get!

"So, why did you not respond to my letters, Black Beaver?" panted Blanche.

Black Beaver ignored the tied down prisoner.

"I told you I would come! Why are you treating me this way?" pleadingly questioned Blanche.

Black Beaver guided his palomino over to the strapped down woman's trotting horse. He didn't say anything for the longest time until his curiosity finally got the best of him!

"You speak as if you know me, fat woman!" tauntingly spoke Black Beaver.

"Look here, Black Beaver, if you don't love me anymore, just say so! If you don't want our baby then at least let me keep it!

You are killing our child by making my body smother my son! How can you do such a thing to your own flesh and blood?" Loudly performed Blanche.

With all of the commotion stirred up by Blanche's blasphemous accusations and being that the Iroquois League forbade its people from any sort of fraternization whatsoever with the whites, it was to Black Beaver's benefit to stop the woman from speaking!

War Eagle's men couldn't help but overhear what Blanche was saying. Breaking that law was a capital offense for your information!

With the speed of an arrow, the scuttlebutt reached War Eagle's ears! He was told there was a 'white' pregnant girl claiming that Black Beaver was the father of their expected child! She had come from the fort looking for him!

This delicious piece of information was War Eagle's chance to knock Black Beaver's odds of becoming Tanacharison's successor for a loop! He kicked his appaloosa sharply in its ribs! He wanted to hear the pregnant woman's story for himself!

Harsh northwesterly winds had begun to sculpt snow drifts as high as a man's eye level. The wagon carrying the half-frozen Princess of the Darkness, was running into all kinds of difficulties.

Massive mounds of fluffy snow were causing the wheels to rise up off of the road thus rendering the wagon to nothing more than a bad sled. And even if the wheels were touching the ground, they wouldn't have worked simply because the wheels' hub grease had frozen up!

With less than a mile further to go, the decision was made to abandon the wagon and mount the 'princess' on top of the delivery horse's slumped back. Cato then asked the men to mix in with the cadets in order to keep their spirits up.

In an attempt to lift everyone's spirits to a tolerable level and taking that same opportunity to construct some sort of plan, Cato flagged down one of their procession's guides. He needed to get permission for them to build a fire in order to prepare for the Princess's sacrifice! Making an even longer stretch of his luck, Cato insisted on their privacy during the 'taking of the heart' ceremony!

To further expedite the speed at which it took the guard to grant that permission, Cato handed the elderly scout a whole jug of rum. The old brave's answer was given in the form of a 'whoop' and a 'holler' followed by the Indian horseman galloping away so he could share his good fortune with his fellow guides.

Crommelin and Samuel Fraunces frantically searched for firewood. James Stanfield took the color guardsmen, Mulligan and Hamilton with him as they tromped through the snow toward the side of a mountain located almost a half mile to the west of them. Stanfield's crew would look for stones the sizes of the one that killed Goliath. Fist shaped rocks when thrown by a shirtsleeve sling, will do the same thing to Indians as it did to a giant.

Little Samuel Woodhull, the drummer boy, was put on guard duty. He was to signal Cato when the drunken scouts returned from their whatever you wanted to call it!

In the meantime, Kimber, Every and Bosman were told to take the delivery horse off, cut its throat, skin it, salvage all of the horse's bones that could be sharpened into weapons and return with enough meat to feed a dozen inebriated Indians! If all of that worked and once the Indians' remains and any scuffling signs were erased, the cadets would return to the fort while Cato and the rest of them made their way to Black Sam's mountain! That was the only plan they had come up with as the crimson line of sunrise reminded them of the time.

Jeffrey Amherst's heart was on fire or so he notated in his diary. He wrote, "Finally, after twenty years of life, I have met my perfect match. Mother, you would have loved him too; he is just so wonderful!

But, Mama, I have a problem! Even though it is just a game, I do not feel that Anton (that's his name) realizes what a prize I am to his research institute! He even suggested (actually mocked me) that one needed warm weather in order to infect a village (so simple to do) with small pox!

Maybe I should just do it (for real!) and then during another stolen moment with him, I'll accept my praise in the end (Ha Ha)!"

At the crack of dawn, Sam Bellamy was awakened by the tingling of what he called, his 'Pigeon Bell'. Whenever one of his carrier birds landed on the coop's sill, the pigeon's weight would announce its successfully completed task for which the fowl was rewarded with a dried plum!

The message from Will Trent a trapper and close friend, promised to ruin Sam's day!

"General Staat's militiamen attacked Tanacharison's warriors two miles across the Iroquois border. Fort Herkimer holds many of the King's College cadets (est.#190) used as Staat's decoy. French troops have been activated with e.t.a. of 12 hours. Attack imminent with Algonquin forces in tow (est.#450)! Take defensive measures immediately!"

Bellamy's skin was cracking open from the dry air. His scar tissue was always a reminder of the fire aboard the 'Whydah'. That was the afternoon when he almost died.

A howling nor'easter gathered. It was one of those surprising storms that seem to just magically show up out of nowhere!

Winds reached more than seventy miles per hour and the sea rose to thirty feet, as Bellamy remembered. A desk lamp slid off of his desk; that's what started the fire!

He was only two hundred yards away from the Nantucket shore when the 'Whydah' hit a sandbar! In an instant, he and his sailors were buried under tons of water or swept out forever into the sea!

It was Tanacharison who had saved his life. A much younger man then, he and a handful of braves happened to notice a white man clinging onto a rock piling; the waves were bashing onto the pirate's unconscious body!

Amid the advice not to enter the ice-cold water, Tanacharison dove into the surf and rescued the nearly dead Bellamy. That valorous move earned for Tanacharison, Bellamy's lifelong loyalty! It was a guarantee that Tanacharison's people would always have the latest weaponry to defend themselves against the white man no matter what language they spoke!

If what Trent had messaged was even halfway accurate, there would be many casualties! Both Staats and Tanacharison were old war dogs themselves so make no mistake about them, each adversarial force was just as lethal as the other!

Sam was all of a sudden overcome by the horrible tragedy happening at Fort Herkimer. Something had gone wrong!

'Somebody from somewhere had started this mess', thought Bellamy. He angrily pulled his way back to the track leading to the semaphore porch.

Hard winds would make it difficult to light the lanterns but Sam knew himself very well, he had to at least try to stop the nonsense!

King George Augustus had not had a single drop of alcohol enter his bloodstream in the past sixty-three hours and counting! Everything seemed to move in slow-motion for Gus. Not only were the people around him irritating but so was everything else!

Life itself seemed flat! It was like viewing one's surroundings in a single dimensional black and white way. There was nothing to look forward to and mostly not worth doing anyway, was George's general attitude. Basically, Gus wanted to quit being the King!

It had taken the better part of the week for King George's men to locate Walpole and bring him back to London. Once George's 'thugs' had pummeled the prime minister back into his senses, he was directed to chair the British Admiralty Board's up and coming meeting!

The primary topic would be the immediate blockade of the British owned ports in North America. New York, Charlestown, Wilmington, Philadelphia and Boston would be the first wave's points of siege. Ground troops would then be assigned to monitor those cities' levels of congruency with the Crown.

From the Leicester House, King George's newly purchased piece of real estate, George Augustus would hold the Kingdom's reins until Frederick, his son, got the swing of ruling the empire and had a chance to get settled into the palace!

Already, the newspapers were calling King George the "absent king"; therefore, him sticking around at least until May seemed like the most noteworthy thing to do.

Meanwhile, Gus claimed he would manage his global war plans from the Leicester property. Actually, his intentions were to hop on the 'Rebecca' along with Captain Dorce and his hundred and some marines, and sink the 'Kitty's Amelia' in the deepest part of the Atlantic ocean!

Much to Abraham Staat's dismay, Governor Burnet had insisted he be included in the general's tactical faint! Politicians, generally speaking, can be great strategists within the walls of a temperature- controlled office; however, with only a few exceptions, most of them perform dismally when they discover what warriors really do!

This couldn't have supported that hypothesis with any greater lucidly than was evidenced by the governor's actions at an extremely dangerous time! Fifteen minutes before General Staat's guerillas were to open fire on the partying Indians, William Burnet out of fear one would suppose, jumped up and threw his weapons down into the snow!

He raised his arms high into the sky and rushed toward the surprised Iroquois warriors! The Governor was asking for a peaceful settlement to the whole matter!

Will's panicky actions in some ways served as a significant disadvantage to the Indians because their focus was shifted toward the anomaly running toward them! Quickly reorganizing, Black Beaver's warriors joined in with War Eagle's men and proceeded to encircle the now prostrated governor! That's when Staat's militiamen delivered a withering volley of lead balls into their war-hooping ranks!

Seeing that a third of his braves had been knocked from their horses and figuring the whites had reloaded and ready to fire again, War Eagle roughly turned his horse toward Black Beaver's supposed paramour and grabbed onto the reins of the horse Blanche was tied on to! As the Indians were retreating, Black Beaver rode up behind his nemesis and severed War Eagle's spinal cord with a swing of his tomahawk!

Black Beaver after assuring himself that War Eagle was dead, reclaimed Blanche's horse's reins and then led his men to a safe place. With the exception of Blanche, Black Beaver was positive that no one had witnessed his deed.

Captain Philippe-Thomas Chabert de Joncaire after admiring the carpentry work Tanacharison's labor force had done for his friend Sam Bellamy, he contracted the Mingo workers to build a fort for the French government! For an astronomical amount of gold, of which fifty percent was paid upfront, Tanacharison promised to have it built on their side of the Ohio River by Spring!

Since it was late January and not one single log had been set, it would be understandable to see why Joncaire was super agitated when his warm and dry unit was ordered to assist in Tanacharison's defense! Supposedly, as his orders said, 'American militia unit attacked an Iroquois detachment'.

The semaphore had signaled that Colonial forces had entered under the guise of a white flag! If that were the case, the treaty signed at Logstown was now null and void!

The days of open passage, safe travel and a right to shoot game for sustenance would become fleeting memories! It would mean 'trust' would die which further meant that war would ooze into the crack!

Joncaire called his brigade of cavalrymen to a sudden halt! He could see people below him making their way along the southern bank of the Mohawk River. A dozen of them were slowly heading upstream.

They didn't talk therefore Captain Joncaire knew they were militarily trained. Strangely though, eleven of the men wore priests' clothing. One woman wore only a pair of boots and a blanket!

The French captain ordered two of his Algonquin scouts to follow the people traveling up the river. The scouts were to report back to him when the party below had reached their destination.

Joncaire's brigade would be camped just outside of Tanacharison's village. They would be within a rifle's shot from Fort Herkimer!

Commander Joseph Coulon de Jumonville had sent Captain Joncaire into the Indian territory for two reasons. The first one was because Phillippe-Thomas Chabert de Joncaire was undoubtedly a first class officer and would follow his orders to a fault. As for the second reason, Joncaire had threatened to report Commander Jumonville for selling an overstock of muskets to Tanacharison's enemies — the Naragansett tribe!

Jumonville apparently thought Tanacharison would never find out about the fifty-rifle sale; but, Joncaire knew that was an impossibility! With Tanacharison's sophisticated intelligence sources, Captain Phillippe Joncaire believed that if a deer farted in the forest, the chief would know about it!

So consequently, as Joncaire understood, if Tanacharison ever caught wind of Jumonville's double-dealing he would smite ole Joseph and everybody else near him! That was why Joncaire never lied to the Indians. They would kill him for doing it!

By eight o'clock, Cal and Alex Selkirk had hired on twenty credential-less crewmen directly from the furthest table to the rear of the 'Three-legged Dog Tavern'! All but six of the hired-on sailors had no luggage to carry onboard so preparing the 'Kitty's Amelia' for embarking took less than an hour.

Once the slave ship passed from the Mersey's gentle pull and into the choppy Atlantic, Ogle, Selkirk and even Kimberly breathed a deep sigh of relief! Kimberly was the first to suggest a toast. Despite her age, she had developed an affinity for the spirits.

With her glass filled to the brim, Kimberly had some rather sagely insight wrapped up within her goblet tapping remarks.

"Here we have a voyage that I shall call, 'the damned if you do and be damned if you don't'! The great 'Kitty's Amelia', a stolen vessel, is now on a journey to America!

Her mission is simply to right the evil doings of an empire which sees itself as a god-fearing benevolent nation. We snarl at their meanness while they smile at their goodness.

So why are we here? Well, I'll tell you why; everyone on this craft is on it for the same reasons! Gentlemen, let us toast to that reason and call it FREEDOM!" Loudly proclaimed Kimberly.

The three of them clicked their goblets together in unison. The winds were favorable and the new crew seemed to be competent. Alex lost the straw drawing consequently, he would take the wheel until midnight.

Ogle and Kimberly crawled into separate corners of the wheelhouse in hopes of getting some sleep. Little did they know that the 'Rebecca' was closing in on the 'Kitty's Amelia' leveraging the price of their freedom to an all-time high!

Black Beaver moved fifty of his warriors to the rear of the retreating Indians. They were to be the first line of defense should General Staats pursue them. In the meantime, he had to take Blanche to see Tanacharison. The chief councilman always insisted on interrogating the tribe's prisoners first.

This offered Blanche ample time to lay out the terms for her silence! She then explained to Black Beaver the small print in their agreement.

"How much time do we have before we reach Tanacharison's place?" politely questioned Blanche.

"You do not need to know these things, stupid woman!" abruptly answered Black Beaver.

"Should I tell your chief where you dragged War Eagle's body?" taunted Blanche.

Suddenly Black Beaver jumped off of his horse, tromped over to the nearest sapling, cut off a three-foot switch and commenced to whip Blanche with it for a whole minute! At the end of the thrashing, Black Beaver remounted his horse and proceeded forward as if there had been no abbreviation whatsoever.

Even louder this time, Blanche spoke again!

"Hey fellows, don't you think that the big and brave woman beater you call Black Beaver ought to kill me before I have the opportunity to spill my guts to Chief Tanacharison? How do you think he will respond when he learns of War Eagle's murder?"

At the conclusion of Blanche's awkwardly yelled accusations, Tupac, the late War Eagle's closest lieutenant, ferociously rode up to Black Beaver's horse and the horse Blanche was tightly tied to! With an awfully frightful frown on his face, Tupac aggressively leaned into the side of Black Beaver's mount and began speaking softly to both Black Beaver and Blanche.

"Fat woman, what you have said will cause your own death or Black Beaver's! If you are not lying about War Eagle's body being dragged away then I will most certainly kill Black Beaver myself! If what you say concerning the murder of my friend, War Eagle is a lie then I shall execute you instead!

So, before we go to see Tanacharison, let us conclude this mystery by applying some good old-fashioned detective work to this much discussed travesty! Black Beaver, untie the woman and remove her boots! She will now determine both of your fates!

Fat woman, take us to the place where you say War Eagle's body was hidden! It should not be hard to find because no new snow has fallen since our retreat!" said Tupac using a threatening tone in his voice.

Blanche rubbed the blistered rope burns on her wrists as she on foot and Black Beaver on his horse, retraced their tracks back toward where Black Beaver's deed was done! Tupac along with sixty- five or seventy tired and hungry braves following about thirty yards behind them, jeered at the two whom they thought were simply looking for their own burial plots!

When Blanche and Black Beaver got to a drop-off in the path they were retracing, Blanche paused while Black Beaver rode his horse around her. In an instant, Blanche jumped onto the rump of Black Beaver's horse and reached around the councilman's waist to remove his knife from its sheath! After Blanche had slit Black Beaver's throat, she swung his horse around and charged at the surprised warriors!

Using Black Beaver's only pistol, Blanche fired it's shot into Tupac's forehead! She then disappeared into a cluster of birch trees!

Cato had seen Joncaire's detachment of horse soldiers on a ridge above him! He figured the French had seen them!

Believing the cavalrymen would come after his crew, he ordered Kimber and Bosman to stay behind far enough so their whole group would not be surprised by a rear assault.

General Staat's map indicated Sam Bellamy's mountain was less than a mile away. Speed at that point became more important than stealth so Cato had the rest of them follow as he sprinted toward the headwaters of the Mohawk River!

Anton von Sporck slammed his gavel for the tenth time on the top of the podium he was standing behind! He was attempting to quell B Group's reaction to A Group's secession from the contest.

Jeffrey Amherst, A Group's leader, and two of their philosophical representatives, George Whitfield and John Wesley had left the institute sometime during the night! The three men had neatly folded their orange jumpsuits on top of their pillows. Their departure had been undetected.

Samuel Bellamy was concerned the fog which had settled on the lake, would prevent his birds from flying. It also made the semaphores into impotent candle holders!

To Sam's surprise, his favorite chess opponent, Joncaire had released one of Bellamy's most tenacious pigeons named, "Carl". There was a message attached to Carl's right leg.

"Am assisting Tanacharison with Colonials' trespass. King's College boys dressed as priests were decoys used in Staats's guerrilla attack. 2 Counsel men and 33 braves dead. 9 militiamen dead. 11 men and 1 woman believed to be trained personnel, were last seen a mile from your location!"

Sam Bellamy took a few deep breaths of the subfreezing air before he settled back down into his wheelchair. He stared out at the colorless abyss as if he were gazing a long way out into the sea.

Black Sam had received a letter from Cato almost six months before. It had been sent from Charlestown. In the letter, after its words were deciphered, the substance of Cato's news translated into a dreadfully clear warning!

"King George had initiated the first prong of his attack on North America. The King sent incarcerated 'pirates' in force, with the intentions of neutralizing Anton von Sporck's (Austrian) ploy to infect the southern ports' with Bubonic carrying flea eggs. I believe King George II intends to exacerbate tensions as a preliminarily designed distraction until he establishes his war cabinet. Expect our arrival by winter. #726."

If Sam had not already been seated, he would have had to sit down once he realized Cato's warning was coming to fruition! This meant King George planned to start trouble wherever there were raw places on America's hide!

He would no doubt, stick the Colonists with additional exorbitant tariffs, George would whack the Indians with all sorts of territorial issues especially if the Indian properties were contiguously located against the French or Spanish owned areas! Cato was right as Sam had surmised, England intended to expand its world dominance and war was the only way in which that could be done!

Captain Dorce's chef nervously tapped on the 'Rebecca's' wheelhouse door. Francois DuPont had some kitchen issues which needed to be addressed!

By the color of Dupont's gin-nose which had turned a deep purple, Dorce could see through the glass window the Frenchman was quite upset about something! He motioned for the chef to come in.

"Hello, Francois, what brings you all the way up here? I hope we don't have to return to England for some ingredient you forgot to bring onboard! joked Dorce.

"Sir, I really hate to disturb you over such a trite issue, but I am having one hell of a time with the King!" said the hangdog chef.

"Oh, how so, Monsieur DuPont?" courteously asked the captain.

"Captain Dorce, he insists on helping me prepare the meals for the ship's crew, Sir!" hissed the wobbling Frenchman.

"Well, that's the first time I've ever heard the famous culinary genius, Francois DuPont complain of too much kitchen help! What's really eating at you, Francois? Tenderly questioned the 'Rebecca's' captain.

"Captain, I'm a little reluctant to say anything, Sir, seeing as how he is the bloody King of England and all!" Whined the Chef.

"That may be true, my Friend; however, you and I will remain partners after that bloke is long gone! Come on, Francois, spit it out!"

"The bastard drank my best jug of scotch! It was twelve years old!"

"Did you say anything to him about it?" asked the Captain.

"He said that 'Timothy' had taken it!" cattily remarked Francois.

"Who in the hell is this 'Timothy' fellow?"

"The King says, he is his roommate, Sir!" Dupont said.

"Have you ever seen 'Timothy', Francois?" genuinely asked Dorce.

"No Sir, I haven't! But as sure as I'm living, I have heard them speaking to one another!" innocently answered the Chef.

"In your honest opinion, Francois, what do you think is wrong with the King?" nobly asked Dorce.

"I believe the man is as crazy as a bedbug, I do!" Dupont said.

"My good Man, I'll rid you of your worries within the day! For now, go about your duties with the knowledge that our meeting 'never took place', Francois! Understood?"

"I understand, Captain, and I thank you, Sir!"

Bartholomaus Girandoni threw his quill like a dart at "Marmaduke", his wife's favorite cat! Once again, the animal had hidden beneath his work bench and launched himself to the top of his drawing board, stolen the sausage from between two slices of rye and escaped into the bedroom!

This time, the quill stuck into Marmaduke's back causing the Abyssinian to squeal as if his tail had been cut off! Thankfully his wife had gone to the market and did not witness his remarkable throw; therefore, Bartholomaus would go unpunished!

The Austrian clockmaker apologized to the wounded beast and paid it off with a piece of pickled herring which had been left over from the previous night's dinner. He then got back to his drawings.

Girandoni had been contracted to design a monstrous twofaced clock destined to be set on top of a courthouse somewhere in Philadelphia. He was six months behind on his promise to have the schematic ready for the actual construction of it. Frankly speaking, Bartholomaus was bored to death with the whole project and didn't particularly care if he completed it or not!

The doctor had been painfully honest with him! Due to his rather rambunctious lifestyle of bygone days and the blistering numbers of things that had lavished him with pleasure throughout his younger years, New England's greatest chronopher was dying.

"They" (his physicians) said he was supposed to be dead two years ago; therefore, Bartholomaus pretty much marched to his own drumbeat! Basically, he did what he wanted to do and like Marmaduke, he didn't much care what anyone thought about it!

But like anything else, life can change at the drop of a hat and thus it did exactly that! At precisely the strike of noon, a green headed pigeon started pecking on his picture window. Sam Bellamy had sent him a message!

"Must accelerate our March reunion. Need 200 windbuchses pronto for peaceful measures. Border dispute involved with 50+ dead. French are in route. Showdown expected at Fort Herkimer. Of dire importance within our ring in twenty days. Cato will arrive at your address with clock box for delivery on that date."

Suddenly, Bartholomaus Girandoni developed a headiness he had not experienced in years! Now there was a purpose to finish off and even celebrate not only the last but conclusive days of his life!

Bartholomaus's mind then drifted back deeply into his past! Beautifully, he recalled the sea's luster at sundown, the electric excitement he would feel seconds before the 'Whydah' robbed another ship!

As if he were slapped by a giant, the ancient pirate collapsed to the stone floor of his study! He clutched his chest in an attempt to relieve the pressure on his sternum.

Girandoni looked upward toward the ceiling. Swirls of purplish colors all mixed together, presented a marvelous backdrop for the warming silhouette of Marmaduke's body lying on top of him!

This left Bartholomaus with a tinge of regret. He had misjudged his wife's cat. Marmaduke liked him after all!

General Abraham Staats breathed a sigh of relief when he saw Robert Crommelin's grin spreading across his copper colored face! Seeing the man meant the boys from the college had made it to the fort.

"Hello, Robert! Please tell me the King's College cadets are in good fashion!" asked Staats.

"That bald headed fellow named 'Cato', outfoxed those Indians like nothing I have ever seen before! That crafty rascal got those dang redskin guides of ours drunk!

That's when he had me and the college boys circle around all of the commotion your soldiers started with the Indians and that's how we got here! All that's troubling those boys right now is just a speck of frostbite!

"Did Cato's people make it through?" strained the General.

"As far as I know! After the shooting started, we didn't hear a peep from them!

I'm assuming they made it! From what I witnessed, they were experienced warriors so I'd expect it would pretty much take ghosts to kill them!" lightheartedly answered Robert.

"Where are the boys now?" asked Abraham Staats.

"They're getting ready, as we speak, Sir!" Said Crommelin.

"Ready? Ready for what, Mister Crommelin?" Asked the shocked General.

"General Staats, one of Samuel Bellamy's pigeons delivered a message for you! We didn't know it was for you until we took it off the bird's leg.

I'll meet you in the Colonel's office in just a minute. You can read it for yourself. We couldn't make heads nor tails of it!" hollered Crommelin.

Colonel Andrew McClelland and Doctor Harold Pollard ran toward General Staat's and his battle scathed foot soldiers. Every one of them had either taken their first life or at least had a hand in a man's killing. It showed on their faces!

Some of the guerillas began weeping when they passed through Fort Herkimer's gates while others, those with no physical wounds, simply fell to their knees and began praying!

The fort's surgeon, Doctor Pollard immediately ushered the severely injured into the triage tent. It had been set up in the middle of the parade ground.

Pots of sterilizing water were already bubbling over causing the "saw water" to hiss when it splashed onto the coals. Pollard's assistants stood ready by the awaiting gurneys. Each of them held blood restrictors as well as tongue depressors for the soon-to-be amputees!

The nine dead were stacked in the southeastern corner of the fort. A burial detail had almost completed their assignment; however, they were to holdoff the interments until Doctor Pollard had completed what paperwork he had to do.

Just the way Governor Burnet glanced up at General Staats told Abraham the man was ashamed of his cowardly behavior! He begged through his facial inflections to not taint his public's impression of him. If they ever caught wind of his displayed panic, he'd never get another vote…ever!

By the glare returned by Staats, Burnet knew Staats had lost respect for him! At best, the General's demeaning gaze would be the end of it but realistically, the Governor conceded his political career on the island was a thing of the past!

Consequently, Burnet declined Colonel McClelland's invitation for him to hear the interpretation of Sam Bellamy's encrypted note. McClelland then turned toward Abraham Staats.

"General Staats, Sir, let's not worry with the debriefing we both know I must report. Tomorrow I'll need to send out a full rundown to England if that would be satisfactory with you, Sir?

Is Governor Burnet not going to join us?" respectfully asked Colonel McClelland.

"'Absolutely', to your first question! Tomorrow will suit me just fine, Colonel!

I would expect that the nervous little fellow's heart couldn't bare the strain if what Bellamy's note says, has anything to do with Indians! I think for that reason, he has opted to sit this one out!

Perhaps Doctor Pollard can give him something for his nerves! Maybe the good doctor could also look in on him every once in a while. Should the wind blow the trees too loudly, the poor soul might just die from fright!" nastily remarked Abraham Staats.

"I understand, Sir! Shall we read the note, Sir?" snapped McClelland.

"#689, #001Roost ^^^>181 Kings+-!."

"What do you make of this, General?" queried the fort's commander.

"Colonel, how did you know this message was for me and how could you have known whom the note was from? Answer that set of questions for me and I shall answer yours secondly, Sir!" said the general as he withdrew his pistol from it's belt.

"General Staats, let's get one thing straight between us right now! Although there is quite a stretch between our ranks, please remember that we are both men and although we are fighting under the same flag, it does not negate the fact we are still civil human beings!

Therefore, Sir, as one man to another, General, if you ever point another weapon at me again so help me god, you had best use it or I shall make you swallow it! Is my point of view understood, General Staats?" flatly said Colonel McClelland.

Staats knew that his card was called. Because the Colonel had every right to react the way he did, General Staats instantaneously re-belted his pistol, snapped to attention and humbly apologized.

Now, please understand that while General Staats was presenting his rather animated gestures of apology, Abraham had a grin on his face the whole time he was doing it; therefore, McClelland's acceptance of the General's pretense was received with mixed internal reviews.

With a little bit of an emotional struggle, Abraham Staats began his climb back to the top of the military pyramid. He did this by obfuscating what was already a confusingly delivered message.

General Staat's name was printed on the band which had secured the message attached to the bird's leg! On the other leg was a similar band but that one had the pigeon's owner's name on it, "Sam Bellamy"!

With that realization, General Abraham Staats proceeded with the verbal deciphering of Mister Bellamy's provocative dispatch. This is how the general decoded Bellamy's note for Colonel McClelland.

"Colonel, "#689" is my code number; the comma explains that the message is to me. "#001" is Sam Bellamy's identification number while the capitalized word, 'Roost' means headquarters.

Each of the "^" symbols signify ten miles of difficult terrain which means that from this fort there are thirty miles of rough country between here and Bellamy's location. The ">" translates into a directive.

I am to go to Sam Bellamy's headquarters with "181" of the "King" ('s) College cadets, "+" (and) "-" (no) and "!" representing soldiers. The "." means 'finality' saying, that this message is of extreme importance and there is to be no deviations from its directive. That exclamation point is also expressing, 'immediacy', Colonial!

It is now eight thirty! I'm going to get a little sleep. Have the boys ready to go in twelve hours. Issue them the rifles they have been clamoring for and be sure each of them have no less than a dozen loads apiece.

Again, Colonial McClelland, I apologize for my earlier bellicosity. I guess I was still fighting Indians when I returned. Forgive me, Sir!

Now, if it's alright with you, I'm going to find a soft spot to lay my head on. Kindly, wake me up at sundown, Colonel McClelland, the boys and I have a thirty-mile stroll to make in a little while and I don't want to embarrass myself in front of them!"

"Sir, what should I do with the Governor?" innocently asked McClelland.

"Don't vote for him!" said Staats.

The raspy voice of one of the cadets first sergeants echoed off of the fort's walls. He was instructing his company as to how to lace their boots onto their snowshoes. They had little time to learn how to survive the subzero conditions.

Thirty miles, traveling at night, one hundred and eighty one very green cadets, two seasoned adult leaders with only a sketchy understanding of the terrain's difficulty! The whole thing was an absolute impossibility thought Colonel McClelland that is, until his sergeant at arms brought him some breaking news!

The fort's guardhouse had just signaled there was a wagonload full of priests, all supposedly playing musical instruments, approaching Fort Herkimer! It was reported that the sign posted on the side of a large box in the wagon bed read, "Blankets for God's Children"!

Captain Phillippe-Thomas Chabert de Joncaire pleaded once again for Tanacharison to spare the life of another one of the men whom had been in charged with the 'Princess of the Darkness's' guidance to the Mohawk headwaters! They did what they were supposed to do; however, they got drunk while they were doing it! For that, all eight were beheaded.

Just as the last body had been tossed into the burial pit, in flew one of Bellamy's green headed messenger pigeons. Furiously, and without opening the bird's mail packet, Tanacharison ripped off the fowl's legs and threw it's body into the fire.

The infuriated Chief then untied the note's packet while adjusting his spectacles onto the bridge of his nose.

"#'s430,+619,#001Roost^^>-!."

Tanacharison looked up at Captain Joncaire with horror in his eyes! His blood brother, Samuel Bellamy, had sent a "code red" message to the both of them. Joncaire also showed signs of distress.

The French commander's face had lost its color. He then whispered a remark to Tanacharison.

"Old friend, I am sure what we had all hoped would not happen has begun! It looks like Sam's about ready to pull the trigger on the British! I knew it would be just a matter of time until he was fed up with the haughty bastards too!" said Joncaire.

"And what am I supposed to do about the men I lost last night?" exclaimed Tanacharison.

"Not meaning to sound callused about the tragic occurrence but under the circumstances, Tanacharison, I would recommend you bury your pain for now and do your reconciling at a later date! My friend, as my father use to say, 'the best way to serve revenge, is cold!', maybe you ought to heed those words for yourself!" gently spoke the French captain.

After an hour's worth of preparation for their trek to the Mohawk River's headwaters, Captain Joncaire and Tanacharison disappeared into the trees. If the moon was good to them, they'd arrive at Bellamy's mountain by midnight.

It was Kimberly's loud squeal which alerted Ogle and Selkirk of the 'Rebecca's' proximity to the 'Kitty's Amelia'. What was thought to become a day of clear sailing was all of a sudden threatening to be their last day of life for them!

In that both ships were under the "Union Jack", Ogle hoped the 'Rebecca' would be satisfied with a 'wave and a howdy-do' but that would only happen if the 'Kitty's Amelia' had not been reported as stolen! Deep inside Chaloner knew full well that it had!

That mystery was solved the second Alex saw a ring of black smoke form off of the starboard side of the 'Rebecca'! A thousand yards later, the cannonball splashed into the ocean just feet in front of the 'Kitty Amelia's' bow!

The King of England's flag was raised, underneath it was a blood red banner indicating the 'Rebecca' was intending to place the entire ship under arrest! They were nearly fifteen hundred miles from London and realizing all the trial work would have to be done onboard the 'Rebecca' plus taking into account there would be no space availability for incarcerations, their chances were better if they made a run for it!

Suddenly Ogle broke into a deep rolling guffaw! With his finger pointed toward the northwest, he drew Selkirk's attention to two peaks appearing to be growing out of the Atlantic Ocean! As soon as Alex saw what Cal was pointing toward, he too cut loose with a mighty laugh and coupled his joviality with a jig!

After enduring several agonizing moments of watching the two men carry on as if they had just been to a hoochie-coochie show, Kimberly spoke up.

"The goddamned 'Rebecca' just happens to be gaining on us, Gentlemen! Would either of you mind doing something to rectify this situation? We seem to have found ourselves in a real shit-can!" Screamed Kimberly Kimber.

"Kimberly, in another ten minutes I will assure you there will be nothing to fear. You are soon to be amazed!

Honey, do you see those two mountains jutting up ahead? Those are the Cape Verde Twins! On the left is called "Fogo" while the peak on the right is named "Brava".

Your Dad and I saw this same sight just a few months ago! A great pirate by the name of Benjamin Hornigold taught your father and me a sneaky little maneuver right here on this very spot!

The 'Rebecca' is wasting their powder on us because we're outdistancing them by the second! What they do not know is, their ship is about ready to run aground!

Kimberly, there are sand bars just waiting for them! If they try to cut us off before we go between the twins, they're going to have the surprise of their lives!" said Ogle in a consoling way.

Barely had Cal gotten his comforting words out of his mouth when a volley of grapeshot ripped through the 'Kitty's Amelia's' wheelhouse! Every single one of the lead balls that hit the ship did some sort of damage to it!

Luckily none of the now petrified crew were injured. There was no crippling done to hamper the 'Kitty's'' getaway. What Commander Ogle had said would happen, happened! The 'Rebecca' suddenly came to a groaning halt!

After suffering only one more shrapnel spray which did kill a man in the crow's nest, Ogle was able to slip through the two mountains and therefore block any future shots from the 'Rebecca's' gunnery banks. It would be hightide before the King's ship would have any chance of escaping its marooning!

Alex Selkirk then politely asked Kimberly to leave the wheelhouse while he "discussed" some personal issues with the Commander! The very second the Kimber girl had shut the shattered door behind her, Alex approached Ogle like a streetfighter. Ogle then got a piece of Selkirk's mind!

"For god's sake, Commander, why in bloody hell didn't you swing around and sink the 'Rebecca'? Do you believe they were shooting candy at us, Sir? We still have time! Let's go back and finish the job, Cal!"

"When Gus and I were kids, eleven years old I think, I fell into an old well while he and I were stealing stuff out of an empty house! Under the incriminating circumstances, George couldn't go for help. If he had, we both would have been in some serious trouble!

It was getting pretty cold as the night began easing in! I had broken my collarbone because someone had thrown a kid's rocking chair down the dry well and that's what I landed on! Therefore, I couldn't climb up the rope that George had thrown down to me.

Already, we could hear our names being called by his father's groundmen! It was dark, foggy and we were two hours late! Gus and I knew they would send out the bloodhounds if King George I's grounds staff came back to the castle empty handed!

We were scared to death, no doubt about it! I reckon most boys would have run back home, admitted their sins, pleaded for leniency and then gotten some adult assistance to fix up the mess they had gotten into, not George Augustus!

I guess you'd call George's father a 'sonofabitch'! When he was in his cups, he would become downright mean and especially to Gus; therefore, other options had to be found! Voices and lights were coming closer!

Finally, I heard Gus talking above me! Between the pain and the poor acoustics in the bottom of the well, I couldn't make out what he was saying to the men up above me. All I know is, whatever he did speak to the grounds personnel about it was done quite loudly and filled with a multiple number of explicative words!

Thirty minutes later, a mule and a children's swing pulled me to freedom! When I got to the top of the well, Gus was sitting on the rescuing beast's back! He bid me a pleasant goodnight and that's the last I saw of the old boy for almost five years!

I don't know any of the details beyond that but I do know, the incident was never mentioned again! For that reason, Alex, I chose not to kill him this time! Should another occasion arise in which he attacks me, I'll not spare his life!" retrospectively stated Ogle.

"Very well! What do you suggest we do now?" snapped Selkirk.

"Hightail it to New York!" rebutted Cal.

"Sir, you know full-well the 'Rebecca' will be back after us as soon as hightide comes in! That means she'll do everything in her power to cut us off between here and New York, Commander!" snapped Alexander.

"Alex, I am aware of your well-founded warnings of which, I could not agree with you more. I expect my old friend Gus to do exactly that! Except in this case, Captain Selkirk, the 'Kitty's Amelia' will disappear from sight!" laughingly replied Ogle.

"How do you propose to do that, Cal?"

"I'm going to pull one of Black Sam's old maneuvers! We shall reverse our course once we get over the horizon to the southeast and then slip up behind the 'Rebecca' about the time they get to the American coastline." cooley said Cal.

"Well let's just hope that Captain Dorce doesn't know of Bellamy's 'old trick'!" sneered Alex.

"Indeed!" sharply agreed the Commander.

Blanche was lost! With no sun or moon she couldn't establish where she was. Recognizable markers were nonexistent; but she did recall someone saying at some time, something about water usually flowing south!

In her attempt to find an unfrozen body of water, Blanche took Black Beaver's horse to a higher point to gain a better look at the surrounding landscape. She was searching for the white bark on sycamore trees. They always grew near water.

The odds of either Staat's crew or Tanacharison's Indians coming after her were close to a hundred percent in Blanche's mind. So, she was very careful about crossing open spaces.

With a snowy background one can spot a horseman from thousands of yards away. Blanche hugged the tree line and followed a distant pattern of white barked trees in the direction away from where the conflicts had happened. It was her only option anyway!

Anne Bonnie had for the most part stopped her shivering. Cato and Every had spotted what they thought was a cave entrance. Fortunately, it turned out to be a well-hidden sanctuary for them to warm up and prepare for what was to come later that night. It was seven o'clock.

From what James Stanfield had estimated, Bellamy's mountain was six hundred yards away from their current location. The trouble with that was, the granite monolith was setting in the middle of a fast-moving river! It could only be reached by boat.

What was thought to be the mournful whistling of the wind, turned out to be the first break Cato's team had had since they got tied up with Staats's men. Bill Bosman upon his return from checking out the mysterious sound they had heard, reported he had not only seen a light blinking near the top of the mountain but he also claimed to have heard someone calling 'Cato's' name!

With that fantastic news still echoing in their minds, they all crept out of their protective cavern in hopes that Bosman's story was more than an exhaustion born illusion! As it turned out, what Bill Bosman had seen and heard was true!

With the use of his telescope, Cato was able to faintly make out what he thought to be Bellamy's silhouette! When Cato and Samuel Fraunces heard Sam's voice blaring out of a megaphone, everyone exploded into a gleeful cheer! Sam was giving them some instructions!

"Cato, follow along the path you are on for two hundred yards. You will come to three white boulders. On top of the quartz rocks, you will see a brass rod protruding from the center stone.

Pull the rod toward you in a slow and easy fashion. Your direction will become obvious from that point further."

Maynard nodded his confirmation of Sam's voice to Anne Bonnie who immediately began plucking her cheeks and patting her hair upon realizing her prayers had been answered!

After eighteen years of separation and not knowing whether Sam was alive or dead, Anne was going to be united with her husband once again.

When Cato pulled the brass rod as Bellamy had instructed him to do, the earth began to vibrate beneath his feet! The noise below reminded Cato of sounds made by chains dragging against wooden planks.

Suddenly, a large slab of granite began mechanically opening in the side of the same mountain that Cato's crew had found refuge within! This opening however, was not a cave at all, it was a tunnel's entrance!

Soundlessly, the eight of them began filing into the mountain's gaping hole. Cato was the last to enter the downwardly stepped entranceway.

He was sure he had heard the rustling of some bushes coming from across the river. Cato waited behind for quite awhile to make sure no one had followed them.

Once confident the noise he had heard was a deer, Cato returned to the awaiting group and proceeded to tiptoe down the tunnel's rocky steps. Henry Every was in the lead because he was the only one who had a functional lantern!

Sporck pretended to be incensed by Jeffry Amherst's and his cohorts' disappearance! Consequently, he put the entire research compound under a lockdown for the sake of national security! He then publicly ordered the armed guards to shoot any person seen walking outside of their billets unless they were carrying a "permission stick"!

The way one could get hold of the 'permission stick' was to personally ask Anton von Sporck for it! Schismatically, as the scientists figured out, one had to walk across a fifty-yard span of open ground without the stick in order to get permission to carry the gold painted piece of wood!

Statistically speaking, a person had an eighty percent chance of being shot while in the process of gaining a ninety-nine percent probability of not being hit by a single guard! However, when a second or certainly a third shooter got added into the algorithm, the ratio of success to failure became dismal!

Therefore, as agreed upon by all, it was better to remain in their quarters than to risk the alternate's odds stacked against them!

Sporck had just finished thumping up a plump vein for an injection into it. When the warm rush came, Ike in a melancholy like fashion, reached over and embraced the pillow on which Jeffrey had laid his head upon. The intoxicating smells stimulated him. He thought about dead Indians!

"State your name and business with Fort Herkimer!" yelled First Sergeant Ben Collars.

"We are here under God's name and we are doing his work, Sergeant! We have no business with Fort Herkimer unless there are souls to be saved within your walls! Our reason for stopping was simply for directions, Sir," piously chimed Jeffrey Amherst.

"And where are you wanting directions to, if I might be so bold to ask?" sarcastically quizzed the sergeant.

"We have been called by the Lord, Sergeant! Our holy mission is to bring aide to Chief Tanacharison's people! We have medicines, blankets, toys and Bibles for them!" Said George Whitefield after standing up on the wagon's seat.

"I, in good conscience Gentlemen, must ask you to turn that wagon around and return to where you came from! Tanacharison's warriors attacked some soldiers just hours ago! It would be suicidal for even priests to show your white faces anywhere around them!" warned the sergeant of the guard.

John Wesley then jumped off of the priests' wagon and tromped to a spot just under the guard tower where First Sergeant Collars was perched. With an eloquent bow, he introduced himself along with his 'brothers' as the official Papal delegation representing King George Augustus II!

"Sergeant, when is the last time you closely listened to the "twenty-third Psalm" in earnest? Perhaps this would be an ideal time for us to set up our tent and include that particular passage in a little program of which I am sure your entire fort's population would spiritually gain a lot from!" joyously yelled John Wesley.

"Do you swear that you are not taking guns or whiskey to them Mingo Indians? If you ain't, then I guess ya'll can move on through! But let me caution you men right now, you'd best just turn around and go back home!

Just because you boys are priests which don't mean a damn thing to those savages, do not think for one moment they won't skin yo'uns alive! As a matter of fact, I doubt if you'd live to see sunrise if ya'll head much further north into their territory!

But, if you do, you sure won't have any trouble running up with them! Actually, to tell you the truth, they probably are waiting for you as we speak!" mockingly stated Sergeant Collar.

"About how far would you say Chief Tanacharison's village is from here, Sir?" earnestly asked John Wesley.

"Son, I'd say it's ten to fifteen miles ahead to the northwest! But I wouldn't worry about that, Father. Tanacharison will catch up with you fellows long before you get close to his village!" said Collars.

"Sergeant, we thank you for your understanding and your concerns! As a token of our blessings upon you, we'll leave with you a blanket identical to the ones our King, Jesus Christ requested we deliver to his unsaved children!

May it remind you of the warmth gifted to you by the savior of your soul and the grantor of your being. God bless you, Sergeant!" wailed John Wesley.

At the tail end of John's miniature sermon, George Whitefield opened the wooden lid to the only unsealed box containing several stacks of brightly colored blankets and ceremoniously withdrew one of them. He then laid the folded blanket into John Wesley's awaiting arms who in turn and placed the gift at the base of the fort's gate.

The three priestly garbed men then proceeded into the Indian lands. It was eight o'clock and very cold.

Captain Dorce was furious! He was angry at himself for allowing a drunk to horn in on his battle plan!

Because of his reluctance to obey a superior's orders, the 'Rebecca's' captain found himself relieved of duty! He was sitting in his quarters with two guards posted at his door.

As Gus had announced, he was now the "Captain" of the 'Rebecca'! His intentions were to cheat the sea of its rightful capture by using ballasts to raise the ship off of its restrainers!

With hightide less than an hour away, the King's genius would in George's mind, shine through thought Captain Dorce. He listened to the King's ravings from the floor above him!

"Unlike one of my predecessors named 'King Canute', I can command the sea to do as I wish! It therefore is my wish that the 'Rebecca' rise as if it were on the wings of a phoenix and come to the aide of our noble cause! Free this ship!" ranted the tipsy British King.

Soon after George's declarations were made, the 'Rebecca' was released by the obeying Atlantic and permitted to leave her prison on its own recognizance! The ship's crew applauded as the King had another barrel of rum rolled out in commemoration of not only their release from their plight but of his birth as well!

Thirty years ago, on that very day, George Augustus had been born! 'Timothy' was slightly vexed because Gus had not had Captain Dorce thrown overboard! He seemed to think, sparing Dorce's life would eventually become one of Gus's greatest regrets. But soon after a few hoists to their good fortunes, most everything else of a negative nature faded away.

Bartholomaus Girandoni blinked his eyes in disbelief! He laid quietly on his study's floor in total amazement. The chest pains had gone and he was still alive!

When he heard his wife's key turn the front door's heavy lock system, Bartholomaus then discovered he had not entirely missed the swipe of the reaper's scythe. Oxygen deprivation rendered his tongue and his right arm useless.

As soon as Grace Girandoni entered their home and realized that Marmaduke was not there to greet her, right away she sensed something had gone awry! From her husband's bluish pallor, she could tell he had had another stroke. This one looked as if it had been a bad one!

Grace in one swift movement, grabbed her clutch bag and went running back toward town to get her husband's doctor. She had not travelled any more than fifty yards down the walk before a loud bang and the ricocheting of a bullet caused the old pirate to stop dead in her tracks!

When she turned around, she saw Bartholomaus leaning against the front door of their home! Grey smoke was still billowing from the pistol that dangled from his left hand. As best as he could, Girandoni was trying to tell his wife something very important!

General Staats was awakened by the sounds of men speaking excitedly to each other! As he sat up from the cot he was fast asleep in, he was met with the point of a spear held by Tanacharison in the flesh!

Behind the Chief was the French captain, Philippe-Thomas Chabert de Joncaire! He had a cocked blunderbuss trained toward Staats's chest!

"How in the hell did you get in here?" asked the astonished General.

"It wasn't difficult," answered Tanacharison.

"I didn't hear any gunshots!" Argued the still disbelieving Abraham Staats.

"We came as a surprise, General," stated Captain Joncaire.

"What do you want with me?" arrogantly asked Staats.

"A meeting has been called by #001! You, Crommelin and the cadets are to come with us!

We have the horses ready. You are to take no weapons with you and we are to leave at once!" commanded the French captain.

"What have you done with my men?" Pleadingly asked the General.

"We have them tied up! They're in the barn!" answered Tanacharison.

"And what if I refuse to allow the cadets to be taken prisoner by you people?" challenged Staats.

"We'll burn the barn!" countered the Algonquin chief.

"General Staats, we have not come for war; instead, Sam Bellamy has summonsed us to a summit meeting! We are to stem the tide of what appears to be the beginning of a world war!

Inevitably it will be our responsibility to stop that kind of tragedy from taking place! Therefore, it is time we get a move on! General, grab a warm coat and let's get going!" excitedly explained Joncaire.

Alex Selkirk spun the wheel of the 'Kitty's Amelia' in order to avoid a massive pod of whales making their way to the warmer gulf waters. He estimated they would pull up behind the 'Rebecca' by sunrise!

Alex inwardly hoped Ogle would change his tune regarding his friend, the King! 'A stitch in time…' kept bouncing around in Selkirk's mind. He knew Cal would come around to his senses but he just prayed it happened before the 'saves nine' part of that old saying played out in truth!

Blanche knew Cato had almost spotted her! She waited practically two hours before she moved another muscle!

When the laurel bush's roots gave way and her leg dipped into the Mohawk River, she was forced to leave it there for fear the movement would draw Cato's attention.

She had seen the lever pull that had opened up the passageway into Sam Bellamy's mountain! Blanche marveled at the lack of feeling she had in her leg as she made her way onto the rocky path leading into the cavern's jaws.

It was like wearing a marshmallow shoe, Blanche thought. It was as if her entire leg were made of wood. Nevertheless, Blanche cautiously slipped into the entrance to her father's home!

CHAPTER 8

NATIONAL BETRAYALS

Robert Dinwiddie had been very meticulous about covering up his past! If the truth about it were to ever reach Walpole's ears, he would be forced to kiss his political career goodbye!

In his early twenties, Robert lived on the British Colony of Bermuda. He thoroughly enjoyed the island's trappings which guaranteed access to the earth's known pleasures!

The young man, and especially because he was a rich one, got involved with an element of people who made their living by hustling others! Therefore, it wasn't very long until something rather startling happened!

One evening after a fairly difficult day of repairing the hull on a customer's fishing boat, "Bob" Dinwiddie locked up his shop and trotted over to his favorite watering hole, "The Queen Anne's Revenge Tavern". He ordered his usual glass of absinthe rum and pineapple juice. He settled into a stool at the bar.

Just as Dinwiddie was flagging down the bartender for another drink, a couple of dozen men straggled into the tavern. After about thirty minutes of reflectively watching the freshly arrived sailors through the Queen Anne's mirror, curiosity finally got the best of young Mister Dinwiddie.

After using what Robert thought was an extraordinary sense of being able to quickly "size a man up", he picked out a certain individual whom he thought to be the most affable. Dinwiddie perceived that his 'mark' had the friendliest looking face out of the whole bunch!

He was planning to coerce the sailor into a game of chance or maybe just a conversation. Either way, Robert was determined to get something off of the handsome mariner!

"Sir, my name is Bob Dinwiddie. I overhaul boats for a living. My shop is right across the street so if you need anything, I'm open every day from dawn to dusk!" Bob said.

"It's only three o'clock in the afternoon! How come you're over here while you say you're over there?" questioned the tall and dark stranger sporting a broad grin.

Stunned by the man's off-the-hip response, Dinwiddie caustically responded with an equally prickly remark.

"Oh, I was just taking a little break! But, do mention to your dad, if he needs the best repair work done on this island tell him where he can find me!" pushed Bob.

"Mr. Dinwiddie, I don't even know who my mother is, much less my father! How about you, are you a bastard also?" softly spoke Black Sam.

The men who were apparently part of Bellamy's crew all of a sudden stood up and quickly left the tavern. That left a few locals still seated. Robert Dinwiddie then answered the obnoxious visitor's question.

"No, sir, my folks are certified! Now, if you'll allow me the pleasure of offering you a drink on my way out, I'll gladly bid you a fair adieu!" said Robert Dinwiddie.

"Sit tight, my friend! I have something I would like to speak with you about! It concerns your future!" said Bellamy with a less jovial look upon his chiseled face.

"No, I think not! If you would excuse me, I'll get back to the shop!" said the addled Dinwiddie.

Faster than a blink, Black Sam Bellamy withdrew two cocked pistols from beneath his jacket and pointed them both at Robert Dinwiddie's chest! He then rebutted with a comment regarding Bob's unwanted departure.

"Look, Mister Robert Dinwiddie, I'm going to be perfectly honest with you! We docked here for the explicit purpose of my interviewing you for a job which is about to become open! Could you spare another minute or two to consider my proposal?"

With that much of an abrupt change in Black Sam's demeanor along with the pistols, Robert nodded his acceptance of Bellamy's proposition.

"Sure, go ahead and say what's on your mind!" said Dinwiddie.

Sam returned his weapons to the front of his belt so the butts of them remained at an easy reach. He then asked Dinwiddie a rather poignant question.

"Robert, if you were walking down a lonely beach and happened to come upon a chest full of English gold coins, what would you do?"

"I suppose I would most likely want to get the chest out of the elements! Wood as I understand it, becomes ruined after long exposures to the sun and rain! But first, I'd make sure the "fairy's" weren't watching!" foolishly answered Bob Dinwiddie.

The next thing Dinwiddie was aware of after his sarcastic remark was looking up at the ceiling of the Queen Anne's Revenge Tavern! Sam Bellamy toasted him as Robert Dinwiddie crawled back onto the same stool he had been knocked off of!

This time, Bob was more focused! He was ready to answer Sam's riddle in a more serious vein.

"I would take it back to my shop and count it. Once I was completely sure that I had not been seen by someone who might have dropped it there, I would bide my time and prepare for a trip to somewhere off of this godforsaken island! Virginia is the place where I would want to go," said the humbled Mister Dinwiddie.

"Then you'll take the job?" spritely spoke Bellamy.

"What job? I thought we were talking about imaginary chests of gold?" asked Dinwiddie.

"They're one in the same, Robert!" briskly stated Samuel.

"Not to be derogatory, sir, but what in the hell are you asking of me?" vociferously exclaimed Dinwiddie.

"I need a more efficient 'Customs Collector', a selectively blind one at that!" blandly stated Sam.

"Sir, that position is already filled and plus, that is a politically appointed position designated by the Crown!" said Bob in a high-pitched voice.

"Do you want the bloody job or not?" pointedly asked Black Sam.

"Well, sure I would but…" said Bob before Sam cut his sentence short.

"Fine! You'll start today!" Sam Bellamy said.

"Respectfully, Sir, by what authority have you that provides this grand opportunity to me?" sincerely asked Bob.

Bellamy stared at an imaginary pinhole between Robert Dinwiddie's eyes! There was little room for misjudgment at that moment; Sam was internally litmus testing Dinwiddie's moxie!

After two brief seconds of 'mind reading', Sam answered Robert's question.

"Bob, from Catherine Point all the way south to Tobacco Bay is my property! I own every house, every harbor fed building, and everything else that King George the first doesn't! And that, my boy, is where your expertise comes into play!

"You see, Mister Dinwiddie, my particular location on this island is of particular interest to those countries with militaristic or commercial designs on the North American colonies! When my ships return to my legally owned dock, their procurements are subjugated to an import tax!

"In years past before this island became such a strategic hotspot, such temporary stopovers were normally taken care of right here in 'The Queen Anne's Revenge'! Without exception, I always paid the Customs Director his handsome tariff by hand, if you catch my drift!

"Up until now, things never went wrong with that arrangement! After all, everyone was getting quite rich from our ongoing understanding and things were wonderful on this island paradise!

"But with the European race to the Americas now under full rally, George has beefed up his tariff squads at all of his ports! Thus, leaving you, Mister Dinwiddie, with a once in a lifetime opportunity!" whispered Sam.

"If I might ask, sir, what kind of shipping do you do?" timidly asked Robert Dinwiddie.

"I am in the import and export business! I am the pirate named, 'Black Sam Bellamy'!"

"Black Sam?" gasped Bob.

"In the flesh, sir!" answered Bellamy.

"Why me, Captain Bellamy?" asked Bob.

"Because of your enterprising skills!" fired back Sam.

"You're speaking in riddles again, Sam! What 'skills' of mine could possibly be of an interest to you, sir?" curiously asked Robert with a friendly smile.

"Demolitionist extraordinaire… a loyal Scotsman… born into a privileged family of merchants… left the family business because of some queries revolving around some missing armaments… an unexplained explosion diminished all shreds of the heist's footprint… and so you are here!" matter-of-factly said Samuel Bellamy.

"I see! So, what do you need me to do for you, Captain Bellamy?"

"At tomorrow's first light, I and my crew will take the 'Whydah' out to the sea. It will seem to the port authorities that we will not return for at least another month. In actuality, we will double back around to Saint George's Town and dock our ship.

"My sailors and I will return to Catherine Point, disguised as a Spanish warship! We'll fire a couple of innocuous shots at Tobacco Bay! In the meantime, you'll have wired up the King's tariff office the night before. I'll supply you with the powder you'll need!

"During the defensive efforts made by the Catherine Point cannoneers, you, Mister Dinwiddie, will light the fuse that will blow the office into parts which should fit into a small man's boot! You will then run up to the cannoneer's turret and fire a misaimed ball at your Spanish ensigned attacker!

"If all goes well, I will create an explosion onboard the imposing marauder and then limp away as if my ship were taking on water! Overnight, Bob, you will become a hero! When all is said and done, and especially once England hears of your valor, I would expect that your political aspirations will be like a pearl found in an oyster! And even if it didn't, you'd still leave this island one very rich man!

"So, Mister Dinwiddie, do we have an understanding? Come on, you've always wanted to be a pirate, haven't you?" cajoled Sam.

"Of course, but what will I owe you for this opportunity? I mean, other than you doing business in a tariff-free zone for a few years, what do you get out of this, Mister Bellamy?" respectfully quizzed Dinwiddie.

"Just a promise, that's all!" said Samuel.

"A promise, sir?"

"If I ever need a favor done for me, you must promise to do it!" said Sam.

"What I can say is, I will do my best to do what you ask! Is that good enough of an answer?" questionably acquiesced Bob.

"No, it isn't! You must swear that under any reasonable circumstance, you will comply with any request I make of you! Is that clear?" pressed Sam.

"Yes, sir!" answered Robert Dinwiddie.

Eleven years later, long after he had forgotten about the agreement with Black Sam, Lieutenant Governor Dinwiddie was alarmed by the presence of a man named "Joseph Brant" who was sitting in the corner of his bedroom one Sabbath's morning in early November. It was 0700.

Robert probably would have never even seen the Mohawk Chief had he not lit up a bowl full of hemp stuffed into his clay pipe. But life in the political orchards had dulled his once lightning- like responses to the point that Thayendanegea (aka. Joseph Brant) had enough time to spring from Bob's dressing chair and hogtie the naked Lieutenant Governor while he delivered a handwritten message from Black Sam!

Once the message was thrown onto Dinwiddie's bed, the Indian exited the house without leaving any sign he had been there at all. Robert had to call Rhoda his housemaid to get him freed from the 'savage's' bindings! He then read Bellamy's note.

"The French are trespassing to the east of the Ohio River. They have built three forts within the Iroquois Confederacy's legally held territory. Fort Herkimer is under siege by Tanacharison and a company of French cavalrymen. Additionally, there are around a hundred Delewares riding with the French. Send a battalion of your soldiers to Fort Le Boeuf at the Ohio Forks immediately! Tensions are high among the divided Indian tribes, the Colonists, the French, as well as the British. Talk of war is thick. The French must leave. Sam."

Jeffrey Amherst found he could stay a bit warmer by sliding between the boxes of blankets, toys, and Bibles destined for Tanacharison's village. Whitfield preferred taking the reins because he felt more comfortable doing it, and truth be told, he would have been on 'pins and needles' if either of the other two had tried to drive a wagon through the snow!

Whitfield and John Wesley were discussing the types of whales that could have possibly swallowed up Jonah without chewing him up first! Jeffrey was in his snug little cubbyhole, sketching out a drawing of Sporck's face on the side of a box containing the contaminated whistles for Tanacharison's people. Professor Amherst surmised by the first of the new year, eighty-five percent of the natives would be hunting gobblers in heaven!

The way Jeffrey had managed to insert the activating agents into the crates without exposing himself was by inserting microscopic larvae into the mouthpieces of the colorful whistles destined for the slobbering mouths of little Algonquins! After that, frantic mothers receiving warm and sincere hugs from friends and family would become the carriers while their musically inclined children would remain as the hosts!

Colonel McClelland had yelled so much his vocal cords became cramped! He couldn't even call for help anymore!

Andrew's last action before he began tearing the wall apart was firing one of his pistols at the skylight window in his quarters! He hoped someone would let him out of the door which had been tied shut!

After an unbearable wait with no response coming from the outside, the Colonel began chipping away at the mortar between the room's log walls with his tomahawk. But then McClelland heard someone faintly calling his name.

"Colonel, I am trying to get myself untied! Are you alright?" cried out Governor Burnet.

"Where the hell are my men?" roughly uttered the Commander.

"I have no idea! But I do know there were Indians involved!" squealed Burnet.

"Do you even know when this happened? Where is General Staats?" asked McClelland with a painful rasp.

"Sir, all I know is after those priests came by with some blankets for the Indians…" yelled the Governor until McClelland cut him off in midsentence.

"What the fuck are you talking about? What goddamned priests? Where in the hell is the first sergeant?"

"Now, don't take this out on me, Colonel! I could have sworn that one of the Indians who tied me up had a French accent! I believe I heard him say something about taking the soldiers to the barn and burning it!" meekly said the Governor.

"Didn't you hear me yelling?" gruffly questioned McClelland. "Yes! But I didn't know if our aggressors were still here!" whispered the cowardly politician.

Colonel McClelland had nothing else to say. Silence followed.

"Hey, Colonel, guess what? I finally got out of these godforsaken binds! Would you like for me to cut off the ropes holding your door shut?" squealed Burnet.

The fort's commander quietly cocked his second loaded pistol and then aimed it at the place on the other side of his billet's door where he pictured Governor Burnet standing. Just to be sure he would make a fatal shot, Andy answered Burnet's ridiculous question.

"That would be a capitol idea, Governor Burnet!" There was no response.

'Timothy' sat quietly in the corner of the wheelhouse drumming his fingers on Captain Dorce's rolltop desk. He had watched the King's silhouette against the bobbing horizon for long enough! He was becoming sick to his stomach. After recognizing his alter ego's ailment because he was pucking too, King George summoned Captain Dorce back to the wheelhouse. George demanded that he take the 'Rebecca' in a circuitous clockwise direction!

Once Gus felt assured Dorce understood his directive, he and Timothy went back to their quarters for a little snort or two. Both agreed they'd run into the 'Kitty's Amelia' by morning so there was no sense in sparing the booze. It was useless just setting in its bottles!

Bartholomaus Girandoni used his only good hand to unroll the message Samuel Bellamy had sent to them. When Grace read that Cato would be arriving soon, she quickly let her husband's malady slip her mind and let him fall backwards onto the kitchen's floor!

Grace knew exactly what "Bart" wanted by what he was pointing at! In the very back of the couple's chifforobe there was a long leather case. In it and all neatly folded, was the schematic for his "Windbuchse".

Beneath the waxed encased blueprint was the prototype of his greatest invention, a 'wind rifle'! Somehow, "Black Bart" and "Grace O'Malley" would have two hundred of them waiting for Cato to pick up at the end of the month!

General Staats was surprised by Joncaire's stature. The French captain was barely four feet in height!

He was even more shocked by the toughness displayed within the King's College cadet corps. They were quite an extraordinary bunch thought Abraham as he watched them pass over a narrow pass above the Mohawk River.

Suddenly, Tanacharison raised his right fist in the air and motioned the procession to an immediate halt. He had smelled smoke!

With the precision of a diving hawk, the Indian chief swept through the staggered line of cadets whispering his orders.

"In the cluster of trees to the left of those twin peaks in front of you, there is some sort of encampment. You must slow your pace down! You must walk like bears to avoid their awareness of your presence. Use the forest to your advantage as we move around them!" whispered Tanacharison.

Right after that, Tanacharison, Crommelin, and the cadets methodically crawled on all fours through the trees. That left the French captain, Joncaire and the British general, Abraham Staats in the rear of the movement.

As the two men waited for the last cadet to bear-walk into the tree line, Philippe-Thomas Chabert de Joncaire jabbed the butt of his rifle into the General's leg. With his finger perpendicularly placed over his lips and an open hand leveled toward the northeast, Staats was made aware of a single individual running toward them!

Joncaire removed his sheath knife while sliding his musket over to Abraham. This meant the tiny Frenchman would take care of the interrogative work. Staats was to stand ready in case there was a mistake made.

A man by the name of Monceau, an apparent deserter, shat his pants when Joncaire rose from the snow and body slammed him onto the ground! General Staats did not hear their conversation but could see upon Joncaire's coat sleeves the Captain had severed the escapee's windpipe!

The French captain then breathlessly whispered the results of his brief interview to the agape British general.

"Commander Joseph Jumonville sent out a 'supposed' reconnaissance squad to report back to him the results of my assigned mission. I, as you know, was ordered by Jumonville to join up with Tanacharison in response to the news of a British invasion!

As poor ole Monceau told me just before he was dispatched, 'our orders were to attack Joncaire's troops upon their return crossing at Redstone Creek. We were to make it appear as if the British had done it!' Which leaves me at this moment, a man without a country!

Nevertheless, I am here amongst France's enemies of whom for whatever reason, the only people on this planet deserving of my trust! Therefore, I suggest we catch up with Tanacharison and figure out just who our foes really are!"

Selkirk hadn't gotten a wink of sleep! He couldn't get his mind off of Ogle's hesitation to smite the 'Rebecca'! The 'Kitty's Amelia's' passengers would pay a priceless fee for the commander's chivalry should the cards fall badly for them!

If the game of one-upmanship was being played between the King and Chaloner Alex, he would have no choice but to take the matters into his own hands. He would be forced to place Commander Ogle under arrest!

Taking over the 'Kitty's Amelia' was the next to the last thing Selkirk would ever want to do but dying on it, seemed like a worse alternative! Alex had made up his mind! He would have a frank discussion with the Commander and from there, he would decide on the best course of action!

Although it was still dark outside, Blanche crawled into the cave's opening in order to lessen her bulbous silhouette. By the deliberate movements the negro had made while pulling the brass lever, she knew he and probably the rest of his cohorts, were more than likely one of King George's special operations units!

Cato suspected someone had followed them into Bellamy's mountain. He instructed Samuel Fraunces to take the others ahead.

He told his brother he was going to wait behind for a while. Cato said he was expecting an unwanted guest to arrive!

Sporck awakened from an almost comatose sleep. Promptly, he walked over to his bedroom's window to check the guard towers before he went out to take a leak. Seeing that all the towers were manned, Ike opened the door and walked out to the patio where his favorite peeing tree grew.

The sounds of wolves precluded his lingering in the subzero air. Ike returned to his room, stoked up his fire, and prepared himself for another injection.

By the time the blue flames from Anton von Sporck's fireplace began keeping beat with the tic tock of his mantle clock, Ike was ready to plan his next strategic move. Already and despite the snow, he had heard soldiers being marched toward the Indian lands. Cannons and wagons followed behind them.

He wasn't sure if the massive troop movements had anything to do with Jeffrey's doings or not. But he did know one thing, if the Indians were knocked out of the equation, King George would have a much easier time managing the Colonies!

Sporck wanted the British to endure as much disruption as possible! He needed to spread Gus's troops out as thin as he could get them!

With winter setting in, that would mean there would be very little combat. If the Indians believed the British had intentionally infected them with Small Pox, they would more than likely forget about the bad weather and burn every fort down from the east coast all the way to the Mississippi!

Once done, it would be easy pickings for the French and the Spanish to take large wedges of the American pie! As long as the Colonists felt as though they had freedom, they would never pay much attention to who actually owned them.

But in all actuality, what really mattered to Sporck was his percentage from every single slave sold to the Colonies. It didn't really concern him who handed that money to him!

Time is cruel enough to the person looking at themselves in the mirror. It is especially hurtful when there is no comparable recognition from someone whom that person once loved!

But there they were, Sam Bellamy and Anne Bonnie! The rest of the world vanished at that very moment as both examined the tolls each had paid.

Sam rolled up to Anne so they could see each other up close. With a sweet smile on her face, Sam's old lover gently reached out to touch his scarred cheek. She then spoke.

"It is absolutely clear to me that you have no business trying to run this nasty house! When was the last time you've had a bath?" squawked Bonnie.

"I can still see the fire in your eyes, Anne! It's been a long time…"

Anne leaned down and kissed Bellamy's hairless scalp and then kneeled at his supported feet. She reached out so their hands touched, Anne then softly whispered.

"Sam, I believe it is now time for us to continue with the promises that were broken out of no fault of our own making! Our vows remain intact as far as I am concerned! I hope you feel the same!

We have much to talk about but for now, Samuel, we've got some company we must attend to! Cato will be along shortly. He is making sure we weren't being followed.

If you'll show me where some food is, I'll whip us up something for breakfast. The sun will be up in an hour!" said Anne.

Virginia's Lieutenant Governor, Robert Dinwiddie, summoned "Baxter", his manservant, to get his carriage ready. He announced his intentions of meeting with a couple of the 'Assembly men' and therefore needed his best riding suit for the occasion.

"Wetherburn's Tavern" unlike the "Raleigh" just across the street from it, offered private rooms for individuals wishing to have 'safe' conversations. When a certain lantern was lit and it was visible from only the southwestern side of the tavern's building, a message was transmitted to the members of a tiny group of men who informally referred to themselves as, "The Owls".

Being Masons, the owls' secret protocol required no originality with regard to subversively instigated meetings. Noon was the time set for the luncheon. The gathering would take place in the "Queen's Parlor".

Precisely at twelve o'clock, James Blair, Sir William Gooch, and Lewis Burwell quickly shuffled into their opulent meeting space. Robert Dinwiddie greeted the men while he finished tidying up a misunderstanding over a previous bill mistakenly unpaid.

Willem Anne van Keppel had been appointed as governor, a posting he never wanted in the first place! Through aggressive passivity, Keppel never showed up for work! Therefore, the responsibilities of running the Virginia territory fell squarely on the shoulders of the men sitting in the Queen's Parlor that November afternoon!

By the tap of his ring on the table, Sir William Gooch stood and asked the three other 'owls' in the meeting room to join him in reciting their creed.

"We are building every day, in a good or evil way; and the structure as it grows, will our inmost self-disclose. Till in every arch and line, all our faults and failings shine; it may grow a castle so grand, or a wreck upon the sand. Do you ask what building this, which can show both pain and bliss that can be both dark and fair? Lo, its name is character. Build it well, what're you do; build it straight and strong and true; build it clean and high and broad; build it for the eye of God! Amen." The owls said in unison.

At the end of their recited opening, the owls slapped their clinched right fists against their left bosoms like Romans hitting their breast plates. Robert Dinwiddie remained standing while the others were seated. He then unfolded a map and spread it out on the table so all could see exactly why he had called the meeting.

"Gentlemen, Operation "Boa Constrictor" has been launched by Black Sam! A mole contacted me less than ten hours ago with some startling news! French commander, Ensign Joseph Coulon de Jumonville out of Fort Le Boeuf ordered an attack on Fort Herkimer! Under the command of Captain Philippe-Thomas Chabert de Joncaire and a couple of hundred Delaware Indians on last account, had the fort under siege! Casualties were reported to be 'minimal'.

"Samuel Bellamy has requested we send a detachment of troops to break up the standoff! And as diplomatically as possible, ask the French to get back on their side of the Ohio River! Bellamy made it very clear, our cavalry unit is not to engage the Indians unless they are siding with the French. Bellamy's messenger stated that King George has already imbedded at least two known agitator teams into the northeast! Ole Gus it appears is making preparations for an all-out war with us!

"Samuel Bellamy has requested us to organize the Virginia militia into a standing army by Spring! Our jobs for now are to put down this French encroachment. We shall also attempt to befriend the willing Indian tribes and to use our operations against the French as a pre-war training ground! #001 is more than positive, George will have ground forces surrounding our cities within six months! What are your thoughts, Gentlemen?" questioned the Lieutenant Governor.

Lewis Burwell stood. After a respectful nod, #623 cleared his throat and began his remarks in a 'drying paint' kind of voice.

"Gentlemen, let me start off by saying, I am one hundred percent in favor of sending our men up to New York! But there is a troublesome question that keeps nagging me, why didn't Black Sam use Governor Burnet's militiamen instead of ours? Hasn't he figured out the correlation between distance and expediency?" sarcastically droned Burwell.

Dinwiddie came to his feet. He pointed at the map of German Flatts and then slammed a salad fork into the island of Manhattan! Robert then answered Burwell's question.

"My Brothers, Governor Burnet is a British intelligence agent! He is just one of many unleashed onto American soil! I'm sorry to say this but there are only a few of us who realize what the Brits are up to and even fewer whom will risk their necks to stop them from doing it! No, we're it! Now with that settled, who can we send to Fort Herkimer?"

As soon as Robert Dinwiddie sat down, Sir William Gooch took the floor. "This lack of polity makes a perfectly good case for exactly what Bellamy has been saying all along, 'if we are to ever gain our independence, we must first get hold of the nation's security forces and in order to do that, as Samuel says, we must establish an air- tight secret service agency to police the heads of state'! I too find it disheartening that we have to risk our own valuable resources all because of a mealy-mouthed governor absent of any sort of scruples or nationalism!" preached the red-faced Gooch.

After a moment of pretending he had a long list of names to consider, Robert Dinwiddie spoke.

"What I feel that we need is someone who is familiar with the territory. There is a young lieutenant, a land surveyor, who is biting at the bit for a chance to show his stuff! Currently he has a battalion of militiamen bivouacked at Winchester. What are your thoughts about him? His name is 'Washington', I believe."

"How long do you think it will take for this Washington fellow to get on the road?" asked James Blair.

"I expect we could have them at Herkimer in two weeks!" said Burwell.

With a unanimous agreement being sealed by toasting the last bit left in the wine giraffe, all four of the Virginia politicians exited the Wetherburn's Tavern through separate entrances leaving the bill unpaid.

Doctor Pollard had chewed his way through the ropes Tanacharison had wrapped around his wrists. He was able to pull out the spikes used to nail the fort's commander in his quarters!

By the time the physician managed to get the bottom half of the Colonel's door open, McClelland slithered out and was off to kill the Governor!

In anticipation of Colonel McClelland's ire, Governor Burnet grabbed one of the fort's horses and skedaddled off to the city! He knew if McClelland ever caught him out in the open, he would shoot him on sight!

King George Augustus was disturbed by a banging noise which sounded like someone was slapping on the bow of the 'Rebecca'! He then heard someone calling for help!

Timothy dismissed it as a puff of wind or just a porpoise racing the ship but the way he put it, Gus knew that Timothy was simply anxious to get back to their jug of rum! George then realized that Tim didn't particularly give a damn what the noise was, as long as he wasn't in personal danger! The tensions between the two were quickly mounting.

Without saying a single word to Timothy, King George barged into the wheelhouse catching Captain Dorce fast asleep at the wheel! With all of the air he could possible retain within his ribcage, the King bellowed out Jesus' name and mixed up a few more unsavory remarks with it!

In response to Augustus's blast of noted irregularities, all the Captain could do was raise his forefinger into the air! Someone had hit the man on the back of his head with a blunt instrument! He had a concussion! Dorce's vomiting told Gus that.

Instantaneously, the sobering King reached for the Captain's Bell but was stopped from doing so by a weather-beaten woman holding Dorce's blunderbuss square at his chest! She was finishing up a turkey leg before she had anything to say to him.

"He'll be alright! I hit him with the flat side of the tomahawk he was using as a paperweight. Get over here and tie him up! This ship is now under my command!" barked the intruder.

George Augustus did as the scraggly woman said. Gus loosely tied Dorce's wrists behind his back and rolled the semiconscious Captain on his stomach so he would not choke on his own puke! Then the King walked toward the emaciated woman to get a better look at her.

As the King was positioning himself so the light would be in his favor, the nimble woman stepped forward while pressing the blunderbuss directly over Gus's heart. Timothy was nowhere to be found.

George Augustus then looked into the desperate woman's eyes. When he realized who it was, Gus reached out his arms and began weeping like a whipped pup! With difficulty, he muttered her name.

"Mary! I thought you were dead!"

"Had it not been for the shoals the 'Rebecca' got caught up on, you'd still have that impression, I'm afraid!" said agent #428.

"Walpole told me that 'Operation Cricket' had failed! He said the mission was a bust!" cried the very sober King.

Mary Read (a.k.a. Mary Hallett) then put the uncocked scattergun on top of the captain's table and held the sobbing king in her arms. In between mouthfuls of food, Mary told her longtime lover exactly what had happened onboard the 'Centurion'!

Embarrassingly, Mary even told Gus how she was left to drown by her daughter and Anton von Sporck! Hallett then disclosed Black Sam Bellamy's influence over the entire matter leaving George II reekingly sick to his stomach.

After learning about Bellamy's hijacking of "Operation Cricket", King George's demeanor completely changed. What was once an imbibing Royal figurehead had transformed into a fierce sea warrior.

With fire in his eyes, Gus turned his head toward Mary. Drawing her emaciated body close to him and with a consoling rock, the King began singing a favorite song of theirs as they danced together in front of the 'Rebecca's' wheel.

They ended their gavotte with a lovely kiss only seconds before George Augustus snapped Mary Hallett's neck! Timothy helped Gus throw Mary back into the Atlantic Ocean. It was 0400.

Grace knew her husband and she would probably not share another Christmas together. Bartholomaus could do very little more than drool.

He had become incontinent and therefore, he knew that he was a burden on his wife's back! As soon as he got the guns built, he, as they had both agreed, would go out in an honorable fashion!

A long time ago, Grace and Bart had made a pact! When one was too difficult for the other to look after, it was the "well person's responsibility" to supply the means necessary to accomplish that "self-delegated" end!

As soon as the windbuchses were done and after Cato's visit, Grace O'Malley Girandoni was going to drive her husband to their skiff and assist him in getting it out to sea! He would take along three things: a Bible, a lantern, and a pistol.

Tanacharison and Joncaire spoke to one another in what could be described as a 'moan'! Although they were in a sound muffling forest, they still hummed their bass toned words so their voices would harmonize with the wind.

The Mingo chief listened as Joncaire gave the high points involving the deserter and his departing remarks! When they reached a point at which the battalion of cadets needed to rest, the Tanacharison raised his arms and called out to General Staats for him to join in with him and Joncaire for a brief meeting of the minds. Tanacharison was the first to say something.

"It appears we are on the brink of war! I am sure Samuel Bellamy has called for us because of that horrible fact! He probably wants representations from the opposing sides of this matrix so as to gain a certain perspective which might lead to peace among the clashing parties involved. I'd bet he wants the cadets to serve as enforcers of some type or maybe he just wanted to shield them from the impending danger! Nevertheless, we must get them safely into Bellamy's mountain before this powder keg explodes!

General Staats, please inform Crommelin that we will be soon crossing over some high ledges! He needs to separate the boys into groups of three; they must prevent the others from falling into the river! With these temperatures, getting wet is a death sentence! We have an hour before daylight so we need to move quickly!" Tanacharison said.

Kimberly timidly tapped on the wheelhouse door. Not waiting for Ogle's permission to enter, she walked into the dull lit space and proceeded to seat herself in the chair facing the map table.

After a few moments of suspense-building silence, Chaloner Ogle turned away from the 'Kitty's Amelia's' wheel in order to determine what was troubling the gimpy girl. With a warm smile on his face, Ogle engaged the little lady in some airy conversation.

"It will be light soon. Couldn't you sleep?"

Kimberly Kimber remained silent.

"Is something wrong, Kim? Are you under the weather, honey?" tenderly asked Commander Ogle.

"It's not that," answered Kimberly.

"Are you scared?" teased Cal.

"Yes, but not in the way you might think, sir!" said the Kimber girl.

"Then tell me, Miss Kimber, what's frightening you?" inquisitively pried Ogle.

"I am afraid that Captain Selkirk and you are going to start fighting!" gushed Kimberly.

"Why would you think that, sweetheart? Alex and I are friends!" briskly responded Chaloner.

"Because you didn't sink the 'Rebecca' when you had the chance to do so! I think he got his feelings hurt when you wouldn't do it!" wailed Kim.

Suddenly, there was a light tap on the wheelhouse door. With a permissive nod from Ogle, Alex Selkirk walked in.

"Commander, if you wouldn't mind, I'd like a word in private with you, sir," said Alex.

"Captain, please come in and have a seat. Miss Kimberly here, has already lambasted me for my behavior concerning my preferential treatment of the King! I too have thought about that and I wish I could reverse my decision at this point; but I can't! George Augustus was my closest childhood friend! I just couldn't drown him! Yes, I should have! I know that now; but I guess I wanted to give the man another chance!" apologetically admitted Ogle.

Alex Selkirk stood and then walked over to Ogle and placed his hand on the crestfallen Commander's shoulder. He then motioned for Kimberly to come stand beside the two men before he spoke.

"Guys, we have a fast ship and a fairly good crew once their sober! Maybe if we would stop playing with dug up 'old bones', we could get on with our mission! Look, I was wrong for second guessing your decision, Chaloner; but I was even more out of order by displaying my disenchantment in front of you, Kimberly! For that, Kim, I humbly apologize! So, what do you say, shouldn't we just stop these hide-and-seek maneuvers and simply haul-ass to New York? If we play our cards right, the 'Rebecca' will never set sight on us again!" exclaimed Alex.

Blanche had removed her boots so she wouldn't stir up any noise. She had her back against the tunnel's side. Her naked left foot inched its way forward trying to feel for any noisemaker which might alert someone of her presence.

With her fingertips, Blanche would after every few steps, touch the granite flooring in search of telltale clumps of snow recently tracked in.

If they were frozen, she was safe, but if the chunks had puddled, then someone had recently gone in before her.

Because of the odor given off by unclean human beings and the measurable hang-times that such smells should linger, Blanche suspected that someone was lying in wait for her! She kept sensing or perhaps even hearing the inhaling and exhaling of a man.

In absolute darkness, Blanche lightly touched the side of the tunnel until she tactilely recognized a turn in the passageway. By sheer intuition, she knew beyond a shadow of doubt that there was someone crouching just a few feet in front of her! But as fate allowed, the last trimester woman's water broke!

Seconds following that splashy event, Blanche's first assault of contractions began! Completely giving up any inkling of self-restraint, she let out a glass-breaking shriek before falling to the tunnel's floor! To the top of her lung's capacities, the birthing woman screamed out a message to whomever was "out there"!

"Listen, you mother-fucker, whoever you are out there, I could care less! Frankly, I don't give a shit whether you kill me or not but before you do, please for god's sake, get this damn thing out of my belly! Oh, help me please! And go get my father!" pleaded Blanche.

For an instant, Cato was not sure if he correctly heard the woman's plea as it involved the word "father" in it. Because of the raw smell now permeating the passageway, Cato knew for sure the woman was telling the truth about the baby thing; but he was still very cautious about exposing himself! He had seen that trick before!

With only nine feet separating Cato from the now writhing woman, Cato could not take the chance of firing his only pistol just for the blink of light the explosion would yield. Instead, he scraped a marble-sized ball of snow from between his bootheel and tossed it at the noise's source much like one would throw a dart.

Cato felt the heat from the lead ball as it whizzed past his cheek! Blanche's exact position was now imprinted in Cato's mind. He had seen she was holding another pistol!

Perhaps it was the "father" word or maybe it was the fact that his "sister" was having a baby that prevented Cato from outright killing the woman but he didn't! Rather, he fired his weapon at the stone ceiling just above Blanche's head causing enough of a distraction for Cato to knock Blanche out with his pistol butt!

Anton von Sporck after giving himself a 'light' injection, ran out to the compound's fire bell and began pulling on its rope like a madman! It was 0600.

Like rats running from a burning building, the guards and the scientists came running toward the quadrant hoping to hear some good news! Sporck had set up a speaker's platform. He had a very important announcement to make!

Before Sporck began his talk and realizing how cold the morning air was, he excused himself to get his jacket and fix a quick pick-me-upper. Fifteen minutes later, he returned with no jacket on. But he had a Bible in his left hand.

At exactly seven o'clock, Reverend Sporck clanged the fire bell seven times, cleared his throat with a swig of corn whiskey, and proceeded to recite his "Ordination Vows"! At twenty-seven degrees outside coupled with a ten mile an hour wind, the thirty-minute recitation probably felt like an eternity for Sporck's congregation.

With the arthritic tightness getting worse by the minute and the siren like call from "Mama Poppy", Sporck cut his sermon a little short to facilitate his relief! He ended his sunrise service with the announcement of a vision (a calling) he had during the waning night's hours!

He said that "Gabriel" had visited him. During this fantastical time the two spent together, Sporck was told a story of what was to be! This angel, 'Gabriel', supposedly commanded Ike to warn the Indians of a "plight" about to befall them!

Gabriel further ordered him and twelve "disciples" to go into the high country, find them, and then spread the "truth" about the "spell" the British had put upon them!

Due to Sporck's health issues and the obvious factor of him being a living angel-elect, he would be unable to lead his flock into the wilderness!

Captains Anson and Wolfe were to lead the ten chosen others into the frozen tundra with the sole purpose of alerting the natives of the venal work delivered by the English! As the guards had been instructed to do, the unchosen, the unfit, or the unwilling to participate in the holy action, were to be executed!

Since there were twenty-three scientists available for only a dozen spots, Sporck said he expected to hear eleven gunshots before 0800! He then retired back to his cabin in the happenstance that Gabriel might return.

Samuel Bellamy was shocked at the size Cato had grown to! Additionally, Black Sam was astounded by what his son was carrying on his shoulder! Everyone gathered around, looking at the unconscious spectacle Cato had laid at the foot of Bellamy's wheelchair!

Blanche looked up at the many faces peering down on her! With a terrified expression which quickly progressed into cries of agony, the birthing mother reached out for Sam's useless legs.

She beckoned him to lean forward as though she had a secret to tell him but instead of a daughterly whisper, Blanche plunged Black Beaver's knife into Black Sam's eye, killing him instantly! Like an acrobat, the spurious laborer jumped up and then spun the blunderbuss out of Henry Every's hands and fired the scattergun into the midst of the nearby faces! Bonnie, Every, and Bob Maynard, all three died right there on Sam's floor.

None of the room's survivors could recall much of what happened next but as Cato later recalled, Blanche had set off Bosman's powder horn. She had used it as a grenade!

When the quarter pound of Bill's black powder exploded, it blew pieces of bullhorn along with other swept up matter, into the dazed onlookers' bodies!

Only seconds after regaining their composure, Cato, Jon Kimber, Samuel Fraunces, Bill Bosman, and James Stanfield, the survivors, swatted through the thick smoke and took after the fleeing murderer in deadly earnest!

Each had already fired their weapons into the tunnel in hopes at least one ricocheted piece of lead would penetrate Blanche's body! No one found any signs of that happening!

With no concern of the dangers facing them, the five remaining men charged down the tunnel, screaming and yelling with all of their might! As soon as they reached the end of the tunnel which opened into the place where Cato had pulled the lever to access the passageway, they heard the large stone door close behind them! Blanche had hoodooed the men! She had never left the scene of her crime!

With a double-duty breath, half being for the extinguishing of his lantern and the other part dedicated to a sigh of relief, Robert Dinwiddie arose from his chair. He set his faithful alarm clock to the number eight giving himself close to three hours to sleep.

At ten, he would dispatch two separate riders to Winchester with orders for Lieutenant Washington. Dinwiddie knew that once Black Sam's "legalized" request landed into the hands of a rank mongering officer, it might as well have been a lighted fuse spewing toward the world's destruction!

Colonel Andrew McClelland marveled at the ingenuity used in sequestering his fort! After a 'forensic walk' around the fort's perimeter, both he and Doctor Pollard concluded that what Tanacharison had done was the most eloquent usurp that either of the officers had ever seen!

Since none of McClelland's men had been killed and it was pretty much a forgone conclusion that Governor Burnet wasn't going to be a 'witness problem', the whole incident would never go on any type of report! With that secret now confidentially stuffed into the 'forgotten' category, the exhausted duo decided to return to Pollard's quarters for a drink before they got the soldiers out of the barn.

King George couldn't help but wish that he had not taken Mary's life! She had been with him even back as far as the "Bow Street Runners" days when they made love under the shroud of England's security force. Those were the times when naivety and the belief of a difference between good and evil were all mixed up in a bowl of chivalry.

In today's world, what was once 'right' for one, was 'wrong' for another! That was why he had elected to escape Britain!

King George Augustus had been transformed into a deity! His disciples, like Timothy, would have to be picked. If he were to be a prophetic world ruler, Gus was convinced he must choose them wisely!

George was quite aware of Ogle's sneakiness on the water! To his recollection, Cal had never lost a sea battle! He was no match for the man!

Timothy thought if the two of them stuck together they could whip the meritorious commander because of the 'Rebecca's' war- class status! After all, the 'Kitty's Amelia' was of the slaver-class and the differences between those two wouldn't take a scientist to explain!

Captain Dorce was a good sailor and his crew were topnotch marines! They could easily overtake the 'Amelia'; but there was still that 'old friend' thing! He had already regretted one decision he had made that day and he didn't wish to do it again!

That's why he called Dorce back to the wheelhouse and commanded him to prepare the 'Rebecca' for a full-sail haul to New York.

'Gus, if you can't depend on others to secure the Colonies enough for you to establish your headquarters, you'll need to do it yourself!' was what Timothy kept saying over and over to him.

Gus was beginning to plot out very secretively Timothy's demise! He could no longer afford the risks involved with befriending an unstable person.

Bartholomaus and Grace had worked around the clock so as to have the rifles ready for Cato to pick up on the last Friday of November. In fourteen days the two of them had manufactured two hundred Windbuchses capable of dropping a man at a hundred yards!

Unfortunately, after test firing the sixty-third air rifle, this had previously happened two days before, ole Black Bart for real this time, died. His wife finished the order up while Bartholomaus sat nearby keeping her company.

Grace would leave the wind-rifles in the shed for Cato along with a note explaining their absence. Hightide would be receding soon! The Girandoni's had a boat to catch.

Tanacharison could see wisps of smoke coming out of the top of a rocky hillside about a mile from Bellamy's mountain. He motioned for Crommelin to have the boys lay flat on their stomachs while he and Joncaire investigated who the people were. They said they'd return within the hour.

General Staats crawled like a serpent over to Robert Crommelin's position. The cadets remained impressively motionless on the side of the ridge that stretched over the Mohawk River. So far, there had been no slips nor falls.

Out of the early morning mist came a voice from above. It was echoed by four more men's voices. They were letting Tanacharison's party know there was no use for them to go any further!

From James Stanfield's mouth came the explanations of exactly what had happened and the who's and the how's of Blanche's japery.

Similar stories were swapped among the menagerie of men! They were all about Blanche!

Tanacharison became furious when he was told that Blanche had invaded the confederate nation's burial vault! He got even angrier when he heard that Blanche was now in control of the almost impervious sacred mountain!

Even if the supposedly birthing woman didn't implement a single weapon from Bellamy's arsenal, it would be nearly impossible to breach Sam's fortress! They would have to come up with another way to retake Sam's bastion.

The 'Kitty's Amelia's' long shadow outraced the ship into the greener gulf stream. Dolphins, close to thirty of them played alongside the slaver as Kimberly Kimber tried to touch their noses. The mammals leaped within an arms-length of her baited hands.

Ogle and Selkirk were in the wheelhouse discussing an alternative plan regarding their approach into the Brooklyn Bay instead of the originally planned arrival at the Long Island harbor. But then there came an amazing calm!

Seagulls no longer darted into the 'Amelia's' backwash! They were flying west toward the safety of land!

Selkirk ran down to the deck to help Kimberly get out of the high winds that were about to come down upon them! The crew moved like trained monkeys as they stripped the sails from their masts.

Waterspouts have been known to lift ill-trained crews along with their ships from the water during weather anomalies such as the one the 'Kitty's Amelia' was facing that morning! The sky was clear in the distance but all around them were sheets of nothing driving rain!

The sea's turquois patina changed into an iodine black. Claps of thunder vibrated the joints in everyone's body!

Ogle began involuntarily heaving up the boiled eggs and sausage he had had at sunrise. Kimberly's pallor was green in color. Alex just sat in the captain's chair drinking directly out of a jug of rum. It was as if a giant were rocking the vessel!

When it stopped, the whole world returned to its natural order. Even the pelicans returned. However, the dolphins were nowhere to be seen.

Ogle, after taking a few swigs of rum for himself and passing the jug over to Kimberly, turned toward the starboard side of the ship and shrieked to the top of his lungs! The 'Rebecca' was setting with fifteen readied cannons aimed at the 'Kitty's Amelia's' stern!

As the British warship passed, Selkirk was the one to point this out, the King, Captain Dorce and one hundred or so marines in full- dress uniforms, respectfully saluted the 'Kitty's Amelia'! A quarter of a mile later, the 'Rebecca' unleashed its mighty load at the open sea. All on board the 'Amelia' quietly bowed their heads with humility!

One of the first things Blanche did as soon as she had secured Sam's fortress was search for opium. With her father's ailments, she thought, he would have had to possess a multitude of painkillers. He did and she found them!

Even with them, Blanche needed to bite down on Every's leather belt when a wave of nearly spaced contractions returned! Her effacing vaginal cavity all the way to her anus, had begun to split open! Soon, the two passages would become one!

Blanche had placed several loaded pistols around her in case Cato and his people returned while she was getting the baby out of her. It was close to doing just that when a blue headed pigeon landed on the room's only window sill! There was a message tucked into the bird's carrying pouch!

Unable to get up and unravel the fowl delivered note, Blanche's eyes rolled back into the rear of her skull as she tightened her stomach muscles! After two or three hours of sweat-drawing pushes along with the earnest damning of all sperm-bearing males, an indistinguishable mass slid from its birth canal! A twin like afterbirth followed seconds afterwards.

After the ordeal was done, Blanche made a beeline for the bird. Lacking the patience to coax the pigeon into allowing her to remove its burden, the childless mother ripped the animal's body a part by not bothering to untie the bird's pouch straps! She then threw the carcass into the bucket where Sporck's offspring was laying and fixed up a hot spoonful of something to rid herself of the postpartum blues!

Blanche then read Grace Girandoni's message to Sam. Despite the coding, she gleaned enough information from the hieroglyphically drawn message to be able to plan for her next move. Four things had been learned: 1) 200 air guns were in the shed behind the sender's home at 2) the address 3) and were to be picked up on the month's last Friday 4) by Cato!

With her exiting strategy still congealing in her mind, Blanche began rifling through Samuel Bellamy's possessions. Money, drugs, and hidable firearms were the endgame of her search!

Traveling now with a spring in her step, Blanche began macabrely decorating Bellamy's place up a bit. She arranged the bodies so the scene would resemble the birthing of Jesus!

Black Sam, Every, and Robert Maynard were to represent the "wise men" while Anne Bonnie played Mary. The pail was laid in Anne's crossed arms.

Having completed that rather entertaining activity, Blanche prepared for what she surmised would be a ten-hour trek into the city. She had plenty of money so once she made it to Manhattan Island, Blanche figured that all she'd need to do after that was wait for Cato's arrival at the Girandoni's house, kill him, sell the rifles to the Indians, and run away to a tropical island somewhere!

After assuring herself that the blue-headed messenger's note would be found, otherwise her trap wouldn't work, Blanche climbed up to the semaphore room where she had earlier discovered several barrels of black powder. Once she had covered the magazine room's floor with about an inch of the granular explosive, Blanche took a lit oil lamp and balanced it on the entrance door's upper edge.

In that, her boobytrap had been set and thanks to Anne Bonnie who had furnished Blanche with some descent clothes, her only remaining task was to climb down into Bellamy's underground escape route, untie his 'log disguised' sloop, and let the Mohawk River take her away!

Blanche crossed herself as she passed by the manger scene. She then opened the bark covered boat's lid, packed in her supplies, hopped into the pilot's seat, closed the watertight top, and let the river's current do the rest.

Because of the height from which Tanacharison and Cato were above the swift-moving Mohawk, there was no way to stop Blanche's escape! Although it was pointless, Crommelin and the cadets did hurl a few hundred rocks at the 'log' as it swept by beneath them!

The bright side of the apparent setback was that the newly formed collaboration of warriors had discovered a way into Samuel Bellamy's citadel! They would need to construct a boat and approach the granite fort from the falls' side! After which, they would 'unroll' the boulder from the entrance so the rest could enter into Sam's old homeplace!

Sporck had once again been visited by Gabriel! During this vision, Ike had been instructed to etch on a piece of slate the number of sacrifices that had to be made in order to fulfill the lord's wishes! Eleven rifle reports equaled eleven scratches on the tally-stone!

When it was all said and done according to Gabriel's words, Sporck's deceased followers would be memorialized for an eternity! Plus, they would be awarded the rank of 'Celestial Angel' once they got settled into heaven!

Anson and Wolfe however were not amused with Sporck's insanity! The man was dangerously psychopathic and had put every one of the egg-rolling "Buzzards" into serious jeopardy! Together, as they had agreed, the British captains would kill Sporck as soon as the opportunity availed itself!

Sensing the rumblings of a proverbial "palace revolt", Sporck decided to clip the potential trouble 'in the bud'! As soon as his service was over, the robe-frocked minister invited Captains Wolfe and Anson to his cottage for a "working brunch".

"Gentlemen, before I explain what King George has requested of us, I would like to congratulate you men on your promotions! I am sorry to say, I do not have the 'Commander's Emblems' for you men to wear; however, in my most recent communique from Walpole, he assured me of the authenticity of the King's citation! It looks like when all of this mess is over, you boys will be heading up a flotilla, somewhere on the seven seas! I can't tell you just how proud I am to have been associated with you both!

"Not only have I had the privilege of serving the Crown with you men, it has been my honor to have you under my command! Unfortunately, this will be your last maneuver in this neck of the woods! When we have completed this final assignment together, you are to report directly to Governor Burnet! You will receive further orders as to where you'll be stationed next. For now, the men under your command must not be told of our last mission. Before I get into the mechanics of the King's assignment, I would suggest we open up a keg of my mama's favorite brandy and enjoy a bit of lamb's loin together," said Sporck.

Once the sun got up over the trees, Jeffrey Amherst could see the signs of a skirmish which had taken place the night before!

A gnawed upon horse rump told the scientist that what remained of the beast's hip would be gone as soon as the wind got the message out to the furry interest groups.

The minute Amherst pulled his wagon to a halt, George Whitfield and John Wesley awakened. Both holy men then jumped from the back of the wagon and in separate directions, searched for their own bushes. The pickled peaches they had eaten during their driving shifts had gone bad thus afflicting their gastrointestinal tracts.

While George and John were struggling with their personal affairs, Jeffrey was having his own troubles unbuckling the wagon tongue from their only delivery horse. Ten or fifteen miles of travel with a brass hasp touching overheated horseflesh meant there was an inch's worth of ice preventing the harness belt's release!

To expedite his cowardly exit, Amherst used his knife to cut the exhausted animal loose from the wagon tongue! Jeffrey then jumped on the back of the horse and rode away!

Corporal Peter Lancaster could see Fort Loudon from atop Fishers Gap. There were Shawnee reportedly all over the Massanutten Mountains causing a great deal of angst for Dinwiddie's messenger!

Through his telescope, the corporal could clearly see there was major construction going on behind the fort's closed gates. They were putting a roof on what looked to be a barracks.

It was a five-mile ride to the fort. Peter's only choices were strategic in nature. He could gallop into Loudon's tree felled perimeter like a comet or the message carrier could quietly ease his way in by traveling along the banks of the Shenandoah River.

A campfire's flicker from a distant mountain on the Allegany side of the valley made Lancaster take the more stealthy approach to the fort! There wasn't a white man alive who would have a fire out in the open like that!

What he saw was an Indian's fire! It was there for intimidation reasons! He would wait until dark before he went any further.

Major Balcombe, Fort Herkimer's bugler, was sternly ordered by Colonel McClelland to "blow" reveille. His new first sergeant, Donald Sweeney, called the bedraggled but freshly untied soldiers into formation.

McClelland standing in front of the flagpole, brought the fort's battalion to a parade-rest. Then as fast as a jackrabbit, Andrew ran to the top of the nearest guard tower so he could see the vast array of perspectives one could gain from such an altitude.

Colonel McClelland would have begun his typical two or more hours of lecturing had it not been for some additional yelling coming from the other side of Fort Herkimer's entrance gate! From the sound of the conversation going on between the fort's commander and the wagon load of men parked out front, the two-digit possibility that something else bad was going to happen became a conclusion!

Two fully uniformed British naval commanders and ten other officially dressed men were wanting to inspect the fort! They claimed the importance of their arrival would be demonstrated once their entry was allowed!

With a wave of his hand, McClelland busted up his congregational styled formation sending the men away to their prewired functions. He then casually walked down the guard tower's stairs leading toward the now opening gate.

The King's examiners quickly jumped from their wagon. One of the privates took their four horses into the same barn the soldiers had been locked in. Other low-ranking souls pulled the wagon behind the barracks.

"Commander" George Anson approached Colonel McClelland with the jutted chin of an angry governmental official! With a big grin on his face, he spoke loudly enough so everyone in the fort could hear him!

"We twelve men are seeking refuge! Over the last four months we have been in captivity! Luckily, we managed to escape under the pretense of serving our captor, Anton von Sporck! Our mission was to warn the Indians of an attempt to contaminate them with small pox! Sporck wanted us to make you believe the British did it when in fact, it was he and a few others responsible for his inhumane effort! Colonel McClelland, I was hoping that all of us could pile into the mess hall together and have a good meal! Your hospitality and a good ear, I promise will yield a very valuable return for your military career! You see, Colonel, we are not the run-of-the-mill escapees, not at all! We were part of King George's "Operation Cricket"! Unfortunately, sir, we fell prey to Sporck and…"

Suddenly, the guard from the north point's tower sent out an alarm! There were two men on foot, running toward the fort! Both were wearing as the watch-out described, "priests" clothing"!

General Staats would have been an engineer if his father hadn't twisted his arm to follow his footsteps. He was expected to make the military his lifetime career.

The problem he was facing had to do with three measurable factors: Water Speed, Buoyancy, Grappling height.

Those variables involved two men floating down the Mohawk at 'X' miles per hour, maintaining a 'livable' body temperature by staying dry and then throwing a grappling hook attached to a rope into an overhead opening 'Y' number of feet above the churning water surface as the craft whizzes beneath it!

The grappler would have only one shot at hooking on to a solid structure. That rope must then hold his weight long enough for him to climb into Sam's window!

Kimberly had become quite proficient with Alex's telescope. She had mastered the art of preventing the shaky-effect of the far- away images. Chaloner found her graciously useful when it came to searching the horizon for sails.

According to the 'Kitty's Amelia's' nautical maps, they were thirty miles east of Tangier Island. Selkirk at the wheel, remembered back a long time ago when an island that size took on the dimensions of the world!

The good memories of valuable things washed up on shore! The gratefulness extended to Woodes Rogers! And the satisfaction of identifying his own personal vulnerability!

Those reflections caused a tear to slip down his cheek. Alex was lucky to be alive and he knew it!

Cape Charles was now sporting several lighthouses that he did not remember being there before. But that was fifteen years ago and there were a lot of things a person should forget over that length of time!

They were five days out from New York. He and Ogle would have to decide on exactly where they would come in to the city. Maybe they'd just flip a coin to adjudicate the matter they joked until Kimberly messaged some bad news!

With her right thumb aimed over her shoulder and five fingers sticking up from her left hand, Kimberly let Selkirk know that the 'Kitty's Amelia' had picked up a follower! She signaled, the three- mast trailer was flying no colors!

Given there was no moon and they were only forty-five minutes from dusk, Captain Selkirk headed into the Chesapeake Bay where they could ambush their pursuer. Ogle, after feeling the ship turn, came out of his cabin to offer any circumstantial guidance.

"Alex, what's the situation?" asked the out-of-breath Commander.

"Five miles behind us, there is a ship with no visible flag unfurled! I thought I'd let it go by me or attack it before we went any further north. Do you agree, Cal?" said Alex defensively.

"Captain Selkirk, there is no more guessing as to whether we will be at war with the Colonies! Virginia's government recently moved that their entire legal system fall under their own parliamentary adjuratory, thus, abandoning the royal legalese! Make no mistake about it, Alex, I'd say these harbors we're passing by will be clogged with British warships within the next eighteen months! Walpole even told me that most of the port cities all along the Americas' ports encouraged privateers to launch pirating activities! The 'privateers' split the plunder with the "state" and then enjoy safe harbor within the blind and deaf populations. Such is the case I fear, with the ship trailing behind us!

"My only concern with circling in the bay would be if there were a couple of his buddies lying in wait for you! I believe we should make them come out into the big water! Once they get out of sight of "home", they'll be very reluctant to chase us out any further than that!" chuckled Cal before he returned to his quarters to finish his nap.

Blanche was relieved to find the Girandoni's home had been left wide open! From the staleness of the two loaves of gingerbread on top of the stove, it looked to her like no one had stepped a foot in the place for at least a week.

A fairly thick coat of dust had settled on pretty much everything in the way of furniture throughout the Tudor house. Blanche searched through everything and in every corner for valuables which might benefit her further travels. Opium, money, clothes, and guns were her prime objects of discovery.

After an hour's worth of rummaging, Blanche injected herself with a full plunger's worth of heroin. Once reaching that "magic place", she set out to find the rifles that "Grace and Bart" had stored up in the barn behind their house. She hoped there would also be a horse in that barn!

Sure enough, when Blanche opened the unlocked storage door, she immediately spotted a wagon with ten casket-sized clock crates tied down into its bed. There was not a horse to pull it with!

Blanche shut the barn up and retuned to Bartholomaus's dwelling to prepare for Cato's arrival. Surely, he would bring the beast she so desperately needed, she thought to herself. She heated up another dose of "magic".

When General Staat's presented to Tanacharison his "X and Y" calculations, an outside onlooker would have thought someone had hit the Confederate Nation's leader square between the eyes with a rock!

Given the cold, the speed of the river, and the "luck" needed to throw a grappling hook ten feet into the air and then getting it into an open window, was an impossibility!

With a gasp fresh from his throat, Tanacharison turned toward the General with a grim smile. That "grim smile" however, was a Janus-faced one!

The happy-half was an applaud for the boat idea while the frowny-side represented the rejection of Abraham's ridiculous notion! It was ludicrous to think that one could toss from a moving boat, a grappling hook ten feet in the air and actually hit something with it! Tanacharison thought before he spoke.

"Engineering is not my bailey wig, General. My intentions are not to make you look like a dunce, sir! I only wish to cast a new light on the age-old Indian problem of getting ourselves into the white man's buildings! May I suggest another remedy?" mockingly said Tanacharison.

"That's enough! We have a potentially deadly task facing us; thusly, we have no time to waste with this sophomoric rhetoric! So, Chief Tanacharison, what do you bring to the drawing board?" scolded Cato.

"My thoughts are this, do the boat thing as planned; however, instead of throwing a rope-held grappling hook, shoot several swiveled arrows into the opening. Each arrow shot will be anchored by strong thread of which, we will pull up into the swivels a grappling armed rope! We then get one of those cadets to swing over and let us in!" said Tanacharison.

In an attempt to salvage his quickly-dissipating "expert's" reputation, Abraham Staats offered a mild yet indefensible, rebuttal. He candy-coated his argument within his single question.

"How do you propose to shoot an arrow into the air and expect it to fly any more than six feet with all of those swivel contraptions taped to the tip of it? Furthermore, how can you hope that a string connected to an unstuck arrowhead hold the weight of an ensuing rope and grapple?" questioned the General.

"Well, actually, General Staats, I was going to scrap your idea altogether! Instead of two men surfing down the wild Mohawk River while madly throwing a grappling hook into a quickly-diminishing target, I propose a trebuchet instead!" spat Tanacharison.

"A trebuchet?" in unison, asked Cato and Abraham.

"Yes! Nobody gets wet and it will take less time to make a bloody catapult than it will a boat! Additionally, we can take as many shots at the opening as we need to and not risk a single soul doing it!" smugly said Tanacharison.

After a second or two of reasoning out the Mingo's plan, Cato nodded at General Staats in concurrence with the Chief's approach to their needed fix. By the look on Staat's face, he conceded as well. Now the problem was, how to build one of the contraptions!

For the past three days, Sporck had done nothing more than attend to his daily needs. For him that meant eating, sleeping, and occasionally giving himself an injection. He did this in order to maintain his self-engineered place at the foot of an ever-present rainbow.

With the exception of a dozen guards, Sporck pretty much had the whole compound to himself. He liked living that way.

After a midmorning walk intended to rid him of the hangover he got from his last two nights of solid potation, Anton decided he needed a hot bath. Ike had to walk out to the woodshed to fetch about ten arm-sized pieces of kindling to heat up his tub water.

A foot of hard packed snow had banked up on the side of the woodshed making it difficult for Sporck to open it up. Once he gathered his logs, he turned back toward the guard towers to discover that not one single one of them were in sight!

After noticing an unusually large number of footprints coming and going out of the institute's gate, it dawned on Sporck that while he was taking his hourlong river walk, the guards had abandoned him! As Ike was entering his cottage's door, he heard something which sounded like someone was calling his name!

Dismissing it as either the wind or an irreverent visit from Gabriel, Sporck continued with his bathtub plans. As the voice became louder and much more recognizable, Anton von Sporck abandoned the idea of bathing and converted his industrious efforts toward loading his blunderbuss!

Jeffrey Amherst was somewhere out there calling for him. Over and over again, Ike heard his name being girlishly hollered. Jeffrey sounded like a jackal!

"I am Corporal Peter Lancaster. I have a dispatch for Major Washington! My pouch contains orders from Governor Dinwiddie. I have come from Williamsburg and must report back there within five days. Permission to enter the fort!"

The twenty-one-year-old major approached Lancaster as though he were welcoming his son home. With a strong embrace and the ushering movement of Washington's hand, Corporal Lancaster was seated behind a large dining table and ordered to eat!

"Corporal, I want to commend you on the obvious tenacity you have displayed! My lord, man, you must be down to skin and bones by now given that you wouldn't have had the opportunity nor the stupidity to build a fire along the way! Some of the areas you crossed through are teaming with some pretty unsavory characters as I am sure you were made aware of! Mister Lancaster, please continue with your meal and do help yourself to as much of that jugged whiskey on the table as you would like! There is a fine bunk in the back with your name on it! We'd like for you to rest up here for a day or two before you report back to Williamsburg!" said Washington.

"Sir, I appreciate your kind invitation, Major Washington! But I'll be leaving at dark! Please feel free to open that satchel laying there beside you! I believe you have been promoted to the rank of Lieutenant Colonel, sir! Congratulations!" said Corporal Lancaster between mouthfuls of stewed rabbit and corn whiskey.

"So, what's the problem with staying over at least for another day, Corporal?" asked Lieutenant Colonel Washington.

"Sir, because of the immediacy of action necessary in this situation, I have been ordered to report back to Williamsburg with your feedback. I, of course, did not read your message from Governor Dinwiddie however he did speak with me regarding certain idiosyncrasies of which you needed to be made aware of! You are to make contact with Samuel Bellamy after you have secured Fort Herkimer! Colonel Andrew McClelland is the commanding officer of that fort. Colonel McClelland will take you to Bellamy's headquarters. It is my understanding that Mister Bellamy is the conduit into the Seneca's leadership! Their chief 's name is Tanacharison!

"The Iroquois Confederacy as it is hoped, will become our allies in the stoppage of the French's further encroachment onto our American soil. It is surmised that Great Britain will soon be sending their warships our way and we're going to need their help! It is to the benefit of both nations, American and Native American, that we, as peacefully as possible, move the French along with their Algonquin helpers back to their side of the Ohio River. This is to be accomplished with little to no bloodshed! To be frank, Colonel Washington, I believe you've been handed a sack of wildcats and expected to tame them with a velvet whip! Honestly, sir, I really don't know how you could ever be expected to accomplish this humongous task! Colonel, what shall I put in my report to the Governor? Better still, why don't you just come on back to Williamsburg with me?" nervously said Corporal Lancaster.

"Sir, when you return, kindly give my regards to Governor Dinwiddie. Tell him that I accept the opportunity to display the talents of my troops in action! Also, I am putting into your satchel a commendation for your promotion to First Sergeant! Any man that pulled off the journey you made, should have the responsibility of training men to rise to your pedigree! It has been an honor having you as my guest, First Sergeant, and I truly hope we have the opportunity to meet again. Please remain seated, sir, and by all means, take whatever you need for your return to the capitol!

"Please convey to your superiors their message has been received. Tell them that I shall do my best to protect every inch of America's blood earned land! I must now excuse myself, I have three hundred men to get ready for tomorrow's shove off. I shall leave a hundred and fifty men here under Captain William Anderson's command. If all goes well, we should return to Fort Loudoun by the ides of March. Let's just pray our results turn out better for us than they did for Caesar!" said George Washington as he left the fort's dining facility.

First Sergeant Donald Sweeney quite zealously brought Fort Herkimer's troops to "Ready-Arms". As the fort's massive gates opened, two priestly dressed foot travelers began pleading for help!

Doctor Pollard knew by the timbre of the men's voices, the uninvited strangers were in need of medical attention! He was convinced both were suffering from advanced hypothermia. He ordered them to be transported to the infirmary!

Upon hearing Sergeant Sweeney's battle command, Captains Wolfe and Anson, along with their ten co-inspectors, ran out of Fort Herkimer's mess hall as if the place had caught on fire! But the real meltdown occurred when the amnesty seekers saw the two half-frozen arrivals right in front of them! They now had someone else to collaborate their stories with regarding Sporck's evil doings!

Even though their face muscles were unable to contract, John Wesley and George Whitfield tried to expose their teeth as a signal of a joyous "hello"! After their brief reunion, the orderlies carried them into Doctor Pollard's operating room.

Captain Dorce saluted as did King George, when the 'Rebecca's' colors were retired for the evening. Dorce had drilled his marines enough so they were worn out! That way they wouldn't stay up all-night in anticipation of tomorrow's furlough to the island of Manhattan!

King George decided he and Timothy would travel together incognito! Gus didn't want anyone to know he was on the grounds of his American headquarters. None of Dorce's men were to wear military clothing of any sort while on their forty-eight-hour leave.

"You, fine sailors, are to represent Great Britain as "Diplomats"! Every one of you are to establish some kind of a relationship with at least five of the common folk living on this island! When you return, I shall expect from each of you a one-page assessment of the dissatisfaction experienced by the current colonial officials. Write their names down of those mentioned as being "unfair" to the colonists! Once we discover who the "people's" complaints point out, we'll hang them right here on the 'Rebecca's' deck! That, by god, will get this show started off on the right foot! They'll quickly learn that their new "King" means business!" Wailed Gus.

Both General Staats and Joncaire commented on how well the cadets absorbed the "shortcuts" Tanacharison had taught them when making something out of seemingly nothing! Along with Crommelin's carpentry skills, those boys had a primitive trebuchet, throwing rocks through Sam's porch window within two hours!

Once the Confederate's chief was satisfied with the catapult's accuracy, he instructed Robert Crommelin to begin wrapping three separate creek stones with a coil of rope made from braded strips of clothing. When slung, the wound ball would unwind while flying through the air and then into the citadel's window.

Tanacharison's first attempt at slinging the coiled "ladder-ball" was an absolute success! It unraveled beautifully, leaving a perfect climbing rope dangling down the sheer granite wall. This would make it a simple task for the drummer boy to shimmy up into Black Sam's window.

Blanche had previously set up a boobytrap involving two kegs of strewn about black powder and a lantern balanced on top of a quarter opened door! This was also the room where Black Sam's control arm which operated the passageway's rolling stone, was situated.

When Tanacharison's amazing trebuchet's shot sent the unraveling 'monkey's-head' through that same magazine's open window, Blanche's diabolical trick bloomed into fruition! When the rope ball smacked into the before mentioned door, the entire top of Sam's mountain exploded!

Boulders the size of houses, flew out in all directions! Everything and everyone for miles around were affected!

Alex Selkirk most certainly knew the ship following them was intentionally tempting the 'Kitty's Amelia' into a commitment to enter the Chesapeake Bay! Just the manner in which the dark running vessel was nudging her into the inviting smooth waters, convinced the captain that Ogle was right on the money! Whomever it was trailing them was absolutely set on boarding their ship!

Selkirk followed the Commander's recommendations to the "letter"! He spun the 'Amelia's' wheel many revolutions toward the deeper waters of the Atlantic. Alex then pulled three short pulls on the Captain's Bell's lanyard followed by three more sets of the same short pulls!

The 'Kitty's Amelia's' crew sprang into action as if they were seasoned mariners. The sails were pulled to full mast!

Neither the intimidating vibrations of barrel-priming cannon blasts nor the royal flag being raised, did anything to slow up their tracker's pace! The ship kept gaining on them!

Blanche had spent hours rifling through the things the Girandoni's had placed in trunks. Drawings, a broken tomahawk, dented bullets, were just a smidgen of the things Blanche discovered. And 'yes', she found lots of opium powder.

While the days dragged by and Cato had missed two Friday's so far, Blanche assumed he never got the note! She was beginning to like living in Black Bart's haunt and sort of hoped he wouldn't come.

Cato's left wrist had been crushed by a flying piece of railing blown from Bellamy's semaphore porch! General Staats had bled out from having had his legs severed. Many of the cadets' bodies were floating in the river's current less backwash while others were caught up in it and taken away.

Crommelin and Joncaire were unquestionably dead! Tanacharison's ribcage was visible from Cato's distant perspective. The Chief was near death!

The concussion that reverberated throughout the Mohawk Valley no doubt, burst the eardrums of every mammal within two miles of the detonation's site. All who could, walked in circular patterns as if they were unable to keep their balance. Everyone was in shock!

Time seemed to stop moving while the blue-tinted happenings ground down to an exaggerated slow-motion. Cato wept as he spied the aftermath caused by Blanche's boobytrap.

It is different when you see the bodies of children than it is when you see dead soldiers. There is no valor to be had by it!

There they were, one hundred and seventy-six mostly intact dead cadets! Cato waved to Hercules Mulligan to catch the boy's attention. He motioned for the lad to come to him.

Buzzards from nearly a mile up in the sky circled around the mushroom cloud that was being dissipated by shifts in the wind. Hercules knelt down beside of Cato.

"Hercules, that's your name isn't it?" whispered Cato.

Hercules nodded.

"How many of us are still alive, son?"

"Mister Cato, this is a terrible thing! The only people who I can count are Hamilton and Woodhull! What do we do?" cried Hercules.

"Cadet Mulligan, something very bad has most certainly happened to us all! Your childhood days just ended! You must act as a man now; we must get all of those that are not dead into the cavern!

Help me get to my feet, Hercules, we'll have to get them out of the night air. Every animal in the forest will be prowling through these rocks with a fine-toothed comb once dark gets here!

Sporck, for the first time in a really long while, was frightened. Jeffrey was outside somewhere, watching his every move. Why his young lover didn't rush back into his arms was the question concerning Anton the most.

Ike was not amused with Jeffrey's approach if what he was doing was for some sort of emotional foreplay. He was going to kill him anyway!

Sporck figured he would coax Jeffrey in close enough to punch a load of lead through his body! Therefore, Sporck called out to his former lover as though he were trying to get a cat out of a tree!

"Jeffrey, Honey, come on in the house! You'll catch yourself a death of a cold out here! I have an entire leg of lamb we can share together in front of my roaring fire. It'll be just wonderful! Please come to me, Jeffrey! I have missed you!" melodically wailed Sporck.

"Ike, I've missed you too! I was very afraid you would be mad at me, darling! We are alone now and I shan't any longer have to share your attention with anyone else!" yelled Jeffrey from the top of the compound's barn.

"Sweetheart, why should I be mad at you?" bated Sporck.

"Because of the bad things I did!" cried Jeffrey.

After shoving two pistols into his belt and picking up a jug of lantern fuel, Sporck proceeded to the back of the barn where he set up a comfortable place to sit in wait for Jeffrey to afford him a clean shot. Once seated, Sporck called out again to Jeffrey.

"You have nothing to feel badly about, dear-heart! I am sure you did your best for me!" softly cooed Ike.

Realizing that the intrigue Jeffrey had built around his surprise arrival was nothing more than a hoax! After listening to Jeffrey's provocative yearnings, Sporck pinpointed his exact location within the stables!

Amherst thought by creating a theatrical scene ending in the barn's hayloft, Sporck would forever remember their very first night together! Jeffrey had already begun to hum one of his favorite love songs as he fluffed up the straw in the corner. He imagined that Ike would want to take him.

With anticipatory yelps being emitted from Jeffrey's lips every second or two, Sporck had no trouble whatsoever creeping up to the barn and quietly slipping a chain through the barn's two door handles. Ike then sloshed the lantern oil on all four sides of the barn and lit the slick fluid with the same match he used to light his stogie! He then sat down and took a bead on the loft's only window.

Washington called Captain William Anderson to his quarters at exactly 1730. There was just a fraction more than an hour's worth of sunlight left in the day. He told Anderson the content of Corporal Lancaster's message from Governor Dinwiddie.

He would take three hundred of the fort's most seasoned soldiers. This left a hundred and fifty to complete Loudoun's barracks construction. They would head out for Fort Herkimer after dark.

CHAPTER 9

KING GEORGE'S WAR

Doctor Pollard along with three field medics attempted to unthaw the holy men's feet. If they could get their blood circulation to resume, amputations would not be necessary!

By chance, if the medics weren't successful, they would receive a formal burial on the fort's parade ground. Herkimer's medical men knew that 'a bad apple spoils the bunch' and so does a rotten foot!

Despite the intermittent hot water treatments going on beneath their seats, George and John were busting at the seams to testify about their impressions of the devil's bastard son named, 'Sporck'! All fourteen of Ike's inmates would have kept McClelland and Doctor Pollard up for another night recalling their ninety-three days of suffering if Sergeant Sweeney hadn't barged into the mess hall with the announcement of there being a man sitting on a horse in front of the fort! Sweeney claimed the man seemed to be having an argument with someone, "who wasn't there", beside of him!

"Hello there! I am in search of General Abraham Staats! I am here to personally deliver a message to him from King George Augustus II!" briskly yelled King George as if 'Timothy' were doing the salutation.

"Sir, if you wish to enter this fort, you must state your name and your business!" Sternly stated a private on duty from atop the guard tower.

"For the bloody second time, I am King George and I wish to speak with General Staats at once! And as far as my business is concerned, it will remain mine and General Abraham Staats's! Now, open this goddamned gate and let us in this instant!" Screamed Britain's king.

"Sir, I'll not be unable to do that without proper identification! I shall repeat for the second time, 'if you wish to enter Fort Herkimer, you must state your name and your business'!" hissed the irritated guard.

In reaction to what 'Timothy' felt was an impudent remark coming from a nave, George II withdrew a pistol from beneath his mink lined riding jacket and without aiming, shot the private's hat right off of his head! He then withdrew another pistol cocked it and spoke but much louder this time.

"Son, if you don't open that motherfucking gate up within the next minute, I give you my solemn word, I'll personally hang you from right where you're standing! Now, go get your Commander and open this gate!" said the King.

Chaloner Ogle had asked the 'Kitty's Amelia's' crew to gather together in the galley before their departure onto the bustling docks of Manhattan Island. He praised them for their valiant service to the Crown. He then gave his crew a brief sermon on the woes of 'demon rum'! They were paid and wished a warm 'fair-the-well'!

Once the crewmen left the ship, Commander Ogle opened the ancient bottle of brandy he had reserved for exactly that moment! After setting out three mugs, Cal unrolled a map of the entire island.

"Kimberly, your father and the men who are his friends, were last known to have met some contacts at the 'Queen's Head Tavern'. As you can see where my finger is pointing, we are docked here at Swamp Meadows.

The tavern is only two miles from where we are at this moment. I suggest we drum up a believable tale and start doing some detective work right away!" Commented Ogle.

"Uncle Cal, how will you know who the bad people are? I mean, wouldn't it be dangerous for you and Uncle Alex to go prodding around a bunch of drinking men in search of someone who might be mad at my daddy's friends?" Innocently queried Kimberly.

Ogle opened up the bottle of brandy and poured each of them a three-finger high amount of the ten-year-old liquid. He gulped his down just seconds before he answered Kimberly's questions with a sugar-coated lie.

"Honey, I don't believe that those 'drinking men' at the Queen's Head Tavern have any bone to pick with your father or with any of his friends for that matter! Actually, there is no reason to even mention Jonn Kimber's name at all! We just have to get ahold of General Abraham Staats and he'll take us directly to him!

Anyway, you don't have to worry your pretty little head about that kind of thing! Your two most favorite uncles in the whole world are looking after you, Kimberly! So, stop fretting, okay?"

Kimberly nodded as she finished off her glass of brandy.

Horace Mann was a mighty fine citizen of the lower Manhattan borough known as "Duck Town". Every morning as the weather permitted, Horace would saddle his Arabian mare and take a ride around Dutchman's Swamp and return back to his home in time to open his downstairs tavern. Fort Amsterdam's thirsty lunch crowd would not appreciate his negligence even if it were because of a lusty widow.

Horace's wife's father had founded the fort's institution based on the creed that the "Pirate's Gulch" was to be a 'home away from home' for the soldiers serving the Crown! Their specialties were everchanging but were all centered around what country moms would have mostly served their young sons. It was a place where good family values were shared by all.

As time progressed, Blanche noticed the almost synchronized pattern in which the tavern manager passed on sunrise mornings. With the boredom of a sedentary life peaking to an all-time high, Blanche elected to mess with the man in order to fill her idol hours.

She was wearing one of Grace's exotic gowns, the kind with all sorts of sparkling sequins on it! Blanche slipped the see-through dress over her naked body. She was hoping Horace would stop to gander long enough for her to strike up a conversation with him!

On the very first day of her attempt at untangling Mister Mann's moral fiber, Blanche struck pay dirt! As it turned out, ole Horace Mann had a regular harem of wanton widows scattered all over the island!

Therefore, when the tavernkeeper roared by the Bartholomaus's house and saw Blanche's naked silhouette through the kitchen's window, he tightly pulled his Arabian's reins forcing the mare to a screeching halt! The "what happened next" part is purely speculative although the aftermath that followed Horace's thirty-six-hour tardiness was not!

The unamused Mrs. Mann along with her father and her three brothers whoes wives were also in tow, had no problems finding exactly the whereabouts of their whoremongering kin! It was a little after four o'clock in the morning when the first set of bare knuckles rapping on the front door awakened Blanche from her drug induced slumber. A woman was calling Horace's full name!

Being new to the mainlining game, Horace would not regain consciousness for at least another half day. But as planned, it afforded an opportunity for Blanche to arrange for some needed materials for her trip. She answered the door.

"Good morning!" cheerfully greeted Blanche.

"I wish to speak with my husband!" snarled the large boned wife of Horace Mann's.

"I'm sorry; but, whom did you say you were searching for?" teased Blanche.

"Oh, Honey, this ain't my first visit to some strumpet's house! He's been running whores since the day that man was born!

Lady, I'm not here to condemn you! I just want you to know that I am dropping his things off here at your place!

I'm done with him and so are my family members! Here we have the King of England docked within a stone's throw from our tavern and the sorry sonofabitch doesn't even show up to open up!

No, we're done with the fool! You tell your chinchilla-dicked munchkin friend in there that all of his belongings are packed in the back of the wagon tied out front! You tell Horace, I'll be taking the Arabian back to my barn! He'll just have to get by with the old nag attached to his shit!" shrieked Mrs. Mann.

"Oh my, Dearest, I most certainly understand all of the confusion now! If I understand what you nice folks believe is happening here, you are under the impression that a Mister Mann is hold up in my place, is that correct? Politely queried Blanche.

"You're bloody well correct there, Missy! I'd bet my bottom shilling the egg-faced bastard is sprawled out drunker than a poisoned dog right in your iniquitous bed as we are sharing these pleasantries together!" hissed the chagrined woman.

"Mrs. Mann, I am sure this is a hard pill to swallow for you but the woman your husband is visiting, lives two houses down and across the street from me! I'm simply not the right "slut" you're after!

But, I too have some very similar reasons to despise the dried-up old cunt myself! If you folks would care to come in, I believe I can show you the way to not only get a pound of Horace Mann's flesh but to slice a couple more clumps off of Miss Caruthers's backside while you're at it! I'll fix us some tea!

Jonn Kimber, Bill Bosman and James Stanfield escaped the initial explosion's spray of rock. The blast's concussion however did a great deal of internal damage to all three of them!

Stanfield was the first to call for help. When he realized Bill and Jonn were also alive he stopped yelling under the assumption the three of them were the only survivors! Their conversations then shifted to apologies and reminiscences!

Cato's muffled voice finally made its way through the ten feet of rubble! A sprinkle of hope spread through the aforethought 'doomed' tunnel!

Poisonous gasses began seeping in from the mountain's subterranean cracks! It made the trapped men aware there would not be ample oxygen to sustain them for long!

The other survivors began tearing away at the formidable tons of rocks and dirt. Two hours later, the conglomerate of 'diggers' had cleared enough of a hole to allow some fresh air to blow into their would-be tombs!

By sunrise, all three of the captains were laying on stretchers. A foot of snow had fallen during the night.

Not only had Cato's cadets dug out Bosman, Stanfield and Kimber they had also broken through to a reasonably stable section of the passageway! Tanacharison swore he smelled gas.

Jeffrey's pleas ended the instant his body filled the cut in Sporck's rear sight! He crumpled like a paper doll when the ball hit him in the chest! Ike had hoped he might have a word with Jeffrey before he passed but the bullet's impact knocked the professor into the blazing inferno!

Sporck returned to his cottage for a little stick of comfort and a tiny congratulatory party for himself on account of the amazing shot he had made at Jeffrey! Shooting a flaming target was customarily celebrated with a cup of the quarry's blood but scotch would do the trick under the circumstances.

Lieutenant Colonel Washington had a very serious situation on his hands! The regiment's cook had inadvertently put lard soap into the stew he had served the night earlier!

Including himself, there wasn't a single man in the entire unit standing on their own two feet! Instead, they had reverted back to being on all fours!

Diarrhea which leads to dehydration, can be as deadly as a pit of vipers! They would have to deal with their dilemma as best they could.

"Paotow", their Mohican scout, appraised the distance to Fort Herkimer from their current location. It was a little under fifty miles away. He refused to take Washington's troops any further due to the increasing number of signs calibrated in the wind!

The scout collected his pay and turned his horse toward the Ohio Territory. Before he left, Paotow drew Colonel Washington a diagram showing the sensed trouble-spots around the headwaters of the Mohawk River!

When First Sergeant Donald Sweeney barged into the mess hall with the story about a pistol packing King and his imaginary sidekick named 'Timothy', the military men inwardly panicked at the realization that if that man outside the gate was in fact the King of England, they may be going to the gallows in a very short while!

Sensing fear which gouged through any hopes of returning the esprit de corps' back to normalcy, Colonel McClelland put on his dress jacket and made a beeline toward the fort's mammoth gate! From over his shoulder he commanded Sergeant Sweeney to "form the men" and then walked toward the entranceway. Andrew's pistol was tucked behind his back.

As soon as 'Timothy' laid eyes on Colonel McClelland, he took an immediate dislike to the man or at least that's what he told Gus!

In response to their now enjoined opinions and at Timothy's advice, the King chose to intimidate the outpost's commander by using threats!

"It is my understanding your name is "McClelland" is that correct?" politely asked King George.

"Colonel Andrew D. McClelland at your service, your Majesty!" barked McClelland.

"Well, McClelland, here's what I plan to do! My friend and I are going to ride away from this fort and return to it in thirty minutes! When I knock on these walls again, I had best have a proper reception or I shall most certainly march you and your officers in front of the business end of a firing squad!" huffed the King.

"As you wish, Sir! We'll certainly be prepared next time, your Royal Highness!" said McClelland.

Because of the subzero temperatures, Gus and Timothy soon returned to Fort Herkimer's gate. Expecting blaring horns and snare drums, George and Tim found only an empty-like log structure!

There was no light nor sound! Fort Herkimer appeared to have no inhabitants whatsoever inside of it!

Samuel Fraunces was blown four hundred feet into the air until the boughs of a hemlock tree snatched him out of his trajectory. With the tips of his trembling fingers Fraunces touched every natural orifice on his body.

He flexed every muscle and he put pressure on all of his bones only to find that deafness was the only cost he paid for the blast! As Samuel Fraunces was negotiating his descent from the hemlock tree's top, he caught the glimmer of a cavalryman's lance!

Samuel Fraunces started counting the number of soldiers surrounding the site where Black Sam's mountain use to proudly set. Fraunces's only option was to remain absolutely motionless and hope the now dismounted cavalrymen wouldn't spot him. The wind picked up.

Tanacharison refused to go into the tunnel until he was positive the cadets' scattered about were dead! Cato dispatched those in critical condition with his tomahawk!

Just as the two 'death angels' were done with the last known one of them, Tanacharison noticed a flash of light coming from the tiptop of a tree more than a hundred yards away! It was a warning signal!

With nightfall still several hours away, it would be dangerous for them to make their way to the tunnel without being picked off by a sniper. Another series of flashes were being sent!

The amplified voice of Lieutenant Colonel George Washington split the evening air.

"Fire-in-the-hole!"

A cannonball whizzed over Tanacharison's and Cato's heads and harmlessly smashed into the river behind their hiding place. Cato looked over at Tanacharison who was lying so still that Cato thought for a minute the Chief had died from his wounds. Fortunately for Cato, he had not.

Tanacharison turned his head toward the blue-eyed pirate with a funny smirk on his face. In a low hum, the Mingo gave his assessment of the situation.

"Cato, they have no idea we're here! White soldiers do everything by their military books which leaves them quite vulnerable!

If War Eagle were still alive, his warriors would already have these gentlemen's scalps on their belts! As it stands, we are currently surrounded by Virginia Regulars and fortunately not the British!

We've got some men freezing to death up there in that tunnel! It looks to me like our best option is to ask for their assistance!

Anyway, you with your smashed wrist and me and my one working lung, would be useless even in a fair fight! How do you see it, my Friend?" asked Tanacharison.

Cato nodded in concession. He knew Tanacharison was correct. There were seriously injured people hiding in Sam's mountain and they had to be moved!

As Cato was about to stand to get the soldiers' attention, a familiar voice rang out from atop the 'blinking' hemlock tree! It was the voice of the Queen's Head Tavern's owner, Samuel Fraunces. He sounded madder than a hornet!

"I can tell you bloody chaps one thing, the next time you Brits ask for my help to guide you somewhere, you can go straight to hell! Look at what you have done!

Get me out of this goddamned tree at once, you limey sons of bitches! You'll pay for this one! Well, don't just stand around playing pocket billiards, get your asses down there and help those kids!"

Kimberly entered the kitchen's entrance to the Queen's Head Tavern in search of her "grandfather", General Abraham Staats! Everyone was busy so no one noticed the ragamuffin crouching behind a stack of ale barrels.

At six o'clock, Kimberly was to sharply pop herself on the bridge of her nose in order to bloody her face. Her story was to be the tale of a grandchild escaping from the merciless talons of an evil stepmom back in Liverpool!

Once her "papaw's" whereabouts was established, two upstanding citizens (Uncles Alex and Cal) would volunteer to protect the child while getting her into the safety of her grandfather's keeping! All that would be needed was an address but then something quite unexpectedly happened!

Thomas Rasmussen, General Staats' fast-footed little slave, was making some money by sweeping up the tavern. He happened to see Kimberly hiding from him!

"And what pray tell do I owe Jesus for him to offer me such a delightful spectacle as I am having the pleasure of looking at with my own eyes? Is it that I am dreaming or have I come up upon something I wasn't supposed to?" queried Rasmussen.

"I'm looking for my 'Grandpa Abraham'!" responded Kimberly.

"Oh yeah, who's "Grandpa Abraham?" pressed young Thomas.

"His name is "General Abraham Staats"! Do you know him?" excitedly asked Kimberly.

"Who'd you say you were, Miss …?" belittlingly asked Thomas Rasmussen.

"Well actually, I didn't! Under these circumstances, I thought it would be rather awkward to say my name out loud!" Bated Kimberly.

"How's that?" Bit Thomas.

"Can you keep a secret?" Kimberly asked in a sisterly way.

"Of course, I can keep a secret and I'm smart too! I'm only twelve years old and I done bought my freedom from Master Staats by myself and the onliest way I done that was to keep my mouth shut about a whole bunch of things!

Even though you ain't answered my question yet, I'll go ahead and introduce myself! My name is "Thomas Rasmussen Staats" but I am called "Mercury" because of my speed and all!" gloated Mercury.

"Mercury, my name is "Kimberly". My last name is still up for grabs at this point! All I can accurately tell you, Mister Staats, I was in a very dangerous situation with the man that was sort of married to my mother! My mother was the illegitimate daughter of General Staats!

This man my mother was tied up with was going to hurt me! I told on him for robbing disembarking passengers coming into Liverpool! That's why I ran away…" said Kimberly as she tightened her line.

"General Staats has gone to Fort Herkimer with some of the local militia in order to settle some kind of issue with the Indians. We've been expecting him back for quite some time now!

Miss Staats, it would be my pleasure to escort you to his home! There is no one there except for a couple of dozen field hands and my mother!

Oh, don't look so surprised, Kimberly, my father has always been colorblind when it came to his lovers! Seriously, I'll be happy to take you there!

I'll be leaving my shift at nine o'clock. I'm sure mom would love to meet you!" Earnestly said Mercury.

"That is a more than gracious offer, Mercury; however, I have a small problem! I promised the two Captains of the "Kitty's Amelia" that General Staats would pay for my passage as soon as we docked in New York!" whimpered the young angler.

"Sis, I have a horse out in the barn that can make that kind of debt vanish in the night! Where are those ship captains now, Kimberly?" bravely questioned Rasmussen.

"They're out front having a drink at the bar! They both are wearing blue seaman's hats.

They have been good to me so please don't hurt them, Mercury! I would be dead by now if they hadn't come to my rescue!" pleaded Kimberly.

"Kimberly, don't worry, I know how to make those guys go away! I'll just put something in their drinks and when they wake up, you'll be gone!" said Mercury.

All Europeans have a righteous fear of rats! Not one single one of them can escape the memory of their grandparents' remembrances of building sized bonfires blazing outside their childhood homes! That was the assumed reason why the Girandoni's had a bag full of "nux-vomica" roots stashed away in their tool shed.

As Blanche was preparing a kettle of "Mama O'Malley's" famous tea, through the reflection in the window pane she noticed the Mann brood exploring every nook and cranny throughout Black Bart's kitchen!

Realizing she wouldn't have enough time to keep their curiosities at bay, Blanche's ingenuity peaked to an all-time high!

Pretending as though she was looking for a strainer, Blanche skipped over to the tool closet like a happy little housewife and while whistling a tune picked up the bag of nux vomica roots and placed it into a pan full of water. She then added two handfuls of kindling to Mary Girandoni's cooking stove while the bag full of the strychnine producing roots soaked for a spell.

The tea kettle began its gurgling boil. While Blanche and the Mann's chitchatted about the fish smelling Ms. Caruthers's slide into her den of iniquity, Blanche casually began walking around the kitchen shutting any of the windows which could permit fresh air to blow into the dining room.

After serving Horace's in-laws a plate of stale gingerbread muffins and a kettle full of nothing but tea in it, Blanche proceeded to shove the soaked root bag into the stove's cooking fire before she walked out of the kitchen door leading to the outside street! On her way out, she turned the damper shut so the poisonous gas would do its job!

Right at sunrise, Blanche returned to the Bartholomaus's home to arrange the entire Mann clan (including Horace) in a way that depicted a family preparing to bury their favorite cat! The Abyssinian tomcat was stretched out on one of Grace's old turkey trays while the frozen faced onlookers looked on in disbelief!

Blanche meticulously went through the Mann family's pockets! Rigor mortis had set in but she was still able to extrapolate a few more valuables to add to what had already been accumulated from the Bellamy and Girandoni households.

With the packing almost behind her and the proper outfit having been chosen for the workday, Blanche pulled out her leather lanyard and drew it tight enough to raise up a plump artery in the crook of her arm.

She waited for the syrupy warmth to catch up with her conscience before she hooked up Horace Mann's fine Arabian to the wagon full of windbuchse rifles. With those casket sized clock boxes filled with deadly silent weapons, Blanche knew she had a ticket to anywhere she wished to go!

After loading up her newly acquired wardrobe compliments of Grace O'Malley, she snapped the buggy whip over the Arabian's ears in order to speed the animal up! The "newly widowed" Mrs. Mann had a tavern to open and she certainly didn't want to keep the soldiers waiting for their hearty breakfasts!

Samuel Fraunces demanded to speak with the commanding officer! The four men who had climbed up the hemlock tree to rescue him had lost their sense of humor! With the back of his flattened hand, the largest of the troopers began rapping the now petrified tavern owner across his mouth every time he attempted to speak! Seven raps later, Samuel got the message!

Much to the chagrin of a handful of Washington's soldiers, Cato and Tanacharison stood up from their skillfully chosen hiding places! The armed cavalrymen who had walked past them several times simply threw up their arms in disbelief of the hoodwinking they got from one single Indian and one blue eyed mulatto!

Fraunces waved joyously when he saw that his brother and Tanacharison were alive! With seeing only two of the adults standing and previously witnessing from atop the tree many bodies being flushed down the Mohawk River, Samuel felt in his heart that a terrible tragedy had occurred! His focus then returned to his captors.

"May I speak, Corporal?" humbly asked Samuel Fraunces.

"Only if you can do it with a civil tongue in your mouth!" barked the boorish trooper.

"Attention!" yelled one of four of Samuel's restrainers.

Lieutenant Colonel Washington entered the scene with the expression of a man- eating wolf! His steel blue eyes seemed to bore right through Samuel Fraunces's body. He approached Samuel Fraunces and then greeted him.

"It never fails to surprise me just how stupid some of the noncommissioned officers they're turning out these days can be! I'll bet you these scholars who assisted you down from that heavenly aimed tree didn't even ask you 'how you got up there?', didn't they?

You'd have thought they could have figured that out by just looking at the tracks or lack thereof encircling the damned hemlock! Man, I can't believe you're still in one piece! How far did you get blasted before you ended up there?" asked Washington.

"Colonel, I figure it was pretty close to a hundred yards I'd expect! I don't know what that Bellamy fella had stored up in his mountain house but I can tell you one thing, it caused the biggest explosion I'd ever seen!

One minute we were shooting rope balls into the mountain's semaphore window and two seconds later, I was hanging on to some branches for my dear life!" Panted the hyperventilating Samuel Fraunces.

"Corporal Fredrick, untie this man's arms and you men go over and help the others! Move those kids to the triage tent! Tell Doctor Arias, I shall expect a full injury report within the hour!

Mister Fraunces and I need to have a little chat together! I'm sure he has a very interesting story to tell regarding the 'how's' and 'why's' which caused a fieldtrip for a battalion of cadets to end so badly!

Samuel, have a seat on this nice soft log here while I pour us a big ole drink! And please, Samuel, go ahead and start with your story! Take it from the top! I want to hear it all!" said Colonel Washington as he refilled Sam's cup again to the brim.

Sporck had just finished giving himself a fairly sturdy amount of 'poppy sap'. He stoked the embers in his fireplace while philosophizing about 'fire' at the same time.

As dilettantes often discover, once they dive into the evaluations of nature's elements, they meet the horrid faces of both good and evil! It is in that murky hole in which their minds are drawn and then quartered!

As far as a weakness in Spork's mind, there actually was none! Anton von Sporck found himself to be a remarkable human being but just one who was at the tiptop of the intellectual pyramid! In all reality, Ike liked himself immensely!

The short hand on Sporck's clock was just about ready to click over to its first digit of a new day when the sounds of marching soldiers rattled the crystal in his cupboard. Sporck put on his jacket and walked out to his cottage's front porch in hopes of getting the latest scoop on things.

By the time he got to the gate most of the brigade had trotted past with only the chow wagon and an artillery detachment switching out a cannon's busted wheel. With his best pastoral grin, Ike threw his hand up halfway to present a show of support while in the other hand he clinched an unopened bottle of muscadine wine! Sporck wanted to buy a bit of information!

"I saw you boys struggling with a wheel that's hub had collapsed on you and I wanted to offer you a little refreshment! I recall how it was when I was in your boots!

Man, I can remember it just like it was yesterday! I don't envy you men one bit, I'll tell you that right now!

Say, would you fellows like to come on inside? I can rustle us up a fine breakfast and more than likely find a little something stronger to drink! It's colder than a 'witch's tit' out here and you guys might could use a short warmup! You all come on in!" gladly said Sporck.

"Governor, we appreciate your hospitality but we've got to pull up the end! We're in sort of a hurry!" said an annoyed cannoneer.

"It's too late in the year for maneuvers! Are the Indians acting up again?" Asked the innocent faced holy man.

"Sir, since King George landed at the fort, all hell has broken loose! I have no idea what's going on! All I know is, we're going to be gone for a while!

Say, you wouldn't by any chance have an extra pair of mittens laying around, would you? With as many drills as we have undergone over the past week, I have completely shredded mine!" asked the complaining British soldier.

"Son, I happened to have some in my jacket pocket! Here take these. Any guesses as to how far north ya'll will have to go?" picked Sporck.

"For sure to Fort Herkimer but beyond that, I'd be afraid to say! Some of the men mentioned they heard the King say that everybody at the fort had been captured by the Indians! But more than a few of them swear that ole George has gone bananas and that the whole crisis up there is nothing more than his twisted imagination!

I do know that Governor Burnet and King George are meeting soon! Come to think about it, I am quite sure it's about the French though and not the Indians!

Personally, I'm like you, I wish to put this army stent of mine into the past! I have grown very tired of people directing my life for me!

Just give me a little plot of good ground and a plump and fertile wife and I'd be out from under the Crown so fast it'd make your head spin! I'll bet you too felt the same way that I do at one time or another, didn't you?" Whined the soldier.

"Hey, I have a terrific idea, while they're changing out that hub, why don't you allow me to give you the money necessary for you to pursue that marvelous dream of yours? Please don't turn me down, young Man;

I have no one to leave my estate to and the doctors tell me I don't have that much longer to walk on this earth!" said the oily voiced Sporck.

"Sir, that's a mighty gracious offering but I really need to get back to my unit! It looks like they got the cannon rolling again and they'll come looking for me directly so I better scoot! It has been a real pleasure speaking with you and I must say, I am honored by your kindness!

Perhaps when I return, I'll come over and you can show me your place! Thanks again, Sir, and once more, much gratitude for the nice mittens!" yelled the departing soldier.

As the young private was tromping away from the compound's gate, Sporck had one last chance to snare the boy into his web. Realizing he had never gotten the artilleryman's name, Anton elected to loudly address the soldier with a subtle remark he knew would cause the lad to stop!

"Just for curiosity's sake, my Son, did your mother ask you to look me up?"

If an onlooker had witnessed what happened next, he would have thought that he was watching a scene from "Hamlet"! When the private felt Sporck's jagged words penetrate his heart, he stopped dead in his tracks and then spun around almost in an attack mode! The soldier then raced back toward the tantalizing stranger standing in the guard tower!

"Mister, I do not take kindly to incendiary comments spouted from an insensitive ogre such as yourself! May I remind you, I am a British dragoon who among many others posted on this godforsaken island, are here to protect you Colonists! Perhaps you might find it a healthier environment futuristically speaking that is, to show more respect for your keepers!

Now I'll be on my way! Have a pleas…,'' the soldier was saying when Sporck's musket ball passed through his brain!

With catlike movements and with a snow rake in his hand, Ike leaped out of the guard tower and dragged the dead boy into his cottage! He then covered any telltale snow tracks with swishes of a bamboo toothed rake and shut the front gate!

Sporck hummed a little ditty as he tied his favorite lanyard around his upper arm. He was preparing to give himself another congratulatory injection for his 'second' superb shot!

The Austrian had placed his bullet so as not a stitch on the soldier's uniform was nicked. To top that off, they wore the same size!

Colonel Andrew McClelland was startled awake by the bugler's call to arms! Seconds later, Doctor Pollard stormed into the fort commander's quarters in a state of confusion! He pulled up a chair at the foot of McClelland's bed and while the colonel was dressing, Pollard started assessing the fort's current status.

"Andy, we got us one hell of a situation going on outside! That supposed crazy man from two nights ago, the one with the imaginary friend named "Timothy", it turned out that that 'delusional' individual was indeed the King!

What's worse, he is back but this time, King George has Governor Burnet and First Sergeant Collars along with a spare horse by his side! Behind them is an entire brigade of Fort Amsterdam's dragoons!

Sir, they have encamped completely around the fort! They have thrown their tents up and they are cooking bacon on their campfires!

Colonel, this leads me to think that ole King George intends on teaching us an etiquette lesson. Sir, I am almost positive we are under siege!" softly spoke the physician.

"Has anyone bothered to find out what they want or for that matter what in the hell they're doing here?" sarcastically questioned McClelland.

"Colonel, as I said, the King and his "friend's" horse, Governor Burnet along with the weaselly Sergeant Collars, are all in front of our gate! They are sitting on their horses and not saying a word! Andy, I believe they want a "ROYAL" reception!" flatly stated Harold Pollard.

"Oh, Jesus! Now I have to eat crow along with the King's bullshit! Alright, if a show is what they want, that's what they'll get!

Doctor Pollard, please summon my first sergeant! We're going to have us a marvelous parade!" shouted McClelland.

Because of the fabrications coming from the mouth of a sleezy governor, King George was led to believe that Fort Herkimer had been overtaken by a band of French soldiers and Tanacharison's Confederates!

From Gus's perspective, none of their verbalized concoctions made sense! A question needed to be answered, 'Since when did the Iroquois Confederacy become friends with Thayendanegea and the French?'!

With this missing part annoyingly rattling around in his mind, George II began his rather skillful search for the truth. By pulling his reins sharply to his left and kicking one of Fort Amsterdam's finest cavalry horses in the rump with his spurred heels, the King was be able to hear an unadulterated version of the Governor's story!

"Tell me, Ben, what really happened at the fort that night? An old brave war dog like you doesn't seem to fit the profile of a fool!

I am quite sure something else was going on you weren't aware of. What puzzles me about it is, how could three hundred of anyone's army catch an armed fortress completely off guard?" gayly queried the King.

"Sir, there weren't any three hundred of anything! Shit, whomever told you that malarkey is a bold-faced liar! At the very most, there couldn't have been over five of them in all toll!

It is my belief, someone let them in the back of the fort while I was gabbing with those three bloody priests! The fools were wanting to take a wagon load of blankets to the goddamned Indians!" sputtered Collars.

"What in god's name are you telling me, Sergeant? Are you saying that three priests in the middle of the night stopped to have a conversation with you regarding gifts for the Indians? Didn't you feel that something was wrong with that?" loudly hissed the King.

"Well, Sir, General Staats had just been in an awful fight with Tanacharison's warriors and frankly everything was in disarray! There was a lot of shuffling going in and out of the fort for a while! Doctor Pollard alone probably performed fifteen surgeries throughout the night!

He saved more than half of their lives; although, I believe that was when we lowered our security measures to a dismal degree! In hindsight, that was most likely when the infiltrators slipped into our walls!" said the downtrodden sergeant.

"Did McClelland do any kind of inspection to determine how his fort was breached?" asked the seething Monarch.

"Your Majesty, when I awakened the next morning, hell, I hadn't slept for two days, and realized all of my men had been tied up in the horse barn and that Doctor Pollard and Colonel McClelland had been nailed shut into their quarters, I immediately left the barracks to find that the only other person left unaffected by the trespassers was Governor Burnet!

But when the Commander started firing his pistols at us and then making all sorts of threats, the Governor ordered me to escort him back to the island! I regret doing that now!" softly said the humiliated first sergeant.

"Do you believe, be careful with your answer here, Ben, that Governor Burnet possibly might have been 'the inside guy' who made this caper a success? And, if so, why would he do such a thing?" sternly quizzed George.

"With all due respect, King George, I would not want to express my thoughts on such a matter! I'll just say, there were some coincidences, more than one of them, which might implicate the Governor! I, most certainly do not feel it is my place to express my suspicions!" piously whined Collars.

"Sergeant Collars, since the cat has a claw stuck into your tongue, I shall ask that your firing squad's marksmen shoot that obnoxious tabby for you! But don't worry, the reprobate you have exchanged your life for will be standing right beside of you!

I was sort of beginning to like you, Mister Collars! I had hoped you could have shown me around this beautiful country up here! It's my understanding, the salmon fishing is superb in these rivers. Such a shame!" mumbled King George.

When First Sergeant Collars heard the King of England pronounce his death sentence he fell off of his horse! Governor Burnet who had eavesdropped their whole conversation, panicked!

Burnet kicked his horse's haunches thus bolting him toward Fort Herkimer's gate! He began pleading for the gate's keeper to open the fort's door.

"I am sorry! I didn't realize…" said New York's governor until Andrew McClelland's musket ball prohibited his apology from moving forward.

A split second later, as the trumpets within Herkimer's logged barrier blared out the King's welcoming, another one of Andy's lead balls did the same thing to Ben Collars! The massive gate then opened.

For only a couple of seconds, Ogle and Selkirk were able to decipher Kimberly's lip movements through the tavern's Dutch door! From their mutual misinterpretation of Kim's message, the blue-capped seamen ordered an additional drink after the 'mickeys' Mercury had just served them!

After gulping down their sworn to be final 'nightcaps', simultaneously both men spun off their stools and onto the tavern's floor! Upon seeing that cue, Mercury grabbed up his "sister" by her waist and headed out toward the stable where his horse was kept.

Four of the nine keys she had filched from the Mann's' pockets were worthless! The fifth one she tried enabled Blanche to enter the "Pirate's Gulch" with little difficulty.

Preparing a couple of boiled eggs and frying up a chunk of meat was about as much culinary experience as the old girl had in the kitchen world. The thoughts of waiting on customers and pulling off her scheme while cooking at the same time, simply made her skin crawl. Blanche had to come up with an alternate plan!

Once Blanche had gone through the restaurant's every crevice that might hold anything of value greater than a dead mouse, she was forced to change the 'Pirate's Gulch's' bill of fare! With a paint brush and a half pint of white paint, the fledgling restaurateur dabbed out on the marquise, "A Middle Ages' Feast"!

The menu read, "Roast Your Own Meal and Drink Ale To Your Heart's Content". The next line read, "Although Gratuities Are Always Appreciated, Your Meal Is On The House."!

As history will loudly proclaim, Blanche knew how to build a good fire! Which is exactly what she did in the Gulch's cooking stove! She sharpened the ends of ten tomato sticks and threw them out on the long line of tables Blanche had shoved together.

Bowls of all sizes were spread out across the vast plain of poorly connected tabletops. A knife was the only eating utensil provided.

Twenty-seven chickens curiously wandered around in their cages. They were stacked up in front of the Pirate's Gulch's roaring fireplace while the vegetables and some secret spices (nux-vomica) were added to the boiling kettle.

With little time to waste due to the sun rising, Blanche hurried through the tavern grabbing things she had missed on her initial sweep. She could smell the sweet gases starting to spread their deadly fingers throughout the building she was exiting!

She gave a foxy smile to the soldiers milling around in front of her freshly painted sandwich board. Horace Mann's solid black Arabian reacted from the sounds of Blanche's expert whip cracking. Blanche was off to sell some rifles!

Sporck moved the full-length mirror from his bedroom into the hallway. This gave him a full-360 degree look at himself!

For a second or two, Sporck reminisced of the times when a uniform attracted the attentions of girls and boys alike! Those were the days of "easy-pickings", he remembered.

Those precious encapsulations suspended in Ike's memory were just that, he must now use his old "jailbait" lure for an entirely different reason on this day in time! Sporck intended to imbed himself within the walls of Fort Amsterdam and wait for the long overdue opportunity to assassinate his archenemy, King George II!

He would pretend to be a messenger from the battle scarred ruins of Fort Herkimer! But before he executed his ruse upon the soldiers of Fort Amsterdam, Sporck deemed it necessary to find out precisely what was happening at the Colonial manned Fort Herkimer.

The Queen's Head Tavern was more than likely the best place on the island to get a fresh scoop of the goings on up at the fort. Because of his slightly blood-spattered uniform, the great pretender launched his scheme. He would enter the tavern as a shell-shocked warrior and one with amnesia!

Washington staunchly walked over to his tent after he had seen that Tanacharison and Cato were being prepped for surgery. He couldn't get to the privacy of his headquarters fast enough!

No sooner had the flap of his tent mercifully shut off the morning sun light, the twenty-two-year old lieutenant colonel dropped to his knees and began vomiting! Never before had he seen such an ugly sight!

George was trembling to such a degree that he found it nearly impossible to even light his pipe! Finally, after failing three times, Washington was able to get a good lungful of opium smoke.

With the additional assistance of a jug of whiskey, Colonel Washington was able to receive the fatality list sent to him from Doctor Rogue Arias! Since the regiment's physician's count took more than two pages to list, George took another puff on his pipe before he read it.

As George's spinal cord began to tingle and he was able to take normal breaths again, Washington began reasoning out the myriad of factors given to him by Samuel Fraunces! He then drew a box on the back of the regiment's surgeon's fatality report.

Starting in the top left-hand corner of his quilled square, Washington wrote the word, "British". To the right top corner, he scribbled a picture of a feather (representing the Iroquois Confederacy). Straight down to the right bottom corner he drew a Tomahawk symbolizing the Algonquin and Mohawk Nations.

For the French, George sketched out what resembled a cannon and put it on the left bottom corner of his chart. In the dead center of the page he wrote the word, "Americans"!

Colonel McClelland was not at all amused by the audacity that King George displayed upon his parade-style arrival! The King even had the Fort Amsterdam's marching band prepare his way through Herkimer's wide open gate! The outside temperature was seven degrees below zero.

When it was time for Fort Herkimer's Commander to meet the King, Gus demanded that a rug be placed in front of his "throne" constructed out of wooden boxes. This had been done so Colonel Andrew McClelland would not have to put his right knee down into the snow when he bowed to his Majesty. The King wanted only bugles, no drums, to be honked during that particular segment of the formality!

A British officer with a voice which sounded like a bullfrog's, announced that the King of Great Britain from the House of Hanover (etcetera) was now seated and prepared to meet the fort's Commander! Colonel McClelland made his way toward the patch of carpet. He kneeled and then greeted the King.

"Your Majesty, we are pleased that you are here! I and my staff will do everything within our power to make your visit a pleasant one!

That being said, Sir, I am sure your soldiers would appreciate the warmth of our barn instead of another night in this dreadful cold! King George, I have a marvelous chef on my staff who would jump over backwards at the opportunity of introducing you to some of America's finest cuisines!

I am also confident, you will find your quarters beyond adequate! Furthermore, if you're not prudent with your compliments of our kitchen staff's efforts, I am quite sure they will roast a pig in your honor!" said the prostrated Colonel.

"Hell's bells you, incompetent idiot! I am here for the second time in order to teach your treasonous lot a lesson! It sickens me how you 'colonists' have forgotten your place on the world's food chain!

All we ever hear from you tools are complaints! You bitch about our levied taxes as if you thought ole Gus here had a bottomless unicorn filled with nothing but gold coins just for you leaching…" snarled the King as a cannonball exploded in the middle of the British "C" Company's midst! Next came the French cavalry right through the gate!

Two hundred yards directly behind the Queen's Head Tavern is a marshy area known by the Montgomerie Ward's locals as, "Dutchman's Swamp". Because of the outside temperature, neither Ogle nor Selkirk drowned in it.

By the looks of the tracks around them, it was quite clear that someone's foul play had led to one hell of a ruckus! Despite the fact that all indications pointed toward victory on behalf of the Alex and Chaloner duo, both had some head traumas from being pummeled, drinking too much, and guzzling down Mercury's mickey!

The problem remaining for the ship captains was of course Kimberly's whereabouts. There were no real clues except for the murky memories of Kimberly being held around her waist as she was being carried out of the tavern's rear door!

Painfully the men got to their feet and began as best they could tracing-back their footprints from the previous night. It was noon.

Hard blowing winds had done a lot to erase the imprints made by the young negro kidnapper; however, Alex found in the tavern's stable the snapped off cap cover of a pocket watch. Upon closer scrutiny, Cal surmised that Kim had left them an inkling of a hint as to where her abductor was taking her! The initials on the gold cap read, "J.F.K.". Kim and her abductor had left on one horse!

Blanche recalled the way in where she had left the island a while back. Fort Herkimer as she remembered, was about a six-hour ride to the northwest once she passed through Kings Forest and across the Rope Walk Bridge.

Horace Mann had left her an amazing horse. The Arabian was one that could close a fifty-mile distance in pretty short order even with a half-ton wagonload of windbuchses behind it! That comforted Blanche.

The sun's reflection off of the windblown whiteness surrounding her caused Blanche's vision to take on a bluish hue which dangerously overlapped everything she looked at! To remedy the harshness of the accelerated sunlight, she raised over her head a parasol she had lifted from the Girandoni's place.

Just as Blanche was turning her rig onto William Street, which put her only a mile away from the Kings Forest Road, she spotted two men warming themselves on the fire they had built beneath the Rope Walk Bridge. Blanche pulled her wagon off of the road.

"Hey Guys! Would you mind sharing a little bit of that nice fire with a mighty cold girl?" asked Blanche in a provocative way.

Alex looked at Cal in a curious manner. Ogle responded to Selkirk in identically the same way. Both men knew the wagon was their lifeline but neither of them had the stomach to kill the friendly traveler.

Alex Selkirk mumbled a remark to Chaloner.

"Maybe we can just take her along, what do you think?"

"Let's wait and see. It'll depend on the chemistry, my good Man!" muttered Ogle.

"Well of course you may, young Lady! Don't you worry none about usun's; We're just a couple of hired hands on our way to the Staats Plantation for some work! He's building a new barn up there and he wants us to tear the old one down for him!" yelled Selkirk.

Blanche in her perusal of the two men determined through various bulges from beneath their matching naval coats, they were arms baring imposters! But they were carrying a boatload of cash on them!

"Would you gentlemen like a ride to the Staats Plantation?" asked Blanche.

Ogle responded to her question but made a novice type of error when he did so. He used words that didn't make sense coming from a man whose partner addressed themselves as "usun's"!

"To paraphrase Shakespeare, Madam, 'Oh alas…'" playfully addressed Chaloner just as Blanche fired her blunderbuss at them from atop her wagon's bench!

Because Horace Mann's Arabian happened to be a jittery kind of animal, the beast anticipated a coming loud 'boom' and therefore jolted forward causing the lead spray to miss its intended marks! Debris and thumb sized limbs dropped from just above Ogle's and Selkirk's heads causing a nasty hiss from their already dying fire!

Blanche with two pistols clinched in her fists, leaped from the wagon and proceeded to race downhill toward them! This gave the sea warriors more than enough time to withdraw their pistols and take aim on their relatively slow-moving target.

Instead of killing the girl right off, Ogle suggested they throw her in the back of "their" wagon and turn her over to General Staats when they got to his farm! Due to Blanche's being knocked out by a Selkirk thrown creek rock, Alex had time to comment on Chaloner's suggestion.

"Cal, have you lost your ever-loving mind? This bloody wildcat is a very dangerous lady! Let's just cut her throat and be done with it!"

"Alex, I am quite sure this 'wildcat' as you called her, is the very same woman who murdered the Queen! It is my steadfast belief, she should be hanged in London! I feel that would provide our countrymen with a "just end" to the terrible hurt this awful creature caused for them!

No, Captain Selkirk, a quick little throat slitting is far too kind of a death for this atrocious thing! She deserves a slow demise, one that might involve some birds, a suspended cage and time!" said Ogle.

With one lightning fast movement, Blanche tossed her powder horn into the marines' campfire! It exploded and she dashed into the current of the Hudson River!

After a series of exchanged deliberations, both men with hopeful prophecies, predicted that Blanche's body would be washed out to sea! Alex nor Cal felt as though it was worth the time to make sure of it. They just prayed they would never have to tangle with her ever again!

Little did they know but as soon as Ogle and Selkirk turned their backs on the ice chunked river, Blanche climbed out of the frigid Hudson and after circling through a patch of birch trees, ended back at the wagon. She carefully hid herself in between two stacks of windbuchse cases and exhaled into a clump of snow so the approaching seamen would not see the vapor from her rapid breaths!

Doctor Arias burst out of the triage tent as if he were on fire! Setting Cato's wrist took less than an hour but Tanacharison's time beneath his knife pushed on throughout the day! It was dusk.

Washington had dabbled a bit with herbs and such and was never in short supply of opium syrups. It was from the effects of this precious substance that Doctor Arias was able to do his battlefield surgeries successfully!

Lieutenant Colonel Washington was standing over him when Cato opened his eyes. With a giant grin, the young commander started picking with the awakening patient as if he were sitting beside of him in a tavern.

"I just spoke with Doctor Arias! He said that your arm would be as good as new but he also mentioned he reduced the size of your penis! It seems that the bloody physician felt the extra ten inches you had were totally unnecessary!

I'll tell you, that ole Rogue Arias is a mighty fastidious fellow, he is! As a matter for future reference, I believe he was a little jealous, don't you, Cato?" laughed Washington.

With a crack of a grin and a snicker emitted from deep within his throat, Cato proved he was not a convicted bowman against the King by raising his good middle finger as high off the cot as he could get it up there! He motioned for Washington to bend down so he could ask him a question.

"How many of the boys are still alive, Colonel?" faintly questioned Cato.

"Eight," answered Washington.

"Oh my god! What about General Staats?" coughed Cato.

"Just six of the adults survived, I'm afraid! When Black Sam's powder stash went off, it blew a million boulders down upon your people with enormous fury! Frankly, I'm surprised there were any survivors at all!" forebodingly said Washington.

"What about Joncaire?" quickly asked Cato.

"Bosman, Kimber, Tanacharison, Stanfield, Fraunces and you are all that are left, Sir!" replied the moved Colonial officer.

"Colonel, you must warn the soldiers at Fort Herkimer of an attack by the French! On our way here, we ran into a scouting party!

From a deserter we learned that the French commander called "Jumonville" and an Iroquois chief with the last name of "Brant", have already begun their strategic onslaught, I fear!" said Cato.

"Cato, we are already working on that! If you think you'd be able to make it, I was hoping that maybe you and your boys might be able to get into the inside of Herkimer and signal to us what exactly is going on within its walls! What do you think?" questioned Colonel Washington.

Cato attempted to sit up but when he tried, Doctor Arias who had just returned to the triage tent, scolded not only him but Colonel

Washington as well! The red-faced physician forbade anymore disturbances of his patients for at least the next twenty-four hours!

"Cuts and bone breaks need time to mend!" Doctor Arias said.

As George Washington was being ushered out of the tent by one of Arias' oversized orderlies, Cato motioned for the Commander to lean forward.

"Have the cadets ready to travel at 0200!"

Sporck had gone through in his mind five times the manner in which he would enter the Queen's Head Tavern! After a quick fix, Ike was able to settle on a 'wounded warrior's' routine.

When he staggered into the tavern, it surprised Sporck that everyone in the establishment were huddled into little groups no doubt chattering about nefarious things. But when Sporck fell to the floor and began a full-blown discussion with the 'lord', he got all the attention he was seeking!

"Come on, Soldier, you're safe now! They're not after you anymore!

Son, you're not in heaven; you are with friends here!" Said an inebriated fat man pretending to know something about warriors' maladies.

"Private, what unit are you with? Can you remember what happened?" asked another goggling expert.

Sporck smiled inside as he pretended to "swear" that Jesus was descending from the tavern's ceiling and was "on his way to take him home!". To further act out the part of a shell-shocked soldier, he rolled over on his stomach and pretended to be running until two of the bar regulars took it upon themselves to pick Sporck up and force-feed some whiskey down his throat!

Pretending the "devils dew" had never touched his lips before, Sporck borrowing from some of his former parishioners rolling out into the isles who were under 'evil-rum's grip', he performed the same antics as did they! But after the third lift to the bar's edge, Sporck caught hold of his senses. At last, he could speak!

"Gentlemen, forgive me but I have no idea where I have come from nor where I was going! All I know is that I have been walking through the snow for a long time!

I do recall an explosion and some strange sounding soldiers' voices but they might have been Indians for all I know! But for sure, there was a big boom!" whined Sporck as he pretended to lose his balance once again.

"I'll bet he was part of the King's bunch from Fort Amsterdam!" said the fat wise man.

"Yea, and I reckon they got tangled up with them Indians up there! General Staats and all them King's College Cadets have been up there for over a week now so I'd lay a year's wage, the King's visit to Herkimer has mucked things up a whole lot!" slurred the man sitting beside of the obese bar-sage.

"I'd cover that bet and double the odds in favor that those two sailors who were here last night! You know somehow they're tied in with all that mess going on at that godforsaken hell-hole!" parroted another sloshed patron.

Miraculously after discovering the King's whereabouts, Sporck immediately regained his senses. With an overly demonstrated show of appreciation toward all the men who helped him during his period of temporary trauma, Sporck threw out two of his infamous magnetizable gold coins on the Queen's Head's bar top! It meant that the drinks were on him for the rest of the night!

He then quite apologetically left the tavern under the pretense he was going to return to his post at Fort Herkimer! The overweight sage volunteered to take the middle-aged grenadier all the way to the fort's gates if the circumstances allowed. The two men ordered a jug of whiskey for the road.

At precisely 2:45 A.M., Cato and the eight surviving King's College cadets left out for Fort Herkimer. Their mission was to glean as much information as possible and to transmit it back to Washington's encampment by way of signal flashes. Hidden soldiers would telegraph to one another Cato's signals over the ten-mile span of icy wilderness.

Joseph Brant (a.k.a., Thayendanegea) and over two hundred tribally mixed warriors, had used knotted rappelling ropes to scale up the back wall of the fort thus making short work of the distracted guardsmen! Not a single defensive shot was fired!

The French commander, Ensign Joseph Coulon de Jumonville who had bravely been the vanguard for his battalion of sword slashing horsemen, arrogantly dismounted his horse before sashaying over to Fort Herkimer's flag pole! The flamboyant Commander raised his right forefinger toward the sky and drew a quick air-circle indicating his dissatisfaction with whomever or whatever didn't make something happen the way he wanted it to.

Finally, one of Jumonville's lieutenants brought him a triangularly folded French flag as the prissy colonel cut the Union Jack loose from its ropes and let it flutter to the ground. He then set it on fire!

Colonel McClelland caught Gus's attention by tapping his boot against the King's ankle! In a low tone, Herkimer's commander had some bone chilling words he needed to say.

"There is still the remarkable chance the French won't discover who you are! If you wish to see London again, I suggest that you mingle in with my soldiers as soon as they move us into the stables!

Your story should naturally spill out that you are one of Doctor Pollard's assistants! You should also say that it has been said to you before that you are a 'dead-ringer' as the King of England's lookalike!

You should even tell your inquisitor your buddies here at the fort, nicknamed you "George"! But if you introduce your little friend "Timothy" to them, they'll immediately know who you are. After all, everyone in the world knows that Britain's King is a madman!"

"Will you help me, Colonel McClelland?" whispered the rattled King.

"Only if "Timothy" isn't hanging around; otherwise, I'll shoot you myself!" softly spoke Colonel McClelland.

Doctor Arias was one angry man when he awakened to find that Washington had allowed, actually coerced, his patients to leave their surgical recovery cots to go out on foot for a simple reconnaissance mission! All of his work as efficiently done as it was, might as well have been thrown into the river! The multitude of sutures were now by this time, done for naught!

Even more disrespectfully, his personal friend and boss, Lieutenant Colonel Washington offered no retribution for Tanacharison's actions! The "goddamned Indian" had tied the doctor up in his sleep preventing him from stopping their exodus!

As Washington untied the strips of silk which had prevented Rogue Arias from ringing the Indian's neck, he began teasing the Oxford man about the wily ways of savages!

"Look at this way, Rogue, Tanacharison was shooting arrows at squirrels about the same time as you were chocking on your silver spoon! They are a hard bunch to fight or so I've been told!

I actually think we finally agree on something, old Chap. Therefore, let us sweep away the crumbs from our "humble pie" and celebrate the dawning of a new tomorrow with a jug of some of my finest whiskey!" playfully prodded George.

"Colonel, have you ever examined your parents' wedding contract? I am beginning to think those papers should they even exist at all, are bogus!

However, being the good sport that I am, I shall take you up on your splendid invitation! But mind you, I shall rid you of something very important to you should I ever get you on my operating table!" jousted the doctor in his typically wry manner.

George Whitfield was the only one of the thirteen "buzzards" that for sure could identify the real King of England on sight! John Wesley along with the surviving scientists had at best, only seen the man at a parade's distance.

Whitfield was the one who taught the King how to roll the egg between his fingers. So, yes, George knew the authentic George quite well!

Jumonville splintered the unlocked doors leading into the Fort Herkimer's mess hall! He and more than a hundred of his soldiers all with fixed bayonets, discovered the chained together "captives"!

The French commander then changed his demeanor. He smelled a rat!

It was then that Whitfield caught King George's eye! With a quick wink exchanged between the two men it was understood the "lack of familiarity" was to be the password for the day.

John Wesley and his newly made friend, Major James Wolfe started working on a plan to extract the King from harm's way. A successful coup such as that, would launch their careers up into the stratosphere!

Commander Jumonville then summonsed Colonel McClelland to the dining room. Four French soldiers ushered the fort's Commander to the front of the mess hall! With tiny sticks from their sabers made Andrew stand on the top of a three-legged milking stool!

The grenadiers then threw a noose over the rafters. Jumonville slipped the loop over McClelland's head and kicked the stool out from under Colonel McClelland's feet! He began kicking!

Very calmly and with no compassion shown toward his dangling American counterpart, Commander Jumonville withdrew his pocket watch and began speaking in English to the former "Cricket" operatives! The French soldiers held onto the other end of the jerking rope.

"By my calculation, your captor the one doing the dance up behind me, has approximately thirty more seconds of worth left in his body! If someone doesn't come forward and tell me what the hell is going on at this ridiculous fort, Colonel McClelland will most certainly expire right before your eyes!"

Even thought there was still a great deal of resentment toward one another, Captain Anson and James Wolfe stood up at the same time! Again, Anson got the jump on Wolfe by getting the first word in on the lie he was about ready to set into the gospels!

"Colonel Jumonville, these men I am connected to were all sent from England on a peace mission to assist the north American Indians! We have brought with us learned men prepared to assist the natives with their spiritual education as well as their medical needs!

It is with great pride that I too may say, I was chosen by our King to serve in his efforts by extending the proverbial olive branch across the Atlantic! Sir, these chains were placed on us only as a precautionary measure! That is until Colonel McClelland had time to question us about our authenticity!

We were scattered by an attack from a band of Indians and fortunately the man you are about ready to murder rescued us from certain death! So, for god's sake, Colonel, lower that good man down to the floor!" screamed Anson.

With an evil slit of a smile jagging across Jumonville's face, the French commander spun around to face the docilly hanging colonel. He then withdrew his pistol from his gold tasseled belt and shot the purple faced man in his temple. In French, he then called for the fort's physician to be brought to the milking stool.

Hearing the muffled pistol's report, the cold sober King of England yelled out to the top of his lungs a message to the French commander! Although spoken in an aristocratic toned vernacular, caused everyone who could hear it to take a deep breath!

Upon hearing George's insults, Joseph Coulon de Jumonville reloaded his spent sidearm and viciously exited through the mess hall's door! When he got back to the flagpole and much to his surprise,

Joseph Jumonville came face to face with King George. It was Gus who spoke first.

"Do you have any idea what Louis Vt's reaction will be when he discovers what you so clumsily have done? I wouldn't be surprised if he were to draw and quarter you the instant he gets his hands around your skinny little neck!"

Just as Jumonville was about ready to have King George hanged, two of his men blew their warning signals on their bugles! A wagon loaded with casket size boxes driven by two men were wanting to be admitted into the fort! They claimed to have a delivery from the King of England!

"Captain Alexander Selkirk and Commander Chaloner Ogle of his Majesty's navy at your service! We have some rifles fresh off the boat that General Staats ordered for Fort Herkimer! Since we were passing by your way, we thought we'd drop them off to you guys!

Anyway, the 'Centurion's' crew left us both with a little silver in our pockets and we thought you may have some card players inside who might wish to try and relieve us of some of it!" jovially yelled Alex.

Without a single response from the French guards up in the fort's watchtower, Herkimer's gates opened. Although inanely tried, Ogle attempted to back the rig up when he saw what looked to be an entire French legion of riflemen aiming their weapons directly at them!

From behind the company of soldiers out marched Commander Joseph Coulon de Jumonville holding his gold braded sabre with a white handkerchief stuck on the end of it! He then raised the tip of the cutlass as if he were readying a firing squad to launch their bullets.

In a mocking sort of way, Jumonville spoke out using a cockney laborer's dialect.

"Why don't you blokes jump out of that mighty fine wagon! Keep your hands in the air so I can see them at all times! Now on your way down to the ground, you bloody dock-scum had best come up with a better story than that!

So far, within this little-known fort stuck out in the middle of the wilderness, I have had the pleasure of meeting a dozen or more scientists all sent to help the poor Indians, the King of England, and now we have two naval officers delivering rifles to this enormously popular place! Doesn't that sound a bit absurd to you?" sneered Jumonville.

As Commander Ogle was about to add his rebuttal, Blanche stood up from her hiding place between the stacks of gun crates. With one sprite like jump, the agile young woman landed just a few feet from where the French commander stood!

After a ceremonial curtsy followed by Blanche dropping to her knees and thrusting her arms toward the heavens, she loudly began her testimony!

"'Brother Sporckian: The Sun is Once Again in the Clutches of the Lion, and the encircling season bids us to the forest—there to celebrate…the awful mysteries!'

I am here to fulfill the promise made to all Sporckians; 'To Resurrect Care' whenever a fellow 'animal head' is pressed into danger. Therefore, it is my duty with respect to the 'Order of Saint Hubertus' to warn you, these so called benevolent Indian lovers are in fact a nest of poisonous vipers bent on driving out the French from North America!

To further make my point and to provide additional proof of my assertions, I exhibit for you a wagonload of windbuchses that were destined to be placed into the hands of Tanacharison's Confederates! These British grenadiers who were ostensibly moved from Fort Amsterdam to here because of an Indian uprising, is absolutely one hundred percent bullshit! Those soldiers were sent here by King George with the sole intention of eradicating the French!

Commander Jumonville, why don't you ask the King himself if "Operation Cricket" wasn't the name used for his intended assaults on your forts to the northwest of us? The bastard is mingled up with those other Brits over there next to the barn! Go ahead and ask the sonofabitch if what I said wasn't the bloody gospel truth!

For me, I've done my duty so Colonel Joseph Coulon de Jumonville, if you would kindly unhook my horse from this contraband toting wagon, I shall get on back to town! Oh, and by the way, a little birdie told me that next year you are to be the voice of the "owl" during the June reunion! Good day!" Blanche said as she rode Mister Mann's Arabian out of Fort Herkimer.

Cato had witnessed everything that had gone on within the fort! He whispered the details to Jonn Kimber who relayed Cato's messages to the spread-out cadets. In turn, the boys signaled the 'happenings' to Washington's mounted troops.

All was going well with Washington's messaging system. Neither the French soldiers nor Joseph Brant's Iroquois had noticed their presence but the successful subterfuge instantaneously was lost when Tanacharison scaled the fort's wall and started running toward the French commander at a breakneck speed!

When the Mingo saw Jumonville accept a sack of gold from Chief Brant he raced so quickly into the midst of the French soldiers that they barely saw him before he buried his war hatchet into their Commander's brain!

Then with the high shrill of an attacking eagle, Tanacharison lifted Jumonville's scalp into the air and arrogantly tossed the bloody patch of hair at the Iroquois chief's feet! Out of nowhere it seemed, Tanacharison's braves sprang over Herkimer's gates like an army of red ants!

Only a few of Jumonville's men were able to fire off their weapons before being brought down by a tomahawk or an arrow. Most of the others surrendered.

Blanche laughed out loud when she thought about the hoodwinking she had pulled off on the French commander! She brought Horace Mann's horse to a complete standstill and started a cooking fire. She treated herself to a hefty shot of Black Sam's pain killer.

The powerful northwestern winds had blown throughout the night which disguised any semblance of a road. All Blanche could see from her position were miles and miles of silver white wilderness!

The sun and the flow of the Hudson River pointed toward the only conceivable place she could hole up in. By Blanche's calculations she was about twenty miles away from General Staats's plantation.

Since it was already two o'clock, she figured by the time the moon was at its peak in the sky, she would be curled up in front of the general's hearth! Blanche looked forward to eating thick slices of ham from the General's smokehouse and drinking glass upon glass of exotic his wines!

As Blanche very well knew, the only thing that could hinder her plans of taking over the Staats house would be the slaves the General kept. That's why Blanche reloaded the firearms she had collected along the way.

When Tanacharison's temper exploded into the swift actions he took against the rifle-selling Jumonville, Cato was left no other choice but to join the fight! Before he did that, he motioned for Bosman to gather the spread-out cadets and get them to safety behind Washington's encampment!

Just as Cato was readying his weapons before he jumped into the boiling fray below, Samuel Fraunces harshly scolded his brother for his flagrant stupidity!

"You mean to tell me, you want to waste your energy on a few unruly Frenchmen instead of going after that she-devil who less than an hour ago, rode away? Let's get out of here and go track the bitch down and throw her goddamned head in a hole somewhere! She killed a lot of good kids you know!"

Without returning any sort of defensive statement back to Fraunces, Cato pointed toward two cavalry horses that were running around outside the fort's walls! Both he and Samuel simultaneously jumped to the slippery ground below before scrambling after the discombobulated animals.

As Cato and Samuel Fraunces rode past Jonn Kimber, Samuel told Jonn to expect the two of them to return by morning. Sam also told Jonnathan what they were intending to do!

As Cato and his brother were about ready to kick their horses in their sides, Kimber asked Cato a question.

"And what should I suggest to Colonel Washington regarding the actions he should enact on Herkimer?"

"Tell him to surround the fort and at sunrise have all of his buglers begin blowing their horns with all of their might! Respectfully suggest to him, he do his best to prevent King George from slaughtering the French and their Indian cronies!" said Cato.

"When should he do this, Cato? I can clearly hear the British shooting them at this moment!

Sir, by the time Washington could get here even if he left at this moment, he couldn't stop the slaughter going on within those bloody walls!" wailed Kimber.

"Exactly, Captain Kimber, exactly!" said Cato as his cavalry horse exploded in pursuit of Samuel Fraunces's lead.

As Cato was riding around the periphery of the fort, he could see the torsos of both Tanacharison's braves and those belonging to

Thayendanegea. They weren't fighting each other; instead, they were acting as spectators watching the bloody massacre take place below!

Ogle was the first to show allegiance to the King by joining by his side! Doctor Pollard along with Selkirk and the "Cricket" gang did the same. At Chaloner's command, the British and American soldiers turned around and saluted them all!

In a different way but none the less a way, the Indians from two different nations lifted their crossed arms into the sky and then lowered them humbly to their chests! Tanacharison stepped forward to speak. Even the subdued French captives craned their heads to hear what the Confederate chief was about to say.

"I speak now to the white man! Several hundred years ago our chiefs for whatever reasons, welcomed the visitors to our shores. Then as time wore on, our forefathers began to trade off particular plots of ground for your great grandfathers to sustain themselves in their typical European fashion of plats and fences!

But when that hospitality was met with distain due to your perception of us as savages which later mounted into disrespect, we objected. And yet still, our late councilmen despite the fact they could not read or write in your languages, errored in listening to the spoken word…and then trusting it!

Because of their blunder, we find ourselves in situations such as this one! So, I shall say this to you and considerate it a warning if you will, stop trespassing on lands that do not belong to you!

Those leagues of forests your settlements so desperately covet are where we harvest our livestock! Your houses, the fine furniture you make and your bloody forts are all at our expense!

Speaking of forts, ask yourselves this question, 'Why would you need to build forts if you weren't doing something wrong to the people surrounding them?' You white bastards build your wooden castles to protect yourselves from yourselves!

Consider this fair warning, what you currently possess you keep! But understand, further encroachments onto our sacred lands will no longer be tolerated!

Where we live and that means all of our holdings, are no longer for sale! Any fighting your disease-carrying rats are involved with will be among yourselves! If you idiots choose to not heed my warning then I swear to you, we so called 'savages', will indeed become just that!

As is the victor's privilege, I proclaim that the Frenchmen be allowed under safe passage to return to Fort Duquesne! Along with their mad King, the British from Fort Amsterdam should also hightail it back to where they came from!

As for these "Cricket" scientists who were chained up in your mess hall, they can go wherever in the hell they wish to as far as I am concerned! What I do care about is that you swiftly deliver my message to your superiors!

From this day forward and so help me god I mean it, the next unwarranted group of you who trespass on 'our' land will be buried in it!" Screamed Tanacharison.

Doctor Pollard had been so overwhelmed by the uselessness of his efforts, he pulled up a chair beside of his operating table and got drunk! All he could do for the two hundred or more wounded was to either turn them over to their exiting units or to the pair of internment ministers, Whitfield and Wesley, who would direct them toward wherever their gods wanted them to go!

Alexander Selkirk, Gus and Cal along with the "Cricket" survivors, mingled in with the British troops preparing to actually walk back to Fort Amsterdam which by the way, whose name had been changed to "Fort George"!

As inconspicuously as Gus's ego would allow, the entire camarilla would make their way back to the King's fort located on the furthermost southwestern tip of Manhattan Island! On the way they would mostly talk about everything except the food from back home.

Tanacharison's warriors did not make it easy on the late Jumonville's cavalrymen as they were being escorted out of Fort Herkimer by Brant's Shawnee braves! Despite the sad fact the lion's share of the Frenchmen had been relieved of their boots, most of them seemed rather anxious to leave Fort Herkimer.

Doctor Pollard staggered out of the surgical tent when he heard his name being repeatedly called.

"Black Sam told me once, your Colonel McClelland was a good man! Therefore, we will leave a horse for your men to ride and enough food for them to eat!

A Lieutenant Colonel Washington will arrive soon! He will be returning with only eight of the cadets from King's College! General Staats and all but six of us died from an explosion!

I shall return to my people and attend to their needs! We too have many dead and there is much grief to bare but I will assure you, Doctor, you have seen but a trickle of European blood compared to what you will see should they ever step foot onto my country again!

My advice to you and to the "Americans" in general, is to follow our lead! Break your ties with the entire European continent! Declare your independence from any and all of those who wish to control your movements and prepare to kill those who feel they own you!" said Tanacharison.

Alex watched King George's face as Tanacharison's remarks echoed off of Herkimer's walls. Selkirk even alerted Cal with a quick nudge when he saw King George's face taking on a purplish pallor.

All who heard the Chief's words especially after his victory tirade, knew he was absolutely correct! But it's impossible to change the place in which a person is born!

The "cricket-men" were as guilty as sin! They were the ones who intentionally set out to do exactly what Tanacharison had said the Europeans were planning to do to North America!

As the effects of Tanacharison's inditement seeped through their minds, the long walk to "Fort George" seemed much further than it actually was. But as soon as the sounds of welcoming fifes and the taps of drumsticks invaded their senses, the reality of their British roots made them wish they were there instead of where they did not belong!

Most if not all of the "Crickets" swore they would never make such a foolish adventure again. The cost of 'freedom' they surmised, just wasn't worth it!

As the sun was just dropping below the treetops, Blanche reached the top of the hill she had set her sights on more than a mile back! She had finally arrived to the point she expected would provide a panoramic view of the Staat's plantation.

A wolf howled from within the grove of trees where she had cut the throat of Mister Mann's Arabian. She needed a low profile once the daylight had died.

SEA BUZZARDS

Even at five hundred yards, Blanche could tell that whatever dogs the inhabitants had were inside. There was no movement whatsoever either in or outside of the Staats' house except for the telltale fluttering of heat waves rising from the chimney. They were expecting her!

From a sudden shift in the wind, Blanche caught the whiff of a cooking fire. Judging from the directions in which the forest's undergrowth was leaning, the smell was coming from behind her!

She hoped her hunch was wrong because that would mean someone was tracking her! If those pursuers were trained soldiers that inviting campfire might very well be a diversion, Blanche thought. She couldn't chance an ambush.

Blanche sprinted across a quarter of a mile of a snow covered plain in less than two minutes! She ended up close enough to the Staats's picture window that she could see Kimberly Kimber staring directly into her eyes!

A split second later, a bullet zipped by Blanche's head! It was a pistol shot made from the front porch! A whole second after that discovery, General Staats's lover laid dead on the steps from where she tried to shoot Blanche from!

Out jumped three of Staats's field hands each with a deadly farming implement in their hands! In mass, the big men attempted to attack Blanche from the top of the wagon she was hiding behind. In midair all three were swept away by a single blast from her blunderbuss!

Seeing that the mansion's door had been left ajar, Blanche ran into the General's home expecting to run into a great deal of resistance! She met none.

There was no sign of anyone within the entire house. But then Blanche heard the sounds of horses galloping by! They were coming from the barn's side of the house!

By the time Blanche could get a bead on them, Kimberly and a black boy were way out of range! They appeared to be headed in a southerly direction and probably in route to Fort Amsterdam thought Blanche.

After a quick going over and packing all the 'light-stuff', Blanche began sloshing lamp oil on every piece of combustible material she could reach until she ran out of it. She then reloaded her weapons, lit the living room's drapes on fire and then went directly to the barn where she set up a sniper's nest!

Blanche knew the house fire would distract those she suspected were following her. It would also provide enough light for an ample sight picture within its glow!

From the top of the hayloft the huntress trained her sights on the only passageway one could approach the barn from but then the loft's floor gave way causing Blanche to fall into an awaiting net!

Cato and Fraunces had watched Kimberly circle back to the barn while her negro friend, "Mercury" pretended to continue south! It was too late to put out the house fire so Cato and Samuel remained hidden while keeping their sights affixed on the barn's openings.

Samuel Fraunces tried to warn Mercury before he dashed into the fire lighted space! It was too late! Even though Blanche was caught in a thickly weaved pig net, she was still able to kill the lad with a shot from one of her pistols!

With an eastern wind kicking up out in the Atlantic, red coals began settling on the top of the barn in which Blanche was suspended within. Kimberly began humming a tune which she and Blanche had harmonized together when they were in adjoining cells. It was intended to be a haunting sound!

"You know, Blanche, you are a very bad person!" said Kimberly from behind the barn's stone wall.

"I am quite well aware of that, Kim, but you would be too if you had undergone the childhood I had to endure! I was a street urchin, Honey!

There was no choice but to be a cleverly deviant girl! Do you believe for one moment that I enjoyed doing what I was circumstantially forced to do?" smoothly said Blanche as she continued cutting the pig net's strands with her boot knife.

"Yes, I do Blanche. Every minute of it!" answered Kim.

"Well I certainly hope you never felt you were endangered by me, Kimberly! I have always considered us sisters, Sweetie! I would never hurt you in any way!" panted Blanche as she touched her feet onto the barn's dirt floor.

"Then why did you push me underneath the Queen's carriage, Blanche?" angrily quizzed Kimberly Kimber.

Blanche did not answer Kim because she was quietly mounting one of Staat's old cavalry horses! She planned to bolt out of the barn on it until Kimberly ran from around the stone wall and latched the barn door shut!

Amid Blanche's angry insults, Kimberly could hear pieces of the barn's roofing rafters cracking! The blade of Blanche's knife darted out between the door's spacings in her attempt to dislodge the barndoor's fastening mechanism!

Twice, the trapped woman attempted to crash through the massive door by racing the General's old cavalry horse into it but it wasn't enough! Blanche's screams increased in pitch as licks of the flames began searching for things to burn.

Pleas attached to all sorts of promises followed when the fire began taking on an angry mode of its own! The barn's roof opened to a moonlit sky but then was filled by an escaping fireball!

Cato cautiously approached the scene from the front of the barn while Samuel came in from the rear of it. Both men closed in on the burning building with the hammers of their weapons fully cocked! Each expected Blanche to appear at any second!

When Cato heard his brother's call for help, he ran to the rear of the fire engulfed barn to find Samuel sitting upright in the snow. A shower of blood had practically encircled him!

He tried to apologize but all Fraunces could do was point toward the direction Blanche rode off in. He then died.

Cato's heart sank when he realized Blanche had taken Kimberly with her! She had also hobbled his horse! The mulatto wept.

The man who had obliged Sporck with a ride back to Fort Herkimer happened to be the grandson of Colonel Benjamin Fletcher. Ben Fletcher as it turned out, was New York's British governor at the turn of the century. He was known throughout the underworld as "the pirate's broker"!

According to the in-transit babblings of Colonel Fletcher's grandchild, his grandfather had taken a 'cut' of every high sea robbery that took place in the north Atlantic from Virginia to Canada! From those trappings he was able to purchase about any governmental seat in the Colonies he wanted to!

He chose Manhattan Island as his permanent stomping grounds because of the deeply imbedded contacts he had made with the local money holders. Plus, he had every dockworker on the eastern shore in his pocket!

This was the Colonel's game: When a shipment left Africa and was due to dock at Williamsburg, if that particular freighter had not paid the Governor's special excise tax and therefore was not flying Fletcher's everchanging banners, one could rest assured, that particular shipment would end up in one of his many "midnight" warehouses!

Sporck realized the obvious tie-in between Black Sam and the former Governor's grandson! Ike made the uncommon decision to allow his obese chauffer to live a little longer!

Because there were a few tidbits of information still left to be answered, Sporck began a foray of questions cloaked within a wardrobe of levity.

"I'll bet that a man of your pedigree must have to carry a stick with him in order to beat the women off! I'm surprised this fine carriage of yours doesn't have bars on it!" said Sporck jokingly.

"There've been a few who've tried to win my heart but when they discovered I was hung like an elephant, most of them ran away! Comically retorted "Fletch".

"So, tell me Fletch, did you ever get to meet the real Samuel Bellamy in person? I use to hear tales of the 'King of the Pirates' from my dad when he was still alive!

He told me once, if ole Black Sam's wealth were to ever be calculated, the accountant would never in his lifetime get to the end of it! Your recon that's true, Fletch?" asked Sporck.

"You darn tooting it is! I've seen where the man lives and I'll tell you right now, his money if what they say is true, is as safe as a baby in his mother's arms! Black Sam resides within a catacomb full piece of rock the size of a mountain! It sets in the forks of the Mohawk River!

I couldn't imagine how someone or even a team of robbers, could penetrate Sam's humongous monolith! It would be impossible for anyone to get to it and doubly as difficult for them to take anything out of it!" mumbled Fletch.

"Just for curiosity's sake, how far are we away from this mighty fortress belonging to the infamous 'Black Sam'?" innocently queried Sporck.

"Well it ain't that far in mileage but it's the company you run into that makes it an impossibility to get to! By the way a crow would fly, Bellamy's mountain is less than twenty miles north of us. Unfortunately, the last ten miles of it goes right through the middle of the Iroquois burial grounds!

Black Sam's mountain is full of dead chiefs' bodies therefore it is constantly watched over by Tanacharison's braves! They're ain't enough tea in China that would be worth that trip, no Sir!" proclaimed the drunken Mister Fletcher.

From about a hundred yards east of their position, Sporck heard men's voices along with what sounded like a squeaking wheel! Fletch and Sporck jumped from their carriage and crawled up an embankment to try and get a better view of the field above them. Astonishingly, they saw hundreds of American soldiers preparing for a battle!

Lt. Col. Washington had been shoring up the battle lines for over two hours. The messages which flickered across the six miles of wilderness from Fort Herkimer had 'said', 'Tanacharison's warriors gained control of the fort and allowed the French survivors safe passage to Fort Duquesne'!

It was hoped there would be no trouble but Washington had to draw the line somewhere! Since his cannoneers had the high ground, this field was as good as any to drive the point home; the French had to get back over to their side of the Ohio River!

Their Parisian government had been formally warned time and time again not to purchase from the Indians anymore of what the British called theirs! "Theirs" meaning, the rich forestlands the British and the Americans had either already bought from the Indians or stolen from them!

But orders were just that, 'orders'! His were quite clear, Washington was to either coerce the French to leave the east side of the Ohio or he was to scatter their ashes into it! George knew he could whip the French on their own but when they were allied with the Delaware, it could mean the tipping point for his men!

"Colonel Washington, Tanacharison has returned with the King's College cadets and a couple hundred of his braves! Tanacharison sends his apologies to Doctor Arias for his nefarious departure and asks that he redo the poorly tied knots the "Shaman" previously attempted!

Sir, Tanacharison in all seriousness, asked where you would like for his men to park their wagon! It seems they have a gift for you, Colonel! Shall I have them meet you at your tent, Sir?" spoke the excited lieutenant.

"I wonder if that means the same as Greeks baring gifts, Lieutenant Fredrick? Why would that cantankerous Chief be bringing me anything at this hour of the morning?" comically asked the Commander.

"Colonel, those who just returned from Herkimer say there are cases of air rifles in the wagon! Some of Cato's crew state that they have an idea which very well may be useful to you! Any response, Sir?" asked Lt. Fredrick.

"Speaking of Cato, did everyone get back safely?" questioned Washington.

"All but Cato and the tree-man, Samuel Fraunces, Sir! It's my understanding that Cato and his pal took out after the girl who boobytrapped Black Sam's mountain! They aim to kill her, Sir!" sharply said the lieutenant.

As Washington was finishing up his discussion with Lieutenant Frederick, up rode Tanacharison. It looked like he had a lot to say!

"Colonel Washington, I fear all hell is going to come your way! Sir, it's not the French that are the worry, it's the bloody British I fear will retaliate!

This may surprise you; but your King is a mad man! I firmly believe when he returns to Fort Amsterdam, he will order an attack on my people!

Judging from what little I could see of him, I would say that King George is a "desperate" man! He is the type who believes the universe spins around him! I feel he is a most dangerous sort of fellow, Colonel!" said Tanacharison.

"I totally agree with your assessment of the King, Chief, but the Colonies are ill prepared to take them on at this point! I do believe however that the day will come and maybe sooner than we hope, when we will fight them but not today! I'm afraid our only choice is to at least appear that we are on their side!" said Washington.

"You are a good man, George. But at some point, during every man's life, that goodness is tested! I, my friend, believe that time has come from you!

Here are the British, your country, now commanding you to do something atrocious to a people who would enjoy a harmonious existence with you! You see, it wasn't such an enigma after all, now was it?" Tanacharison said as he turned his horse around and headed toward Doctor Arias' tent.

An hour after Tanacharison's departure, Washington returned to his headquarters with intentions of getting some much needed sleep. As he entered his tent, he smelled tobacco smoke and whiskey vapors. They were emitted from the mouths of five drunk men!

From left to right, sitting in a jury's fashion behind the maps table were Jonathan Kimber, William Bosman, James Stanfield, Tanacharison and Doctor Arias. Except for Tanacharison, they seemed to enjoy watching Doctor Arias' final stitches being weaved in the Indian's side! Washington pulled up a chair.

Jonnathan Kimber wasted no time on salutations. He skillfully unrolled a map of the "Wilderness" Tanacharison's braves confiscated. He then marked an 'X' on Washington's soldiers' exact position!

Like a magician, Kimber opened a box containing a dozen windbuchses! He picked one of them out of the clock box and pumped the "wind-rifle's" stock five times.

After that, Jonn dropped a tiny lead ball down the muzzle's barrel and tapped it down with a ramrod. He shot the rifle at the candle he had set up for the demonstration's sake. It exploded into a thousand pieces!

Still without saying a word, Jonnathan walked back over to the map and placed two 'X's' on both of Washington's flanks. He then looked across the table at the young Lt. Colonel and spoke.

"With an hour's worth of training, I can have two hundred of Tanacharison's braves hidden behind your cannons! While you nor your men are engaging the King's men, the Chief's braves will be 'silently' I might add, picking them off one by one!"

"Captain Kimber, I am not questioning your strategy not at all, as a matter of fact I like it very much! I would appreciate however some clarification as to why you believe an attack by the King of England is eminent? Why here and why now?" George Washington asked with a high-pitched tone.

Jonn Kimber then smiled at Washington as he walked away from the marked-up map. He returned to his seat. James Stanfield then stood before he began explaining to Washington the reasons for Kimber's incendiary statements.

"Colonel Washington, beyond a shadow of a doubt, George Augustus II has made several efforts to undermine as well as to sabotage the Colonies' efforts to gain any semblance of interdependence! He knows America will not forever tolerate the exponentially mounting tariffs placed upon them nor will they allow for much longer, being squished under Britain's thumb!

King George as you may or may not know, has executed two operations aimed at disrupting any plans the Colonies may have at establishing their self-dependencies. Colonel, the King's intent is to create a new empire, one in which he will rule from Manhattan Island!

Ultimately, George feels that America will turn toward him for his prophetic leadership at which time, he will declare himself the ruler of it! Although he is quite mad, he still has the capability of unleashing his navy onto these shores and consequently turning the Americas into little more than a complex of feudal villages!" said Stanfield.

"Captain Stanfield, what you have stated leaves me totally flabbergasted! Are you saying, Sir, that King George has become somewhat of a rogue agent now operating outside of his own empire?" quizzed Washington.

"Precisely!" sharply answered Stanfield.

"I respectfully must ask you, how would you know of such intimate details regarding King George?" asked Colonel Washington. William Bosman stood up so quickly that Tanacharison sprang from his chair causing Doctor Arias to drop his pair of scissors to the tent's floor! Bosman then stepped in front of Captain Stanfield so his face was within six inches of Washington's! Bosman then spoke with a high shrill in his voice!

"Sir, it would take three days to appropriately answer the question you asked Captain Stanfield but let me assure you, what was told to you is the absolute gospel truth! Factually speaking, there are hundreds of dead boys who would gladly attest to King George's diabolical attempt to gain control of this continent!

Tragically, Colonel, King George is not America's only evil suitor! France and Spain are certainly the top two contenders for its resources but those aren't the countries the Colonies should fear the most!

America's greatest nemesis happens to be an Austrian named, "Count Franz Anton von Sporck"! He was one of the Habsburg Empire's sad bastards cast away from the royal family at the turn of the century.

"Sporck" however, was one of the few who took his 'hush money' and turned it into a fortune! He purchased the Royal African Company.

Based out of Liverpool, Anton von Sporck over a couple of decades, built what is still probably the largest slave trading operation in the world. He also holds himself out to be the second most powerful next to the Pope, religious leader in all of Europe!

Although cloaked as the founder of the "All Saints' Church of Childwall" and passing himself off as a "Reverend Green", he established within its hallowed walls, Europe's largest laundering organization! It caters mostly to pirates and road bandits!

As a recruiting tool built around the prestigious "International Order of Saint Hubertus", Sporck has been able to sew into America's plantations an army of supporters. Most of his members also known as "animal heads", are the sons of plantation owners with whom he sells his slaves to!

'Ike's' dubious efforts are geared toward elevating the value of his human cargo and providing the high seas pirates a place where they can turn their pillaged trappings into "innocent" coins! We discovered that Anton von Sporck attempted to "seed" the Charlestown coast with flea larvae with the intention of killing off a good share of its population with bubonic sickness!

Such a disaster would have made the per head value of his "uninfected" cargo quadruple in worth at the block! Ironically, King George caught wind of Sporck's venal plot and supposedly sent out a team of assassins to foil Sporck's plan!

Fortunately, they were successful but not before one of the vials contaminated a few hundred of Charlestown's citizens! Even more tragically, a slave named 'Jemmy' escaped and made it to New York where he caused a lot of mayhem before he and his cohorts were killed!"

"So where does King George come into play?" questioned George Washington.

"Sir, the King never expected Jemmy to be stopped!" flatly stated Stanfield.

"I'm confused, Captain, why then did he even make any effort at all?" asked Washington.

"Because he and Sporck have the exact same agenda! We suspect they are in cahoots! They pretend to be enemies but not so ironically, they both have their sights set on identically the same goal!" excitedly said Stanfield.

"So, your team came to Manhattan Island in pursuit of this renegade 'Jemmy'? Pressed Washington.

"Well sort of, Colonel! Captains Kimber and Bosman and I set out in the 'Thomas' on our first leg from Liverpool to pick up our typical load of slaves from the western coast of Africa. We were contracted by the Royal African Company to transport a few hundred negroes to Charlestown. We were "guaranteed" an enormous bonus for doing so!

When we embarked on our second leg out of Africa, we noticed we were flanked by two escort ships, the 'Fancy' and the 'Happy Return'! All was going well up until the point where the Atlantic meets the Caribbean waters. That was when we came under attack by the 'Whydah' under the command of Commander Chaloner Ogle of his Majesty's navy!

To make a long story short and several hundred deaths later, the three of us were rescued by Commander Ogle! It was then that we were able to piece together the real intentions of both Sporck and King George!

Our conclusive findings were exactly as I stated, King Augustus George as well as Sporck, intend to cripple the American colonies and eventually take control of the whole goddamned continent!" screamed Stanfield.

Doctor Arias rushed over to Washington's side as the American commander's pallor cautioned him to do so. Bosman stepped forward to assist the physician as Colonel Washington crumbled to the canvas floor. The man was in shock!

Fort Herkimer's physician Doctor Harold Pollard, sat on the milking stool which had been an intricate part in Colonel McClelland's hanging. Whiskey offered no assistance to him; the anguish Pollard felt was beyond extinguishing!

The fort's soldiers walked around the logged perimeter like aimlessly wandering catatonics. The French survivors of less than fifty men had left with Thayendanegea and his Iroquois warriors. The only dead they took with them was Captain Joncaire's scalped body. The rest of corpses were left for Herkimer's soldiers to bury.

Britain's King insisted his dead soldiers be stacked onto the beds of three of Fort Herkimer's wagons. The fourth one was for him and solely his to occupy on their retreat back to Fort Amsterdam.

The horses, guns and cannons originally belonging to the attacking French and British cavalrymen, had been divvied up between Tanacharison's and Thayendanegea's braves. They got all of Fort Herkimer's stable full of fresh horses too!

Though the temperatures had dropped well below the teens, King George ordered even the officers to tow the four wagons. Gus did offer Ogle and Selkirk a ride in his wagon but they declined. Major James Wolfe who alibied he had a military strategy to privately discuss with the King, took their places.

Given that Wolfe had the wise foresight to grab a couple of jugs of rum from the mess hall, he had no difficulty obtaining King George's invitational alacrity. Once Major Wolfe got settled into the wagon's seat and shared a half dozen ladles of rum with his new best friend, Gus, he saw that King George was speaking with a 'Timothy' as well as with him; so, he listened!

"I am not a goddamned coward, Tim! Despite what you say, those redskins were all over us! Those French would have hanged me you know!" said the inebriated King.

Timothy did not answer.

"Of course, I will retaliate, you damn fool! But with no weapons and no horses, I'm afraid I'll have to wait until I get back to Fort Amsterdam to mount a proper offense!" cried Gus.

Again, Timothy did not respond but Major Wolfe did!

"Your Majesty, may I respectfully offer you a possible solution to this seemingly unsolvable conundrum?" obsequiously asked the British major.

After a relatively long pause presumably because of a whisperingly secret discussion with Timothy, the King responded to Wolfe's titillating question.

"Certainly, Major, what are your thoughts?" asked Gus.

"Your Highness, there are two men actually two evangelists, assisting the pull team of the last wagon in our caravan. There names are George Whitfield and John Wesley!

Sir, they will know the whereabouts of a professor named Jeffrey Amherst. I know for a fact, Amherst conjured up a nasty little concoction that he swore would annihilate the Indians from here to the Ohio!

I am sure if you were to get your hands on Doctor Amherst's pogrom, it would not even be necessary to use an army to defend your honor! If I might be dreadfully honest, your Majesty, if I were in your shoes, I'd use it on both the savages and those impotent lot at Fort Herkimer! I'd then repeat the process on the French and anyone else who could possibly recollect the tragedy of this day!

Afterwards, I believe I would sail back home and tell the tale of how the great warrior King singlehandedly defeated the wild Indians of North America! Just think of how such stories might embolden you in the eyes of both your friends and enemies throughout Europe!" slurred Major Wolfe.

King George suddenly stood up from his wagon's seat and commanded that the human drawn wagons be halted. They stopped beneath a grove of old red oaks.

He then hopped into the back of his wagon and stood up on a box. George forcefully summonsed Wesley and Whitfield to appear before him while he 'royally' sat in the back of the wagon. He wished to ask the holy men a couple of questions!

While John and George were making their way toward the King's wagon, Major Wolfe whispered another suggestion submerged within a question to King George.

"Your Highness, wouldn't it prudent to ask the highest ranking officer in our midst to deliver any punishments to these ministers in case they for some reason, refuse to provide our desirable answers?" leered Wolfe.

After another long pause, two gulps of rum, and a short sidebar discussion with Timothy, Gus requested that Commander Ogle come to his wagon for an abbreviated conference. Chaloner approached the wagon.

"Reporting as requested, Sir!" barked Ogle.

"Cal, I am officially turning this detachment over to you! Under your command your first assignment will be to extrapolate some much needed information from Misters Wesley and Whitfield!

Because of our obvious time constraint, I'm afraid we will need to enact the same 'truth or death' procedures we use when questioning a captured enemy. Therefore, kindly have your sidekick, Captain Selkirk prepare a couple of nooses for our god-fearing constituents!

Should their memories fail them and let's just pray they don't, we'll hang them right off of the wagon I'm standing in! If they are able to recall the whereabouts of one Professor Jeffrey Amherst, we'll set them free!

Once Selkirk is done with his rope tying, have him throw the nooses over the big limb above this wagon! Fit the boys with their necklaces into heaven and then begin your questioning, Commander?" slyly stated the King.

"Isn't this a rather draconian approach to take, Gus? After all, these are our own countrymen, Sir!" sharply said Ogle.

"Chaloner, do not forget with whom you are addressing, Sir! And please do not forget, it is almost as easy to hang three people as it is for two! Do you have any more questions, my old Friend?" quipped George II.

"No, Sir!" responded the naval commander.

"Then I expect you will have these 'two' ready for their hearing within the next few minutes?" stoically asked the King of England.

"I'll do as you commanded, your Highness!" Ogle said.

After dragging Samuel Fraunces's body as close to the fire-consumed barn as possible, Cato tossed as many boards on top of his brother before he began his pursuit of Blanche and her hostage, Kimberly. He didn't have the heart to kill the hobbled warhorse so he removed its bridle and wished the beast well.

Cato was fully aware of the danger Blanche presented to him! He knew that her cunningness was as deadly as that of a cobra's bite; therefore, it was evident that extreme caution had to be exercised at every turn of the trail she left in the snow.

Following a hunch, Cato assessed that Blanche's options were limited because of the outside temperature. A fire would put him on top of her in a heartbeat!

Her choices were limited. His guess was, since Blanche and Kimberly were riding on the same horse, they could travel no more than twenty miles before their cavalry mount would give out on them!

By inferential reasoning, Cato guessed Blanche would circle back toward Fort Herkimer and commandeer the first farmhouse she came to. She would likely pick one that was defensible!

Logically he thought, Blanche would want to approach a place where there was enough traffic so her tracks were indistinguishable. No one would be unable to pinpoint her and Kimberly's exact location then.

The only town between Fort Herkimer and Manhattan Island was a little speck on the map known as "German Flatts". If Cato's assumption was correct, Blanche would more than likely go there but that hypothesis if proven wrong, would cost little Kimberly her life!

Finally, after that inner argument had exhausted itself within Cato's mind, he decided to play it out by entering the farming settlement from the east. He guessed that Blanche would expect him to follow her westerly tracks.

With Blanche no choice was a good one; nevertheless, Cato headed out with the sun over his right shoulder. If the weather held up, he would arrive about an hour before sunset, Cato thought to himself.

Washington's soldiers were busy sharpening the logs they had freshly cut from the forest on the south side of the field. Sporck and Fletch agreed it was time to make their way out of what obviously would become in the very near future, a battlefield. Neither of them wished to spend another night out in the cold anyway!

"Hey Fletch, tell me, where is the closest town other than Manhattan to us right now? Not that I ever intend on going there but I was just figuring that maybe we could buy a jug or two of liquor before we headed back to the island!" whispered Sporck.

Mister Fletcher curiously turned toward the suspected imposter with a look of distain on his face! He then grabbed Ike's jacket and pulled him close enough so that both men could smell the other's rancid breath! Fletch then spoke.

"Look, Mister, I could give a rat's ass about your reasons but I'm going to tell you, I ain't the kind of man who supports cowardice! If you're going to desert the British army or for that matter any outfit, you will not use me as your scapegoat!

I've a good mind to throw you in the back of my carriage and turn you over to the authorities myself! I got no stomach for any 'yellow-backed' bastard who would abandon his own men!" spat Fletch.

Anton von Sporck then withdrew his boot knife and inserted the blade an inch into the soft tissue below Fletch's sternum. With a fatherly tone in his voice he leaned close enough to the stunned man's ear so there would be no misunderstanding of what he was about to say.

"If you wish to see another day, you will need to answer my question regarding the location of German Flatts! Otherwise, I shall pierce your heart with the remainder of my dagger! Do you understand, Fletch?" nonchalantly asked Sporck.

"Oh my god, Man, don't kill me! It's just four miles to the southwest of us, just let me …" gurgled Fletch.

Washington and Doctor Arias sat quietly on their horses as they watched Tanacharison instruct his braves how to shoot their windbuchses. Both marveled at how quickly the Indians were able to pick up on their deadly use!

"George, do you really believe the King will come?" questioned the physician.

"Rogue, if there is an inkling of truth behind what those three slaver captains said, then I hope so!" retorted Colonel Washington.

"I gather from your somewhat bellicose answer, you think methods of genuine negotiations are 'out the window'?" inquisitively stated Arias.

"Doctor Arias, you saw as I did the bodies of those cadets, did you not?" flippantly responded Washington.

"It was the most tragic sight I have ever seen, George!" Doctor Arias said.

"Then my answer is this, from this day forward, I intend to enrich the American soil with the blood of anyone who opposes our earned right to be here! With every bone in my body, I shall do my very best to extinguish the lives of as many of its foes as is humanly possible!

I will no longer respect British law! I shall only obey the words of God and the wishes of the American people! Any schisms to that personal creed of mine will be met with lead and the sharp edge of my cutlass!" said Washington.

Suddenly the sound of a screeching eagle echoed across the massive wilderness stretching in front of the Virginia regiment. Tanacharison had sent out the warning of an approaching horseman!

Colonel Washington gave the command for his soldiers to ready their arms. A lone rider holding a white flag was galloping at a rapid pace toward the freshly constructed picket line. It was Fort Herkimer's physician, Doctor Harold Pollard.

"Halt! Halt!" yelled a sergeant with an Irish accent.

"Hold your fire! I have an important message for your Commander! I am Lieutenant Colonel Pollard from Fort Herkimer!" screamed Pollard.

Four of Washington's soldiers immediately surrounded the jittery physician and demanded that he dismount his horse! A sentinel requested the American officer to raise his hands! Two of Washington's cavalrymen grabbed the reins of Doctor Pollard's mount in an effort to settle the animal down!

Washington and Doctor Arias rode their horses over to the place where Doctor Pollard had been apprehended. Colonel Washington was the first to speak.

"Colonel, please follow me to my tent. We'll get you a fresh horse and warm you up with a good meal and some of the best Virginia whiskey you ever put in your mouth!" said George Washington.

"Sir, I'll gladly take you up on your kind offer of the fresh horse but I must return to my men as soon as possible! Colonel Washington, as I am sure you have already heard, our fort was ransacked by the Indians! We have been left with no medical supplies, no horses, no food and no guns!

Also, it is my belief that King George intends on attacking our fort as soon as he returns to Fort Amsterdam for reinforcements! What is left of his company of grenadiers of which most were killed by the French, he is planning to use as scapegoats by annihilating them for witnessing his debacle!

Colonel, I am sad to say this but I believe King George has become psychotic! I say that because of a conversation I had with one of the scientists he supposedly had sent here under the pretense of helping the Iroquois! Sir, King George is plotting to kill them off as well!" Cried Doctor Pollard.

"Under those circumstances, Colonel Pollard, we will move my men into your fort and give this mad King of ours the surprise of his life!" exclaimed Washington.

"Colonel Washington, considering what I have experienced from the actions demonstrated by my country's ruler and compounded with the aftermath caused by King George's duplicity, I can truthfully tell you, I shall declare myself at this very moment an expatriate and therefore will provide my undying allegiance to the American colonies!

I will say, if killing British troops can be averted, I would promote that avenue first. But if those efforts are decidedly for naught, I shall do everything within my power to destroy their beings!" proclaimed Harold Pollard.

In a somber way, Colonel Washington quietly nodded his head in acceptance of the doctor's words. With the wave of his hand, Washington's forces including those belonging to Tanacharison, broke camp.

From there and to Pollard's amazement, over four hundred horse backed men emerged from their hiding places! They began their journey to Fort Herkimer.

What had started out to be a quarter moonlit evening turned into a snowy deluge. Flakes the size of thumbnails began filling in the tracks made by King George's hand drawn wagons.

Although the temperatures had risen into the mid-twenties, the defeated soldiers from Fort Amsterdam began complaining about the effects of frostbite as well as the stupidity of pulling three wagons through the snow! Not only did several of the British grenadiers run off but there were certain overheard grumblings about killing the King and writing his death off as a war casualty!

Realizing the tumultuous dangers that were brewing, Ogle cautiously approached King George.

"Your Highness, upon questioning both Wesley and Whitfield, I determined that they believe Jeffrey Amherst after abandoning the two of them, took his wagonload of blankets to the nearby town of German Flatts! Sir, they suspect that Amherst was intending to take refuge in the town's only tavern there!

In perusing the map that I am showing you, the place I have circled indicates that German Flatts is less than a mile from us! King George, in that I am only a man of the sea, perhaps Major Wolfe's expertise might be of great benefit to us all, Sir!" flatly reported Commander Ogle.

Gus took the last swallow from the rum jug and then threw the empty container into the snow. With a scowl on his face the King turned toward his childhood friend and spoke.

"Cal, I shall confer with the Major but in the meantime, I expect your men to continue their course but at a faster pace! We'll resume our inquiry of those 'righteous' idiots when we get back to the island!" yawned George.

"King George, Sir, through my experienced eyes, I too conclude that German Flatts is about a mile and a half to the southwest of us! I might propose that we temporarily leave the two body wagons behind and have an all-hands tow to the village! If my calculations are correct, we should be sitting in front of a crackling fire within a couple of hours!" surmised Major Wolfe.

"Son, I believe you have the makings of a general! That's a brilliant suggestion, James! Kindly take Ogle's command and let's get to that tavern in double-time!" said the painfully sober King.

At Lieutenant Colonel Washington's direction, Tanacharison led his braves, the cadets and the slaver captains in an inconspicuous manner toward Fort Herkimer. While the Virginia regiment approached the fort frontally, the windbuchse baring others would encircle Herkimer and remain unseen until the fort was entirely surrounded.

They were not to fire on the British until signaled to do so! A flare shot from within the fort would do that!

Kimberly had begun to cry. Blanche refused to stop when the child first stated she needed to do number two! Stomach cramps had set in.

Through a stand of cedar trees, Blanche could see a line of houses which had been built on both sides of German Flatt's only road. By the sounds of men's distant voices, she figured its population was about ready to call it quits for the day!

Blanche counted eleven lit lanterns throughout the village which she concluded would be a good time to allow Kimberly to relieve herself. After removing Kimberly's boots, she allowed the little girl to do just that.

Due to the close proximity of the German Flatts' dwellings, Blanche reasoned that a disturbance from any individual house would alert the entire village of her presence! There was however one place that might offer to them some shelter. It was a newly constructed church.

Although roofless, the stone walls would at least provide them some blockage from the wind. They would wait until dark before they crossed the open field to it. More snow was falling.

Cato's focus on the evening's movements in German Flatts was rapidly decreasing by the second. His body's core temperature had dropped considerably due to his now freezing sweat. He had crossed close to three miles of foot deep ground and it had overheated him.

In his attempt to fight off the nagging sleepiness which had set in, Cato rubbed an ice clump over his eyelids while counting the milliseconds it took the water to refreeze on his face. However, when he saw Blanche and Kimberly cross the greyish span of an open field, his adrenalin flow allowed him to get back to normal. They disappeared within the walls of a roofless church!

Cato knew if Blanche were threatened, she would use Kimberly as a trading token! The odds of salvaging the girl's life would rest upon the accuracy of a single shot!

The stonemasons had laid a thirty-foot-high square-shaped steeple. More than likely, it had scaffolding constructed on the inside which gave Blanche the higher ground.

Cato's vantage point from behind an empty pig sty provided only the hint of someone within the half-built construct. Should Blanche climb to the steeple's top as he guessed she would, Cato would be detected upon his first movement toward her!

His only choice was to get closer. He needed to be in a position which would allow him a clean shot!

The distance between the sty and the rock steeple was a little more than a hundred yards. There were two possibilities as Cato surmised, the first was a grain silo but that would require risking a run-in with a shotgun toting resident. The other option was the forest from where Blanche came in from!

After weighing out the odds, Cato elected the woods. He had spotted the top of a hemlock tree that would fit the bill. The only problem with the tree idea was crossing the open road in order to get to the wood line. A diversion would be necessary!

Like the same stones used in the construction of the town's church so were the limestone rocks used to build the wall around the swine pen. Cato grabbed a couple of handfuls of doubloon sized pebbles and stacked them on the ground in front of him. He then removed his waist sash in order to make a sling.

Although grossly out of practice, Cato was able to throw a barrage of speeding pebbles onto the porches of the nearby houses! As hoped, the ill-tempered occupants emerged! A fist shaking contest ensued giving Cato his chance!

Sporck without drawing the Virginia regiment's attention, made it around the fort. The road leading from Fort Herkimer to Manhattan Island had close to six inches of freshly fallen snow on it.

Ike came across the two soldier filled wagons. He could see the signs explaining the horseless method in which they were dragged.

This was an opportunity to make his way into the walls of Fort Amsterdam! He then followed the footprints preceeding the wagons' tracks in pursuit of the answer to a big royal question.

When Fort Herkimer's lights came into Colonel Washington's view, he drew his cavalrymen to a halt. He requested that Doctor Pollard vanguard his regiment's approach offering Tanacharison's braves an undetected opportunity to implant themselves around the fort. The cadets along with the three sea captains, were to remain at the rear of Washington's forward moving troops.

Upon sounding off a loud command commensurate with the rat-a-tat of Samuel Woodhull's drum, several hundred sabre drawn cavalrymen began their intimidating affront toward Fort Herkimer!

Alex Hamilton and Hercules Mulligan rode behind Doctor Arias' wagon. Kimber, Bosman and Stanfield rode on the munition's carriage.

First Sergeant Sweeney ordered the weaponless soldiers of Fort Herkimer to sharpen sticks into pikes! The exhausted men began yelling earsplitting 'hoorahs' upon realizing the approaching cavalrymen were not French! Frenetic screams followed that when they heard their fort's physician's voice.

"First Sergeant Sweeney, kindly open these gates and allow these fine Virginia gentlemen the opportunity to enjoy our gracious hospitality!" glibly hollered Pollard.

"Certainly, Sir! By god you've returned in the nick of time, King George just after you left, took all but one of our wagons! He put his dead into two of our wagons and made his soldiers pull without any horses, the three flatbeds he stole from us!

Two of Fort Amsterdam's boys escaped from the mad tyrant's march and returned here! They're in pretty bad shape, Sir, but they were able to tell us that the King intends on destroying our fort! They're in the mess hall!" squealed Sergeant Sweeney.

Washington then spurred his horse toward the opening gate. He looked up at the first sergeant and saluted the petrified man before he spoke.

"Sergeant, in which direction did they go? You say these men were on foot and pulling three wagons full of dead soldiers? Did they have weapons?" calmly questioned Washington.

"Colonel, they were planning on pulling two of the wagons full of the deceased soldiers all the way to Fort Amsterdam by dark! One of our wagons was used to tote that mental King George!

According to the deserters, they abandoned their trek to Fort Amsterdam. Supposedly, they pulled the King's wagon to German Flatts instead!" wailed Sergeant Sweeney.

"Sergeant Sweeney, with your permission, Sir, may we enter your fort?" graciously requested Washington.

Realizing the Colonel's disposing etiquette was simply a show of respectful gentility, Sweeney returned Colonel Washington's salute along with a cheerful, "Yes, Sir!".

Once the Virginian's were within the fort's walls, Doctor Pollard with Sweeney by his side, turned over Herkimer's command to Colonel Washington. Upon the acceptance of it, the American officer relieved Fort Herkimer's pike baring soldiers and requested they immediately report to the mess hall!

After Herkimer's men had eaten, Colonel Washington, Doctors Arias and Pollard as well as the slaver captains, sat down to dine with the British deserters. Their names were Pinkney and Scroggs. They offered no resistance to Washington's inquiries.

"Colonel, as soon as King George docked the 'Rebecca' at Fort Amsterdam, the very first thing he did other than drinking up all the whiskey was change the fort's name to 'Fort George'! The second thing he did was order an attack on Fort Herkimer under the premise it was under French control!

With no planning, the King ordered the grenadiers to haphazardly attack it by the dawn of the next day! The sad thing about that was, the royal idiot refused to take our commanders along with us! Under his command, the bastard split our regiment up into four parts and commanded us to converge on Herkimer from all directions!

Gentlemen, it was the biggest 'goat-roping' any of us had ever seen! We had no maps, no guidance, nor any clue as to what our adversaries were planning in the way of their defense! Basically, we were sitting ducks!" gasped Scroggs.

"On top of that, King George stopped on numerous occasions to ask for directions to the goddamned fort! It scared us to death if you really want to know the whole truth about it!" butted in Private Pinkney.

"Corporal Scroggs, at what point during the King's retreat to "Fort George" did you boys escape?" pleasantly inquired Washington.

"Right after Major Wolfe told the King that German Flatts had a tavern in it! You see, Colonel Washington, they had run out of the rum and they couldn't wait until we dragged their worthless carcasses back to the fort to get more of it!" grumbled Scroggs.

"Could you take us to the exact place where they crossed over to German Flatts, Gentlemen?" pressed the Virginian.

Both men nodded their heads but then Private Pinkney spoke up.

"After what that son of a bitch'n king was going to do to those two holy men, we'd crawl to the place on hands and knees to show you where he went!"

"What do you mean, Corporal?" pointedly asked Washington.

"Sir, if it hadn't been for Commander Ogle, Major Wolfe would have hanged those religious fellows right then and there!" spouted Scroggs.

Jonnathan Kimber then slammed his flattened hand onto the tabletop! With a ferocious demeanor, he leaned across the dining table and emphatically yelled.

"Now listen here, why in the hell would Commander Ogle have anything to do with the King and those men Wolfe wanted hanged?"

"Because they knew the whereabouts of a wagon full of 'tainted' blankets, Sir!" sheepishly replied Private Pinkney.

"What fucking blankets?" screamed Kimber.

"The ones that a fellow named Sporck had sent to the Indians!" timidly replied the private.

Sporting sheet-white faces, the three sea captains glared at one another in disbelief. Stanfield then turned toward the two field doctors sitting at the table and capsuled an accounting of the past year's experiences starting with the bubonic episode in Charlestown!

When James Stanfield completed his sum-up coupled with the compilation of their theories regarding Sporck's and King George's ulterior motives, Rogue Arias stood. With the seriousness of a snake bitten man, the military physician began speaking directly to his commander.

"George, I believe much to my vexation, what these men are saying is the truth! Therefore, it is my thought that we must do two things; i.e., we must find and destroy that blanket wagon and we must kill both Sporck and King George!" said Doctor Arias.

"I most certainly concur, Rogue! Do all of you sitting at this table agree?" firmly asked Colonel Washington.

They did.

"In that case, we'll take a hundred of our cavalrymen and go after the King! Half of my remaining soldiers along with Tanacharison's braves will spread out to find that goddamned blanket wagon!

The remainder will stay here at the fort! After all is said and done, we'll meet back here in forty-eight hours! Any questions?" asked the American Colonel.

No one had any.

King George ordered the remaining few left in the regiment to stop pulling his wagon! German Flatts was just around the next bend in the road and he didn't wish to ride into the village without the folks having enough time to prepare for their welcoming of the King of Great Britain!

He summonsed Chaloner Ogle to come to his wagon. He wanted to instruct the commander as to what to say to the towns' people!

"Cal, I would appreciate it very much if you would run over to the tavern and let the fine folks of German Flatts know of my arrival! Kindly ask them to greet me at their tavern's entrance for I have some uplifting words to share with them!

Because of the inclement weather, please inform the good people of German Flatts there will be no expectations of pomp; however, I would expect they will want to roust their children out of their warm little beds for the rare opportunity of meeting a real King!"

"By all means, your Highness! I'll even take Selkirk with me due to his grasp of the German tongue. Shall I bring you a sample of the tavern's top drawer's finest?" pleasantly replied Cal.

"Indeed! But, let's let ole Alex stay here! In case you don't return say within the next hour, I'm going to hang your bosom buddy from the nearest tree!

So, if you will, Chaloner, let's beat-feet and say 'hello' to the great folks of German Flatts! I'll look forward to your swift liquor baring return!" smartly commented Gus.

Tanacharison became livid when Sergeant Sweeney told him about the tainted blankets sent by an Englander! He was so disturbed with the white man in general, he had the braves who had been issued a windbuchse to stick them, barrel first, into the snow!

To accelerate his protest even further, Tanacharison refused to allow Washington's detachment to enter his tribe's property! As he and his warriors rode out into the wilderness, Tanacharison once again, swore his people would eat every white who in the future, crossed into the Indian lands!

Alexander Selkirk felt that Ogle was up to something! It was his departing glance that reassured Alex that whatever was about to happen would soon take place!

Selkirk had become worried about Wolfe. The major seemed much more concerned with his rank climbing than he was with his men's attitudes toward him! It was that lack of leadership skill which was responsible for the ocean's floor being littered with the bones of thoughtless naval officers!

Alex knew from deep down in his soul, the young major would never live to blow-out the twenty candles promised to him on his next birthday! Secretly, Selkirk was planning to expedite his prediction!

He watched Commander Ogle weave his way through the trees while he scooped out the miniscule village of German Flatts. There of course was no tavern nor anything else resembling a store of any kind!

It was simply a settlement made up of German immigrants just hoping to live long enough to bury their parents. Nevertheless, Alex knew that Ogle would spin the story in such a way, it would avail them both the opportunity to escape!

Blanche knew that Cato would try to track her down! Her inner alarm system warned her he was close by!

The coincidences revolving around people simultaneously coming out of their homes was all telling in Blanche's mind. In her bones, Blanche could feel Cato closing in on them!

She debated as to whether to cut Kimberly's throat and bolt away or to keep the girl as an 'ace in the hole' should the need arise for an old-fashioned hostage exchange! After a few moments of some serious thought, Blanche elected the ladder option.

With the expression of a doting mother, Blanche invited the eight-year-old to come into her arms to warm up. The candle she had placed in the corner of the square steeple helped some. Then with a velvety tone in her voice, Blanche laid out their situation.

"Sweetie, your daddy will be here to pick you up in a little while! But there is a very mean man trying to hurt him! This terrible person believes that your father knows where a secret treasure is hidden and he is planning to use you to make your dad tell him where it is!

Kimberly, I have an idea, if you place this candle on the window sill over there and you stand behind it, your papa will see you and come after you! When that mean person comes after your daddy, I'll shoot him with my pistol!

Kim, it is most important that you remain at this window or our plan will never work! Pretty soon you and your father will be basking in the sun together on some exotic island in the Caribbean!

I'll be hiding in the bushes just below us so if you need me, just holler! I love you, Sis!" raspingly whispered Blanche.

The winds had pushed the clouds away exposing a very bright three-quarter moon. Cato had climbed to the first cluster of branches of the hemlock tree he had spotted from behind the pig 'sty. He was seventy-five yards from the rock church's steeple and dead even with it!

He found a perfect prop for his rifle barrel and was preparing to twist the tang to the appropriate setting when he saw Chaloner Ogle walking toward the semiconstructed church! The Commander was whistling while he nonchalantly tromped through the fluffy snow.

Cato filled his peep sight with the body of the illuminated figure standing behind the lighted candle! The blade of his front sight was leveled at the image's chest! His right forefinger lightly touched the rifle's trigger.

Ogle began singing in a piercing falsetto tune about a woman impatiently awaiting her groom at the cathedral's steps. Cato got the message but it was too late!

Blanche quickly stood up from behind the shrubs she was crouched behind and fired one of her pistols directly at the naval commander's head! Cato by this time, had taken aim on Blanche's body and squeezed the trigger but all that happened was a metallic 'click'! His weapon's frizzen had iced over and did not ignite its powder charge.

With one man already lying face down in the snow and another some thirty feet up in a tree, Blanche stepped out into the open and placed her other pistol into the crook of her left arm. She took her time while carefully aiming at the darkened clump in the hemlock tree!

A stone block landed squarely on top of Blanche's crown causing the unfired pistol to drop into the snow-covered shrub beneath her! Kimberly climbed down the scaffolding and ran outside to help her "Uncle Cal".

Blanche started scrambling for her weapon! Cato attempted to fire his rifle again but his powder was still wet making his rifle useless.

Suddenly, Washington's cavalrymen more than a hundred of them, came riding in from all directions! The King's men immediately surrendered!

Blanche dropped down to one knee and took careful aim at Cato as he was shimming down the hemlock tree. Kimberly screaming like a wild banshee, maniacally attacked Blanche!

Kimberly tore her fingernails into the witch's eyes! The pistol exploded but fortunately ended up putting a hole through Blanche's right foot!

By this time, the men from German Flatts had come out of their houses! They saw that Washington's troopers had pretty much encircled their village!

King George and Major Wolfe were forced to join Fort Amsterdam's lot while Blanche was draped over a horse.

Kimberly hopped into the King's former rolling throne along with Cato, Selkirk, and the highly perturbed Ogle. Chaloner had sustained only a superficial wound but his favorite telescope was shattered which was the real reason for his anger!

Sporck was discovered hiding amongst the dead British soldiers which had been piled into the King's abandoned wagons. He too was forced to march with the rest of the apprehended troops back to Fort Herkimer!

First Sergeant Sweeney was shocked when he saw Washington's Virginia Regiment appear on the moonlit horizon. Doctors Pollard and Arias were also surprised when they realized there were no casualties!

When Jonnathan Kimber saw his daughter sitting in the back of the wagon he began uncontrollably weeping. He was speechless until Kimberly commented about his loss of hair.

Sergeant Sweeney was ordered by Colonel Washington to have the cooks prepare a hardy meal for his men but as soon as their suppers were completed the Commander asked that the mess hall be transformed into a courtroom! The fort's first sergeant then boldly asked Colonel Washington a very dicey question.

"Sir, shall I prepare the gallows? It's my understanding that the little 'she tiger' we have locked up in the stockade was the one who blew up General Staats and all those cadets! I'd be honored to drop her myself, Colonel, if you'd allow me to, Sir!"

"Sergeant, let me answer that question after this evening's hearing! In the meantime, Lieutenant Sweeney, how about seeing my quartermaster and ask him to fit you into one of our uniforms! I'd like you to return to Williamsburg with me!" jovially remarked Washington.

"Gus, you've really got us in a mess this time! Had you taken my advice and not let that dilettante Major Wolfe suck on your ear, we'd be on our way back home!" imaginatively said 'Timothy'.

"What was I supposed to do, just sit back and cowardly allow the French to ooze their way into my colonies?" deliriously yelled King George.

"Well, you can argue with me all you please! The facts still remain, your ass is chained up in this godforsaken hell hole and they're more than likely going to hang you tomorrow morning!" 'Timothy' said.

"You idiot, they'll do no such of a thing! They have no reason to do that; plus, once the word got back to England our marines would flood the continent and burn it into ashes!" wildly screamed the cold sober King.

"Who's going to say anything, your pompous ass? What's to prevent Colonel Washington from killing us all?" argued 'Timothy'. A guard banged on the stockade's door with the butt of his rifle.

"Keep your mouth shut in there! We'll come and get you when it's time!"

"You see what I mean?" mocked 'Timothy'.

"My old friend Chaloner won't allow that to happen; after all, we played together as young boys!" whispered the panicking Royal prisoner.

"Oh, you mean the man you tried to kill a few weeks back? And isn't he identically the same person whom after discovering your and Sporck's sinister bubonic plot to weaken America, did not follow your orders by preventing the 'Thomas's' crew from drowning?

Do you really believe that same man would lift a single finger to stop your inevitable rope dance? I think not, Augustus! The best thing for you to do for yourself, my Friend, is to ask for mercy and hope they shoot you in the head!" said 'Timothy'.

Kimberly Kimber told her father everything that had happened to her since his departure on the 'Thomas'. She left nothing out!

Kimberly spoke of the cruelties inflicted upon her but she also included the kindnesses shown to her as well. At the conclusion of their reminiscent chat and recognizing that his daughter had prematurely evolved into a wise young woman, Jonnathan reached out his hand and did as she had requested him to do.

The two of them went to Colonel Washington's quarters and tapped gently on his door. They then asked that the Virginian hear what Kimberly had to say.

An hour later give or take a few minutes, George Washington emerged from his room. He called for "Lieutenant" Sweeney.

"Lieutenant, I have decided to break from the normal military protocol! Without causing a bunch of commotion, kindly ask the good doctors, the three sea captains, Cato, Commander Ogle and Selkirk and most importantly the cadets, to gather in the mess hall at thirteen hundred hours! Explain to them that I have an important announcement to make," softly spoke Washington.

At precisely 1:00 a.m., with a roaring fire behind him, Lt. Col. George Washington began his message.

"The time has come for us to take the European threat seriously! It is inevitable that many of us will die in the coming endeavors; however, the defense of the American colonies must become the most paramount of our concerns!

We can no longer allow ourselves the luxury of naivety to ignore what any intelligent being can clearly see! Granted, it took an eight-year-old girl to fit me with the proper spectacles but now that my visual impairment has been corrected, my gaze has been cast across the Atlantic!

Even the old folks in this room have seen far too much! I can say nothing that will balm the wounds of the present youth in our midst except to say, thank you!

At sunrise, I shall allow Major James Wolfe and the remaining soldiers from Fort Amsterdam to leave this fort along with any of Fort Herkimer's soldiers who wish to go with him! They will be given weapons in order to defend themselves along with an adequate number of horses to haul their dead back for burial.

Those of you who wish to remain on American soil may return with me to Williamsburg! In reverence to Tanacharison's wishes, my soldiers, their horses and those of you who wish to swear allegiance to us will board the 'Kitty's Amelia' and sail southward.

Finally, King George, Blanche, and Sporck will be nailed into three separate gun boxes and placed into the bed of Fort Herkimer's last remaining wagon! Once we set this fort on fire, we'll push it over onto the Iroquois' lands.

Are there any questions?" No one raised their hands.

Lightning Source UK Ltd.
Milton Keynes UK
UKHW011832040621
384966UK00001B/33